The Ring

The Ring

Sylvia Halliday

KENSINGTON BOOKS

KENSINGTON BOOKS are published by

Kensington Publishing Corp.
850 Third Avenue
New York, NY 10022

Library of Congress Card Catalog Number: 95-081476
ISBN 1-57566-014-8

First Printing: March, 1996

Printed in the United States of America

The author wishes to acknowledge dear friends Liz and John Denning, gracious hosts of the *real* Burghope Manor, Winsley, Bradford-on-Avon, Wiltshire. She treasures the memory of many a warm and rollicking evening spent before the fireplace of the historic Cranmer Room.

Chapter One

⚜

" 'Od's fish, Pru, but I'd rather stay a Cheapside whore than do *that* to myself every day!"

Prudence Allbright made a face at her friend Betsy and finished wrapping the wide muslin band around her breasts. She held her breath for a moment, gave a final tight, sharp pull on the fabric, then tucked in the ends. If only she weren't quite so full-bosomed, she thought with an edge of discontent. Then chided herself for surrendering to even a momentary vexation. Papa would have been displeased. Didn't God have a purpose in everything he did?

"If my meeting tonight at the tavern goes well, Betsy," she said, "I shall be more than delighted to dress as myself again. With a pretty gown and stays. But in the meantime . . ." She slipped her shift over her head, tied it high against her throat, and stepped into her petticoat; then she donned a ragged, faded gown and laced it tightly across her bound breasts. Her figure appeared as straight and shapeless as a boy's. Tying on a worn apron, she smiled at Betsy and shrugged. " 'Tis safer for me on the London docks to be a sexless old woman."

Betsy grunted and reached for her pot of rouge. "I suppose. But not near as profitable." She stroked the vivid color on her cheeks and into the hollow between her breasts to accentuate the curves of her rather modest bosom. She giggled. "Look at us. I try to make more of what *you* have in abundance, whilst you suffer to disguise your charms."

Prudence twisted her long auburn hair into a knot on the top of her head, fastened it with a small comb, and put on a stringy gray wig. She added a large, soiled cap with lappets hanging over her ears, which further obscured her fresh young face, then folded a tattered neckerchief across her chest. "What else am I to do, Betsy?" she said with a sigh.

Betsy puffed in exasperation. "By all the banners of the Tower, you can put on a proper gown and join me in the streets! With your looks, you'll have your passage to Virginia in no time. Instead of trying to earn a farthing here and there as an old hag selling gewgaws."

"Lord have mercy! You know I could never be a seaside doxy and . . ." Prudence stopped abruptly. Betsy was the only friend she had in this world. Who else could she have turned to when she came to London? She scarcely wanted to hurt Betsy with her intemperate words. Besides, if her friend was to be believed, she enjoyed her calling.

Betsy clucked her tongue. "Oh, Pru, you always were a scarebabe. All the time we were growing up in Winsley. You always cared more for doing right than I did."

"That's not so! I had my share of naughtiness. I was marched to the dairy on many an occasion. To stand in isolation and repent my ways. And those times across Mama's knee, with a stout switch to my backside . . . But I hated to disappoint Papa."

Betsy rolled her eyes. "And all that psalm-singing. While you knelt in church, I was stealing kisses from the village lads!"

Betsy's words sounded like a reproach. "I was raised to be God-fearing," said Prudence. "Is that so terrible? And now you want me to forget all of that and join you on the streets?"

"Sweet Mother of Mercy, Pru, 'tis not as though you're still a virgin!"

Prudence flinched and fingered Jamie's ring, feeling the shame burn her cheeks. The florid JA carved into the dull gold seemed to mock her hopes.

Betsy smirked. "What was that song you used to sing?" She raised her voice in a wavery soprano:

"Bobby Shaftoe's gone to sea
Silver buckles on his knee
He'll come back and marry me
Pretty Bobby Shaftoe."

"Well, he *will!* Didn't he even kneel and pledge me his troth? We belong to each other in the eyes of God, he said. We'd be married already if he hadn't been called away to his plantation in Virginia."

"And why should your great Lord Jamie—a viscount, so you say—marry a country girl? Even with a dowry from your grandpapa?"

"Because he loves me so," Prudence said with some heat.

"And the letters you wrote to him in Berkshire? That he never answered?"

"Mayhap he had already left for the Colonies. And they haven't reached him yet." She held out her fist, displaying the gold band. "But he gave me his *ring.* That counts for something. He said it means we're nearly married already."

"Pshaw! A man always expects to pay for a woman's favors. 'Tis the way of the world. A gift for a treasure. *That's* why your Lord Jamie gave you the ring."

Prudence felt an unfamiliar pang of doubt. Betsy was wise in the ways of men, and she herself knew so little. But Jamie, sweet Jamie, with his handsome face and earnest gaze . . . "No! I love him, and he loves me. He'll be pleased that I couldn't wait on his return. That I came all the way across the ocean to join him. And then he'll marry me." She clutched at her belly and bent over in pain. "He *must* marry me!" She sighed, straightening, and managed a thin smile. "You wicked Betsy. You'll have me doubting my Lord Jamie in another moment. But the sooner I can raise my passage . . ."

"You'd do better to pawn his ring, then," said Betsy dryly.

"Fortune preserve me! That my dear Lord Jamie gave me? When he kissed me and . . ." She felt the blush stealing into her cheeks again.

Betsy chuckled—the sly, knowing laugh of a practiced whore. "Did you like what he did? You never told me."

Prudence turned away. Her face was now burning. It had been only those two times with Jamie. The soft, misty rain on the hillside, the sheep nuzzling at her bared legs, the mud on her skirts, the fear and the pain . . . "His words and his kisses held the sweetest promise I've ever known," she murmured.

Betsy swung her around, her hands firm on her shoulders. She raised a skeptical eyebrow. "And the rest of it?"

"I . . . I was so frightened we'd be found out and . . . and surely God was watching . . . And the second time, we had so few hours. A sad, hasty parting." She gulped and rubbed at her eyes. How could she confess that she'd found *that* part of Jamie's love less than perfect?

Betsy folded her into a warm embrace. "You poor sweet innocent. How can I make you see? Your eyes are filled with stars." She sighed. "Maybe 'tis best you earn your passage money as you do, however long it takes." She turned to the broken mirror that sat atop the mantelpiece in the small, cramped garret room. "As for me"—she frowned at her reflection—"I look like a ghost on All Hallows' Eve. I need a bit more color. Hand me my pot of cerise, love."

Prudence watched her friend corrupt her fair young beauty with two garish spots of crimson, then brush on a thick layer of powder with a rabbit's foot. Dear Betsy, she thought. Too pretty to waste her youth on the dregs of the London docks. She could only wish her a true love someday, as she herself had found with Jamie.

"Are you 'most ready?" asked Betsy, giving a final pat to her blond curls. She fluffed out the skirts of her fine silken gown and perched a saucy straw hat atop her head.

"In a moment." Prudence knelt to the cold fireplace, took a handful of soot, and rubbed it on her face and arms. She smiled, her natural optimism returning. "Well, if all goes well with your Mr. Crown at the tavern tonight, I'll get to Virginia sooner than I had hoped, by God's grace."

Betsy snickered. "He's a clumsy John-among-the-maids, but a gabbler. 'Od's fish, not a moment of silence the whole time! But when he said that he was going to Williamsburg with his family and his wife needed a maid to help with the children, I thought of you at once."

Prudence bared her teeth to the mirror. Taking up a small pot of tar, she blackened her front teeth, then picked up a large basket and swung it over her arm. "I'm ready. Wait! My Lord Jamie's ring." She stroked the ring with loving fingers, then reluctantly pulled it off. It never left her hand when she was in this room, and when she lay in bed at night it was her comfort in the dark.

Kneeling to the humble flock bed that the two girls shared, she lifted the cheap mattress stuffed with wool refuse and rags. She kissed Jamie's ring and placed it next to her meager sack of money. All she owned in this world. She frowned, then rummaged in the pouch and removed a few coins. "I shall need to buy more ribbons today. The sailors always like them for their doxies in foreign ports."

Betsy nodded smugly. "To be sure. Just as I said. A gift for a treasure. A trinket for the chance to poke a woman." She sighed. "Never mind, love. Don't pout. Your Lord Jamie loves you. Now, will you come back here to change before you meet Mr. Crown?"

"Yes." Prudence indicated her unkempt clothing. "He would never hire *this.*"

"Come before seven, then. I might have my lustful solicitor for a bit of diddling tonight."

Prudence grimaced. "Must I sleep outside in the doorway, then?" The passage to the tiny garret was close and dark and filled with bad air. She hated it when Betsy had a customer all night.

"No. The man's a becalmed ship. Full-rigged, but with damned little wind to keep his sail puffed! An hour, at most." Betsy reached into her bosom and pulled out a sixpence. "Here's a spare tester for you. For pocket money. Get yourself a Cornish pasty while you're waiting to come home."

Prudence pocketed the coin, then gave Betsy a fervent hug. "What would I do without you?"

They descended the steps of their lodging house and emerged onto Shoe Lane. Here were the many sponging houses, where the bailiffs kept debtors crowded in until they could be transferred to a larger prison. It was a forbidding street, filled with squalid taverns and shops. They hurried to the corner, passed Fleet Market—pausing for a moment so that Prudence could purchase her ribbons—then parted at the corner of Old Bailey Road. Betsy turned north to Newgate Street and Cheapside, where young bucks were always on the prowl, while Prudence made her way toward the river Thames.

The sweetness of the August morning air was nearly overpowered by the choking smells of the port. Even at this hour, tobacco smoke wafted from the taverns, drifting up to the tankards that hung from their eaves to advertise their wares. The stink of fish lingered at every corner of the narrow, cobbled streets, where fishmongers hawked the day's catch. Dead dogs and rats lay decaying in the gutters, to be preyed on by an occasional foul-odored pig. A pie shop gave momentary respite, its belching chimney redolent of baking crusts and good English roast beef. Prudence lifted her skirts to step across a small ditch, where sausage-makers had flung their malodorous garbage, and wrinkled her nose in distaste. The city was not for her, so crowded and filthy.

She looked up at St. Paul's as she passed. Even the beauty of that magnificent church was marred by the crowding that prevented a person from seeing it whole, in all its glory. She sighed. But Papa would have liked to see it, particularly the splendor of its interior. She sighed again. She had been to church only once since she'd come to London, creeping into St. Paul's on a dark, rainy afternoon. Like a wicked sinner who didn't deserve to plead to her Maker after all she'd done.

She passed the Custom House, reached the Tower stairs, and descended to the wharf. She felt giddy from the growing warmth of the day, breathless from her long walk with her breasts so tightly bound.

There were fewer ships than usual in the Pool, that part of the Thames that stretched from Tower Bridge to Limehouse at the turn of the river. A couple of sturdy merchantmen, their masts sharp against the clear sky. A flyboat carrying coal, a few small coasting vessels, and three or four cutters ferrying provisions from the docks. The wharf itself was crowded, with porters and watchmen and merchants bustling about like so many busy bees in a hive. Not the sort who would stop to buy a trinket from an old woman. As for the sailors lounging in the doorways of taverns and gin shops—they seemed more interested in wasting their money on the prancing harlots who dotted the waterfront than in spending a penny on a bit of tobacco or a tin of tea. The air was fouled with their lewd comments and bawdy shouts.

"Harkee, Doll, will you lay alongside me vessel?"

"I beseech thee, pretty one. Hoist yer sails. Have a dram o' pity for this poor tar's aching cods!"

"You there, hussy! Will I catch a pintle blossom if I boards ye?"

The crudeness of their language made Prudence blush. She was grateful that the words were not directed at her, but it shamed her to hear them. In all her twenty-one years, she had never heard such talk until she had come to London.

She thought of poor dead Papa. "Kitten," he would have said, "you have no one but yourself to blame. God shows us many paths, but 'tis we who make the choices." But how could she have chosen otherwise?

There was a flurry of activity next to one of the wharves. Prudence recognized a blowsy bum-boat woman of her acquaintance, standing in the middle of her boat and gesticulating wildly. A dozen girls, tricked out in gaudy laces and ribbons and feathers, shrieked back at her.

Prudence made her way through the crowd and frowned down at the woman. "What's in the wind, Grace?"

The red-faced woman huffed in annoyance and pushed back a greasy curl from her forehead. "There be a fleet o' men-o'-war at Deptford, ready to sail. I told these bawds I can take 'em there for tuppence each. But there be room for only two of 'em in my boat, lessn' I leaves my victuals behind." She pointed to the baskets of fresh produce and livestock that crowded the bottom of her tiny boat. "Where's the profit if I leaves my goods? But how am I to choose among these painted sluts? One's as good nor t'other!"

A fleet of ships! A whole fleet of His Majesty's sailors, needing candles and soap and tobacco for their long voyage. Prudence could sell everything in her basket! Calling up all her reserves of boldness, she reached into her pocket and took out Betsy's sixpence. She held out the silver coin to Grace. "Here's a tester, if you take me instead."

Grace grinned and snatched the money. "Done!" While the harlots complained loudly, the bum-boat woman helped Prudence into her boat, sat down between two cages of live chickens, and applied herself to the oars.

Deptford lay a few miles up the Thames, a small village dominated by the Royal Dockyard, military storehouses, a marine barracks, and several offices of the Admiralty. The dockside was crowded with a dozen men-of-war, tall and proud and freshly painted. Bright banners and ensigns hung from their masts, and every deck teemed with scurrying sailors engaged in final preparations for the voyage. Large davits swung over open hatches, delivering last-minute supplies to the holds.

While the bum-boat woman stayed in her little vessel to barter her goods through the open portholes and gun ports of a third-rate man-of-war, Prudence was passed hand to hand to the main deck by a group of cheery tarpaulins, all eager to buy the wares of the "old grandam." The deck was a chaos of men and their tearful wives, brazen whores, traders of goods of all sorts, stiff-necked officers, brightly uniformed marines, and lowly sailors in various states of excitement or dismay. The sea could be an adventure but, with the French beginning to challenge the British in the Colonies, as Prudence had heard, this could be the last voyage for many a man, and they knew it.

Prudence did a brisk trade, nearly emptying her basket in little more than an hour. Her pocket was filled with coins. She peered over the side of the ship; Grace still had half a boatload to sell, and had moved on to another ship. It would be hours before she was ready to return to the city. Prudence swayed against the railing. The heat and the crowd and her tight bindings were beginning to stifle her. Perhaps she could find a bit of shade and quiet inside.

She steered a path through the milling crowd toward the forecastle and shelter, skirting the ship's boats filled with caged fowl, avoiding the cannon that punctuated the open deck, and dodging a crew of seamen storing the last of the supplies in a nearby hold. She heard a shout above the din on deck and turned just in time to see a large crate, swinging on a davit, come hurtling toward her. She tried to duck, but it was too late. The box crashed into her head with a sickening thud that set bells to ringing in her skull. She clutched at her forehead and sank to the deck. She could feel the warmth of her blood seeping from beneath her wig.

"Grandmother, be ye bad hurt?" A sunburned young tar bent over her, his eyes dark with concern. He held out his hands to cradle her face.

She eluded his grasp and struggled to her feet. Dabbing at her cut with a corner of her apron, she shook her head. "No, no." It wouldn't do for him to examine her more closely. "I'll just seek a bit of rest within."

Still trembling and shaken, she staggered to the forecastle and inched her way inside. She found herself in the upper gun deck. It was almost as crowded as the deck outside, with seamen availing themselves of the services of the whores before their long, enforced celibacy. The sight of the grunting couples made Prudence's stomach turn. Still in a daze, she backed up to the steep stairs of a hatchway. Perhaps the deck below . . .

She felt her foot miss the step. Felt herself tumbling down the stairs head over heels, felt the jolting blows of the wooden planks as she struck her head, her arms, her body.

The fall seemed interminable, like a long, agonizing drop into a dark tunnel. She was powerless to stop her descent. She landed with a heavy thud.

When she raised her head at last, she saw that she was in the lower gun deck, which was quite deserted. She felt nauseated and dizzy, desperately blinking her eyes to clear her head. And the air was so close, and she could scarcely breathe . . .

The sun streamed in at the open gun ports. *Air!* she thought. If she could only reach fresh air . . . Crawling painfully across the rough deck, she dragged herself to one of the cannons that sat, well lashed down, before a port. She clawed at it with bloody hands and tried to haul herself to her feet. But her head was spinning. She heard a loud buzzing in her brain and felt her body bathed in an ice-cold, clammy sweat. With a sigh, she pitched forward.

She felt the cold barrel of the gun crack against her skull as she fell. And then . . . nothing.

Chapter Two

"Damn my liver, sir, if ever I've seen a face so beslubbered with tears." Doctor Ross Manning scowled down at the young lieutenant and finished stitching the gash in the man's scrotum. He admired the neatness of the stitches. A fine job, he had to admit to himself. Even the fussy examiners at Barber-Surgeons' Hall would find no quarrel with that.

Lieutenant Elliot sniffled and rubbed his sleeve against his dripping nose. "A man has a right to tears when it hurts," he said, sulking.

Ross contemplated Elliot with his cold gaze. "A man has no right to *any* tears. Ever. Not if he's a man." Not even when his dear Martha . . . He gritted his teeth and hardened his heart against the pain. No point in dwelling on the past.

He watched Elliot haul himself painfully off the surgeon's table and pull up his bloodied breeches. "Next time," he said, "be more careful when you're showing the ratings the use of a cutlass. Bathe your wound often. Salt water will sting like the devil, but the cut will heal faster. Use it. I'll remove the stitches in a week or so. You should be walking sans pain in two or three weeks."

Elliot scuffed his buckled shoe against the deck and cleared his throat like a man reluctant to speak. "And what of . . ." he murmured at last.

"By the time we reach Williamsburg, you should be primed and ready to board any doxy you find. If that's your fancy," he added in disgust.

Elliot looked horrified. "I have a wife, sir!"

Ross shrugged. "More power to you. Now leave me. I have other work to do."

He watched Elliot make his tentative way out of the cockpit, shuffling and limping by turns. Then he emptied the basin of bloody water into the slop bucket for his surgeon's mate to dump, neatly put away his instruments, and washed down the table. The boy had even pissed as he'd operated! What would he do in the event of a battle, if his leg had to come off?

Ross let his gaze wander over the quarters that would be his for the next month or so. As on most men-of-war, the cockpit, where the surgeons operated, was tucked into the orlop deck, nestling snugly aft just below the lower gun deck. It held the surgeon's table, a large medicine chest—well stocked on Ross's orders with powders, potions, knives, and saws—and a long, shelflike table fastened to the mizzenmast. If there were a battle, this platform would hold the most seriously wounded. There were lengths of canvas nailed to the beams on two sides; they warded off the draft and screened the cockpit from the quarters of the midshipmen and quartermasters, who were lodged within the cable tiers on either side. Two rolled hammocks leaned against a far wall; at night, they would berth Ross's surgeon's mates.

He crossed the passageway to his own cabin. It was far roomier than his quarters on his previous ship, and he'd furnished it to his exacting taste—a wide box bunk with wooden side boards, a comfortable padded chair, a broad bench, his sea chest and food cupboard, and a desk large enough to hold his books in a small rack, serve his meals, and still have room to spread his sketching folios. Several lanterns hung from the beams; at this level, below the waterline, the cabin was perpetually in darkness.

He crossed to his sea chest, pulled off his white tye wig, and folded it away in its own box. Now that they were under weigh, he'd have no need of it, except for the officers' mess. And unless this captain was more rigid and formal than most. He was curious to meet the man; the purser had suggested that Captain Hackett was a man out of the ordinary.

Ross found a ribbon and tied back his light brown hair. It was of an indeterminate color—like wet sand on the beach, Martha used to tease him. Which had always disturbed him in some odd way: he didn't like to feel that any aspect of his person was less than perfect in her sight.

He rolled down his shirtsleeves and put on his uniform coat, meaning to inspect the ship and ascertain what seamen might already be in the sick berth.

There was a soft tap on his door. At his bidding, a pale-skinned midshipman, scarcely into his teens, stepped into his cabin and tugged at his forelock.

"Begging your pardon, Mr. Manning, but Cap'n Hackett wishes to see you in his quarters."

"Thank you." He surveyed the pallid face before him with a practiced eye. "Take a little sun whilst we're still in the northern latitudes, boy. Else you'll scorch to a turn when we reach the Azores."

He dismissed the boy and climbed the three levels to the great cabin under the poop deck. The bright sun coming through the gratings above the aft hatchway showed him that it was still afternoon. With a brisk wind, he noted, stepping out onto the quarterdeck and leaning against the railing. They were making good headway. He could see the harbor of Sheerness already well aft of the ship. The sky was beginning to cloud over; it promised rain, but not a heavy storm at the moment. He crossed the quarterdeck, knocked on the captain's door, and was admitted by a servant, who discreetly vanished.

The purser had been right. Captain Sir Joseph Hackett was a man of extraordinary good looks, far beyond those of other mortals. Ross was struck at once by the fineness of his features: a lean, saturnine jaw, a perfectly shaped, straight nose, glittering dark eyes surmounted by black eyebrows that rose to sharp peaks in the center. Though he seemed to be about thirty-five, his deeply tanned skin was smooth and scarcely touched with lines or weather. He had put aside his powdered wig; his glossy raven hair was tied in the back with a large black silk bow, and the side pieces had been meticulously curled and pomaded. His uniform was expensive and exquisitely tailored, serving to accentuate his wiry—though no less masculine—body. His nails were trimmed and carefully buffed.

Ross glanced around the spacious cabin. The costly furnishings seemed to have been chosen to flatter the handsomeness of its occupant. The polished mahogany wall paneling and furniture, and the scarlet plush chairs were the perfect background for the man's dark good looks. Ross suppressed a cynical smile. If Hackett wasn't lacking in beauty, neither was he lacking in vanity: several gilt-edged mirrors hung on the walls, interspersed with paintings and a carved coat of arms.

Without rising from his chair, Hackett responded to Ross's salute with a civil nod. "Doctor Manning. I trust you're settled in?"

"Yes, sir."

"Have you met the other officers?"

"Most of them, sir."

"You find your quarters to your liking?" At Ross's acknowledgment of his comfort, Hackett smiled in smug satisfaction. "Better than your last ship, I'll warrant. I'm told you served for a year aboard the *Thunder.*" His well-formed mouth curled into a sneer. "A fourth-rater in every way, I'm told. With a fool for a captain."

Ross clenched his fists at his sides. Not only a man of vanity, but pompous besides. "I served for ten months, sir," he replied stiffly, forcing himself to remember that this was his superior officer. "As for the *Thunder,* I found captain and crew to be agreeable comrades, to a man."

"In faith? That's scarcely what *I* heard. 'Cold-hearted Manning.' Wasn't that what they called you in the dark recesses of the carpenter's walk?"

Ross had heard the whispers, but had ignored them. What did it signify in the scheme of things? But to have Hackett throw the insult in his face . . . "My task is not to earn the seamen's approval," he said, his jaw clenched, "but to cure the sick and infirm."

Hackett brushed at his ruffled cuff in an indolent manner. "A proud answer. I trust your pride and mine don't clash on this voyage. I'm a tolerant man, as befits my noble birth and breeding. But even I have limits. I have wealth enough to live out my days in comfort on my estate. Instead, I chose this calling out of a sense of duty to my sovereign, his most esteemed majesty, George the Second. Whilst you . . ." He waved a languid hand toward his coat of arms. "Without a crest or a title, what is left for a man of education except to stoop to medicine or the law to earn a living?"

Ross sucked in a deep, steadying breath. It felt like a blast of icy air pouring into his lungs. "Did you have a reason for summoning me, Captain Hackett?" He measured out his words.

Hackett leaned back in his chair and tapped his fingers together. "In point of fact, I did. The master-at-arms tells me that you had the handcuffs removed from the pressed seamen in the forecastle. Even before we sailed."

"I did."

"Did you know you were countermanding the orders of the officer on duty?"

Did he think Ross was a fool? "By the beard of Aesculapius, of course I did. The men had been savagely beaten when they were taken. I wished to tend their wounds."

"Damme, sir, you had no right to take such action."

"I spoke to the midshipman on duty and explained the men's needs. He chose to behave like a stiff-necked ass."

Hackett's eyes flashed. "And so you went against his orders? On a military ship?"

Ross felt his anger rising. Was his judgment as a surgeon to be questioned? "In matters of health and safety aboard ship, I hold that *my* orders take precedence. Especially over the petty whims of a callow junior officer."

Hackett sprang from his chair in a rage and faced Ross toe to toe. "Now, by God, sirrah, will you defy me? If you speak to me like that in the presence of others, I'll have you flogged! Surgeon or no."

Ross held his ground and responded to Hackett's challenge with a cold stare. "I don't intend to cross you, Captain, but the sooner you give me leave to conduct my business as I see fit, the sooner you'll have a healthy crew ready to engage in battle for you."

They stood facing each other for a long, tense minute. A surgeon was vital to a warship, and they both knew it. At last Hackett's piercing gaze wavered and he turned away, his shoulders set and rigid. "In matters of health, I shall trust your judgment, Manning. But I expect a great deal less defiance in return. Even surgeons can be thrown into a locked hatch!"

Ross gave him a bow that owed as much to mockery as deference. He'd won his point, though the captain seemed loath to admit it. "Will that be all, sir?"

Hackett preened in front of a mirror for a moment, allowing his anger to cool. Then he turned, his face relaxing into a patronizing smile. " 'Twill be a long voyage, Manning. Let us begin as friends, if not equals." He indicated a chair and picked up a small bell from his desk. "Sit down. I'll send for some Madeira."

The man was making an effort to be civil; Ross responded in a conciliatory tone. "I have no doubt the voyage will go smoothly." He seated himself and accepted the Madeira when it was brought.

Hackett sipped at his wine with studied casualness—his head tilted to the side, one hand resting languidly on his sword hilt—as though he were posing for a portrait. "You'll find the *Chichester* a good ship. The men have learned not to cross me. Not that I don't work them hard. We should be prepared for a new war with the French any time now. There have been skirmishes off the coast of the Colonies. And open fighting, 'tis said, in the boundary between French Canada and Nova Scotia. We have a complement of one hundred marines on board. Unless we lose them in a sea battle, they are to replace the troops that were sent north from Virginia. We could face daunting challenges before we ever reach the Colonies."

"Your pardon, sir, but I'm not a novice. I saw battle aboard the *Thunder*. And my surgeon's mates seem competent. We spent last night ashore discussing their duties."

Hackett clicked his tongue. "What a waste of an evening." He suddenly grinned—a leering, satyr's smile. "I spent *my* last night in the company of several charming creatures. One of them stood upon a table stark naked and danced and danced . . ." He licked his lips at the memory. "Odds my life, I had not thought the female form was capable of such gyrations. All the while, the other bawds kept my attention from straying too far from those vital parts of a man that need constant refreshment."

"A most amusing evening, no doubt." Ross fought to keep the falseness from his voice.

"With no regrets, God willing. I have not suffered claps in years. I can afford a splendid, clean house at fifty guineas a night. But I trust you have brought aboard cures for the loathsome distemper, should they be necessary."

"Of course. But you might consider sheathing yourself with armor when you visit the whores of London."

Hackett's face was flushed with excitement. Clearly his love of women was nearly as great as his love of self. "Ah, but the adventure, the risk! There is an establishment on Half Moon Street . . ." He crossed the cabin to a chest of drawers and pulled out a small leather-bound volume. "The good madam of that house has such an array of beauties that, between the lot of them, I've been able to perform in like manner each and every position." He opened the book and ruffled the pages before Ross. They contained dozens of pictures of naked couples fornicating.

Ross was now actively swallowing his disgust. "How clever," he managed to say.

Hackett laughed and tapped at a particularly lewd illustration. "Does it not stir your loins, man?"

Not in the slightest, thought Ross with revulsion. He fixed the captain with an icy stare. "I take no interest in women." God knew *that* was so.

Hackett shrugged. "Each man to his own taste. There are more than enough powder monkeys aboard. Soft young lads of eleven or twelve. I trust you can find a few to play catamite to your needs. For a shilling or two."

Ross rose to his feet. If he didn't leave now, God knew what he'd be tempted to do. "By your leave, sir, I have my duties," he said in a choked voice.

"Captain Sir Joseph, sir." Hackett's servant stood at a side door of the cabin, his body bent in a deferential bow. "There's a rater outside who says he has a message for you."

"Send him in."

The man who appeared at the door, clutching his shiny tarred hat in his hands, was as unhandsome as the captain was beautiful. His head, anchored upon a massive neck, was too large even for his barrel chest, and his short, bandy legs made him appear to be squatting. He had a bulbous, red nose with several deforming growths on it, and his eyes were small and set uncommonly close together. His fleshy lips drooped on one side, and his weather-beaten face was pockmarked. His black hair, tied back with a leather thong, was stringy and thinning on top.

He saluted awkwardly. "By your leave, Cap'n, the first lieutenant wishes you to know that we be comin' up to Margate in an hour or so, by his reckonin'. And did the cap'n, sir, want to heave to and send any last messages to London? 'Tis our last landfall, d'ye see, afore we tacks back through the Channel."

"Do you think me ignorant of these waters, you scum?" growled Hackett.

The seaman shook his head vehemently. "No, sir. Not I, sir. I be a good honest seaman, sir, and polite to my betters. That I be, sir. That I *certainly* be, sir."

"Hold your babbling tongue, you dog! Are you new aboard this ship?"

"Aye, sir." A frightened whisper.

"What do they call you?" asked Hackett, as though he felt that the possession of a name was beneath the wretched creature before him.

"Wedge, sir. Tobias Wedge."

"What's your station?"

"Gunner, an't please you, sir."

"Do you know how I treat insolent dogs who insult my intelligence?"

Wedge was now trembling. "Aye, sir. That I do, sir. There be talk in the fo'c'sle. And I seen the stripes on my mate, Gawky, what you give him on the last voyage."

"Then be warned, Wedge. Tell Lieutenant St. John that he may proceed full speed ahead. I have no messages. And tell him further that he is not to send you to me again. *Never!* Do you understand?"

"Aye, sir, I w-will," stammered Wedge, saluting and backing out of the door.

Hackett swallowed the last of his Madeira and shuddered. "I can't abide ugliness. It makes my guts turn."

Ross scowled. "The man can scarcely be blamed for an accident of nature."

"The dog would do well to keep out of my sight." Hackett rose from his chair. "Now, Mr. Manning, if you will leave me to my charts . . ."

"Sir." Ross bowed and made for the door. If this interview with Hackett was any indication, it would be a long voyage.

"A moment, Doctor. All the officers will be dining with me this evening. 'Tis a custom of mine. Noblesse oblige. First night out, and once a week thereafter. I expect you in attendance, of course. Come here to the great cabin at first watch. Eight bells prompt. I don't take kindly to laggards."

"As you wish, sir."

Ross made his way onto the deck and drew in great breaths of fresh sea air, as though he could cleanse his body of the foulness of Hackett's presence. The man was vicious and vain, flaunting his title, his station, his wealth. Most captains didn't take on the expense of entertaining their officers at table. A few senior men, once or twice during the voyage, perhaps. But not the full complement of officers. And not by the week, certainly. As for Hackett's disgusting preoccupation with women . . .

Ross moved down to the main deck, his brain crowding with dark thoughts. How imperfect was mankind. How useless to struggle against cruelty and evil, when there was always another weak or venal or stupid creature to take the place of the last.

He nodded to himself. He was right to make his decision as he had. And Hackett had only confirmed the rightness of it. There was no ridding himself of his black humors so long as he traveled in the company of man. He had thought that devoting himself to medicine this past year would help. That the care of others would fill his days and blot out his nightmares. But it had been useless. Even as he'd tended and patched and healed, he had been aware of his chilling indifference toward his patients. God preserve him, he'd cared little if they lived or died, prospered or suffered. He'd doctored them as best he could, proud of his skills. But he could no longer see them as human beings.

And the carnage of battle. Was there anything more inhuman than that? That engagement with the French near the West Indies last May. He had tossed overboard enough severed arms and legs and hands to feed a school of sharks. He was tired of seeing death in every face, no matter how robust. Tired of the awareness that life was brief, and struggle was futile. What was the pettiness of a man's life against the inevitability of death?

Yes. He had made the right choice. He was firm in his resolve. His surgeon's warrant was only for the year. And, despite the harassment of the French, England was not yet at war. He would resign his commission in the Colonies, abandon civilization, and find a hermit's cabin in the wilds of Virginia to live out his days. He still had the last of his mother's inheritance—enough to survive in the wilderness. Perhaps he could find peace at last. Nourish himself on the few sweet memories he had of Martha, and forget the pain and bitterness that gnawed at him like a cancer. *Oh, God,* he thought, rubbing his hand across his eyes, *let me find peace in solitude.*

Or a bottle of poison to end his days.

Chapter Three

❧

The afternoon sky had turned dull and threatening; the clouds were now the color of steel. A bad beginning to the voyage. Still rankling from his meeting with Captain Hackett, Ross started down the hatchway in the forecastle.

It was dim on the stairs, the light fading as he moved farther away from the open grating above. He considered lighting the lanterns that sat in niches beside the stairs, but remembered that he'd left his tinderbox in his cabin. He stopped suddenly on the staircase, peered into the gloom below him, then knelt. He hadn't been mistaken.

The flash of red that had caught his eye proved to be a length of ribbon. One of the harlots had dropped it, no doubt, before she'd disembarked. He was about to pick it up when another object caught his eye. And then another. There seemed to be a trail of trinkets and small objects—tins of tea, a candle, a few quids of tobacco—leading down to the bottom of the stairs. And when he reached the lower gun deck he saw a basket, half-crushed and lying among the racks of cannonballs.

He heard a noise, a soft rustle, coming from somewhere amid the guns. By the Lord! Were there conspiracies among the malcontents so soon into the voyage? He strained his eyes against the dimness of the gun deck. Despite the open gun ports, the deck was gray and shadowy.

He spied a pile of rags, half-hidden under the nearest gun. As he stared in disbelief, the ragged mass moved and stirred. A dog or cat, smuggled aboard by a lonely tar? It emitted a sound that was very like a human groan.

He was beside it in a minute, kneeling before the prostrate form of what seemed to be an old crone, to judge by the matted gray hair that spilled out from beneath her cap. A poor ancient peddler, no doubt, who'd had the misfortune to tumble down the stairs before the ship sailed. Or perhaps, given her age, she'd had a seizure on the hatchway and dropped her basket, only managing to drag herself to this spot.

Aware that she might be badly hurt, he turned her over as gently as he could; her dirty face was almost completely covered with blood. He muttered an oath. It was too dark here to see her clearly, let alone to find the source of her injury. But if she was still senseless after all these hours, her wounds could be severe, her condition grave.

And then, even with all his skills, he might not be able to save her.

He scooped her up and carried her down the last flight of stairs to the cockpit. He hadn't lost his sea legs since his service on the *Thunder;* his steps were sure and steady, even with his burden. Placing the woman carefully on the table, he noted how thin she seemed, even under her voluminous rags. Perhaps she had fainted from hunger. The trinket-women along the docks often had large families to support. A penny saved from an unbought piece of cheese for breakfast might mean food on the supper table for the children. He considered sending for one of his surgeon's mates to cook up some hot broth in the ship's galley, then changed his mind. There would be time for that when he'd discovered the source of the creature's affliction. He was a doctor first.

He filled a basin with water, found dressings, brought some sponges to the table. He frowned in annoyance. It was still too dim to tend her properly; he'd have to light a few more lanterns. He hung them from the beams, then turned back to his patient, scanning her body quickly with an experienced eye. Her limbs didn't seem to be twisted, nor was there blood anywhere but on her face and hands and the corner of her apron. He hoped it indicated that there were no compound fractures—an agony to set, with the patient screaming in pain. Doubly so if it was an old woman.

Strange, he thought, feeling for her pulse, which was strong and steady.

Her hands, though mottled with blood, were smooth and long-fingered. Not a sign of gnarling. A fortunate old woman, not to suffer the deformities of age. Well, first things first. He couldn't find her wound unless he cleaned her face. He took off his coat, rolled up his sleeves, and reached for a sponge.

Suddenly, she began to gasp, her face twisting with the effort to breathe. She inhaled with little painful cries, and exhaled shallowly on a moan. He dropped the sponge and bent over her. Her head would have to wait. She might have broken a few ribs in her fall, or punctured a lung. Clearly, the pressure was building in her chest and causing her great difficulty. He would have to work fast.

He tore her large neckerchief from her body and tossed it to the floor. She was even thinner than he'd imagined; scarcely a curve to her bosom. He reached for scissors and cut the laces of her bodice, pulling open the gown to her waist. How odd, he thought. In contrast to her ragged outer clothing, her shift was clean and seemed quite new.

Her distress was increasing by the minute; she was now thrashing in breathless pain. He had no time to concern himself with the niceties of the woman's apparel. Clutching the top of her shift with both hands, he tore it straight down the middle and spread it wide.

"By the beard of Aesculapius," he muttered. "What mummery is this?"

A band of cloth was wrapped tightly around her bosom; moreover, the skin above and below the muslin was soft and pink and young. But the band was keeping her from breathing—he'd have to get it off in a hurry. Again he reached for his scissors and snipped. The band fell away.

Compressed as they had been, and bearing red marks from the tight fabric, her breasts were still magnificently full and alluring, with small, rosy nipples and sensuous curves. He remembered when such a sight would have excited him. But now . . .

She sighed in relief and relaxed against the table, gulping in great draughts of air. He watched her dispassionately for a moment, assessing her with a surgeon's experienced eye. She still seemed befogged, but the steady rise and fall of her chest reassured him that he'd cured her breathlessness with one cut of his scissors. However, there was still the matter of the cut to her head.

"What else are you hiding, 'old woman'?" he asked mockingly, although she seemed not to be aware of him yet. Indeed, her eyes were still closed.

He slipped his hand behind her neck to raise her head from the table, and pulled off her shapeless cap. He could see clearly now that the gray hair was merely a wig. He removed it from her head and heard a sharp click as her comb dropped to the deck. At once his hands were covered by a thick, silky mane of hair. The color of leaves in autumn—a rich, burnished red.

"Damn my liver," he murmured, taken aback. Surely the face under all that blood must be as exquisitely beautiful as the body and the hair. He was filled with a burning curiosity to see her clear—a curiosity that had nothing to do with Ross Manning, surgeon. And what color eyes, he wondered, would go with that glorious hair?

He squeezed out the sponge in the water and stroked it across her forehead. At the touch of the cold liquid, she cried aloud and opened her eyes.

They were green, as he knew they had to be. Soft and green. And filled with terror.

Prudence stared at the man in horror. Even before she'd opened her eyes, she had been dimly aware that her breasts were uncovered. But to find a man bending over her, his face so close to hers . . . She remembered the things Betsy had spoken of. Of men and their lewd ways. She felt panic rising in her throat like a choking tide. "What are you doing?" Her voice shook.

He had the coldest blue eyes she had ever seen. Like icicles hanging from the eaves, hard and glittering. "Be still," he said. "You've been hurt."

She tugged at her torn clothing in a vain attempt to cover her bosom. "Wh-what kind of a man are you, to take advantage of a helpless woman?"

"God Almighty. Ever the cry of the female sex. As though a man can have nothing deeper in his thoughts."

"And *your* thoughts?" She could read nothing in his face.

"Young woman, I'm a surgeon," he said with a tired sigh. "You've been hurt, I told you. Do you remember what happened?"

She felt chastened by his tone. How foolish, to jump to such a ready conclusion. But after Betsy's stories . . . and then her accident . . . She closed her eyes for a minute to struggle against the wave of dizziness that swept her. "I fell. The stairs. The cannon . . ." It was so hard to remember. "There was a crate, when they were loading. It hit me." She touched the spot on her forehead, just within her hairline, and cried out.

"Good." He gave a dispassionate nod, as though her pain scarcely concerned him. "You've saved me the trouble of searching for it." He picked up a moistened sponge and brought it to her forehead.

"Wait," she said, aware for the first time that the lantern above her was swaying, and she along with it. "Where are we?"

"H.M.S. *Chichester.* Third-rate man-of-war in the King's Navy."

"Are we under sail?"

"Of course."

Sweet merciful heaven! Asea? "I can't be here!" she cried, struggling to sit up and ease herself off the table on which she seemed to be lying. Her head pounded with every movement. "I must return to London." She tried to stand on unsteady legs, found it impossible, and collapsed into his arms.

He placed her back on the table and scowled; his eyes reminded her of a frigid sky in winter. "I've been known to tie my difficult patients to the table. Will that be necessary with you?"

She felt real terror at the thought. To be tied and helpless with a strange man? "No. Please," she murmured.

"Then do as I tell you. Lie down. We can concern ourselves with returning you to London later." Considering his unsympathetic tone, his hands were surprisingly gentle as he pushed back her hair and sponged the cut on her forehead.

Curious, she watched him as he ministered to her. Save for his icy, discomfiting eyes, his face was pleasant. Even handsome, she had to admit to herself. His wide forehead bespoke intelligence, his jaw was square and strong without being belligerent. His long, proud nose was a little less than symmetrical, with a small bump on the bridge, which—rather than detracting from his looks—made him seem appealingly vulnerable. His mouth was firm and wide, set now in a rigid line of concentration. She wondered what it looked like when he smiled. *If* he smiled. Ah, but those eyes . . .

Though she'd kept her hands modestly crossed against her bosom all the while he worked, she wondered if it was necessary. Those eyes had shown not the slightest flicker of interest in her as a woman. That thought was reassuring; still, she felt an odd pinprick to her pride. Even the bumpkins in Winsley had turned their heads as she'd passed them on the High Street.

Oh, Prudence, she thought, hearing her father's gently chiding voice. *Vanity, Kitten. Vanity.*

Vanity, indeed. This doctor was a strange, distant man. He looked at her, but she had the uncomfortable feeling that he didn't really *see* her.

" 'Tis not too grievous a wound," he said, putting down the sponge and frowning. "But I should put a stitch or two in it, so it heals properly." He turned to his medicine chest and removed a small, curved needle and a length of catgut. He threaded the needle, then bent over her once again. "Keep still. Don't move," he ordered.

She felt the sharp stab of the needle in her forehead and winced. She closed her eyes and gritted her teeth until he had finished his work and snipped the ends of the catgut.

"Good girl," he said. "You were very brave."

His patronizing tone grated on her ear. "Did you expect me to scream?" she asked sharply.

Again that cold, unemotional gaze, and a long, disapproving silence. "Do you have a name?" he asked at last.

"Why shouldn't I?" she snapped, angry at how uncomfortable he made her feel. "Am I simply a cadaver to be probed and pricked and poked at?"

He gave a dry snort. "Scarcely that. Cadavers are silent."

A pox on his rudeness! "Prudence," she muttered.

"What?" He looked bemused.

"My name. Prudence Allbright."

He was capable of smiling after all, though it was only a smirk. "Doctor Ross Manning. Mine. Now"—he freshened his sponge in the basin and brought it to her face—"do you think you can keep still while I see what other injuries you may have sustained?"

She agreed with a sulky nod. He washed the blood and soot from her face, commenting on a small scratch on her chin and a bruise on the edge of her cheekbone. "Scarcely worth troubling about," he said. He sponged the blood from her hands and frowned down at her. "How were you hurt? The cannon, the crate, the stairs?"

"All of them, I think." She felt foolish, as though she were admitting to the sin of clumsiness. "The crate hit me on deck. I was bleeding and came below. I fell down the stairs. I remember getting up, then fainting. I think I hit my head against the cannon then."

He seemed to be fighting a smile. "A veritable Job, afflicted from all sides. Where did the gun hit you?"

"I'm not sure. Somewhere on my head."

He ran his fingers through her hair, probing her scalp. She yelped in pain as he touched a spot just above one ear. He separated her tresses and peered closely at the spot. "A very large bruise, though the skin wasn't broken. A mild concussion, perhaps. No doubt that is what kept you insensible for so many hours. That," he added, "and that absurd band that nearly squeezed the air out of your lungs." His voice had darkened with disgust. "You don't seem like a rattlebrain. What in Satan's name possessed you to do such a thing to yourself?"

She hated having to defend herself against his mockery. "I needed money," she said with some heat. "I could either disguise myself as an old woman to sell trifles, or appear as my own young self. In which case, I have no doubt that I would have been expected to sell . . . other things." She stopped abruptly, feeling the blush burning her cheeks. What had possessed her to be so immodest? To talk brazenly of such matters to a stranger?

"To sell 'other things'?" he repeated dryly. "You needn't be so coy. I'm old enough to understand the ways of men and women without turning scarlet." He raised a quizzical eyebrow. "But are you, I wonder?"

She felt challenged by the question, by his overbearing superiority. She wasn't an empty-headed child, after all. "I'm twenty-one!"

"And filled with all the knowledge of life, no doubt," he drawled.

She blushed even harder. This past year had taught her—and with a vengeance—how little she knew of life, of herself, of all the verities she had taken for granted up till then.

He gave a humorless laugh, reached out, and tossed back her skirts to her thighs.

"Sweet Mother of Mercy! What are you doing?" She sat up with a jolt that made her head pound afresh. She didn't know what to clutch first— her aching head or her bosom, which was once again exposed by her movements. And still she'd need a third hand to pull down her skirts.

Doctor Manning sighed, a man at the edge of his patience. "Don't act like a ridiculous child. You took a tumble. I want to be sure your limbs aren't broken or sprained. Now lie down, damn it, and let me examine you."

She obeyed meekly. She was behaving like a skittish fool. He must think her a perfect ninny! She relaxed on the table and stared up at the ceiling beams, covered with pitch. Lord have mercy! Her blackened teeth! Not only behaving like a fool, but *looking* like one! She glanced at Manning, then surreptitiously rubbed away the tar.

He seemed not to have noticed. He untied her garters and pulled down her stockings to her ankles. He pressed and squeezed with sure hands, watching to see if any of his movements caused her pain. He found a scrape on her knee and bathed it. "I expect you to keep your garter tied below your knee for a few days until it heals."

She felt like a little girl being admonished by a nursemaid. Why did everything he did or said seem to put her at a disadvantage? From the first moment she'd opened her eyes. "I *have* had scraped knees from time to time," she said sourly. "When I was a child."

"Indeed? And were you always so difficult? As a child?"

His calm demeanor was infuriating. She glared at him and let him finish his examination in silence.

"Some bruises, of course," he said. " 'Tis to be expected. But nothing that won't heal itself." Without even bothering to cover her legs, he moved upward toward her head and peered down at her again. She felt like a specimen on a botanist's tray. "Where else do you hurt?" he asked.

She moved gingerly and groaned. "Everywhere. When I fell . . ." She chewed at her lip in dismay; her whole body was sore.

"Can you sit up?"

"My head hurts more when I do. But yes."

He waited until she had carefully eased herself into a sitting position. Then he reached out to her gown and began to pull it down from her shoulders.

"You lecherous villain!" she cried, and slapped his face as hard as she could.

He recoiled. She had not thought his eyes could grow any colder, but he froze her with his gaze. His jaw set in a hard line, the muscles bulging tautly beneath the skin. "If you do that again, I'll return the favor. But it will *not* be on your face."

She had a sudden memory of Papa scolding her when she'd been naughty, and nearly apologized to Manning. Then her pride reasserted itself. What did she have to be sorry for? Hadn't the lustful devil attempted to lay hands on her? "You'll not touch me again," she said boldly. "I'll not abide it."

"Damn my liver, but you're a vexing creature! Let me remind you again. I'm a surgeon. You've had a bad fall. I merely want to be sure that no ribs are cracked." He waited while she mulled his words, then crossed his arms against his chest. "You're behaving like an infant. Must I undress you like one?"

Imagining the humiliation of *that* scene was all the prod she needed. She had no doubt he'd make good his threat. Carefully she pulled down her gown and shift to her waist, managing to shield her bosom as she did so. When she was finished, she raised her chin in haughty defiance. "I give you leave to examine me now, Doctor."

"Put your hands down, damn it," he barked. "I've seen a woman's breasts before."

She hesitated and glared at him.

"Do as you're told! I'm losing patience." It was the first flash of anger she'd seen him allow himself.

She dropped her arms and sat stiffly while he pressed his long fingers against her ribs, just beneath her breasts. "A large bruise here"—he pressed against the side of her ribcage—"and here." He touched her shoulder and she winced. He moved around to her back and repeated his minute examination. His touch was delicate; when she didn't see his cold eyes, she could stop to admire his skillful care. His hands were almost as gentle as Jamie's had been when he'd caressed her. Jamie. She sighed.

"Do I hurt you?"

"No." The pain she bore was far deeper than her bruised flesh.

His fingers stopped at a spot just beneath her right shoulder blade. "You have a scar here."

"I fell out of a tree as a child and hit a rock."

He finished his examination and moved around to face her once again. She didn't even bother to shield her body this time. She no longer felt embarrassment. She might have been half-naked before Grandpapa's cows in the barn, for all the human feeling that emanated from the cold doctor.

"You were very fortunate when you fell," he said. "Save for your head, of course. I found only a few bruises and abrasions on your back." He stared down at that small part of her that was still decently covered. "And the rest of you?"

She colored. "I wasn't hurt there, and you'll not touch me further." She jammed her hands on her hips for emphasis and grimaced in unexpected pain.

"What?" he demanded.

She rubbed the top of her hip bone through her skirts. "It feels like a bruise. Nothing more."

"Show me."

"Will you not rest content until you have me naked?"

"I don't want to 'have' you, I merely want to examine you." He sounded like a parent explaining a simple problem to a child.

She drew herself up. She had her limits, after all! She was a woman of modesty. Not even Jamie had seen her completely naked. "You've seen all I intend to allow you to see."

He hesitated for a moment, then shrugged and turned toward the medicine chest. "I shall give you a powder of willow bark for your aching head. You should sleep for a few hours. Have a doctor in London take out the stitches in a fortnight. Mind you don't forget. I've done a tidy job. There should be little scarring."

She gave him a halfhearted smile of appreciation. The man was thorough as a doctor, at least, if not very civil as a human being. "Thank you, I . . ." she began.

"Gad's curse! You sly devil, Manning!"

Prudence turned in surprise at the voice that came from the doorway. A strikingly handsome man in a splendid uniform stood there, his dark eyes narrowing and his mouth curving into a wicked smile.

While Prudence stared, too stunned to move, he gave a sharp laugh. "So 'tis true, Mr. Manning. A woman. And by the looks of her, a veritable treasure."

Chapter Four

Doctor Manning stiffened. "Captain Hackett. Sir." He saluted smartly. Then he scooped Prudence's neckerchief from the deck, hurried to her side, and pressed it into her hands and against her breasts. "Cover yourself," he said in a low voice.

She smiled her gratitude and wrapped the neckerchief around her shoulders, folding the ends across her bosom and tucking them into her petticoat. Then, aware of her exposed legs, she quickly smoothed down her skirts.

The captain laughed—a silky laugh that seemed to hold hidden meanings. He was a marvelously well-favored man—it was the first thing she'd noticed about him, despite her alarmed surprise. Genial and agreeable. Then why should she feel a shiver of unease? "You surprise me, Mr. Manning," he said. "I did not think we shared the same diversions."

Prudence had been chilled more than once by the cool demeanor that seemed to be Manning's normal aspect. But this time she was certain that the calm face he turned toward Captain Hackett was feigned, hiding unfathomable emotions. "What brings you to the cockpit, sir?" he asked.

Hackett indicated the lengths of canvas that screened the cockpit from the cable tiers. "The timbre of a woman's voice can be heard through that. So when it was reported to me, I thought to investigate for myself." He stepped closer to the table, his dark eyes scanning Prudence. His smile held a look of warm approval that she found oddly flattering.

"I'll not begin to ask why you brought this flower aboard," he continued. "But I must admire your taste. She's a beauty. I trust that you are a . . . How shall I put this delicately? A generous man, Doctor. Democratic in your views of property rights."

Prudence frowned. Property rights? What did he mean by that?

"Not in this instance, sir," said Manning in the same genial tone. He turned his back on the captain and grabbed Prudence's left hand. He fished surreptitiously in his waistcoat pocket, pulled out a ring, and shoved it onto her fourth finger. His eyes held a silent plea, begging for her cooperation. "This young woman is Martha Symonds Manning, sir. My wife." He draped his arm around Prudence's shoulder as though to emphasize the point.

She swallowed her astonishment. *Wife?* Perhaps it was the odd look on Hackett's face, or the fact that she'd been taken by surprise, but Prudence allowed Manning's arm to stay. She even managed to gaze up at him like a devoted spouse, though she couldn't imagine why she was helping him in this mad deception. Why should she trust him over the captain?

"Egad!" exclaimed Hackett. "Wife? I don't believe you!"

"See for yourself." Manning thrust Prudence's hand before the captain's eyes. He smiled at her. "Give him your ring, my dear. Let him look."

The ring was a wide, shiny band of gold, engraved with floral tendrils and scrolls. Prudence admired its workmanship even as she slipped it off her finger and handed it to the officer.

"You may note the inscription inside," said Manning. "POR TOUS JOURS." He smiled again at Prudence. "Do you remember, my dear?"

Hackett turned the ring around in his fingers, squinting at the fine carving within. "The spelling is unusual."

Prudence found her voice at last. If she was to be a party to this bizarre charade, she should bestir herself. " 'For always,' " she translated. " 'Tis early French."

The captain eyed her with approval. "Not only beautiful, but educated."

Ross nodded and returned the ring to Prudence's finger. "Yes, she is." He seemed mildly surprised, as though her behavior up to now had almost convinced him that he was dealing with a simpleminded child.

"Wife," muttered Hackett, his face set in a sour frown.

Prudence could scarcely understand why he seemed so disconcerted. Indeed, the charged air between the two men was bewildering. Why had Manning—a calm, seemingly rational man, if nothing else—suddenly reinvented her as his wife? It was madness! Upon reflection, she decided that there was no reason for Hackett not to know the truth of her predicament. "Oh, but . . ." she began.

Manning cut her short with a frosty glance. "Yes. My *wife*. For three years now, sir. I regret I cannot produce the papers, since you seem to doubt my word. But I do have a handkerchief with our names entwined. Would you care to see it?" His eyes held a bold challenge, for all his agreeable tone.

Hackett wavered. "That will not be necessary for now," he said at last. His jaw hardened. "But can you explain how she came to be aboard, Mr. Manning? I don't take kindly to stowaways." He glared at the surgeon. "Nor to accomplices, sir."

"I'm as displeased as you are, Captain, sir. But an educated woman does not, of necessity, mean a wise one. This creature is quite young, as you can see. Lacking in mature wisdom. She foolishly decided to come aboard in disguise and surprise me. Then had the misfortune to fall in the gun deck, where I found her."

Prudence shook her head. Heaven alone knew why she was going along with this pretense. And enduring Manning's insults, to boot! But it seemed a little late to expose the game and embarrass herself further. She smiled as innocently, as helplessly, as she could—the "young" and "foolish" wife. "Your pardon, Captain . . . Hackett, is it not? I've quite forgot my manners, or I should have apologized at once for stealing aboard your ship. But I struck my head. And it seems to have addled me. You see?" She pulled back her hair and showed him her stitched wound. She glanced at Manning. Would she be expected to address him by his given name? She decided to chance it. "Ross . . . my dear husband . . . has been patching me together."

Manning smiled in acknowledgment—a patently false smile—and patted her head.

Hackett whirled to the surgeon. "Damme, sir, but I don't believe this masquerade!"

Manning's face was a mask of control. "You doubt my honesty, sir? Would a strange woman let me do this?" He put his arm around Prudence, tilted up her chin, and kissed her full upon the mouth.

His kiss was long and thorough, his mouth moving over Prudence's with a firm and demanding pressure. She was too startled and alarmed at first to react, but then she remembered that Hackett was watching. She contrived to play her part; she reached up and rested her hand on Manning's shoulder. In response, he folded her into a close embrace. She was dimly aware of the strength of his arms around her, the solidity of his chest pressing against her bosom, the warmth of his hands on her naked back. She felt her cheeks flooding with heat, and wondered if it was because of this shameful scene—or something else. Something she didn't dare to think about. She struggled to push him away. "Please," she whispered, as he freed her lips.

If she had wondered about his reaction to the kiss, his cold, unfeeling eyes answered her, despite his tender words. He stepped back and gave her a small bow. "Forgive me, wife. I scarcely meant to affront your modesty and bring a blush to that lovely face." He turned to the captain. "Are you satisfied, sir? That I had to humiliate my wife in order to content you?"

Hackett looked uncomfortable. "Gad's curse! But you said . . . in my cabin. I mean to say, sir . . . you take no interest in women. Is it not so?"

Manning shrugged. "I merely meant aboard ship. Separated from my wife. She is always in my thoughts. And her virtue governs my own virtuous behavior."

Hackett's handsome lips curled in an odd twist. "A paragon among men, it would seem. How fortunate you are, Mrs. Manning. But I have my duties." He gave a formal bow to Prudence. "Your servant, madam. I should be honored if you came to supper tonight with your husband. The other officers would be pleased to meet you. Eight o'clock. In my cabin."

"No." Manning shook his head with finality. "My wife is not herself yet. The blow to her head, you understand. I fear you must excuse us both from your table tonight."

Prudence frowned. How dare Manning presume to speak for her? And the thought of spending the evening alone with this overbearing, unpleasant man, when she might have the company of the charming Captain Hackett and a host of young officers, all eager to please her . . . ! She gave Hackett her most winsome smile. "I should be delighted, Captain. I feel sure that, if I rest for a few hours, I shall be as bright as a Michaelmas daisy." She deepened her smile when she saw Manning scowl. So much for the old crosspatch! She hesitated, then held out her hand to Hackett. "Till later, sir. I can scarcely wait," she added, simply to discompose Manning further.

The captain's eyes widened in pleased surprise. He bent over her hand and kissed it warmly. " 'Twill be a pleasure to have such beauty grace my table. You shall sit at my right hand, of course, dear lady."

"By your leave, sir, I should like to be alone with my wife," Manning said. His voice was a strangled growl.

Hackett's mouth curved in a smirk. "I quite understand. I envy you, Doctor."

"To scold her, sir." Manning threw Prudence a look of disgust. "I'm not sure I shouldn't beat her," he muttered.

The smirk deepened to a leer that puzzled Prudence. "Ah, yes. I too have my little amusements, from time to time," said the captain. "What pleasure to dry the tears and comfort the hurts. Afterward."

"If you please, sir," said Manning through clenched teeth, "the child needs her rest."

"Of course." Hackett bowed again to Prudence. "Until eight, madam. I await your charming company." He turned on his heel and left the cockpit.

As soon as he was gone, Prudence glared at Manning, thrusting forward the hand that held the ring. "Now, sir, if you will explain this . . ."

He silenced her with a scowl and a finger to his lips, then pointed to the thin canvas walls.

She nodded her understanding; if there was to be a quarrel between them, let it be in private. She started to climb down from the table, but he abruptly picked her up and carried her through a passageway to a cabin, where he deposited her on the bunk. When he turned and slammed the door shut, she sat up in alarm.

Sweet Mother of Mercy! Surely she had misread his earlier indifference! *This* was why he had invented the story of their union. To get her alone. To have his way with her, the lewd villain! "Do you think I can't scream?" she sputtered. "If you dare to touch me? All that nonsense about being your wife . . . only to satisfy your own disgusting pleasures . . . !" She tore off the ring and hurled it across the cabin.

His eyes darkened in fury, deep blue and hard as sapphires. "By God, if you *were* my wife, I'd be tempted to tuck back your skirts and beat a little sense into you!" He pointed to the cabin door. "There are three hundred men out there—three hundred! And every one of them thirsting for a woman! And a captain with the appetites of a whoremaster. I heard from him such stories as would not lead you to wish to be a single woman aboard this ship, and at his mercy. The man's a crude voluptuary!" His lip twisted with scorn. "And you. You little fool! You smile at him, give him your hand, accept his invitation as though you thought to attend a garden party! Take care at supper, lest you find his hand up your skirts. Is that what you want?"

She stared at him, her indignation cooling. Could she believe him? She had found Hackett charming enough. Given to saying odd and mystifying things, to be sure. But scarcely the villain Manning was trying to portray. And, in the meantime, she was in a closed cabin, on a strange ship, with no means of escape. Locked in with this disagreeable surgeon, not the captain she was supposed to fear. A surgeon who had not hesitated to strip her nearly naked! "And you?" she demanded. "What of *your* appetites?"

"I have no interest in women. I'm a doctor."

"Are doctors not men?"

He sighed, his angry expression fading. "I carry in my heart the love of a good woman. 'Tis enough to warm my nights. To think of my wife, Martha."

She bit her lip, filled with doubts. "Do you really think the captain . . . ?"

"I do." He scowled and sank to his knees, searching for the ring.

Could he be right? And she so young, so inexperienced in the ways of men that she had failed to appreciate what Manning was trying to do for her? He was a doctor, after all, accustomed to saving lives. Perhaps he had saved her with his ruse, and she had been too stupid to realize it. Lord protect her, what did she know of men aboard a ship? What did she know of men at all, save for Jamie? She felt humbled and ashamed as she watched Manning grope almost desperately to find the ring.

The silence was heavy with her guilt. "Thank you for all your kindnesses," she whispered at last.

He straightened with the ring in his hand and slipped it back on her finger. "That's the first sign of gratitude you've shown," he said with a dry laugh. "But I invented this deception as much because I dislike the captain as to save you from him."

"How gallant of you, sir," she snapped. Could the man not even accept her apology with any grace? She wondered how any woman could ever have married *him!* She twisted the ring on her finger. "And where is your wife, Martha? Pining at home for your return?" She found it difficult to keep the sarcasm from her voice.

"Dead now for a twelvemonth." His voice was flat and distant.

"Oh!" The shock of his words made her cover her mouth in dismay. "I'm sorry."

"Why? 'Tis not *your* grief."

Despite the cold rigidity of his person, the dispassionate look in his eye, she felt a pang of sympathy. "You must have shed a great many tears since then."

"I mourn in my own way," he said frostily.

"How . . . how did she die?"

She could hear the crunch of his teeth. "Because of one man's stupidity and overweening pride."

"What do you mean? Who . . . ?"

He brushed aside her question with an impatient wave of his hand. " 'Tis time you rested. I liked not the size of the bump on your head. I'll bring you that powder." He went into the cockpit and returned a few minutes later, bearing a small glass. "Drink it," he ordered.

She stared at him for a moment. If there was a warmhearted man hiding behind that doctor's facade, he was buried deep, somewhere in the recesses of the man's soul. She swallowed the contents of the glass and made a face. "It tastes like bitter apples."

He frowned in sudden curiosity. *"You* tasted of tar. When I kissed you."

" 'Twas part of my disguise, to appear toothless." She giggled and bared her front teeth.

"There's still a bit of stain. Hold still." He perched on the edge of the bunk and pulled out a handkerchief. "You can scarcely charm the captain's mess with blackened teeth." He knit his brows in concentration as he held her chin in his hand and rubbed at her teeth with the snowy linen.

His face was so close. She found herself remembering his kiss. *He* had tasted of tobacco and mint-suffused tooth powder. A very agreeable taste. A very pleasant kiss, now that she had time to think about it. Not like Jamie's, of course. But then, there was no one in the world like Jamie.

"There," he said, satisfied, repocketing his handkerchief. "You shall appear at supper in all your pristine beauty."

"Supper? Oh, bother!" she cried, as a sudden thought struck her. "I shouldn't have accepted the captain's invitation. What am I to wear? Look at me! These torn rags. And I could never fit into your breeches and coat, even should you have a spare, without looking ridiculous." She blushed. There was her wicked vanity again. Papa would be ashamed of her.

"I can do better than that," he said. He crossed to his sea chest, opened it, and rummaged around until he had found what he was looking for. He pulled out what appeared to be a gown and stays and petticoat, in the softest shades of striped green silk, trimmed with embroidered roses. He thrust the gown toward Prudence. " 'Twas a favorite of mine," he said gruffly. "She looked like a queen in it."

She took it with reluctance. "Oh, but . . . you don't mind if I wear it?"

His blue eyes were empty of emotion. "Why should I? 'Tis merely a gown."

"Yet you kept it for a remembrance."

"A moment of weakness. 'Tis not your concern. Now, I want you to sleep. I'll speak to the captain about allowing you to disembark at Portsmouth or Plymouth in the morning. If he doesn't wish to make for land before we leave the Channel, we'll be stopping at the Azores to take on supplies. I'll find a ship to take you back to England. If you haven't passage money, I can afford to pay for your voyage."

"Why would you do such a thing?" Was there a spark of warmth in him after all?

He shrugged. "Because I can afford it."

She sighed in disappointment. And then once more, because the time was passing. It would be weeks before she returned to London. Another delay in her quest. And poor Betsy would be frantic with worry.

Wait! What had he said? The Azores? But perhaps she could find a ship to take her to America from there! Oh, what joy! By God's grace, she could join Jamie sooner than she had dared to hope. "You stop at the Azores?" she said, her spirits brightening.

"On our way to Virginia. Yes."

Oh, sweet heaven! *"Virginia?* But that's where I want to go!"

He raised a mocking eyebrow. "What? Is London not to your liking? All those dirty streets and rogues and painted slatterns?"

The man was impossible. A cold cloud that descended on everything around him. "I was in London only to earn my passage to Virginia," she explained impatiently. "I have a . . . a friend I wish to meet. That I *must* meet."

He looked bored with the conversation, with her distress. "I wish you well."

"Dr. Manning, I . . ." She found herself groping for words. The man didn't make this any easier, with his indifferent eyes. "When we get to the Azores . . . It could be weeks before a merchantman arrives on its way to Virginia."

"True enough. And so?"

She twisted her hands together. "Why . . . why can't I stay on this ship until we reach the Colonies?"

"Good God. As my 'wife'?"

She was desperate. She had to reach Jamie as soon as possible. It was the only way. Her life's happiness depended upon it. And here was her chance, like a blessed miracle dropped from the heavens. "I know 'tis impertinent of me, even to ask. But I so want to reach Virginia."

"To see your . . . friend," he drawled.

"Yes." An aching whisper. "I know it will be a burden on you. To pay for my food and keep. But I have a little money." She fished in her pocket with shaking hands and held out the coins she had earned this morning. "Take it. As for the rest, I feel sure that my friend will repay you for your trouble."

He studied her intently. "A man, of course. Your friend. A sweetheart?"

She blushed and lowered her eyes. His searching gaze was more than she could endure.

"And when you find him?"

Her eyes filled with tears. "We're to be married."

" 'Tis a long way to go, for a marriage."

She felt pushed to the edge of desperation. "I can't wait for him to return to England!" she cried.

"Ah! I understand now." He scanned her with the cold, dispassionate eye of the physician. "And how many months will it be, before your friend"—his lip curled in scorn around the word—"is forced to marry you, willy-nilly?"

She felt her face burning anew. What she had done was shameful. Sinful. And Manning was waiting—with his cold eyes and his cynic's heart—for her to confess it all. Well, let her feel the fires of Hell before she'd tell this unsympathetic man her secrets!

"Well? Speak up," he said. "Do you carry his child?"

She stared at him, shocked at his frankness, and wondered if he really cared. Perhaps he was only hoping to find out if she was a virgin. Men liked virgins, Betsy always said. She sighed. She felt so young, so ignorant of life. So lost and alone that Manning could devastate her with one sharp question. "I . . . I know he waits for me with longing," she said, her lip trembling. Jamie, her sweet Jamie . . . She was suddenly overcome with her memories, her suffering. She buried her face in her hands and wept. "But if it's too difficult for you . . ." she said in a choked voice.

He took her by the shoulders and lifted her tearful countenance to his. There was unexpected compassion on his face as he stared into her eyes. "You're very young. And very foolish, I suspect." He sighed and dropped his hands. "This is madness. But I think I can invent a plausible story for

Captain Hackett. A reason why you must stay aboard for the whole voyage."

She sniffled and wiped at her eyes. "Oh, thank you, Doctor Manning. Thank you!" In an excess of gratitude and emotion, she got to her knees on the bunk, raised her arms, and threw them around his neck.

"God Almighty!" he said, pushing her away and straightening in alarm. At her bewildered frown, he laughed dryly. "I assume you don't intend to barter yourself in payment."

She gasped in horror. "Sweet merciful heaven. No!"

His eyes had frosted over once more. "Then kindly do not do *that* again. I shared my last embraces with my wife. 'Twill suffice me until we're reunited beyond the grave. As for 'Doctor Manning' . . . since I'm to be your husband, you should accustom yourself to calling me Ross. I shall, of course, address you as Martha. Try to respond to that name as if it were your own."

She nodded in agreement. "Of course."

"Now lie down and take your rest," he said. "I'll gather your scattered trinkets while you sleep." He laughed, a harsh, sardonic sound. "You can present them to your young man as your dowry."

She felt the need to defend Jamie, as though Manning were somehow seeing him with a jaundiced eye. "He doesn't need them," she said with pride. "He's a viscount."

One eyebrow angled into the smooth expanse of his forehead. "And you're a duchess."

"Do you enjoy being cruel?" she said softly.

He smirked. "I'm neither cruel nor kind."

"What are you, then?" Surely far from human!

"You may think of me as . . ." The mocking smile faded, to be replaced by a look of such desolation that it tugged at Prudence's heart, in spite of herself. "That cadaver we spoke of before," he said, his voice thick and hoarse.

She touched his hand in sympathy. "Ross . . ."

He flinched at her soft touch and snatched his hand away. "Go to sleep," he commanded.

———

She woke to a bell sounding the hour. There was a small clock on Manning's desk. She struggled to sit up, and blinked at it. Seven o'clock. Her body was stiff, but not as sore as she'd expected it to be, and her head had ceased its throbbing. The doctor's powder had done its work.

She eased herself from the bunk and stood up. Her basket sat on the edge of the desk, filled with its trinkets. Beside it lay her comb. Martha's gown had been lovingly placed across the chair; she examined it more closely, holding it up to herself. It was a trifle short; she guessed that Martha had been an inch or two shorter than she. But the stays would fit, if she laced them tighter. And the petticoat could be drawn in by its string.

She glanced down at her own clothing. Her simple gown could be washed and patched for everyday wear, if she cut a strip from her petticoat to mend the ragged hem. But her shift . . . She clicked her tongue. Brand-new when she'd left Winsley! Had it been necessary for Manning to be so hasty? So careless of her garments? The shift was torn all the way to the waist. Well, she'd have to find his sea kit and repair it if she could.

She turned to the small mirror on the wall and gasped in dismay. Her face still held traces of blood, and her hair was a tangled mass around her head. She had looked better as an old hag! Well—she squared her shoulders in determination—the sooner she began the restoration, the sooner done.

Manning had thoughtfully provided a basin of water, a towel, and a small firkin of soap. She set to work with water and soap and comb, and pronounced herself satisfied with the results a quarter of an hour later. Her face was pink and shiny from its scrubbing, and her auburn hair was securely knotted on the top of her head and fastened with the comb. She had left a few tendrils loose to fall against her forehead and hide her wound.

Am I beautiful? she thought, peering into the mirror. Jamie was the only one who had ever called her pretty—until Captain Hackett. He had pronounced her a *beauty*. Not that Ross Manning would notice or care!

She found his sea kit in his chest, removed needle and thread, and stitched her shift with a neat hand, as Mama had taught her. She turned it back to front, so that the mended seam would be hidden beneath the back bodice of the gown. She finished dressing, noticing that the faint scent of lavender still clung to the silken folds of Martha's gown. She wondered again how the poor woman had died.

"God Almighty." She whirled at the sound of Manning's strangled voice at the door. He stood gripping the door frame as though he feared to topple over. He was clad in a dress uniform of dark blue with a white satin waistcoat, and his light brown hair was covered with a formal, powdered wig, tied neatly behind with a black silk bow. His face was as white as the curls at his temples.

"Are you ill, Doctor Manning? Ross?" she cried in alarm.

He drew in a ragged breath. " 'Tis like seeing a ghost."

She saw that he was trembling violently. *I should never have taken the gown,* she thought. How could she have been so stupid—not to know, not to guess, that even a cold man could feel grief in his deepest soul?

He groaned and covered his eyes with his hand. "Christ Jesus, I must be mad."

She fumbled to unfasten the lacings of her gown. Martha's gown. "Perhaps I oughtn't . . ." she began.

He lifted his head. The chilling mist had descended. He held out his arm for her to take, and bowed in deference.

"Come, *Martha,*" he said. "To table."

Chapter Five

"Shall we have rain by morning, do you think?" Prudence shivered in the chill wind that swept across the quarterdeck. It smelled of salt, a sharp, damp tang that seemed to promise rain.

She glanced at Ross Manning beside her. He hadn't spoken a word since they'd left his cabin, and his profile—by the yellow glow of the lanterns that hung above the poop deck—was harsh and stiff. Distant and bleak. She felt a twinge of guilt. How difficult this must be for him.

"Rain?" he said, shaking his head as though he were freeing himself from a dark mist. "Rain? More likely a heavy storm, the master seems to think. 'Tis one of the reasons I was able to persuade the captain to my views. And with so little trouble. He wants to get beyond the Channel before the tempest hits and we face the danger of being driven into shore." He frowned. "You should know that I've told him you have relatives in Virginia that you wish to see. Martha had family in America. Symonds cousins, if Hackett should ask. I'm not certain he has completely accepted our little fiction." He seemed still to be far away, speaking to her from some remote corner of his being.

She held his arm more firmly and gave it a little squeeze, hoping to bring him back. "Shall I play the devoted wife through supper?"

He shrugged. "As you wish."

The captain's table was crowded when they entered the great cabin. Prudence counted six officers, besides Hackett. They rose to their feet and nodded their greetings or extended their hands as she was introduced. She wondered if she'd remember their names. They were all so alike: so young and eager and fresh-faced, so straight and tall in their braid-covered uniforms—like shiny new pins in a game of skittles on the village green.

She would remember the name of Lieutenant Elliot, of course. Unlike the others, he was pale, and he seemed to have difficulty rising from his chair. The man next to him had passed a whispered, seemingly jocular comment as he struggled to stand, which had brought a hot blush to Elliot's face.

And how could she forget the name of the first lieutenant, Mr. St. John, when the smile he gave her was so dazzling, and his hearty greeting so filled with compliments?

"By George, Doctor!" he exclaimed. "How did such a glout as yourself—a morose devil, if we're to believe Elliot . . . How did you ever win the favor of this glorious creature? No offense, sir, but I warrant you scarce deserved such luck!" he added with a grin. He bowed to Prudence. "Madam, with your beauty to grace our ship, we shall have sunshine for the entire voyage."

Prudence blushed as brightly as Elliot had done a moment before.

And surely she would remember the purser, Mr. Slickenham, whose name seemed to suit him. He had the sly look of a ferret, and the oily demeanor of a self-seeking bootlicker. He reminded Prudence of her grandfather's steward, who had tattled on her many a time.

"We welcome the doctor's wife aboard," he purred. "Is it not so, Captain Sir Joseph?"

Captain Hackett took her hand, kissed it, and guided her to the seat beside him. "You're looking charming this evening, Mrs. Manning," he said, his eyes appraising her and coming to rest, if only briefly, on the rounded swell of her bosom. "How clever of you to have brought a fine gown with you. I suspect, dear lady"—he winked—"you were prepared to plead your own cause had your husband not spoken for you."

She remembered her part in the game. "I so longed to see my relations in America," she said. "And then, you see, I dislike being separated from my husband," she added, managing to pout in a fashion that Jamie had called "adorable."

She was rewarded with another kiss on her hand from the captain, and with such a welcoming smile that she began to doubt Manning's warnings. After all, hadn't he said that he was protecting her only because he disliked Hackett? *She* wasn't finding the captain to be the evil man Manning had portrayed! She ignored the surgeon's scowl and returned Hackett's smile with one of her own. "How kind you are to let me stay aboard, Sir Joseph," she said. "I shall be forever in your debt."

"I shall remember that pledge," he said firmly. "Make no mistake about it. I expect to be repaid." He smiled mysteriously and signaled to his servants to begin serving the meal.

His attentions never flagged throughout supper. Indeed, seated between the gracious captain and the charming Lieutenant St. John, Prudence felt like a princess. It was such a new and heady experience, to be flattered, to be admired, to be waited on and served, that she found her head spinning, her cheeks flushing with nervous excitement.

Papa had concerned himself only with the development of her character as she grew, and Grandpapa—with his Methodism and his pious, pinch-faced new wife—had threatened a beating if she so much as looked at the young village lads, let alone encouraged their interest. Now she found herself responding to all this attention with artifices she had scarcely imagined she possessed. She giggled whenever the captain passed a witty remark, and smiled her thanks at each of St. John's kindnesses.

"I fear you'll turn my wife's head, gentlemen," grumbled Ross at last, from his isolation at the far end of the table, where Hackett had directed him to sit.

The captain laughed and refilled Prudence's wine cup. "Is that jealousy I hear, Mr. Manning? Perhaps we should have put this dear lady ashore after all. For it is *we* who envy *you*. Is it not so, gentlemen? A long, lonely voyage, without the company of a woman . . ." He laughed again. But this time the laugh had an odd, ugly edge to it that bewildered Prudence.

"Except for Elliot, here, of course," said one of the other officers, which elicited a round of sly laughter that was even more mystifying to her.

"Gentlemen, if you please," said Ross, half rising from his chair. His eyes were dark and stormy. "My wife is very young and innocent."

Prudence glared back at him. Why did he always make her feel like a child? Whatever was the secret joke among the men, *she* certainly hadn't felt insulted! She decided that he was too disagreeable to be paid any mind. She put her hand on Hackett's sleeve and smiled radiantly at him. "The *Chichester* seems like a fine ship, Sir Joseph. How proud you must be of your command. Have you been asea for long?"

He beamed back at her, clearly flattered. "I've served in the King's Navy with reputation for half a score of years. The *Chichester* is a sixty-gun third-rate. Fine enough, as she goes. But I expect to move up in the ranks. I had the occasion to go fox hunting with John, Earl of Sandwich, on my last stay ashore."

Hackett paused and assessed the reaction of the men at his table. Several of them nodded in understanding, and Lieutenant Elliot's eyes opened wide in undisguised admiration and awe. Hackett turned to Prudence with a smile of smug pride. "Sandwich is the First Lord of the Admiralty, Mrs. Manning. And a discerning man who appreciates and rewards the skills of his captains." He smoothed the curls at his temple. "And of his personal friends, of course." His voice darkened for a moment. "I count on my officers to help me realize my ambitions."

He smiled expansively at Prudence, lifted her hand from his arm, and pressed his lips to the soft flesh. "All generous deeds should be rewarded. Don't you think so, dear lady? And I am prepared to show my gratitude to all those who please me. In whatever manner."

Ross uttered a strangled sound from deep within his throat. "I shall do my best to keep my wife out of your path, then, sir. Lest she turn you from your ambition."

Prudence stared at him. What was vexing the man now? She herself had found Hackett's remarks harmless.

The captain's dark eyes narrowed to slits. "Why do I always feel you are challenging me, Mr. Manning? Are you afraid I'll steal your wife from you?" He laughed. There was no mistaking the animosity in his tone. "Gad's curse, I wonder if she *could* be wooed."

Before Ross, eyes blazing, could respond, the captain waved his arm toward the other officers. "Did you know, gentlemen, that I was of the opinion that our fine new surgeon here had . . . inclinations in an entirely different direction? His own words at our first meeting seemed to confirm it. We must all watch him carefully on this voyage."

Ross took a deep, steadying breath, ignoring the snickers and guffaws from the men around him. Prudence bit her lip in bewilderment. Would she ever begin to understand men? Ross reached inside his waistcoat and pulled out a square of lace-trimmed silk. "I thought this might interest you, sir," he said. "You will note the names, Ross and Martha, stitched into the corner. Done by my wife, with her very own hand. Scarcely a gift for a man with inclinations." He passed the handkerchief down the table to Hackett, his eyes glinting in triumph.

Hackett peered at the square of cloth, then smiled at Prudence. "A skilled piece of work, dear lady. When did you give it to him?"

Prudence caught her breath, aware of the sudden gleam of suspicion in Hackett's eye. "For his birthday," she said, thinking quickly.

But it was too late. Ross had already burst out, "For our wedding anniversary."

A sly smile spread across the captain's face. "How peculiar. A treasure such as this. And you can't agree on the occasion?"

Sweet heaven, Prudence thought in a panic. Ross had warned her that he thought the captain doubted their story. If they were to be found out now, it would mean serious difficulties for Ross, at the very least. Arrest, perhaps. And for her? Transport to the first ship bound for England, no doubt. She managed an innocent smile. "I'm a giddy fool. Too much wine tonight, mayhap. Or the lingering effects of my accident. Forgive me, Ross. Of course it was the anniversary of our marriage. I remember how I stayed up for hours the night before, to finish the stitches in time." She smiled again at Hackett, praying he would accept her explanation.

His dark eyes were still shadowed with suspicion. "How did you and your husband come to meet?" His tone was more sharp than friendly.

She saw the expression of unease on Manning's face and shot him a wild look that begged for silence. "No, Ross. I'll tell it. Have you so little faith in my memory?" Heaven alone knew that this was a story she could tell more convincingly than he, with his cold demeanor and his dark, grief-tinged memories.

" 'Twas in my village in Wiltshire," she began. "I was in the hills, tending my grandfather's sheep. Ross was visiting a friend of his. A lord in the next parish, I think. I was singing." She smiled innocently at Hackett. " 'Tis a lovely way to spend an afternoon. Among the sheep and the fragrant thyme, with naught but songs to break the sweet silence."

Ross nodded. "I remember the day."

Her memories were beginning to stir and clutch at her heart. "He came riding up on his horse and asked about my song. It was an old one my mother taught me, about love and loss and the sweet sadness of autumn." She choked on the words, nearly overcome.

Lieutenant St. John put his hand over hers, clearly moved. "You must sing for us sometime, Mrs. Manning. I have no doubt you have a beautiful voice."

Hackett glared at him. "And then what, Mrs. Manning?" he said sharply. "When you met your husband."

"We frolicked in the sunshine, like children. And plucked the wild primroses that grew among the rocks. He laughed about my heavy clogs. I felt like such a country girl. And he a great . . . gentleman." She gulped. She had nearly said "viscount."

Ross cleared his throat. "You looked charming in them. But I think these gentlemen have heard enough. Will you tell all our secrets, my dear?" He seemed to want her to stop.

It was too late. She was lost in her sweet memories, the tender recollections. "He came many times after that," she said dreamily. "In fair weather or foul. We would sit and talk and laugh. And once, in the soft rain, he . . ." She stopped, feeling the hot tears begin to flow. Oh, Jamie! Had there ever been a sweeter day since time began? Had there ever . . .

She looked at the captain and saw the odd expression on his face. What was she doing? Had she so completely forgotten herself? She brushed at her wet cheeks and managed a soft laugh. "It was so sweet a courtship that it still makes me weep."

Whether Hackett believed the story or not, the other officers were clearly affected. They stirred in their chairs, murmured words of sympathy and understanding.

"Your sensitivity does you credit, Mrs. Manning," said St. John. "We have no right to be privy to your intimate secrets."

Hackett leaned back in his chair and raised a skeptical eyebrow. "No. I'll hear more."

"Indeed. 'Tis a fascinating story," said the purser, Slickenham, bobbing his head in fawning agreement with his captain.

Prudence chewed at her lip in dismay. In another moment she'd be blubbering like an idiot, all her griefs bubbling to the surface to overwhelm her. And then what would Hackett think? She cast a look of desperation in Ross's direction.

He stretched in his chair. "Confound me for a gaping puppy, how I yawn," he drawled. "I think these gentlemen must forgive us for tonight, wife. I should seek my bed. And you need rest, after your fall." He stood up and held out his hand to her. "Come." He bowed to Hackett. "By your leave, Captain, sir. I think my wife's soft recollections will have to wait for another time." Before Hackett could protest, he had moved around the table and helped Prudence from her chair.

The officers rose and bade them a good night. Only Hackett seemed piqued at their abrupt departure. "You'll tell me more at another time, I'm sure, dear lady," he said. His jaw tightened. "I count on it."

The air was fresh on the deserted quarterdeck, crisp with the smell of tar and brine. Prudence stopped when they reached the main deck and breathed deeply. She could hear the creaking of timbers, the flapping of canvas high over their heads. The laughter of seamen gathered on the forecastle. Commonplace sounds. Soothing sounds. They calmed and cheered her. Reminded her that she was on a ship, flying through the night to her dear Jamie.

"Have you quite recovered?" Ross's voice was warm and surprisingly gentle at her ear.

She sighed. "Yes."

"You must love him very much, your viscount." He echoed her sigh. "I met Martha at an assembly ball, before I went to the university. I suspect your memories are more romantic than mine. She despised me at first sight." He sighed again. "But Hackett is suspicious. We shall have to be vigilant. Exchange stories, so he doesn't catch us unaware again."

"I shall be pleased to hear about Martha," she said with sympathy.

He snorted. "I shall be less than pleased to tell. Make no mistake. I like very little about this venture. Not the least of which is revealing my life to a stranger. A reckless chit of a girl. But you?" He gave a scornful laugh. "My little shepherdess. I suspect you could share your love of your viscount with the world."

It sounded like a condemnation. She eyed him with reproach. "I could speak of my love for my Lord Jamie until the end of time!"

"Ah. So he has a name, this lover who planted his seed in you and then absconded."

Filled with the warmth of the wine, and the attentions, and the good fellowship at supper, she had almost forgotten what a cold cynic Ross could be. " 'Twas not his fault," she said in Jamie's defense. "He had to go away. But his promises were as true as his love is pure."

He laughed again, a snicker of disbelief. "I should like to know what *truly* happened on that hillside."

"Oh!" she cried, filled with anger and shame in equal measure. "You blackhearted man with your evil thoughts! How can you think . . . ?"

"And you?" he interrupted with a sneer. "A wide-eyed naïf who can't see truth when it confronts her! I wanted to shake you at supper. Encouraging that lecherous dog with your every smile. Didn't you hear, didn't you understand, what he was saying? Good God, he as much as invited you to be his mistress!"

She clicked her tongue. "What foolishness! He was merely being gracious."

"Christ Jesus," he muttered. "Is that all you saw and heard?"

She was beginning to doubt herself in the face of his certainty. "Well," she admitted, "some of his talk was bewildering. What did he mean by your 'inclinations'?"

"He meant he thought I was a sodomite. A lover of men and boys," he explained dryly, as she continued to look puzzled.

"M-men and boys?" she stammered. "What . . . how can a man . . . ?"

"By the beard of Aesculapius!" he burst out. "Where were you raised? In a cocoon?"

"Oh!" She stamped her foot in fury. She'd had enough of his insults, of feeling like an idiotic child. "I was raised to be a God-fearing Christ-

ian!" she cried. "To take people at their word, without reading ugly meanings into everything that . . ."

"Hist!" He grabbed her arm to silence her. "Hackett is watching from
the quarterdeck. He shouldn't see us quarrel."

She hesitated. They had a mutual interest in keeping Hackett fooled.
He might not be the villain that Ross insisted he was, but he was a proud
man. He would surely take vengeful action if he thought he was being
gulled. "What should we do?" she whispered.

"I think we ought to kiss." Without waiting for her consent, he pulled
her into his arms and planted his lips squarely on hers.

His mouth was firm and sweet, with an insistent pressure that took her
breath away. She sighed and melted against him, sliding her hands around
his neck. She clung to him, her head spinning, aware of every thrilling
sensation. The warmth of his hard body against hers, the strength of his
possessive embrace, the burning mouth that claimed hers with such assurance. She was light-headed and dizzy by the time he released her.

Oh, Prudence! she thought in alarm. *How wicked!* To enjoy another
man's kiss when Jamie never left her thoughts. She was confused and bewildered. Ashamed of her disloyalty. Papa had never looked at another
woman, let alone kissed her with pleasure, in all the years that Mama had
lived. Wasn't that what love was supposed to be? Forsaking all others?

Shaking and frightened, she turned away from Ross, lest he see the look
on her face.

"You're trembling," he said. "Is your head troubling you again?"

She was frantic to cover her shame, to hide her guilty pleasure in a forbidden kiss. Doubly shameful, because *he* seemed not to be affected.
"Yes!" she blurted. "My limbs are weak. My bones are beginning to ache
again."

"I shall give you another powder before you sleep. Come." He put
his arm around her for support and guided her down the hatchway
to the cockpit. She was dimly aware that the seamen they encountered
on the stairs smiled slyly, or buzzed with low-pitched, eager talk as they
passed. Three hundred men, Ross had said. Hungry for a woman. Was
this to be the tenor of the whole voyage? She remembered Betsy's
stories of rapacious men. Men to be feared. She shivered and leaned

more closely into Ross as they made their way through the ship.

They stopped in the cockpit, where Ross mixed a fresh powder into water and watched with a professional eye as she drank it down. "You'll sleep well," he said, and led her to the passageway.

The door to Ross's cabin opened. A seaman came out—the ugliest man Prudence had ever seen. As ugly as the grotesques carved into the dark corners and columns of the old church at Winsley. She felt a pang of sympathy. How sad to go through life with a face that would cause children to run and hide.

He stopped, abashed, and tugged at his forelock. "Beggin' your pardon, Mr. Manning. I bean't up to no mischief. Not a bit of it, sir!"

Ross scowled. "Wedge, isn't it? Tobias Wedge?"

"Aye, sir. Though my mates call me Toby."

Ross's blue eyes glittered like cold steel. " 'Tis not your duty to tend my cabin. I have a servant for that. What are you doing here? Stealing?"

Wedge shook his massive head. "Oh, no sir! Me and Gawky, my messmate, wished to welcome your lady aboard. I be leavin' her a little gift inside, d'ye see, sir?" He jerked his thumb in the direction of the cabin. The soft, warm eyes in the unlovely face glowed with sincerity.

Ross hesitated, then nodded. "Be on your way, then. Stay away from the quarterdeck," he added. "The captain's taking the air."

"Thankee, sir." Wedge's face melted into a wide smile of gratitude that almost transformed him. "He has it in for me, that he do. I can feel it in my bones."

"What have you done to anger him?" asked Prudence with soft concern.

"Naught that I can tell, lady. But, d'ye see me, a hare crossed my path when I were ashore at Deptford. A bad omen, that. My Maw, God rest her soul, always told me that were why I be born so ugly. Body o' me, 'twas a big black hare what frighted her, and her so close to her time . . ." He stopped, glanced uneasily at Ross's frozen expression, and backed down the passageway. "But I be keepin' you from your rest. Your pardon." He saluted again and disappeared.

Prudence frowned at Ross. "Why should the captain dislike him for no reason?"

His handsome face registered disgust. "Because the captain, having confronted beauty in his mirror every day of his life, scorns the lack of it. But come into my cabin. This is not the place to hold a private conversation."

The cabin was softly lit, with a single lantern left burning. The blankets of the bunk had been turned down, and two pillows had been placed side by side at the head of the bed. On one of the pillows was Wedge's gift—a small dish carved of whalebone, and piled high with hazelnuts.

"How generous of them!" exclaimed Prudence, cradling the bowl in her hands and smiling down at it.

Ross laughed dryly. "They're superstitious children, not high-minded samaritans. Hazelnuts betoken fruitfulness in marriage."

"Oh!" She sank to the chair, her cheeks burning. The reality of their situation, the uncomfortable intimacy they would be forced to share for the next six weeks or so, was only now beginning to seep into her consciousness. In another moment, she was certain, Ross would produce a hammock from somewhere and string it up to the beams. If nothing else—and to her chagrin—he had made it abundantly clear that he was aware of her innocence. Her inexperience.

But in the meantime . . . She felt awkward and embarrassed, uneasy as to how they should proceed. She made a desperate effort to sound natural, to pretend that she wasn't flustered. Perhaps a bit of small talk . . . ? She smiled brightly at him. "The officers seem like an agreeable lot."

"I met them only briefly, when I came aboard this morning. The usual complement. Ambitious, but good-natured. Only a battle will prove their mettle."

"I liked the first lieutenant. St. John."

He grunted. "So I noticed. As did he. You would be wise to . . ."

She refused to endure another paternal lecture! "Is Lieutenant Elliot ailing?" she cut in quickly. "He scarcely seemed fit all evening. So pale and wan. And the other men seemed to make sport of him. 'Twas quite puzzling. Can you explain it?"

Ross cleared his throat and straightened the papers on his desk. "He . . . sustained an injury, which I was forced to repair."

"Oh, the poor man." She frowned. "Then why did they twit him so cruelly?"

" 'Tis not for you to know."

She glared at him, indignant at his high-handed tone. "I'm not a child, Mr. Manning!"

He raised a mocking eyebrow. "Very well. If you insist on knowing. He was practicing his skills with a cutlass this afternoon. And received a cut to his balls."

She gasped, feeling her face flame anew. She stared at the lantern, the ceiling, the deck. Anything to keep from seeing the triumphant gleam in the man's eye. He had enjoyed shocking her, the rascal!

If he was aware of her discomfort, he chose to ignore it, for which, at least, she was grateful. "Now," he said briskly, "do you wish to chatter all evening, or shall we get to the matter at hand? Except for Captain Hackett's weekly suppers, you'll take your meals here, or in the wardroom with the other officers. It's on the upper gun deck, just beneath the captain's cabin. I should prefer that you allow me to accompany you to meals. Unless you can prove yourself less susceptible to St. John's charms." He pointed to the covered chamber pot in the corner of the cabin. "If you should wish more privacy than that, there's a necessary on the quarter gallery, just off the wardroom. Though I'll spend most of my days in the cockpit, or at my duties, and not disturb you here."

"Am I to spend my days isolated in this black hole?" She jutted her chin at him.

He hesitated, clearly gauging the depth of her defiance. "No. Of course not," he said at last. " 'Twould be unhealthy with the close air. And you so unaccustomed to it. I shall allow you to go on deck in fair weather. You may spend the rest of the time in the wardroom. 'Tis bright and airy, the officers genial company. Though I charge you not to forget you're supposed to be a married woman."

She glared at him. When he wasn't treating her like a child, he was behaving as though he thought her a strumpet!

He ignored her scowl. "As to the difficulty of dressing and undressing in privacy," he went on calmly, "it would scarcely do for me to withdraw from the cabin, and risk being seen by my mates, who sleep in the cockpit. Instead, you have but to ask me to turn my back, and I'll oblige you."

She appreciated his concern for her modesty, if not his brusque and imperious manner. Not even *Grandpapa* had ordered her about so much. "Thank you." She tried to sound as sure of herself as Manning.

"Well?" He folded his arms across his chest. He seemed to be waiting.

"N-now?" she stammered, all her boldness vanishing. "You want me to . . . *now?*"

"When did you intend to go to sleep? It will be a long day tomorrow. I, for one, need my rest."

She felt like a child being chided for obstinacy. Obediently, she rose from her chair. At once, he turned away from her and pulled off his wig, shaking his head to let his sandy blond hair fall loose around his shoulders. She gulped. It would be as embarrassing to watch him undress as to take off her own clothing in the same room with him. She averted her gaze and quickly shed her gown and petticoat and stays, then sat to remove her shoes and stockings. She had never felt more shy in her life, not even when Jamie had lifted her skirts.

Foolish Prudence! Where was her courage? Hadn't Manning seen her practically naked? And her full shift covered her decently enough. She glanced up at him. He had stripped down to his shirt. His legs were long and muscular, covered with a fine drift of brown hairs. She gulped again. What a mad, foolish adventure this was! "I'm ready," she whispered.

He turned, examining her with his cold, distant eyes as she twisted her hair into a long braid down her back. "Is that not the shift I tore?"

She showed him her back. "I've mended it, you see. But I wish I had another."

"Mr. Slickenham may have a length or two of fabric in his stores. If you're handy with a needle." He folded his clothes neatly and laid them across the bench, then crossed the cabin to his sea chest, carrying his wig.

Ah! thought Prudence, exhaling with relief. She had begun to grow concerned. But that was where he kept the hammock, of course. In his sea chest.

He opened the chest, pulled out a box, and carefully folded his wig before putting it away. He closed the chest and turned to Prudence.

"Well," he said, pointing to the bunk, "will you take the inside? Or the outside?"

Chapter Six

⁓⧉⁓

"You scoundrel!" she sputtered. She didn't need Betsy to tell her what was in the man's thoughts! "You expect me to lie in the same bed with you? First the kisses—that you pretend not to care about! And then . . . then *this?*"

He puffed out his cheeks in exasperation and released his breath in a long hiss. "Damn my liver, but you're a trial! You could sleep in my sea chest, for aught I care! But this is a ship. It affords little privacy. The man who makes up my cabin would soon guess if we didn't share the same bunk! And tell our doubting captain, of that you may be certain! Have you forgot how quickly the presence of a woman in the cockpit was reported to him? There's many a man, I'm sure, who would like to curry his favor by playing spy!"

She chewed at the edge of her fingernail and eyed him with continuing suspicion.

"Look," he said more calmly, " 'tis a large bunk, and you have my oath that I shall stay on my side."

Perhaps she could trust him. "Do you swear?"

"I swear." He sighed. "I have almost forgot the enjoyment of a woman. And happily so. I rest content with my memories." He pointed to the bunk again. "Take the outside. That way, should you wish to make a ready escape from the scoundrel's clutches . . ." Unexpectedly he chuckled—a warm, good-humored laugh that revealed even white teeth and two small dimples.

She looked down at the deck and twisted her fingers together. "Forgive me for being foolish."

His voice was soft with understanding. It took her by surprise. "Not foolish," he murmured. "Only young. And perhaps a little frightened." He shook his head. "You needn't fear me, Prudence Allbright. You have my word on that."

He crossed to the bunk and took down a candle and a tinderbox from a shelf attached to the bulkhead that adjoined the bed. He struck flint to steel, lit the candle, and set it back on its shelf. Then he folded back the blankets and climbed into the bunk, placing himself as close to the wall as possible, his back up against the bulkhead. "Come," he said, patting the mattress beside him. "Put out the lantern. I'll snuff the candle when you're settled in."

She hesitated, then dropped to her knees and closed her eyes in prayer, her hands clasped before her. She prayed the prayer that had been on her lips for so many aching, tearful nights. That God would help her to find Jamie quickly. That he would marry her. She sighed, stifling her longing. She had no wish to shame herself by weeping before Manning.

She extinguished the lantern and climbed over the high side planking of the bunk, managing to turn her back to Ross as she did so. She winced. The bruise on her hip pressed painfully against the thin mattress. *It must be very large,* she thought, *to hurt so much.* She would have to remember to examine it in the morning.

"Good night," he said, and blew out the candle. He stirred for a moment, making himself comfortable, covered them both with the blankets, and then was still. True to his word, he had taken care that no part of his body should touch hers.

The cabin was as dark as pitch. Prudence could feel the gentle rocking of the ship. It was disquieting, rather than soothing. A steady rhythm that beat against her conscience like a condemnation. Though Manning's even breathing told her that he had fallen asleep almost at once, her own blessed release eluded her. *What am I doing here?* she thought, anguished. She must be losing her reason. Surely grief had addled her brains.

She thought of Mama, dead for nine years now. And dear Papa—two years in his grave. What would they think of their good little girl now? Lying beside a stranger. On a mad quest.

She dared not think about what Grandpapa would say. Papa had been strict, but fair. Seeing the rebel in her, he had yet tried to turn her to God's ways through the example of his own virtuous life. She had never quite lived up to his expectations of Christian piety, but he had been loving and forgiving.

But with Papa's death, there had been no one left to protect her from the righteous wrath of her grandfather. A pious wrath that was as hypocritical as Papa's faith had been pure. Grandpapa. A terrifying man, who had demanded perfect obedience of her. She had trembled and obeyed him—all the while her heart burned with rebellion—and known that sooner or later they would clash.

But how could she have guessed that Grandpapa would emerge so completely the victor?

She sighed and fingered the ring on her hand. She missed the sweet comfort of Jamie's ring. The promise of their union. He had been her only joy, in that dark, lonely time that had followed Papa's death. And then he had gone. And the days that had followed . . . She covered her mouth to stifle the sob that rose from her aching heart.

She heard the sound of the ship's bell, echoing from a distance. A ship. She was on a ship. Sailing to America . . . and Jamie. Why should she give herself over to despair? Hadn't Papa said many a time that God had given mankind the gift of hope? A comfort when life seemed unendurable? She would hold that hope against her soul, to cheer her. Soon she would be in Jamie's arms. She was sure of it.

That sweet thought calmed her. She felt herself drifting on a warm tide, teetering on the brink of sleep. Soon she would see Jamie. How foolish, to give in to thoughts as black as this cabin. How foolish to doubt God's purpose. Jamie, she thought, feeling the heaviness of her eyelids as they closed. Sweet Jamie . . .

She shrieked as she felt a warm arm curl around her waist, a strong hand press against the softness of her stomach. Terror-stricken, she bolted upright and scrambled from the bunk. The high side caught at her leg and she fell, landing heavily on the deck with a loud crash.

"Good God," came the mumbled oath from Manning. She could hear him fumbling in the dark, hear the scratch of the tinder. The cabin was suddenly bright with the glow of the candle. Ross was sitting up in the bunk, blinking in the light, his eyes bleary with sleep and bewilderment. "What the devil is the matter?"

"The matter? The *matter?*" She rose to her knees, too indignant to do much more than sputter. What could she possibly say, when the lecherous rascal pretended ignorance?

He scrubbed at his eyes and stared at her. "What is it?" he demanded. Then his expression softened, the harsh planes of his face relaxing into a look of concern. "Did you have a bad dream? Is that it?"

She felt a moment's doubt. Perhaps he *was* innocent, reaching for her in his sleep without his consciously willing it. "I . . . I heard strange sounds in the dark," she said lamely. What else could she tell him? "They startled me."

He swore again. "And so you cried out loudly enough to waken the dead! Thanks be to God I have a strong heart, or they'd be pitching my corpse over the side of the ship at dawn."

She glared at him in the gloom. Innocent or not, *he* had grabbed *her*. And now he was compounding the insult by using that arrogant, superior tone of voice again! " 'Twas not deliberate," she snapped.

He grunted. "Your hysterics tore me from a sweet dream. A dream about my wife."

She understood at once, and felt a stab of guilt for her hasty anger. He had thought she was Martha, of course, in the bed beside him. The poor, bereft man. "I'm . . . I'm sorry," she stammered, beginning to feel foolish.

He shrugged. "A ship is alive at night, with many sounds. Frightening to someone not used to them. Come back to sleep."

She got to her feet gingerly, relieved to discover that her fall hadn't damaged her bruised body further.

"Wait," he said, gesturing to a lantern in the far corner of the cabin. "The dark belowdecks can also be frightening. Perhaps you're still accustomed to sleeping with your childhood candle. Put a low flame on the oil lantern over there. We shall have it every night, for your comfort." He held out his candle to her.

She ignored his disparaging suggestion that she was still a child, and took the candle. It was probably for the best that he saw her that way—as a child, not a woman ripe for the taking, should he suddenly have a mind to it. She lit the lantern with the candle flame, blew out the candle, and returned to bed, again turning her back to him and shrinking up against the side of the bunk.

He stirred restlessly for a few minutes, and then sighed. "Damme. Now I can't sleep."

She stared at the flickering lantern. It gave the room a somber glow. "Was it such a sweet dream?"

He sighed again. "It always is. As predictably sweet as was our life together."

She hesitated. "Tell me about Martha."

"Why?" The cold distance had returned to his voice.

"I shall have to know. For Captain Hackett." No. That wasn't entirely true. "I should like to know," she added softly.

"She was an angel. Beautiful and kind and good. And now she sleeps with angels." His voice was husky and dark, pausing over the words as though he were reluctant to speak them.

"And she disliked you at first sight, you said."

He laughed sadly. "I think I wrote as many love letters to her, in my years at the university, as I wrote papers for my professors. And when I did my surgeon's apprenticeship, I could scarcely concentrate on my work for thinking of her. But at last she agreed to be my wife. We were married in the spring of 'forty-seven. And danced in the orchard, among the drifting blossoms. We had two years of bliss. That was all." He groaned, then cursed softly, as though his momentary weakness offended him.

Prudence brushed at a tear on her cheek, feeling his pain. "How . . . how did she die?" she whispered.

"Must you know all?" he growled.

"Only if you wish to tell it."

"There's little to tell. Life is simple—both the pain and the beauty." He had lapsed into his familiar tone, curt and cold. "She had a tumor in her womb. I thought it might be benign. She wanted me to operate, to cut it out. She hoped someday to bear our children, if I could rid her body of the evil growing there. But I hesitated."

Prudence marveled at the dispassion in his voice, as though he were telling someone else's story. "And it killed her?" she murmured in sympathy.

"No. A proud, arrogant surgeon killed her. A man so sure of his talents that nothing would dissuade him once he had decided to operate. He severed a vessel and she bled to death."

Her eyes opened wide in horror. Was he speaking of himself? "But how could he . . . ?"

"Enough," he said tiredly. " 'Tis not a pleasant memory."

"How you must have wept at her loss."

She could hear the crunch of his jaw. "I have *never* wept. 'Tis a weakness I'll not allow."

A man who doesn't weep? she thought. *Surely he must be awash with tears deep within his soul.* She was eager to give him comfort. "But surely you'll find another woman. In the years that God has left you."

He laughed without humor. "The years I have left? Good God, how old do you think I am?"

She turned to face him. He lay on his back, staring up at the ceiling beams. His profile was rigid, his mouth set in a tight line, his brows drawn together in a scowl. She thought of Papa, with his stern ways and his sometimes disapproving frowns. "Oh, very old!" she blurted out.

He laughed again. She had never heard such a bleak sound. "Then life has taken its toll. And I'm a man who has seen enough of it."

She was alarmed at the finality in his tone. "But you're a fine surgeon, I think!"

"And a little less than a man," he muttered. "Who finds naught but disgust in the company of other men. Do you know what I intend to do when I reach Virginia? I shall go out into the wilderness of the Shenandoah Mountains and build a cabin and let my my beard grow."

"And do what?"

"Sketch a little, and wander the woods. And wait for death."

She gasped in dismay. "Oh, no! You must not! To cut yourself off from the world?"

He turned his head and stared her full in the face. His mouth curved in a mocking smile. "Do you have a better plan?"

He was so cold and remote it tore at her heart. "In my village, when I was a little girl," she said softly, "there was an old woman who remembered the old ways. She used to make winter wine, she called it. She would set her crocks into the snow and let them freeze. And what was left—the ruby liquid within—was strong and rich and pure. I would play truant from my lessons, and tramp through the deep snow to taste the forbidden brew." She sighed with the remembrance of a magical time, when she had lived—secure and loved—with Mama and Papa together.

He snorted. "A charming story. And so?"

"Don't you see? Perhaps your heart is like that wine—encased in ice. Waiting to be released, stronger and purer than it was before."

"A fanciful thought. But to what purpose?"

"Why, to live and love again! Your life is scarcely over. I found love with my Lord Jamie, because I never gave up hope that it would come to me. And now I put my trust in God—and keep my hope alive. My sweetheart is waiting for me in America. I know that with a certainty. Have *you* so little faith in God's plans for you? That you can bury hope?"

He raised himself on one elbow and took her chin in his hand. "Great God Almighty," he muttered, peering deep into her eyes, "does such innocence and faith yet exist in this world? You poor benighted child. I buried hope, and everything else, when I buried Martha. When we get to Virginia, your life will begin. Mine will end. 'Tis what I long for." He released her chin and lay back down on his pillow. "Above all else," he added fervently.

She turned away in sadness. What more could she say? Her face felt warm from the touch of his fingers, but her heart was chilled by his despair. It was too difficult for her to understand—that grief could so overwhelm a person as to quench the spark of life. Her sufferings had made her strong and determined, while Ross . . .

God forgive me, she thought, *I have no right to judge him.* She, at least, had someone to live for. Someone to love.

She hovered on the edge of sleep for what seemed like hours, her thoughts churning. She heard him stir and turn, and mumble "Martha" in his sleep. And when she felt his arm around her once again, she let it stay. It was warm and comforting.

She wondered if she was granting him this tender, unknowing embrace merely to ease his heart. Or her own.

Chapter
Seven

⚜

"I've brought your breakfast."

Prudence struggled to sit up in the bunk and stared sleepily at Ross Manning. He held a small tray upon which was a bowl of thick gruel and a mug of steaming cider. She groaned. Her head was pounding again, and her stomach churned alarmingly. "Sweet merciful heaven," she said, clutching at her belly. "I couldn't swallow a mouthful this morning. I fear I'd cast it up again."

"Yes, of course," he said. "I had quite forgot."

She resented the sly, disapproving edge to his voice. "What do you mean?"

He smiled blandly. "I feel sure 'tis only the motion of the ship, of course. You'll soon grow accustomed to it."

"And my head hurts." She felt too sulky to return his smile.

"The close air of the cabin. When you're dressed, I'll take you up on deck. We seem to have missed the brunt of the storm. There's only a light rain." He set down the tray on the cupboard. "But you must have something to eat. Some tea and a few biscuits, at the very least. I insist upon it." He indicated a basin of water on the desk. "Get up. While you're dressing, I'll make the tea."

Did he leave her *any* choices? She waited, peevishly refusing to move, until he had turned his back. A small victory. Then she eased herself out of the bunk. The water was warm and refreshing on her face; she was beginning to feel better already, her headache abating. She lowered her shift, one arm at a time, and washed her armpits, then splashed herself with the scented rose water he had thoughtfully provided. Beside the wash-bowl, she found as well a glass of cold water, a toothbrush, and powder. She brushed her teeth, spit into the bowl, and drank down the rest of the water. It was soothing to her queasy stomach.

While she dressed in Martha's gown, he busied himself preparing her breakfast. He took from his locker a small brazier, which he lit, boiled some water, and brewed the tea. He turned and presented a cup to her while she was combing out her auburn curls. " 'Tis very beautiful, your hair," he said.

It sounded like an observation, not a compliment. She chose not to acknowledge it. She finished pinning up her hair, then took the cup from him. "Do you think it wise . . . ?"

"A full belly is better than an empty one on a rocking ship. *Whatever* the cause of your distress. Wait." He turned and took a small vial from the cupboard. "A little oil of pepperment should help," he said, pouring a few drops into her tea.

The tea was warming, and the dry biscuits sat well on her stomach. "Whatever it was, it has quite gone away," she said.

"I knew it would. These episodes are fleeting, so I've found in my prac-tice. A little nausea in the morning. Nothing more." He pointed toward the bench, upon which lay a large packet. "Mr. Slickenham had a goodly quantity of muslin. And I've left you scissors and needles and thread. He had no stockings. But I've given you several pairs of my own."

"Thank you." She chewed at her lower lip. "You've been up for hours, it would seem. But how did you contrive to . . . ?"

"Get out of bed? I climbed over you."

That thought set her to blushing. His body so close to hers . . .

He chuckled. "I must have done it with care. You never stirred."

Somehow, that didn't seem proper. "Oh, but . . ."

"Come, come," he said impatiently. "You survived the night un-touched, didn't you? You shall have to accustom yourself to my rising be-fore you. But if it disturbs your modesty, sleep on the inside."

"I *shall,*" she said with defiance. She had to show him that she wasn't a passive ninny who took kindly to being ordered around!

He motioned toward the door. "Come up on deck now."

"No. I'll not. I want to cut out my shifts first. And mend my gown. I intend to be here the whole of the morning."

He shrugged. "If you choose to be petulant. Seek for me in the cockpit when you're ready to take the air." He turned and left the cabin, his face registering displeasure.

As soon as he had gone, she remembered the bruise on her hip. Tucking up her skirts, she examined it carefully. It was still painful to her touch—a red patch, several inches across, just at the top of her hipbone. She was surprised that it hadn't begun to empurple, as bruises usually did. But perhaps it was less serious than that, despite the soreness. She smoothed down her skirts; there was work to be done.

She shook out the lengths of fabric that Ross had brought and laid them out on the floor. Fine muslin. And he had paid for it, no doubt. She would have to keep a ledger, so that Jamie could reimburse him. She cut out the few simple pieces that her shifts would require and was pleased to see that there was enough fabric left over for the hem of her gown, without sacrificing her petticoat.

She frowned as she folded the last piece and made a neat stack on the bench. She shouldn't have been so stubborn and refused Ross's offer of a turn around the deck to clear her head. But she hated acquiescing to him. Hated even more his easy assumption that she would obey, like a little child.

But stubbornness *is* childish, Kitten, Papa used to say. And foolish. And now her head was thumping like a Persian carpet being beaten in the kitchen yard. She swallowed her pride and turned to leave the cabin.

Just then, there was a soft tap on the door. At her bidding, a young seaman came into the cabin. "Mornin', ma'am," he said, making a leg to her. "I be Thompson, what makes up Mr. Manning's cabin. But if I be comin' to anchor at the wrong time, you've but to pipe me out, and I'll be gone faster'n a worm on a fishhook when the haddock is runnin'."

She was grateful for the excuse. "No, no. I'm just leaving."

She crossed the passageway and entered the cockpit. Ross sat at the table, with half a dozen seamen lined up in front him. Near the medicine chest stood a ruddy-faced man, more finely dressed than the seamen, in a plain coat and waistcoat, with a round wig on his head that had clearly seen better days.

Ross rose to his feet as Prudence entered, and tried to hide the smirk on his face. "So soon?"

She blessed Thompson for his interruption. "I didn't want to disturb Thompson at his work," she said loftily. "So I thought I'd accept your kind offer of a walk on deck."

He gestured toward the man with the wig. "Let me introduce you to Bailey, here. He's one of my surgeon's mates."

Bailey beamed and nodded a greeting. "Wecome aboard, Mrs. Manning." The smile deepened. "I'm the *first* mate, you understand. 'Tis my pleasure to serve under your husband."

Ross snorted. "Wait until the voyage is over before you say that." He pointed to the door through which Prudence had just entered. "Now, wife, if you'll wait outside until I've finished with these men . . ."

She didn't intend to be dismissed offhand! "I shall wait here," she announced in a firm voice. " 'Tis too close in the passageway. Unless you prefer me to go up on deck alone. *Husband.*"

His cold blue eyes narrowed. Prudence shivered at the look, prepared to flee the room. Then he seemed to reconsider, and held out his chair for her. "As you wish."

She seated herself with as much pride as she could muster.

Ross crooked a finger at the first man in line. "Come forward."

The man was flushed, his skin dry and taut. Ross felt his pulse, put his hand on his temple, and shook his head. "You have a fever. Is there a reason for it, that you know?"

"Aye, sir." The seaman rolled up his sleeve to display a large wound on his forearm; it was red and swollen, oozing a thick, yellowish fluid. "I took a broken spar in me arm two days ago, sir."

Ross's lip twisted in annoyance. "And thought that God would heal it without man's help." He glanced at his mate. "Suck out this foulness, Bailey, and put a compress on it. Then send the man to Richards in the sick berth. He can't stand watch until his fever breaks."

While Bailey took a syringe to the wound, Ross examined the next man. The seaman sighed and groaned, and complained of a hundred maladies. But after a thorough examination, Ross folded his arms across his chest and glowered at the man.

"Now, by God," he growled, "you're nothing but a lazy, lubberly son of a dog! There's not a bloody thing the matter with you. Get back to your duties before I report you to the boatswain for a shirker. And thank your Maker that you have your health!"

The seaman hung his head and skulked away. He was followed by a man who hadn't stopped scratching his wrists all the time he was in the cockpit. He held out his arms to Ross. The flesh was covered with green crusts that looked to Prudence like hairy moss, interspersed with red, oozing pustules. She gulped at the sight, beginning to regret her folly in staying.

"I can't hardly do me work, Mr. Manning, with this tormenting itch," said the seaman.

Ross gave him a cursory inspection. "If every man who had the scabies in the army or navy was excused from duty, we should not have more than a handful for a fighting force. Stop scratching, man! The water from the pustules spreads the disorder to other parts." He took up a pen and scrawled a few lines on a paper before him, then handed it to his mate. "Bailey, mix up this prescription for our twitching friend here."

The next seaman shuffled forward, bent in pain, and glanced uneasily at Prudence.

"You have a complaint?" said Ross impatiently.

The sailor cleared his throat and rubbed the back of his neck. "Well, sir, there I was in London, yardarm to yardarm wi' a fire ship, and she not letting on the whole time! And now . . ." He looked down at his groin and muttered an oath.

Ross rolled his eyes. "Damn my liver. Do you expect honesty from a whore? Well, show me."

"But sir . . ." The seaman blushed and cast another furtive glance toward Prudence.

"Show me!"

The man sighed, dropped his trousers and lifted his shirt. Prudence fled.

She stood trembling in the passageway, trying to forget the sight of the man's genitals, deep red and distended and covered with sores. Papa had died quickly, and Mama had wasted away with a hidden, silent disease. She had never before been exposed to the corruptions that the human body could endure.

She was still shaking when Ross strode out into the passageway. She lifted tear-filled eyes to him. "I . . . I hadn't imagined . . ."

If she was hoping for comfort, there was none to be found in his icy stare. "I deal in reality," he said. "Not in that world of dreams and faithful lovers that you envisage. If you're too squeamish for the rudeness of medicine, stay out of the cockpit unless you're invited."

She felt chastened and humbled. He had tried to spare her by asking her to leave. Unlike Grandpapa, he had meant his orders for her own good. "I'm . . . I'm sorry," she said, her lip quivering.

His expression softened. " 'Twas a raw awakening. *I'm* sorry." He proffered his arm. "Come. The deck."

She slipped her hand through the crook of his arm, feeling strangely comforted. Now that the shock had passed, she was filled with curiosity. "What will happen to the man with the fever?"

"If his wound turns to gangrene, as I fear it might, we'll have to cut off his arm."

"How dreadful! The poor man." She looked up at his impassive face. "Does that not distress you?"

"Very much. There should be more that a doctor can do to cure infections."

That's not what she had meant at all. She tried again. "What's a fire ship?"

He crooked his eyebrow at her. "Do you really want to know?"

"Of course."

" 'Tis what the seamen call a whore with gonorrhea. Must I explain that to you as well?"

She shook her head and kept silent until they had reached the main deck. She wasn't *that* ignorant. Betsy had been forever treating herself with salves and elixirs to forestall the diseases of her trade.

The rain had stopped. The air was clear and fresh, and the clouds had begun to break, revealing small patches of brilliant blue. Prudence felt refreshed, her spirits lifting with every soft puff of wind on her face. Above them, the sails billowed in the breeze; below, the glistening waves slapped against the ship in a soothing rhythm. And she was on her way to Jamie.

She spread her arms wide to the shining day and grinned at Ross. "I feel newborn! Does it not delight you, this day?"

He stared at her, his expression desolate. "I wish to God I could still see the world as you do."

"My dreamworld, as you called it?" *And not without a certain contempt,* she thought.

He cupped her chin with his hand. His fingers were warm and gentle. She thought for a moment he would kiss her, as improbable as it seemed. "Your heart is as pure as your face is lovely," he said. "I wonder . . . if I could bottle your essence, could I save the world? Or myself?"

"Ross . . ." she whispered, trembling at the softness of his touch. Why should he have the power to move her?

"Beggin' your pardon, Mr. Manning. Lady."

They turned. Toby Wedge stood before them, shyly scraping his shoe against the deck.

Ross frowned. "Yes, Wedge, what is it? Do you have some illness that needs to be treated?"

"Oh, no, sir. But, d'ye see me, here's my messmate, Gawky, what wants to see the lady up close. 'Gawky,' says I, 'she's as pretty as a picture. Fine rigged.' " He bowed clumsily. "An't please you, ma'am."

"It pleases me very much." She found his awkwardness oddly touching.

Wedge gestured to the man behind him, a tall, gangling fellow in a check shirt. "Don't lag astern, Gawky," he said. "Come an' make your compliments to the lady, and say your piece."

Gawky hitched up his wide breeches, puckered his lips, aimed a stream of brown saliva over the side of the ship, and stepped forward. His bow was even more ungainly than Wedge's had been.

"Your servant, ma'am," he said, shifting his quid of tobacco from one cheek to the other. A blush showed beneath his tanned complexion. He jerked his finger toward Wedge. "Me and Toby here, hearing as how you was cast up on the ship without so much as a trinket box . . . Well, we jawed fore 'n' aft with our messmates for a bit . . ."

"Good gunners they be, all of 'em, d'ye see," interrupted Wedge.

Gawky glared at Wedge, clearly piqued to be cut off in the middle of his declamation. "The long and the short of it, ma'am, is that everyone, to a man, put in what he could. Gewgaws and stuff you might be needing. We left 'em in your cabin, Mr. Manning. And that's all I'll say. I've said my piece." He stared down at the deck, his long face redder than ever.

Prudence felt the tears well in her eyes. "How kind you are. Thank you. And thank your messmates for me, as well."

"Have you managed to steer clear of the captain, Wedge?" asked Ross.

Wedge nodded his massive head vigorously. He looked like a marionette on a string. "Aye, that I have, Mr. Manning, sir. But he were born under a dark moon, Cap'n were. So I've heard tell. A bad omen, that. It bodes ill for the voyage. More ill for poor Toby Wedge." He jerked his thumb in his mate's direction. "And Gawky, here, still wearin' his stripes what he got last year from Cap'n."

"Just stay out of his way."

"Aye. That I will. I be mightily feared of him."

Prudence was about to protest the injustice of Hackett's animosity toward Wedge, when a shrill whistle rent the air.

"There's the boatswain, piping to dinner," said Ross. "Go and join your messmates. And thank them again for their kindness to Mrs. Manning." He turned to Prudence. "Wife? Shall we dine?"

Wedge and Gawky scurried away to their mess, and Ross led Prudence to the wardroom.

It was crowded with men when they entered—senior warrant officers as well as the commissioned officers Prudence had already met. They gathered around the long dining table, laughing and joking. Mess-boys bustled about, laying a cloth and pewter plates. There was a bank of windows at the stern, which made the room bright and cheerful. Beneath the windows, there was a long, padded locker upon which sat First Lieutenant St. John and another man, engaged in lively conversation. A large, octagonal table was situated just in front of the window bench; Prudence knew enough about ships to know that it covered the rudder head.

Perched gingerly on it was Lieutenant Elliot, scraping away on a fiddle, a pained expression on his face. Remembering his troubles, Prudence felt a pang of sympathy.

St. John bounded to his feet when he spied her. " 'Pon my word, Mrs. Manning! A pleasure to see you again." He bent to kiss her hand. "Though I should prefer to have you all to myself, without your husband glowering at me!" He grinned at Ross. "Do you know, sir, that your wife has the prettiest green eyes in all the world? If I didn't know how she chanced to come aboard, I should guess that she was a mermaid, sent to enchant us all!"

Prudence blushed, too overwhelmed to say a word.

St. John rummaged in his coat pocket. "I noted last night that you wore no buckles on your shoes. If you would do me the honor of accepting a small token? In exchange for the gift of your beauty on this voyage." He held out a pair of silver buckles, finely chased and polished.

She gasped in surprise and took the proffered gift. "How kind you are, Lieutenant St. John."

He beamed. "You must call me Edwin. And may I be permitted to address you as Martha?"

She lowered her eyes, too shy to look him in the face. Never before had she known such sweet attentions. Not even Jamie had been so fervent—at least not until the moment when he'd told her he loved her. "Of course you may," she replied to St. John. "How can I not consent, after such a fine gift?"

Beside her, Ross made a peculiar sound, as though he were choking. "Shall we go to table?" he said, his voice tight and cold. "The mess-boys are ready to serve."

St. John held out his arm to her. "May I, Martha?"

She took his arm and allowed him to seat her next to himself. There was a scramble among several of the officers to take the seat on the other side of her. But Ross stopped them with a frigid glare and reached for the chair.

It was a lively dinner. She soon learned the names and ranks of the senior warrant officers—the master, the officer of gunnery, the boatswain, and the master carpenter. Even the captain of the marines was there. She gave Slickenham a polite nod, and thanked him for the muslin. But she found it difficult to like the man. And when he mentioned in passing the price of the cloth, she liked him even less. The finest *silk* in Winsley was less dear than that!

Though Ross was quiet and remote, St. John kept up a bright conversation, constantly turning the talk back to her charm, her beauty, her grace. And when the meal was finished, and the officers had begun to return to their duties, he put his hand on her arm.

"Don't go yet, Martha," he said. "I've been longing to hear you sing, since you spoke of it last night." He gestured to Lieutenant Elliot. "Come, man. Pick up your fiddle for this sweet lady."

She hesitated. "I only know the old country songs." And even they had been forbidden her in the house, after Papa's death.

Elliot frowned in thought. "Do you know 'Madam, Will You Walk'?"

She smiled, ignoring Ross's scowl. "Of course."

"But that's an air for two," said St. John. "May I join you?" At her nod, he signaled to Elliot.

It was a courting song, with the verses alternating between an imploring suitor and the reluctant object of his affections. Prudence sang it with all the coquetry suggested by the lyrics. St. John matched her artistry, clutching one hand to his breast, his eyes burning with unrequited love.

They were rewarded with applause and lighthearted laughter when they had finished.

St. John bowed to Ross. "Your wife is the most delightful creature I have ever met, sir!"

Ross gritted his teeth. "My wife, sir, is . . . my *wife!*" He grabbed Prudence in his arms and ground his mouth down on hers in a possessive kiss.

She swayed against him, overcome with the passion of his lips on hers. She felt frightened, helpless, light-headed, drowning in the wonder of his kiss.

"Are we to have these constant displays of matrimonial affection, Mr. Manning?"

Prudence whirled to see Captain Hackett in the doorway, glaring at them.

Ross bent his head in a stiff salute. "I only wished to make clear to these gentlemen that Mrs. Manning has a husband."

Hackett's lip curled. "And a jealous one?" He shrugged. "No matter. I came to pay my compliments to this dear lady." He lifted Prudence's hand and brought it to his lips. His eyes glittered with unfathomable thoughts. "You slept well, Mrs. Manning? Was it your first time? Sleeping aboard ship, that is."

Prudence blinked, her head still spinning from Ross's kiss. But she recovered her wits soon enough to realize that Hackett was again suggesting that he suspected their charade. She managed an innocent smile. "Yes, Captain. And such a small bunk. Our bed at home is ever so much larger." She would have to remember to ask Ross where "home" was.

Hackett returned her smile, his mouth curving in a tight grimace. "Ah, yes. I, too, miss the comforts of home and hearth. And bed. *All* the comforts." His eyes swept Ross with distaste. "But we are forced to suffer aboard ship. At least, most of us. Is it not so, Mr. Manning?"

Ross's smile was as false as the captain's. "But in a few short weeks we shall be in Virginia, sir. With all the attendant pleasures that can be found in a proper . . . house."

"But, in the meantime, I must deal with my deprivation. 'Tis my hope that you, Mr. Manning, may provide a cure."

"Alas, sir. I have nothing in my possession to ease your distress."

"Nothing, sir?"

"For a certainty, sir."

Prudence stared at the two rigid faces. What in heaven's name were they angry about *now?* The captain's longing for home and hearth? A sensible desire, to her way of thinking.

Mercifully, their simmering quarrel was interrupted by the boatswain. "Do your orders still stand, Captain?"

Hackett scowled. "Indeed, they do. I like not this crop of pressed men. Nothing but a bunch of freshwater, wishy-washy, fair-weather fools! I'll not tolerate the lazy, lubberly sons of bitches . . ." He caught himself and bowed to Prudence. "Beg pardon, Mrs. Manning. These rogues, who are good for nothing on board but to eat the king's provision. And while we're about order on this ship," he beckoned to St. John, "I'm disgusted at the slovenly condition of some of the midshipmen and petty officers. You will issue an order that they are not to appear on deck in check shirts or soiled linen. They are to follow the king's new proclamation, and wear the proper uniforms. At all times. I'll not endure disorder or ugliness around me. Do you understand?"

"Aye, sir."

"Speaking of which, Doctor Manning, did I see you on deck speaking to that grotesquerie of a man? Wedge. Was that his name?"

"You did, sir." Ross's jaw was set in a hard line. He reminded Prudence of a pugilist at a country fair, preparing to lay out his adversary.

"In truth, Captain," said Prudence quickly, putting her hand on Hackett's braid-covered sleeve, "Wedge had done me some small service. 'Tis I who spoke to him. Only to thank him." She dimpled prettily at him, hoping to soften his anger toward Wedge.

The captain smiled down at her hand on his arm and relaxed his rigid body. "Why then, dear lady, I must excuse the man's presumption this time. For your sake. How can I refuse such a charming advocate?" He took her hand and kissed it, his lips lingering on her flesh. "I could wish to do you some service myself. If circumstances allow." He bowed. "Your servant, ma'am. Come, St. John. We have matters to discuss."

And I have my sewing, thought Prudence. "Will you accompany me back to the cabin, Ross? Or shall I go alone?"

He took her firmly by the elbow. "I think you need an escort," he growled.

The sky was clear when they emerged on deck. The clouds had blown away. The summer sun was high in the blue heavens. Hot and bright.

But Prudence was chilled by the aspect of the man who held her arm so tightly—a cold column of rage. She felt as she ofttimes had felt with Papa: as though she had somehow displeased him, but didn't understand the reason why. Because she had been civil to the captain, while Ross had seemed determined to be quarrelsome?

They made their way to the cabin in silence. But when they opened the door, Prudence smiled in pleasure, her dark thoughts vanishing. On the floor were the gifts from Wedge and the other gunners. She ran and knelt before a battered sea chest, sifting through the items within and exclaiming in delight over each one. Humble gifts, but treasures, no doubt, to the men who had parted with them. A bunch of onions and a small slab of salt pork, wrapped in oiled paper. A gallipot of butter, beginning to turn rancid. Two hair combs, crudely carved of whalebone, and a blue ribbon. A tin mirror, worn and scratched, and a cockleshell on a braided cord, to tie around her neck.

"Oh!" she cried. "How lovely! How dear of them." She smiled up at Ross, hoping to share her delight.

He merely shrugged. "I suppose it's an occasion to men like that, when a woman is aboard ship."

She clicked her tongue. "Well, if you choose to be a dog in the manger about it . . ." She turned to her sewing, vexed that he had taken all the joy out of the gifts. She lifted a piece of the muslin. "Can you imagine? Six shillings a yard? That wicked Mr. Slickenham!"

He snorted. "I never knew a purser who didn't try to line his pockets. I wouldn't give you a farthing for the accuracy of his weights and measures."

"Nonetheless, I'll see that my Lord Jamie pays you back for the muslin."

"That's not necessary."

"Oh, but he must."

His eyes flashed. "No!"

He was already in a foul enough mood. She wasn't about to do battle over a few pounds and shillings. "Very well," she murmured. "I thank you for the muslin."

He acknowledged her thanks with a nod. Then he pointed to the sea chest on the floor. "I will, of course, see that Wedge and the other gunners are repaid for that."

This, at least, was worth quarreling over. "Most certainly not!"

He stared at her in disbelief. "By the Lord, why not?"

"Don't you understand anything of human kindness?" she chided. "How can you degrade those men by *paying* for a gift? Merciful heaven, why did you become a surgeon, if not to do good?"

His mouth curled in a cynical smile. "It was interesting. A challenge to my intelligence." Before she could respond, he turned to the door. "I have my duties."

"And I, my sewing." She hoped her tone was as cold as his.

He paused, one hand on the latch. "By the bye, while we're on the subject of gifts—you will please to give back the shoe buckles to St. John."

"I shall not!" He was really going too far with his high-handed orders.

He whirled to face her. "Damn my liver, are you as blind as all that? You blush and mince and simper around him! Do you think he'll not expect something in return? By God, if you insist on flirting with him in such a shameless fashion, we'll take our meals here. Alone! I'll not have you compromising yourself for a pair of damned shoe buckles or an easy compliment!"

She chewed at her thumbnail, momentarily thrown into confusion. A gift for a treasure, Betsy had said. Was that what St. John expected—her favors? Was she as naive, as dense to the workings of a man's mind as Ross suggested? No! It was only *his* way of looking at life. "You think that every admiring glance is a prelude to a . . . a . . . !" She couldn't even say the word.

"A rape?" he said with a sneer. "No. But I think you put yourself into the sort of situation that will virtually ensure it, one of these days!"

"How can you say that? Lieutenant St. John—yes, and the captain as well!—have been perfect gentlemen. Kind and thoughtful. I see no sign of the lechery that you're always predicting. Not in them, at least. Whilst *you* . . . You take every opportunity to . . . to kiss me. In a most unseemly way."

His face was a mask of cold indifference. "Those kisses meant nothing to me. I behaved as I did only to remind the other men that you're a married woman, since you yourself seem incapable of remembering it. I fear that if *I* don't kiss you, the captain and St. John will certainly begin to do so!"

"Fiddle-faddle! They are kind to me, and I can do naught but be kind in return. How can you imagine anything more?" She swallowed hard, her heart suddenly twisting in her bosom. "Don't you understand? I love my Lord Jamie. And no one else. I long for the day when we'll be wed." She glared at him with defiance. "And if you suppose that *your* kisses mean more to me than simply a device to fool the captain . . ."

"Ah, yes. The absent Lord Jamie, who has so bedazzled you that you'll chance all this to fly to his side. Do you really think, in that dreamworld of yours, that a nobleman will stoop to marry you?"

She turned away, the hot tears springing to her eyes. Sweet Jamie. Had she gambled everything on a losing game? This mad charade, the companionship of a cold, unfeeling man? "You said you had your duties," she said in a choked voice. "And I have my sewing. Please go away."

He turned her to face him, his hands strong and warm on her shoulders. His eyes had grown soft, the blue of the summer sky. He brushed a tear from her cheek. "Prudence. You innocent child. I only meant that you shouldn't put so much hope and faith into what awaits you in America. I . . ." He stopped and frowned, as the sound of a drumbeat reverberated through the ship. "Damme!" he swore, and turned toward the door.

"What is it?"

"All hands on deck. I order you to stay here."

"Is it a battle? In these waters? I want to see."

"I forbid it," he growled. "Stay below." He went out the door, slamming it behind him.

Forbid? she thought, feeling her anger stewing like a hot pot on the fire. She had entered into this masquerade as an equal, not an underling! She turned to her sewing, tried to work, but found her hands shaking with rage as she threaded the needle and began to stitch. At last she threw down the shift. No! She would not allow him to order her around!

She marched out the door and made her way up the hatchway. It was deserted, and the steady drumbeats grew louder as she reached the quarterdeck and came out into the sunshine. She stared in surprise. Every man aboard seemed to have been assembled topside. The gangways were lined with seamen, and the forecastle was crowded with the rest of the crew. Ross and the other officers stood at attention on the poop deck above her.

Ross came racing down the stairs and grabbed her savagely by the arm. "Damn it, I told you to stay below!"

"But why?" she stammered, bewildered. "Why can't I . . . ?"

And then she saw him. A man tied to the ratlines of the ship. His shirt had been torn from his body, and his back was covered with red, bloody

lines. As she watched in horror, the boatswain's mate lifted a frayed rope
and slashed it across the man's back, leaving another oozing cut. The man
cried out in agony.

"Sweet merciful heaven," whispered Prudence, and collapsed into
Ross's arms.

Chapter Eight

⟋⟋⟋⟋⟋

Prudence yawned and opened her eyes. The cabin was in darkness, save for the lantern on the desk at which Ross sat. He seemed to be writing, deep in concentration. "What time is it?" she asked. Her voice sounded oddly cracked and dry.

He looked up from his work and smiled. "Near to six bells, and suppertime. Seven o'clock," he explained, when she looked bewildered.

"I've slept a long time."

"You've slept longer than you know. You've been abed for two days now. I think it was the lingering effects of the blow to your head."

She rubbed her eyes. "Two days abed? And you?"

The smiled deepened. "You didn't disturb me."

She was about to reply sharply when she realized that she was now on the inside, next to the bulkhead. Whatever else Ross Manning was, he was good to his word. She noticed the large folio on the desk before him. "What are you doing?"

"Drawing. 'Tis a pastime of mine."

"Show me."

Reluctantly, he lifted the folio from the desk and carried it to the bunk. Prudence raised herself on one elbow, the better to see. The page was filled with sketches of hands—mostly his, she guessed—and executed with remarkable skill.

"But these are wonderful," she said, surprised by his refined talent, a sensibility she would not have suspected in him. She reached out to turn the page. "I should like to see more."

He slapped his hand on the folio, preventing her. "No."

She giggled. "Are there pictures that would offend my modesty?" Betsy had had a book like that. For her customers who needed encouragement, she'd said, mystifying Prudence. She had glanced at it once, and shuddered in disgust.

"Of course not." Ross looked decidedly uncomfortable. Then he shrugged, took his hand from the paper and allowed her to turn the page.

To her astonishment, it was filled with drawings of her: lying asleep in the bunk, several sketches of her hands, the side of her face, her profile. There were even a few small drawings, grouped together, where he had clearly tried to capture the particular curve of her eyebrows. She stared up at him, then looked away, suddenly shy. To know that he had examined her with such care as she slept . . . It gave her an odd thrill. "This is . . . very flattering," she stammered.

His laugh was cool and distant, reminding her that she was foolish to indulge her romantic fancies where Ross Manning was concerned! "Good God," he said dryly, "don't begin to suppose that I'm as susceptible as those young sparks in the wardroom. You simply make a charming subject. And a welcome change from all the men on board."

The men. His words reminded her of something she had tried to put out of her mind. "That poor seaman, the one they whipped . . ."

He closed the folio quickly and returned it to his desk. "He'll recover."

Her lip trembled. "But . . . *why?*"

"He was one of the pressed men. Captain Hackett wished to make an example of him."

"That's barbarous! And you tolerate it?"

"What would you have me do?" he growled. "This is a ship of the King's Navy. 'Tis how things are done." His voice deepened in anger. "I warned you to stay below."

She glared at him. "As I recall, you *forbade* me. Like a child."

"And was it not childish of you, to disobey me?" He shook his head in disgust. "To swoon in my arms like that . . ."

"I wonder how Martha enjoyed being ordered about all day long," she said petulantly.

She was sorry she'd uttered the words almost as soon as they left her mouth. He stiffened, his jaw tightening, and turned away. "I shall attempt to put my commands into requests henceforth," he said at last. When he turned back to her, his eyes were cold. "Do you feel well enough to dress and come to supper in the wardroom? Or shall I have it served here?"

She felt remorse for her thoughtless words. "No," she said meekly, "I'll get up." She sat upright in bed, then gaped down at herself. Instead of the shift she had expected to see, she was wearing nothing but a shirt! His shirt, no doubt. "What have you done with my clothes?"

"Since you were scarcely in a fit condition to sew any new shifts, I gave yours to Thompson to wash. And the gown and apron you came aboard with. He has contrived to mend the hems, as well."

"Oh, but you should have allowed me . . ."

"Most seamen are handy with the needle. They mend enough sails."

She eased herself out of the bunk and stood on shaky legs. She dared not dwell on the thought of Ross stripping her shift from her. Thanks be to God she had been insensible at the time! But she had a fleeting moment of unease, wondering what other pictures of her might be in that folio of his. He had been quite eager to take it away from her.

Ross handed her her freshly washed shift and Martha's gown, then turned his back without being asked.

She took a moment before she dressed to examine her injuries. The large bruise on her shoulder was still quite black, but beginning to turn yellowish around the edges. A good sign. Her hip was even better. Though it was still tender, the spot was scarcely red any longer. She peered into the mirror. The cut on her head was healing nicely; she assumed that Ross would remove the stitches in a week or so.

As she was pinning up the last curl on her head (and blessing Wedge and his messmates for the additional combs!), she heard the ship's bell clang six times, followed by the sound of the boatswain's whistle, piping the crew to supper. She cleared her throat delicately and Ross turned around. "If you'll please give me your arm," she said. "I'm still a trifle unsteady."

They ascended the aft hatchway, stepping aside for the mess-boys who came running from the galley; they carried platters of steaming food and cried "Scaldings!" as they hurried down the stairs, to warn of their presence.

Prudence found her spirits dampened during supper. Despite St. John's lavish attentions, she couldn't help but remember Ross's words. What if the lieutenant's warm flattery was less benign than she had supposed? She scarcely wished him to misread her conduct. Besides, with Ross glowering at her the whole time, she half expected him to snatch her up and carry her to their cabin, if she should give St. John the slightest encouragement! She resisted the lieutenant's entreaties for a song, pleading a lingering weakness, and allowed Ross to lead her onto the deck as soon as the supper plates were cleared.

There was still a glimmer of light in the evening sky, but several stars glittered brightly in the soft blue heavens, and the silver sickle of a new moon floated just above the horizon.

Ross reached into his coat pocket. " 'Tis too pleasant a night to go below yet. By your leave . . . ?" He pulled out a pipe and a pouch of tobacco.

She smiled and nodded. She had always liked the smell of Papa's pipe.

He found his tinderbox, lit his pipe, and stood leaning against the railing of the deck, lost in thought. The pale blue smoke drifted above his head, was caught by a gentle breeze, and wafted past Prudence and out to sea.

She stared at the clear sky, awed—as always—by its majesty. Perhaps Jamie was gazing up at the same moon. She had never shared the beauty of the moon with Jamie; Grandpapa had always expected the sheep to be in their pens by sundown. But soon, she and Jamie would stand together, her head on his shoulder, his ring—sanctified by the blessing of marriage—back on her finger, where it was meant to be. And then . . . and then . . . She sighed heavily. All would be right in her world again. She put her hand to her abdomen. She could almost feel the joyous pain.

Ross's voice cut through her reverie. "Have you made your wish on the new moon?" He laughed softly. "Of course you have. What is he like, your Lord Jamie?"

"He has black hair. And his eyes sparkle, like those stars. And he laughs, oh so merrily, and teases me." She sighed again. "And tells me that he loves me."

He gave a mocking laugh. "Before, or after, he seduces you?"

She turned to him, her eyes filling with tears. "How can you begin to understand? With your cold heart?"

He seemed startled by her words, and slightly abashed. He nodded his head. "Forgive me. You're quite right, of course. 'Tis too sweet a night for you to suffer the dark thoughts of a man who has grown weary of mankind."

The despair in his voice touched her heart. "How can you have dark thoughts, when the night is so lovely, and God's hand stretches over all? Come. You must make a wish on the new moon. A wish filled with hope for the future." She tugged at his sleeve for encouragement.

He strode to the side of the ship, knocked his pipe against the outside planking, and watched the bright embers blow away. "I already have," he said at last. " 'Tis my wish to be free of this world. This weary life. And— absent that sweet release—I hope for solitude in the wilderness." He turned and offered his arm. "Come. If you're not tired as yet, I have books that might entertain you for an hour or so."

She moved toward him, but the rocking of the ship, and the weakness she still felt in her limbs, contrived to make her steps unsteady. She stumbled and would have fallen, but for his arms.

His face was in shadow, close above hers. She could hear the deep rasp of his breath. His arms were warm around her body, with a strength that set her heart to pounding. When he bent to kiss her—as though it had been ordained, the most natural act in the world—she offered her mouth willingly. She felt her face flaming with the hot pressure of his lips on hers.

"Gad's curse, Mr. Manning! I begin to think this supposed 'marriage' is a mockery. No husband kisses his *own* wife with such regularity."

Ross released Prudence's mouth, but kept a firm hold on her waist. "Captain Hackett, sir. Can you fault me, with a wife such as this?"

"I can only envy you, sir." Hackett bowed to Prudence. "Your servant, ma'am. You'll soon have every man aboard feeling hatred for your husband."

The way Hackett had said the word troubled Prudence. *Hatred,* with a sneer in the utterance. She smiled her most disarming smile at him. "But not you, Captain, surely!"

His responding smile was strange and puzzling. "Whatever . . . understandings that might be arrived at between Mr. Manning and me need not concern you, dear lady." He bowed again and vanished into the wardroom.

"That lecherous cur," growled Ross. "I'll settle with him, by God, before I'm through."

"I don't know why you dislike him so. He spoke of reaching an understanding with you. Does that sound like a man who wishes to be your enemy?"

"It sounds like a man who wishes to possess . . ." He stopped and shrugged. "No matter. I doubt you'd understand. *Your* world, I warrant, never entertained villains."

She remembered his unexpected kiss, and with more than a little guilt. If Jamie should ever learn of it, what could she tell him? That she accepted it? Nay, that she had welcomed it? What had Papa said, whenever she had given in to temptation? Get thee behind me, Satan.

"That 'villain' wasn't the one who kissed me, and with no cause," she said sharply, feeling an inexplicable anger.

"I saw the captain coming across the deck."

He left her no target for her vague discontent. "Well, you didn't have to take pleasure in it, you scoundrel!" she said, and flounced away.

She felt his hand on her sleeve. And then she was jerked around and pulled into his arms, none too gently. He held her close to the length of his hard body, and ground his mouth down on hers. His hands were firm on her back, her waist; her bosom pressed against his solid chest. She trembled and moaned beneath his possessing lips, gasping in helpless pleasure. His tongue slipped between her parted lips and explored her mouth with tantalizing, maddening strokes. She was lost, quivering in every fiber.

God forgive me, she thought. To enjoy another man's kiss, and Jamie still fresh in her mind. She was as wicked, as godless as Grandpapa had said she was. *Get thee behind . . .* But it was no use. She surrendered to the rapture of Ross's kiss and slid her arms around his neck.

When he released her at last, she could scarcely stand. She swayed with the movement of the deck, praying she wouldn't tumble at his feet. And she had accused *him* of taking pleasure in their kisses?

He laughed, a low chuckle that held mockery in its depths. And a clear understanding of her weakness. "Nor did you," he said.

She burst into tears, filled with shame and humiliation. "Masquerade or no, you'll not kiss me again! *Ever!* If you do, I'll tell the captain the truth. And you'll be put in irons, and I'll rejoice, and . . . and . . ." Sobbing, she raced down the hatchway to the refuge of the cabin.

By the time he entered, she was already in bed. She turned her back on him, flattening herself up against the bulkhead. Plague take the cold-hearted rogue, who kissed like a lover, yet looked at her with his indifferent eyes.

If she so much as felt the heat of his body near hers tonight, she would push him out of the bunk!

Ross looked up from his bowl of porridge. "We shall reach the Azores in three or four days, I think. And lie in the harbor of Ponta Delgado until the fleet catches up with us." Hackett had driven the men hard, with more than one flogging to encourage them. They had outrun the rest of the ships after the third day.

Prudence sipped at her mug of beer. There had been no tea for days now, the water aboard ship having begun to turn foul. But Ross had a store of his own brandy and beer that he had brought aboard. It even served for brushing their teeth. "I shall be glad of solid land," she said.

"If there's opportunity, I'll take you to the mineral baths. The island of São Miguel is noted for them." He glanced at her empty bowl and nodded in approval. "You finished your coddled eggs in no time. Shall I send Thompson for more?"

"No." She reached across the desk, which was laid for breakfast, and took hold of the jam pot. "But if you'll pass me another biscuit . . ."

She nearly giggled aloud. *Look at us,* she thought, *like a couple of old married people.* The proximity of their living arrangements had produced a comfortable easiness in a remarkably short time, a familiarity that had become quite natural as the days had passed. Ross no longer bothered to turn his back when she dressed, unless she was changing into a fresh shift. And the sight of him stripped to the waist as he shaved and washed himself no longer disconcerted her, despite the overbearing power of his torso.

He had never kissed her again since that unfortunate night, nor had he spoken of it. Upon reflection, she was glad of that. She had no one but herself to blame, as Papa would have scolded her. She had accused Ross of wanting to kiss her—perhaps to hide her own desire from herself. But any fool could see that he took no interest in her; his cool demeanor when they were away from curious eyes attested to that fact. Perhaps he had meant his impassioned kiss to be a rebuke: if anyone was weak, it was she.

She had grown quite accustomed to his cold, remote ways. It was just his nature, she supposed. The nature of a man who had already removed himself from the world.

But he still held her in his sleep, almost every night. She would waken, and find his arm around her. And sometimes he mumbled "Martha," and the word tore at her soul. The poor man. She never had the heart to push him away and destroy his tender dreams.

To protect themselves against Hackett's prying, they had fabricated a few stories together, made up of bits and shreds of their lives—Ross's practice of medicine in London, the country house in Gloucestershire, a village fair she had visited with Jamie.

But whenever the talk turned too intimately to his life with Martha, he retreated into his distant world. And she had no wish to cause him anguish by pressing him further. He seldom called her "Martha," even in front of others—as though the mere mention of the name was too painful. She answered to the name of "Wife," and let it go at that.

They ate more grandly than she would have supposed aboard ship, from the stories she'd heard of the common seamen who visited Betsy. Every officer, including Ross, had brought his own supply of food and drink aboard, to augment the ship's diet. Most of them kept laying hens as well, sheltered in cages on the main deck, within the protective shadow of the forecastle.

They took dinner and supper in the wardroom, except for the weekly suppers with Captain Hackett—twice more since that first night. Ross was always tense at the captain's table, darkly hinting afterward that the man was out for no good. But Prudence never saw anything untoward in Hackett's manner.

She spent most of her days in the bright wardroom, sewing or reading. The young officers were pleasant company. They played whisk and backgammon with her, and Lieutenant Elliot had even taught her to play hazard, with a set of dice. She often sang to his fiddle playing, but there had been no repetition of any duets with St. John. She didn't want to tempt Ross's anger.

Sometimes, like little boys trying to dazzle the village queen, the officers practiced their fencing before her, with much bravado and leaping about; on bended knee, they begged her to choose them as their champions before the match. They still flattered and complimented her. But she remembered Papa's admonition—Pride goeth before a fall—and refused to allow them to turn her head.

She had grown quite weary of St. John and his excessive praise. Whether or not he was only trying to seduce her, as Ross claimed, she found it tiresome to treat with a man of so little intellect that he was incapable of holding a serious discourse with her. Ross had reluctantly allowed her to keep and wear the shoe buckles, but only because they seemed too trifling a gift to precipitate a quarrel.

Ross finished the last of his beer. "What will you do today?"

She pursed her lips in vexation. "I don't know." She had finished sewing her shifts long since, had even taken the care to frost them with embroidery. The books on Ross's shelf were dry and uninteresting, though she'd read them through to pass the time. Ross had said that a storm was blowing up this morning; the upper deck would be too cold and windy for a stroll. And the thought of listening to St. John chatter in his mindless way was more than she could bear. After an hour or two in the wardroom with him, she always welcomed the comfortable silence of Ross's company.

"I don't know," she said again, dreading the boredom of the long day.

"What was your habit at home? In your village?"

"I tended my grandfather's sheep. And went to church. And read."

"You enjoy reading? A rare quality in a woman."

"While he lived, my father was the schoolmaster in our village," she said, feeling the need to defend her humble life.

"Ah!" He seemed pleased with that. "Then you can read Latin."

"Of course."

"You might wish to help me for an hour or so in the cockpit, then. Mixing up my medicines."

"In point of fact," she said, "I've been thinking of late that I should like to help you minister to the men."

He frowned. " 'Tis not a pretty chore. I'm minded of the last time . . ."

She blushed, remembering the seaman with his foul distemper, his swollen groin. "I promise to leave the cockpit if . . . anything should distress me."

He suppressed his smile. "And will you faint at the sight of blood?"

"No. I've watched the cook slaughter a sheep many a time. And rip out the guts with her bare hands." She pointed down to her plain gown and apron. "And I'm dressed for hard work."

He rose from his chair. "Come along, then."

The ship was beginning to pitch as they made their way to the cockpit. The storm had increased in fury. They passed a line of seamen waiting to bring their complaints to the surgeon, and entered the cockpit. Prudence nodded a greeting to Bailey, who gaped at her as she took a seat, and scratched at his shaven head beneath his wig.

The first sailor to appear was Gawky, accompanied by Toby Wedge. The gunner's eye was nearly swollen shut, with a huge, inflamed stye on his upper lid.

Wedge made a leg to Ross and pointed at his companion. " 'Tis my messmate, Gawky, d'ye see me, sir. For a week, now, his starboard peeper be swellin' like a puffer fish. And him not payin' it a mind. 'Body o' me, Gawky,' says I. 'It be time to see the surgeon.' But he were mulish, sir. Till he wakes up like this. 'How can you stand your watch,' says I, 'with one window out?' So here we be." He pushed Gawky in front of him.

"It looks ready to burst," said Ross, examining Gawky's eye. He wrote something on a piece of paper and handed it to Bailey. "Give him a little steam to break it open. And then mix up this salve."

Prudence cleared her throat. "If you'll but show me where you keep your brazier, husband . . ." She smiled timidly when he raised a questioning eyebrow to her. " 'Tis a task not unknown to me. Farmers on dry land get sties as well."

While Bailey mixed up the prescription, Prudence lit a small charcoal brazier. When it was burning hotly, she took a pitcher of water and poured a thin stream on the coals. She directed Gawky to lean his face as close to the steam as he could endure.

All the while, Wedge kept up a mournful babble, his coarse face twisted into a grimace. " 'Twas meant to be, d'ye see me, lady. Old Gawky, here, he broke a shoe latchet a se'ennight ago. A bad omen. And there he were, my messmate, bendin' on the deck to fix it. He looks up, and who do you think be there, not an eyelash in front of him, but Cap'n Hackett, with a dark cast in his eye. 'Gawky', says I, when I heard tell of it, 'you be touched by that man. Same as poor Toby Wedge.' " He pointed to his suffering messmate. "And here be the proof on it, d'ye see me?"

Prudence smiled at his innocent superstition, and poured more water on the fire to maintain the steam. In a few minutes, the stye had burst. Gawky grinned, rubbed his eye with a handkerchief several times, took the salve and pronounced himself well satisfied with the doctor's cure.

He was followed by a man who needed bleeding, a pale, emaciated creature with the ague, and a seaman with a pleuretic stitch, spitting blood. Ross treated them, prescribed medicines, or sent them off to the sick berth to be cared for by Richards, his second mate.

There were several men with gashes, and a little powder monkey—the lads who fetched fresh gunpowder during a battle—with a bad cold. A groaning seaman limped in with a distended belly, suffering from dropsy. While the man gritted his teeth in pain, Ross tapped his abdominal cavity with a large, sharp probe, releasing a thin, watery fluid.

Prudence did as Ross directed, wrapping bandages and applying ointments, or helping Bailey with his mixtures. She discovered that she was less squeamish than she had expected to be, though she was troubled to see so many men in distress.

At last, no more sailors appeared at the door. Ross tiredly rubbed the back of his neck and looked at her, his eyes warm with a new respect. "Go to the wardroom. You've done enough this morning."

"And you?"

"I'm for the sick berth."

"Let me come."

" 'Tis an unlovely place. Men are dying there, and there's little I can do to save them. And the air is foul with their sickness. Vomit, and worse. Heat and filth and overcrowding. 'Tis a well-known fact that the stenches in the sick berth can bring on illness."

She stood up and smoothed her skirts. "I shall come."

"By the beard of Aesculapius, but you're stubborn."

"No more stubborn than you! And who is this Aesculapius you always swear by?"

"He was the Roman god of healing. And I could wish for his powers, God knows." He gestured toward the door and sighed, conceding to her. "Come along, if you must. But I warn you. 'Twill be a revelation, not an adventure. The world is not as pretty as you view it. Be prepared."

The sick berth was on the deck above. They climbed the hatchway with care, clinging to the railings to keep their balance in the worsening storm, and inching their way past guns and sailors preparing the ship for bad weather.

The sick berth proved to be a large space, walled off from the guns with canvas. It was crammed with swaying hammocks and their occupants—men so close to their fellows that one could breathe contagion upon another. A sharp wind blowing through the open portholes helped to dispel the sickening odors of corruption and disease, but the rising sea splashed in without cease, drenching those unfortunates who lay closest to them.

Ross turned to his second mate. "Well, Richards, how goes it?"

The man shook his head. "We shall lose Nash within the hour, I fear."

"Not unexpected," said Ross, without passion. He shouldered his way through the crowded hammocks.

Cringing at the sights before her, Prudence followed, noting the feverish faces, the wasted bodies, the missing limbs covered with bloody bandages, the splints that encased broken arms and legs. Some men moaned in their sleep, and others thrashed about or wept with pain. One seaman coughed piteously, as though his lungs would burst. *Sweet Mother of*

Mercy, Prudence thought, wishing she could cast a magic spell that would heal them all.

They came to the hammock of one who had the pallor of death. Prudence suffered just to see his gasping breaths, the glazed look in his sunken eyes.

"Well, Nash," said Ross bluntly, reaching for the man's pulse, "have you made your peace with your Maker?"

"Aye, sir." Nash's dark eyes were filled with resignation, but Prudence could see the terror lurking in their depths.

" 'Tis just as well," said Ross. He dropped Nash's wrist abruptly and turned to the fellow beside him, pulling down his blanket to reveal the man's bandaged leg. He pushed his trouser leg above the knee, frowned down at it, and pressed gently. The man cried out in pain.

Ross muttered a curse and turned to his surgeon's mate. "Richards, I like not the look of this leg. Take the man to Bailey, and have him make preparations. I'll be down anon to cut it off."

"Must I be docked? No, sir! Not my leg, sir!" the seaman cried in panic.

"It must come off before the gangrene spreads. 'Tis either that or strike your colors to Death's ship, man." He gestured briskly to Richards. "Get a few ratings to help you, and carry this man to the cockpit." In a few moments, the seaman was carried, screaming, from the sick berth.

Shaken as much by Ross's cold efficiency as by the tragedy of the young seaman, Prudence stood frozen beside Nash's hammock. At the sound of the other man's cries, he had begun to twitch in an extremity of agitation, his face beading with sweat. She lifted her apron and dabbed at his brow, murmuring soothing words.

He smiled wanly at her, his quivering subsiding. " 'Tis not that I'm afeared of death, ma'am," he said, his voice a low croak. "But there's me wife. And the new babe that I've seen but once. I should have liked to dandle him on me knee once more."

She fought back her tears. "God will see you united in Heaven some day." She fetched him a tin of water, settled his pillow more comfortably beneath his sweat-drenched head, and held his hand while he wheezed his last breaths. He gasped, gave a final quiver, and was still, his eyes open and staring.

Feeling helpless, and nearly overcome with grief and pain, Prudence signaled to Ross. All the time Nash was dying, he had been moving among the hammocks, examining each man in turn and stopping to write instructions and prescriptions for Richards, who had returned from the cockpit.

"Ross," she whispered, as he pushed his way to her side. She could say no more, only watch dumbly as Ross felt for Nash's pulse and shook his head. He closed the man's eyes, pulled his blanket over his face. Then he took Prudence firmly by the elbow and steered her out of the sick berth. "You've seen enough for one day. Go back to the cabin."

Her lip trembled. There were poor unfortunates to be succored. "No."

"Damn it, you're as white as paste. And the ship will soon be pitching so much that you'll not be able to stand. I have work in the cockpit, before the storm breaks."

He had called it merely "work." But what he meant was that he intended to cut off a man's leg in cold blood. "How can you heal, and not see the man?" she cried.

" 'Tis not my task to be kind," he growled. "I'm meant to heal the sick, if I can. And nothing more."

"You're kind to *me,* "she said. " 'Tis not a sentiment unknown to you. Don't you care what happens to these men?"

"More men die in sick berth than in a battle," he said tiredly. "In the space of a week, half those men inside will be dead of a fever."

"We'll all be dead, one day. Does that mean we must forfeit our humanity? Our compassion? A little human kindness would ease their suffering."

He stared at her, then groaned and rubbed his hand across his eyes. "I shall be glad to leave all of this behind. Life is too imperfect." He sighed. "Now go to the cabin. I have an amputation to perform."

"I'll help you. The man might need tender comfort."

He laughed, his blue eyes cold with mockery. "There's no 'tender comfort' that you can give. Bailey will have filled him full of brandy by now. And he'll faint at the first cut, God willing. Save your compassion for the men who die, and leave me to my work."

His words reminded her of poor Nash, who would never see his child again. She was suddenly overwhelmed with the horrors she had seen, with Nash, and his child, and her own griefs. She turned away and sobbed into her hands.

"Now, by God," said Ross, "you *will* take to your bed." He picked her up and carried her down the hatchway to his cabin. He laid her on the bunk and scowled. "I expect you to rest until dinner. There will be no more visits to the sick berth. Do you understand?"

She sniffled and wiped at her tears. Was he angry at her for her weakness? Or angry at himself because her chiding words had hit the mark, reminding him that he might be a doctor, but not a man with a heart.

As soon as he had left the cabin, she stumbled out of the bunk, bent over, and vomited into the chamber pot.

Chapter Nine

❦

Prudence sighed and pushed the damp hair from her forehead. Her bones ached from weariness, and her heart was heavy. She glanced back into the sick berth from which she had just emerged, and sighed again. The air was close with the heat of summer; she could smell the reeking odors even from here.

The storm had abated at dawn, just before the morning watch, but the violent rocking of the ship had caused more than a few of the unfortunates to cast up what little sustenance their stomachs could hold. She had spent the morning rushing to their sides with buckets, and stilling their trembling, and mopping their damp brows when they had finished retching. She had helped Richards change the bandages of a man who had torn them in his frenzy, and sung a lullaby to a young midshipman who lay dying. She had quieted the fevered thrashing of the seaman whose leg Ross had removed yesterday.

And still so much more work to be done, so much suffering to alleviate. So much misery that all her tender care couldn't ease. For the first time, she began to understand the dark cynicism that drove Ross. Surely a man could go mad if he allowed himself to care too much.

Yet she herself had not lost her faith. There was always hope, even in darkness. A seaman whom Richards had given up for dead had stirred and opened his eyes and smiled at her. And after she had fed him a little hot broth, the color had actually begun to return to his face.

But the smells! Sweat and filth and rotting flesh. It had been all she could do to keep from gagging. She needed fresh air, bright sunshine, to restore herself. She headed up the hatchway to the wardroom, praying that St. John was not there.

The wardroom was deserted. Prudence reckoned that most of the officers must be at their navigation class, or supervising gun drills. There was always the danger of a belligerent French ship in these troubled times.

She was grateful for the solitude. She opened a small window and seated herself beneath it, taking in deep breaths of sweet air. She'd heard seven bells sounding a short while ago. Eleven-thirty, by the clock. It would soon be time for dinner, and she knew she couldn't eat until she had refreshed her body and her spirit.

"I ought to wring your neck!"

She turned in alarm at the sound of Ross's harsh voice. He stood in the middle of the wardroom, his fists jammed on his hips, his face twisted in a frightening scowl. "What have I done?" she asked tremulously.

"I've just been to the sick berth. Richards tells me that you spent the morning there. Did I not expressly forbid it?"

She gulped and found her courage in the face of his terrifying anger. "You may play at being my husband," she said, fighting to keep the quaver from her voice, "but you're not."

His eyes glowed like blue crystals. "I forbade you as the *surgeon.*"

"Why? Do the men not need tending, Doctor Manning?"

"Not by you!"

"Is it such a difficult chore, then?"

"Of course not, but . . ." His piercing glance wavered.

She pressed her advantage. "And do I look helpless to you? Do you think me such a ninny, such a dreamer, that I shrink from cold reality?"

"Damn it, there is contagion in the sick berth that can lay you low."

"And do you, and Bailey, and Richards not risk it every day? I'm as hale as you are, I warrant."

He was beginning to sputter, seeing himself losing ground. " 'Tis no place for a woman, and I had not given you leave, and . . ."

She waved her hand at him. "Fiddle-faddle. You're just angry because I didn't obey your orders. I acquitted myself very well in the sick berth—you may ask Richards. And I intend to go back."

"In the name of God, why?"

She thought of the aching emptiness of her arms, the hollowness of her days until she and Jamie should be reunited. Her eyes filled with sudden tears. "Because it gives me someone to love," she whispered.

He sighed, defeated, and relaxed his rigid body. He sat beside her and took her hand in his. "I wish you a husband and many children some day," he said in a gentle voice.

It was too much for her to bear. Why had God punished her so? She covered her mouth to stifle a sob.

He seemed disconcerted by her grief. Helpless in the face of strong emotions he himself had denied. "Come, come," he said gruffly. "In a few short weeks, you'll be with your Lord Jamie." He patted her awkwardly on the shoulder. "Richards tells me you were a ray of sunshine in the sick berth. I was proud to hear his account."

His words of praise, so unexpected, cheered her. She dabbed at her wet cheeks and managed a wan smile. "But so much misery. 'Tis hard to find hope there."

He took her chin in his hand and stared deep into her eyes. "And yet, I suspect that you do."

She nodded. Not even the horrors she had seen could dampen her optimism for long. "Peterson—the one whose leg you cut off—was quite cheerful, despite his pain. He joked that he was tired of being a foretopman, and would welcome the stationary life of a cook."

"I'll have the carpenter make him a wooden leg as soon as the stump heals."

She had noticed something more on her rounds this morning. "You're a very good surgeon and apothecary."

"Thank you. I do what I can."

"Nay, 'tis more than that. When I changed the dressings on some of the men, I couldn't help but notice how cleanly you'd stitched their wounds. And several of the men seem to be recovering, thanks to your prescriptions. I've known more than one doctor to kill a patient with his nostrums. But you heal, not kill."

He seemed almost embarrassed by her praise. "I do what I can," he said again.

"You must have had a good master, when you were an apprentice."

The familiar cloud, the screen that shut him off from the world, descended over his eyes. He jumped up from the bench and paced the room, clearly agitated.

She stared in dismay. What had she said to disturb him? "Ross?" she said hesitantly.

He whirled on her. "Why must you pry?"

She refused to be deterred. "Tell me," she insisted.

His lip curled in bitterness. "The man who taught me was the man who killed my wife." He sank to the bench and covered his eyes with his hand. "And the man I used to call father."

"Sweet Mother of Mercy!"

He continued, his voice cold and unemotional. "I had been called away to see a patient. He operated while I was gone. I came home to find her dead."

"Oh, alas! What did you do?"

"I told him I was no longer his son. He was no longer my father."

"But that's dreadful! The poor man. How he must have suffered. To lose his daughter-in-law, and then his son."

He lifted his head and glared at her. His eyes burned with rage. "God Almighty! The poor man? 'Tis a marvel I didn't run him through on the spot!"

"But surely he was consumed with guilt, needing your forgiveness. Can you not find it in your heart? God tells us to forgive even those who harm us."

His jaw tightened. "I shall never acknowledge him while I take breath. Nor forgive him. Let him rot in Hell."

"And you've been asea ever since?"

"Yes."

"Are there oceans wide enough to distance you from your thoughts?" she asked softly. "Or wilderness deep enough to swallow up the past?"

"Christ Jesus! Must I suffer again your rose-colored view of life?"

She fell to her knees in front of him, understanding at last the depths of his sorrow, his bitter anger. To lose a beloved wife and a father all at the same time. "Ross," she implored, gazing earnestly up at him, "forgive your father, as God would wish it. 'Tis black hatred that is corrupting your soul. Not grief. With God's help, we can reconcile ourselves to grief, and endure. But hatred is a creeping disease that eats away at a life. As cruel as any malady that infects those unfortunates below."

His mouth twisted in a sneer. "Spare me your sermons. What have you known of tragedy to begin to understand? The little shepherdess with her extravagant dreams of marriage to a lord! You would do well to go home to that village of yours and find a simple country lad to marry."

She struggled to her feet. The man didn't deserve a crumb of sympathy. Why was she humbling herself, trying to resolve a quarrel that was none of her concern? "My Lord Jamie is the only man I want," she said, thrusting out her chin in defiance.

The sneer deepened. "That ruttish aristocrat who turned your head? I have no doubt he found you an easy mark. And still you pine for him. Till I tire of hearing your lovesick praise."

" 'Od's blood," she said contemptuously, "you sound like a jealous husband. Does it offend you, my love for Jamie? Are you jealous? Is that why you attack my sweet dreams of him? Or does your hatred of your father spill out onto the whole world?"

He went rigid, and a small muscle twitched in the corner of his eye. He stood up, strode to the door and turned back to her, his face set and cold. "I may call you 'wife' in this farce we play, but I have not given you leave to examine my soul." He bowed stiffly. "Make my excuses to your silly admirers. I shall dine alone today."

"I admire the way you've drawn the billow of the sail. But the ship's bell is a trifle large, I think."

Ross, kneeling on the quarterdeck, his folio and crayon in his hands, turned and smiled up at Prudence. "Am I to have a critic, on such a lovely afternoon?"

Prudence looked up at the sparkling blue sky. Not a cloud to disturb the day. It was nearly the end of August, and far warmer in these latitudes than it would have been in Winsley. It filled her heart with a joy she couldn't even begin to explain—the crystalline sky, the summer sun, the sea like blue-green glass, except where the bow cut a path and cast up white foam. She returned Ross's smile, pleased at his sunny mood.

It hadn't been so, before the Azores. After their quarrel in the wardroom, he had been more cold and distant than ever, his silence a condemnation. She had had no right to speak to him of his father, no right to probe his wounds. She had gone about her work in the sick berth, but had found less pleasure in it, with no one to share her triumphs and griefs.

By the time they had landed at the Azores, and they were going ashore, she could endure his coldness no longer. She had shyly slipped her arm through his and told him that she missed his friendship, which she had come to rely on.

He had hemmed and hawed for a bit, remarking on the peculiar volcanic formations of the island, before admitting with reluctance that he, too, had missed their comfortable familiarity. Then he had taken her off to the town of Ponta Delgado to see the sights.

She had strolled beside him, aware for the first time in her life of the stir her appearance caused. She had lifted her chin and walked proudly. Was her newfound self-confidence due to the unending praise of the *Chichester*'s officers? she had wondered. Or the tall, dignified man who walked beside her, his arm possessively through hers?

He had bought her a straw hat for the sun and a new petticoat. And—over her protests—a plain blue muslin gown to wear when she tended the sick. She had declined a visit to the mineral baths; she was too shy to undress before strangers. But she had allowed him to take her to the theater to see a foolish comedy, and had found more pleasure in his hearty laughter than in the antics on the stage. In the week since they had set sail again, their friendship had flourished.

Ross finished his sketch of the forecastle and sighed. " 'Tis not what I had wished."

She thought it was skillful and splendid. "Must you always achieve perfection to be satisfied?"

" 'Tis my curse, I suppose. Do you draw?"

"Not very well."

He turned his folio to a fresh page and held it up to her. "Show me."

She took the folio and sat cross-legged on the deck, near the railing. She resisted the urge to flip through the pages of the book; he had kept it out of sight and hidden in some unknown niche since the night she'd seen the pictures of herself. "My best subjects were trees and people," she said. "Absent a sturdy oak, I fear I must turn to you."

He smiled, a charming, crooked grin that flustered her. "Do you think you can do justice to a 'very old' man, as you once called me?"

She bent her head, feeling her cheeks redden. "I'm sure you'll be a fit subject, no matter your advancing age, and . . ."

"I'm only twenty-six," he interrupted dryly.

"Oh!" She found herself babbling to hide her surprise and embarrassment. "I would have thought that you were far older . . . that is . . . you don't seem like a man in . . . Oh, mercy." She bit her lip. "You're *very* handsome," she finished lamely, praying she hadn't insulted him too much with her witless chatter.

The grin deepened, making him look like a mischievous little boy. She wondered how she had ever thought him old. "Am I, now?"

She tossed her head at him. "Well, don't get peacockish about it! You're not near as handsome as Captain Hackett."

He tried, unsuccessfully, to hide his smile. "Who is?"

His teasing was so new and unexpected that she scarcely knew how to deal with it. "And now that I know you're not so much older than I, I'll not allow you to lecture me like a father, ever again," she announced in a dignified voice.

His answering laughter deflated her dignity and made her blush anew.

"You're a rogue, Ross Manning. Behind that . . . that proper facade," she sputtered. This time, she *meant* to insult him!

"I?" His eyes were wide and clear blue and innocent. Then he squinted up at the sky. "I think the moon will rise before you begin your picture."

She made a face at him, put the folio on her lap and picked up the crayon. "I can't draw you if you keep talking." He immediately looked contrite, closed his lips and composed his face. She began to draw the outlines, sketching in the pleasing squareness of his jaw, the high cheekbones that sharpened what would have been too soft a shape for his face. His eyelashes were remarkably thick and long, further accenting those striking eyes. She wished she had color to do justice to them. She glanced again at his face, then down to the folio, then back to his face once more. She frowned. "Your nose is crooked."

"Indeed it is. A schoolboy brawl. The jackanapes had the effrontery to laugh at my drawings."

"And bested you, to judge by your nose."

"To the contrary. They had to carry him home on a litter. The schoolmaster thrashed me soundly, of course. And my right hand was too bruised from the fighting to use a drawing crayon for a week." He smiled with the pleasure of remembered satisfaction.

"I was forever being thrashed by my Mama. Or forced to stand in the dairy for hours as punishment." She giggled. "I wonder if she knew that I spent the whole time kicking the wall. It delighted me to scuff the whitewash in revenge."

"A rebellious little chit, it would seem. And no doubt as stubborn as you are today," he said, shaking his head.

She was suddenly sober, humbled by her memories. "I was not nearly so good as I should have been. Papa tried to curb my ways, after my mother died." She sighed. "But I failed him often. I'm not sure he would be pleased at the way I've governed my life since his death." She stared off across the sea. *Oh, Papa,* she thought with longing. Would any of this have happened if she had had his wisdom to guide her? His understanding?

"Tell me about your village. In Wiltshire, I think you once said."

She smiled dreamily. "It was lovely. Snowdrops in the spring, along the paths and shady lanes. Our house was down the lane, just beyond the old church. Built in the time of Henry the Third, so they said. There were weavers' cottages tucked away amid the hawthorn hedges, and a pond filled with geese. Marsh marigolds in summer. I always liked to pick them, though my shoes got wet and Mama scolded me."

"And primroses, with your Lord Jamie."

"Yes. They grew beyond the farmland, on the hills where I took my sheep. It was so pleasant at twilight, with the sky turning pink. The High Street would fill with lowing cows coming home from pasture. And at the end of the High Street was Papa's schoolhouse." She bent her head in sorrow. All lost to her now.

"It makes you sad to think of it?" he asked, his brow furrowing in concern.

"It makes me sad not to be there."

"Then you must tell me a happier story of your village. One that cheers you."

She thought for a minute, then smiled. "I always liked the green." Grandpapa had forbidden her to go there, of course. But she had managed to sneak away from time to time, and sit in the shade beneath a large tree, hidden from the view of her grandfather's tale-bearing steward. "Farmers would come with their fiddles and pipes, after their work was done. There was music and gaiety. The village lads would wrestle with one another, and play games and boast in front of the girls. And sometimes they danced, laughing and happy. My friend Betsy always had half a dozen swains at her feet."

"And did you dance, my little shepherdess? And turn the boys' heads?"

"Mercy! I dared not. Grandpapa would have been in a rage. But I would remember the steps, and go home and practice them in my own room."

He leaned his hands back on the deck and stared up at the sky. "Martha danced like an angel. I remember once we went to an assembly ball. There was a fat old squire, who was quite taken with her. However much she tried to avoid him, he would pounce whenever they played a lively reel. She was too much a lady to refuse him, though I tried to intercede more than once. Upon my word, but he was a clumsy dancer! He trod on her foot with every other step. We laughed about it, going home in the carriage. But when she pulled off her stocking, I saw that her toe was broken."

"The poor creature," she murmured.

"We learned, the next day, that he had fallen down the stairs and broken his leg. Tripping over his own clumsy feet, so they said. I owned as how the oaf had deserved it, but Martha, ever forgiving, called upon him and brought him beef jelly to ease his misery." He laughed softly. "He sent her trinkets for a month, thinking that she was partial to him. Until I wrote him a note explaining that—while I could appreciate his admiration of my wife—any further pursuit could be dangerous to his health. He caught my drift. And that was the end of Martha's suitor." He chuckled. "We laughed for days about it."

She stared at him. "This is the first time I've seen you smile when you spoke of Martha."

" 'Tis a sweet memory." He smiled wistfully, then pointed toward the folio. "Have you finished?"

She had quite forgotten her drawing, lost in the pleasure of seeing him smile. She applied herself to her work again, filled with a happiness she couldn't explain. She began to hum softly. One of the old songs that Papa had taught her.

"No. Sing it aloud," he said. "You have a charming voice."

She blushed, then nodded and began to sing:

" 'Twas in the pleasant month of May,
In the springtime of the year.
And down by yonder meadow
There runs a river clear.
See how the little fishes
How they do sport and play,
Causing many a lad and many a lass
To go there a-making hay."

"That be a fair song, lady. And you sing it with a right good voice."

Prudence looked down to the main deck to see Toby Wedge grinning up at her. "Why, thank you."

"We call you the little skylark, in the fo'c'sle. Always singin' for joy." He shook his large head. "But you never sing a sea chantey."

"And is that a bad omen?"

His brow wrinkled in bewilderment. "Lady?"

"Never mind. I was only teasing. What would you like me to sing?"

He reached into the pocket of his wide breeches and pulled out a pipe. He put it to his lips and began to play. The pipe was so fragile and his fingers so massive and coarse that Prudence was astonished at the delicacy of his playing.

It was a lively air. Prudence listened for a few moments, and then nodded. "A-roving," she said. "Of course I know it." She lifted her voice and began: "In Plymouth Town there lived a maid . . ."

"You vile gargoyle! You dare to be familiar with your betters?"

The whistle of the pipe faded away on a thin wail. Wedge looked up in terror at Captain Hackett, who stood glowering down from the poop deck. "No, sir. I be but playin' a tune for the lady, d'ye see me, Cap'n, sir?"

Hackett marched down from the poop to stand at the quarterdeck railing. "And you have nothing better to do, you lazy lout? Do you fancy a round dozen at the gangway?"

Wedge gulped. "No, sir. I be on my way to my watch, sir, when I hears the lady singin' . . ."

"I heard eight bells sound not a minute ago. Is this how you stand your watch, you dog? Or salute your commanding officer?"

"I . . . I . . ." Wedge fumbled with his pipe, desperately trying to stow it and bring his hand to his forehead at the same time.

"Please, Captain," said Prudence, rising to her feet. " 'Twas entirely my fault. I asked him to play."

The smile he turned to her was tight and forced. "Dear lady, I must ask you not to interfere in matters that don't concern you. Nor take upon yourself the blame that rightly belongs on this ugly dog's head." He whirled again to Wedge. "Get aloft and stand your watch, you deformed villain, before I find cause to make you regret you were ever born!"

"B-b-but Cap'n, sir. I bean't a foretopman, sir, an't please you. I be a gunner."

Hackett pounded the railing with his fist. "By God, sirrah! Will you raise a squall with me?" He gestured to a man on the gangway, who held a small rattan stick. "You! Master-at-arms! Clap this lubberly son of a whore into leg irons! A day or two exposed to the elements might make him regret his insolence. And give him a bit of starting with your jack, while you're about it!"

Ross had risen to his feet and now stood glaring at the captain, his hands curled into tight fists at his sides. "I do protest, sir. This man . . ."

"Is *my* affair, sir!" Hackett's handsome mouth curved into a sudden, sly grimace. "Will you challenge me openly, Mr. Manning?"

Ross ground his teeth together, then bent his head. "No, sir," he muttered.

Prudence stared in horror as Wedge was dragged to the forecastle and shackled to the deck. She could hear the smack of the master-at-arms's cane, and the muffled grunts from Wedge that followed each blow. And still Ross did nothing? She looked at him with accusing eyes. He gritted his jaw and turned away.

Hackett smoothed the ruffles of his cravat and relaxed into an expansive smile, as though nothing untoward had happened. "Now, dear lady. St. John tells me you're a superb backgammon player. Would you care to join me in my cabin for a game?"

She didn't know who angered her more—Hackett with his cruelty, or Ross, who hadn't the courage to defend poor Toby Wedge. "Forgive me, Captain Hackett," she said, fighting to control her rage. "I fear I have a headache."

"I'll mix you a powder," said Ross.

"I can mix it myself," she said coldly. It was a little late for him to atone! She glanced down at her hands. She still held the folio and crayon. "I never finished my picture," she said. She drew a large, black X through Ross's face, threw down the folio, and stormed below.

The sunny day had lost its glow.

Chapter
Ten

Prudence shivered as she entered Ross's cabin and closed the door. The sooner she got out of her wet gown, the sooner her trembling would cease. She glanced down at the large, damp stain on her skirt. She was grateful her bodice had been spared when the seaman had upset that basin of water on her; she had only Martha's rose-embroidered stays to wear. But her petticoat was as soaked as her gown.

The clock on Ross's desk showed the hour of eleven—more than enough time to change before dinner. She shivered again. She should have left the sick berth as soon as the accident happened, instead of staying and fetching a fresh basin of water to bathe the poor man. But somehow his needs had seemed greater than hers. Now she hoped that she wouldn't come down with a cold.

She stripped off her gown and petticoat. Thankfully, her shift had escaped the drenching. She reached for the blue muslin gown that Ross had bought her. Perhaps she'd wear it open for a change, and lace her stays with a pretty ribbon. She fished in the sea chest that the gunners had given her and pulled out her trinket basket. She had a cherry red ribbon that would look pert.

The sea chest reminded her of Toby Wedge. The poor creature. He had stayed shackled to the deck for three days, his legs immobile, his large head baked by the sun and battered by the winds. She had visited him whenever she thought the captain wasn't nearby, and brought him food and water, and bathed his sunburned face. He had been so cheery, despite his ordeal, that it had almost broken her heart. He seemed resigned to his ill luck aboard the *Chichester;* in his simple mind, bad omens and Captain Hackett were intertwined, and the whole voyage was cursed for him.

Prudence had sulked around Ross for two days, holding him somehow responsible for what had happened to Wedge. But after a while, she had decided to forgive him. He might have protested more forcefully, but Hackett was still the captain, after all.

She finished lacing the ribbon through the eyelets of her stays, and gave a sharp tug to the ends. She winced. The bones of her stays had pressed against her hipbone and sent a throbbing pain shooting through her. *Mother of Mercy!* she thought in alarm. She hadn't looked at the spot in more than a week, assuming it had long since healed. She unlaced her stays and threw them down, then lifted her shift to examine herself.

The spot on her hip was bright red and swollen, rising to a peculiar point in the center. The edges of the spot radiated thin, pinkish streaks. She had seen enough boils on farm boys to realize what had happened. Instead of healing normally, the bruise had become a dangerous infection, the hard, central core filling with pus.

She bit her lip in dismay. Perhaps she could borrow one of Ross's instruments to lance the boil. But it was in an awkward place; it would be difficult to reach.

She gave a start as she heard the sound of the latch being lifted, and quickly smoothed down her shift. She wasn't about to be found half-naked by Ross, her skirts raised to her waist!

He stopped in the doorway and frowned. "Your pardon. I didn't know you were changing."

She felt like a little girl, caught stealing sugar from the larder. " 'Tis no matter . . . my gown . . . I only . . ." The words tumbled out in a nervous stammer.

He closed the door and strode to her. "What's the matter?"

"Nothing!" Why had she answered like that? She sounded even more guilty.

"Your cheeks are flushed."

She crossed her arms protectively against her bosom. " 'Tis . . . 'tis only my modesty."

"That's not a blush, damn it," he growled. "And your eyes are too bright." Though she tried to duck away, he put his hand on her forehead. "Great God Almighty! You have a fever. I *warned* you about going into the sick berth!"

She sighed. There was no way she could avoid telling him. He would harry her until she blurted it out. "I have an abscess," she said. "I think it happened when I fell down the hatchway."

He swore softly. "And it has been festering all this while? And not a peep from you?"

His anger was intimidating. "I . . . I thought it would go away."

"Show me."

"I can treat it myself."

"Damn it, I'm a surgeon! Show me!"

Reluctantly, she lifted her shift, sliding it up her leg to expose as little of her flesh as possible. She kept one hand firmly on the fabric at her groin and belly.

He bent to peer at her hip. "Christ Jesus. The poison has already begun to spread. This is no simple boil or abscess, but a carbuncle that could kill you." He looked up at her, his lip curling in disgust. "When did you plan to tell me? When there was nothing for it but to amputate your leg?" He waved aside her timid protests and swept the books and papers from his desk. "Place yourself here."

She climbed up onto the desk, keeping her wound uncovered and her modesty intact, and watched him as he angrily tore off his coat and rolled up his sleeves. "Will you lance it?" she asked, venturing speech at last.

"It needs more than that. A proper evacuation, before it spreads further. Lie still," he ordered. "I shall get what I need from the cockpit."

He left the cabin and returned a few moments later carrying bandages, a lancet, and a cupping glass. "This will hurt like the devil before I'm through," he said, "but you only have yourself to blame." She flinched when he made a deep incision in the center of the swelling. He seemed to show no concern with her distress—only her folly. "I mind that bruise hurt you on the first day. When you were too prudish to let me examine it," he grumbled.

Prudence watched uneasily as he took down his brazier, lit the charcoal, poured a bit of water into the glass, and placed it over the hot coals. When the water had boiled away and Ross seemed satisfied that the glass was heated enough, he grasped the bottom of it with a wad of bandages. He scowled at her. "Lift your shift farther, damn it. And be quick about it, while the vacuum holds."

She frowned back but obeyed, careful still to keep most of her lower body covered with her shift. She wondered if the father who had taught him was as cold and unsympathetic in his doctoring. She wondered . . .

And then there was no time left to wonder. There was only agonizing pain as the hot glass seared her skin, and the vacuum sucked the poison out of the carbuncle with a sickening sound. It felt as though the very flesh was being ripped from her body. She cried out in anguish, tears springing to her eyes.

He removed the glass and its foul contents, then dabbed at the spot with a fresh bandage. "You'll have a scar," he said. "But it can't be helped."

The pain was beginning to subside. She struggled into a sitting position, the better to see. The wound looked like a volcano with a crater in the center, oozing blood instead of molten rock.

He made a small dressing of gauze and pressed it firmly to the carbuncle. "I'll bandage it," he said, "and give you something for the fever. But, for your health's sake, you will stay abed for at least two days. Do you understand? Now lie back and lift your shift to your waist."

She stared at him in outrage. What new indignity did he have in mind? "I'll do no such thing!"

"Damn my liver! Are we to have modesty, even now? I can't put on a bandage unless I wrap it around your flanks."

She felt suddenly foolish and childish. He had seen her breasts and legs weeks ago, and she had survived that with no loss to her pride. She sighed and adjusted her shift, carefully avoiding his glance.

He leaned close, bandage poised, then gave an involuntary jerk. His eyes opened wide. "God Almighty," he breathed, "you've had a *child.*"

She shook her head vehemently. "Don't be absurd!" She pursed her lips in anger. "Now, do you intend to stare at me all morning, or will you finish your work? I scarce enjoy lying here like a London tart!"

"Your pardon." He wrapped the bandage as quickly as he could, smoothed down her shift, and helped her from the table.

She turned to walk unsteadily to the bunk, but his hands on her shoulders prevented her. "Prudence," he said, his eyes grown suddenly soft. "I'm a doctor. Do you think I don't know what a woman's belly looks like when she's borne a child?"

She was beginning to quiver. "I told you, that's absurd."

"A child," he insisted. "And quite recently, I should guess."

She felt herself losing control of her emotions. Choking back her tears, she closed her eyes and turned her head away. "No."

He gave her shoulder a gentle shake. *"Yes,* my poor foolish lass. Was it your Lord Jamie's?"

She hesitated, then nodded at last, all her grief and shame welling up in her breast—like her carbuncle, about to burst. She had never spoken of it except to Betsy. Had even forced herself not to think of her babe for days at a time.

"A boy," she whispered. "Such a pretty little thing. With a birthmark on his shoulder. Like a butterfly, as though an angel had kissed him there."

"When was he born?"

Her voice trembled on the edge of shrill hysterics. How many more prying questions could she endure? "In . . . in May."

"And where is he now?"

The agony of her suffering broke forth unchecked at last, overwhelming her. "I l-lost him," she sobbed, collapsing against Ross. "I lost him. God punished me for being wicked and sinful." Her body shook with weeping.

"Oh, Lord," he muttered. He picked her up in his arms and sat on the chair, cradling her gently as she moaned and wept against him. "Don't cry, little Prudence," he said over and over again. "Don't cry. You'll find your Lord Jamie."

She had thought there were no more tears left in her to mourn her loss.

But the comfort of Ross's arms seemed to encourage the release of her suppressed pain. She wept until she was exhausted.

He carried her to the bunk and tucked her in like the tenderest of nurse-maids. Then he left the cabin. She lay, spent and empty, until he returned with a large beaker filled with a milky fluid, which he ordered her to drink. She swallowed it, unprotesting; she felt numb, like an automaton mechanically responding to the control of the puppet-master.

She drifted into sleep, and dreamed of cuddling her little boy.

Ross sighed wearily as he climbed to the quarterdeck. He dreaded this interview with Hackett, to speak about his charges and defend his skills. So many men lying fevered in the sick berth, and so little he could do about it. Thankfully, there was at least small chance for scurvy on such a short voyage. A sure killer. Aboard the *Thunder*, he had seen far too many sailors go to Davy Jones, their eyes sunken in pale, toothless faces.

He was grateful, at least, that Prudence was growing better. He had kept her under heavy sedation for two days now—as much to allow her heart to heal as her wound. He had changed the bandage while she slept, noting with satisfaction that the red streaks were gone from her flesh and the incision seemed to be healing without infection. She had wakened for an hour or two this morning, and had managed to swallow a little hot broth and a glass of Madeira, though her eyes were haunted and the soft lilt was gone from her voice.

He shook his head. A babe! He still couldn't believe it. While he himself had trumpeted his grief with every dark word he spoke, every sour frown and cold glance, she had gone about singing and laughing. And her heart heavy with a grief he couldn't begin to fathom. A grief that dwarfed his own. To lose a child that she had carried in her womb! Small wonder she had nursed the seamen with such tenderness. She needed someone to love, she had said. He didn't have the courage to ask her how the child had died.

He emerged on the quarterdeck and knocked at the captain's door. Hackett neither rose nor smiled when he entered. In private, at least, they had long since stopped pretending that there was aught but animosity between them. "Mr. Manning," he said. "Your wife is recovering, I trust?"

"An unfortunate fever. But it has passed."

"May I expect her charming presence at my table tonight? She is too . . . tantalizing to shine for your eyes alone."

Ross gritted his teeth. It always made his blood boil to see Hackett's lustful eyes lingering on her bosom, to hear his veiled hints of seduction that, mercifully, she was too innocent to understand. "I doubt that she will be well enough tonight, Captain," he said firmly.

"A pity. But tell me about the men in the sick berth. On to three dozen, now, Slickenham informs me."

Ross scowled. Slickenham was a spy and a truckler, as well as a double-dealing purser. He despised the worm. But men like Hackett depended upon men like Slickenham to keep their masks of goodwill from slipping. "You needn't have had Slickenham sneak around, sir," he growled. "You could have asked me direct."

Hackett's dark eyes glowed; he was clearly fighting his anger. "And is his account true? Three dozen?" he demanded coldly.

Ross responded in the same measured tones. "Thirty-four men, to be precise, sir. With various fevers and maladies sharpened by the summer sun and a poor diet. The seamen can't work in this heat when they're on short water rations."

"They get their full measure, per diem, as naval regulations require."

" 'Tis a 'purser's quart,' short by a half pint," he said with a sneer. "And every man aboard knows it. Moreover, they are being served cheese that should have been condemned and thrown overboard. You might remind Mr. Slickenham of *that* regulation."

Hackett bristled. "Do you presume to tell me how to run my ship, sir?"

"Not at all, sir. But you want healthy seamen, and so do I. The choice is between Mr. Slickenham and his bulging pockets, or sailors who get enough decent food and water to withstand sickness."

Hackett leaned back in his chair. "Though I scarce credit your report of Slickenham's cheating, you understand, I might be persuaded to ensure that the men get all the rations that are due them." He tapped his fingers together, a slow, crafty smile spreading across his face. "For a price."

"Must I now pay you in coin for what the men are rightly owed?" he snarled.

"Not at all. But Slickenham has been very helpful to me in other ways. The matter of your . . . wife, for example. The purser had the discernment to speak privately to your man, Thompson. It seems, when he makes up your bunk, he has never found any telltale signs in the bedclothes of . . . marital bliss, shall we say. An odd discovery, that. With such a beautiful . . . wife. And yet you *do* sleep together. Can you explain the paradox, sir?"

Ross was choking on his outrage. There had been a night, he remembered, when he had wakened to what had seemed to be the sound of the cabin door closing. Had it been the purser, warned by Hackett's suspicions? He thanked God he had not strung the hammock as he had originally intended. "The traffic between my wife and myself is our own concern, sir," he said tightly.

"Of course. But in view of your own remarks to me about women that first day, you must admit that I have a right to be suspicious, and doubt the legitimacy of your passion for the woman. For *any* woman. No matter your tender kisses. Were they merely for my benefit?"

"I am devoted to Martha."

"Yes. All well and good. And quite proper. But I digress. You want well-fed men, sir. Whilst I find myself quite obsessed with your beautiful . . . wife. Since she seems to be of little use to you—in the way that a man should use a woman—I thought that you and I could come to some agreement. I shall speak to Mr. Slickenham about the rations. In exchange, I should expect you to advance my cause with that exquisite creature you choose to call your wife."

Ross clenched his fists. He wondered why he didn't throttle the man where he sat. But of course that was what Hackett was waiting for. He bowed stiffly. "Is there anything more, Captain?"

Hackett waved his hand in dismissal. "No. But think about what I've said, Mr. Manning. I see no reason why we both can't get what we desire."

Ross stormed out of the cabin and gripped the quarterdeck railing, fighting his towering rage. Prudence was in more danger than she realized, and he was helpless.

Yet how could he put her on her guard, tell her what the captain had proposed? She was too innocent, too trusting to believe that any man could be so vile. He could only protect her by keeping his temper in the face of Hackett's disgusting provocations.

He shuddered, picturing Hackett slobbering over her pale flesh, touching the soft, sweet perfection of her full breasts, running his hands through the scented fire of her hair. Stealing kisses from the honey that was her mouth. Caressing her body and claiming at last the treasure that lay beyond that seductive triangle of red-gold hair. Plunging himself into . . .

Christ Jesus! He gasped in breathless astonishment and rubbed at the sweat that had beaded on his brow. What was he thinking of? It was not Hackett he had pictured in that scene. God help him, it was himself! He felt his loins stirring with a hunger he hadn't known in a year.

He took a deep breath and willed his overwrought body to cool. *Forgive me, Martha,* he thought, anguished. *Forgive me for being weak, if only for a moment.*

He laughed suddenly. How mad of him, to even consider touching the girl. She was too young, too innocent. If he gave in to his momentary physical need, the depth of his passion would frighten her half to death. And he would live with the guilt of betrayal to Martha's memory for the rest of his days. Better not to waken the sleeping dogs.

Besides, the girl was besotted with her Lord Jamie. Bent on marriage, come what may. It was scarcely up to him to speak against the man, though he doubted the rogue was more than a dallying aristocrat who had seen the opportunity for an easy conquest, and had taken it. He saw nothing but grief ahead for Prudence—whether she failed to find her lover, or found him and persuaded him into marriage.

Ross frowned in sudden thought. *Marriage.* But why—if there was no child—did she need marriage? Simply to make a new life for herself? The frown deepened. He remembered her first morning on board. She had felt queasy. The motion of the ship? Or something else?

"By the beard of Aesculapius," he muttered. Perhaps she wasn't so innocent after all. Perhaps she was carrying another child, so soon after the first. He shook his head in disgust. A man could seduce a naive woman *once,* perhaps. But a second time? Not without her willing, open-eyed consent, perfectly aware of what the results might be. Scarcely the behavior of an innocent.

The devil with her, he thought. She had unsettled his life too much already. Muddled his thoughts, his plans, his future. He was tired of thinking of her. Tired of being drawn into the intrigues of her life. The sooner the voyage ended, the happier he would be.

The safe, mind-numbing solitude of the wilderness suddenly seemed more desirable than ever.

Chapter
Eleven

❦

Prudence carefully shifted her body in the bunk, avoiding pressing her wound against the mattress. She couldn't sleep, no matter which way she turned. Why was Ross angry at her now?

She had insisted on dressing and going to the captain's supper this evening, hoping it would cheer her. Ross had ordered her back to bed, as her doctor, but she had been adamant.

Was that why he was angry? But surely he was accustomed to her occasional stubbornness by now; indeed, she sometimes felt that it amused him, to give in to her willful demands. Or perhaps his discovery of her recent child had turned him against her—an unchaste woman who no longer deserved his friendship.

She had found no cheer at supper. Her spirits were still too low, and St. John's attentions had been cloying. Ross had been mystifyingly rude to Hackett; she had become quite vexed with him. Although she herself still felt a lingering resentment toward the captain for his treatment of Wedge, there was no reason to be uncivil. This was a military ship, after all, and such harsh punishments were to be expected.

They had retired early from the captain's table. Ross's cold manner had held even as they undressed for bed and wished each other a good night.

She had prayed with more fervor than usual tonight, desperate to recapture her optimism, her hopes for the future. St. John had said that they expected to reach Virginia in little more than a fortnight. Surely that was cause for rejoicing.

Virginia . . . and Jamie. Perhaps if she thought of him, it would settle her nerves and help her to sleep. But it was no use. She could scarcely conjure up his face anymore. His features were blurring in her memory, like the reflection of a tree in a pond when the wind ripples across it.

She felt lost and lonely, aching for the warmth of a human touch. She eased her body closer to the sleeping Ross, molding her back up against his chest. And when he mumbled in his sleep and held her close, she sighed in contentment. She felt secure and soothed, as though she belonged in his arms. She closed her eyes. She would sleep now.

When she awoke to the sound of the boatswain piping the men to breakfast, Ross's arm was still around her, his hand on her breast. She let it stay. She needed his warmth. She was still trembling from her bad dream—a vivid, fanciful recapitulation of all the horrors of the last year. She hoped that it would be as comforting to sleep with Jamie when she was troubled; she couldn't imagine being alone in a bed ever again.

"Great God Almighty!" Ross jerked his hand away and leapt from the bunk. She turned and sat up. He stood staring at her in alarm, his chest rising and falling with heavy breaths. His bare legs were planted wide on the deck, as though he would never move from the spot. She thought that they were the most well-formed male limbs she had ever seen.

"Your pardon," he said gruffly. "I had not meant to touch you. You have a right to reproach me, though I was not aware . . ."

She shook her head and gave him a reassuring smile. " 'Tis no matter. You do it all the time in your sleep. You must be dreaming of Martha. You call out her name, sometimes, and then put your arm around me."

That confession seemed to disconcert him. "Nothing more?"

"No."

"Damn it, you should wake me! You should . . ."

"Why? To disturb your sweet dream? To disappoint you with reality, that I am not the one of whom you dream?"

"You innocent fool," he growled. "Aren't you afraid that it might lead to other things?"

She swung her legs over the side of the bunk, preparing to rise. "Why should I? Don't you think I trust you by now?"

He was staring at her bare legs, his face set in a strange expression. Then he muttered a dark oath, reddened, and turned his back on her. But not before she had seen an odd bulge at his shirtfront. "I'm only a man," he said in a choked voice.

"And a good man. I fear you not."

His back was rigid through his shirt. "Martha was the only woman I ever loved. I think 'tis God's way—that we have but one spiritual mate in this life. It is so for me. I shall never love another."

She saw his shoulders rise with a steadying breath. "But the flesh can be weak," he went on. "I must insist that you waken me whenever I hold you."

"No. It harms no one. And it brings you comfort."

He turned to face her, his mouth twisting with sarcasm. The bulge was gone. "How benevolent of you. To understand my weakness. And you can, of course, pretend to yourself that the man who holds you is the one in *your* dreams."

She bit her lip. She had almost thought to tell him of her sad dream this morning. But not now.

"What?" he said. "No words in defense of your lecherous Lord Jamie? No dreamy-eyed tales of how he'll marry you?"

Plague take him! She would *never* tell him. Not ever! He would twist her story, sharpen her pain with his cynical words. She turned in vexation and reached for her petticoat.

He began to dress hurriedly, pulling on his stockings and his breeches. "I'll have Thompson bring you breakfast. Unless, of course, you prefer the company of your sparks in the wardroom."

She stared at him. He seemed to be pushing her farther away with every cruel word he uttered. "Why do you deny your humanity?"

His eyes were cold. "I have very little humanity left in me. I've renounced it—and the world—long since. Have you forgot my wish to live alone?"

"And until then? Have I become such a burden to you?"

He tied his cravat and buttoned up his waistcoat. "Only when I must

suffer the same 'tender comfort' you give to the others. 'Tis suffocating."
He reached for his coat and gave a short laugh. "But perhaps you're only
soft and sympathetic because you need my help. And my purse."

"Oh!" He was impossible this morning. And all because of an uncon-
scious embrace? She stooped and picked up his shoes, then marched to
the cabin door, tore it open, and tossed the shoes into the passageway.
"You may finish dressing out there," she said. "Let the men think what
they will. I have no doubt they know that married people quarrel from
time to time." His icy glance enraged her further. She wanted to hurt him.
"Except, to be sure, you and your sainted Martha!"

He stiffened. She thought for a moment that he would strike her.
Then he bowed and gave a cold smile. "Your servant, madam. Martha,
to her credit, was not a shrew." He stormed out of the cabin before she
had a chance to throw something at him.

But when he had gone, she sank onto the chair and covered her eyes
with her hand. He had never wanted the bother of caring for her. He had
hidden his true feelings until now. But the closer they came to Virginia,
the more his thoughts, no doubt, turned to his longed-for solitude. And
she had become an intrusion on his cold world, a burden he could no
longer tolerate.

Wasn't that what Grandpapa had said? "You're a trial in every way, Prudence Allbright."

Grandpapa had never forgiven his only daughter for marrying a humble schoolmaster against his wishes. He had hoped for a match with a pros-
perous squire like himself. He had raged at their elopement, Mama told
her, and refused any traffic with them—though Papa struggled to eke out
a living in the village school. They had lived in a crumbling little cottage,
with scarcely enough to eat, or wood to feed the fire. But Prudence still
remembered those days with warm affection. There had been love, and
laughter, and the joy of learning at Papa's knee.

It was only when Mama's health had begun to fail that Grandpapa had
relented, and allowed them to come and live with him in his manor
house. And even then, he had never let Papa forget that he was a failure
in his eyes. Unable to properly care for his family.

Prudence supposed that Grandpapa had hated her from the first: a mere girl, instead of the grandson he longed for. And the product of a union he abhorred. He had never shown her the slightest warmth.

It had been even harder for her with Papa dead, and Grandpapa's new wife as mistress of the house. A woman who followed the new teachings of John Wesley. Stern and unforgiving, pious to the point of hypocrisy, she had turned Grandpapa even more against his granddaughter. Every harmless escapade had become a sin against God, every thoughtless word a reason for punishment. She had been scolded for her godless singing, and chided for her frivolous laughter. And when they had learned that she carried a child in her womb . . .

Prudence trembled, remembering her dreadful dream. She was on her knees again before Grandpapa, begging him not to send her away. She would marry anyone he chose, if only he would let her keep her child.

"You have brought shame and dishonor to this house. You are no kin of mine." She clapped her hands over her ears to still the voice in her head. She had heard the terrible words over and over again, in her dreams, for months. Shame and dishonor.

She stared up at the beams of the cabin, tears misting her eyes. "But the father of my child is a great lord, Grandpapa," she whispered, caught once more in her dream. "And he loves me."

"You have no child," he had said—last night in her dreams, and on that terrible June morning. *"You have no child.* He belongs to me now. I shall raise him as my own, unblemished and free from your sinful taint."

She wiped at her wet face with the back of her hand. She had shed more tears in the past few months than there were clouds in an April sky.

Oh, Jamie, she thought. *Only you can give me back my babe.* She clutched her arms across her breasts. She could still feel the soft mouth, suckling. Still smell the sweet odor of her newborn—the most precious perfume to her.

"A great lord?" Grandpapa had said with a mocking sneer. "More likely a country bumpkin, who played upon your wicked, immoral nature. But if he *is* a great lord, let him come and claim the child himself."

And he will, Grandpapa, she thought. *Just you wait and see.* She and Jamie would march into Grandpapa's house as husband and wife, and take back what was theirs.

Her grandfather couldn't refuse. Not with Jamie's noble title to persuade him. To intimidate him, if need be. She was sure of it. What else had kept her going through these long, painful months, but that certainty?

Heartened by the thought, she dried her eyes and finished dressing. Perhaps she'd take a turn on the deck, if the weather was fair. She didn't feel strong enough yet to go to the sick berth and tend the men. Besides, she didn't want to see Ross again this morning.

She sighed. She was sorry now that she had told him anything about her child. There was no sympathy to be had from him. He was too cold, too quick to stand in judgment, too bent on his need for perfection to understand her weakness in succumbing to Jamie. And too indifferent, perhaps. A man who would choose to be a hermit would take little interest in a woman beset by a misfortune of her own making. She had shamed herself enough by what little she had already said.

She would speak no more about it, no matter if he pressed her. She would find Jamie, and all would be well. "Forgive me, dear Lord, for my sins," she whispered. "And deliver this imperfect creature of Thine to a future of Thy choosing."

But how long did God wish to punish her? How many weary months until she could hold her beloved child again?

"I fear you'll gammon me, Martha!"

Prudence looked across the backgammon board at St. John and gave him her most winsome smile. She cast down her dice, furrowed her brow as though she were deep in concentration, then deliberately moved her stones into a vulnerable position. Even a dolt like St. John could scarcely fail to take advantage! "I'm not nearly a good enough player, Lieutenant," she simpered.

He tried to hide the triumph in his eyes as he rolled a double and put two of her pieces on the bar at once. She contrived to pout. "There, there," he said, reaching across the table to pat her hand. " 'Tis only a game. And you play it very well, for a woman. But I mind you promised to call me Edwin. And you forget as often as you remember."

She sighed. " 'Tis so difficult, when one is only a woman. How I should like to be a big, strong man, and play with confidence, as you do."

He preened like a peacock. "Dear Martha. You have your own singular charms."

"Oh, Edwin." She buried her face in her hands, as though she were hiding a blush. But it was difficult not to laugh aloud. He was so solemn, and so earnest. And so easily gulled.

She was quite enjoying this new game of hers. The discovery of her power as a woman. The effect her smiles and frowns had on St. John. Perhaps it was easy for her because he was a simpleton. But it made her feel confident and beautiful—to play the charmer, as she had seen Betsy do on the village green, many a time. She had envied her friend, wondering how a woman learned to bewitch a man. But St. John had responded at once to her forays into coquetry, which gratified her spirit.

The good Lord knew she needed reassurance. Ross's deepening estrangement from her these past few days had brought her low. She felt as though she had lost a friend, and didn't know why. She had found herself responding to his icy demeanor with petulance, deliberately going against his wishes. When he held her in his sleep, she found herself pushing his arm away. And, in a perverse way, it pleased her that her coy games with St. John seemed to infuriate him. She tried not to think of what Papa would have said about her willful behavior.

She glanced up. Ross had just entered the wardroom. He nodded at the several officers who still lounged at the supper table, and strode over to where Prudence sat with St. John. " 'Tis an hour since supper was done, wife. Do you intend to come to bed?" His voice was tight and controlled.

She smiled sweetly at him. She felt reckless and contrary. He never spoke to her except to order her around! "Why do you never call me by my name, husband? Do you find it so difficult to say the name Martha?"

The blue eyes glowed with cold heat, like the edge of a flame. " 'Tis only a week since your fever, *Martha.* I insist that you get enough rest."

She turned to St. John and gave a silvery laugh. "He says my name almost as nicely as you do, Edwin. But he seeks to spoil our lovely evening."

St. John closed up the board. "And we haven't even had a song from you. Come. While Elliot is still here." He gestured to Lieutenant Elliot, deep in conversation. "Come, man, pick up your fiddle, and Mrs. Manning will pleasure us with a song."

She pouted in her most charming way. "Only if my husband will allow. He's been such a bear of late."

Ross opened his mouth to speak, but was silenced by the pleas of St. John and the others, urging him to agree. What was the harm in one song before his wife retired? And they were all perishing to hear her sweet voice. He clamped his jaw shut and reluctantly nodded his head.

"What will you sing tonight?" said Lieutenant Elliot.

"Do you know 'Black Is the Color of My True Love's Hair'?" she asked, rising from her chair.

Ross's eyes narrowed. *"Black,* madam?"

She thought of Jamie, with his dark curls. "Yes, black," she said dreamily. "And brown eyes."

He frowned in warning. "But 'tis only a song, of course."

"Of course!" she responded, recovering herself.

He bowed, his body rigid. "Then I leave you and these gentlemen to your song. And trust you have the wisdom to retire in good time." He stalked angrily out of the wardroom as Elliot scraped out the first notes.

Prudence soon regretted that she'd chosen that song. Every line seemed to remind her of Jamie, and waken afresh her unhappy memories. By the time she had finished, there were tears in her eyes.

St. John hurried to her side and took her elbow. "A sad song. You should not have chosen it, Martha." He urged her toward the door. "Come. The night is sweet. Let the soft air restore you."

She allowed him to lead her up to the quarterdeck. The sky was brilliant with stars, glittering like jewels on black velvet. She gazed up at the tranquil night, her thoughts filled with Jamie and her son. She had never felt so alone, lost among the multitude of stars, a speck of humanity aching to find the one other human who could make her life whole again. She sighed.

"You must know I worship you, Martha."

She turned to see St. John leaning toward her, his arms outstretched. "Edwin, I . . ."

He slid his arms around her waist and pulled her close. "You beautiful, desirable creature. I long for your sweet favors."

She struggled halfheartedly in his arms. Tonight, with Jamie so fresh in her thoughts, yet so far away, St. John's tender words struck a chord. Jamie had wanted her—desperately. Had told her so in almost those very words. She felt weak and vulnerable. "I . . . I'm a married woman, Edwin," she stammered, grasping at the last straws of common sense.

"Devil take your husband. He scarcely appreciates you. Give me your sweet love, and I promise you'll not regret it."

Was she mad? So far sunk into sinfulness that she would weaken, even for a moment? "I *cannot*. 'Twould be against God."

His arms tightened around her. "Then one kiss, I beg you. It has haunted my dreams, the thought of one sublime kiss from those tempting lips."

She wavered. One kiss. What was the harm? She had never known a man's kiss, save for Jamie's. And Ross's. Was every man's kiss the same, filled with such delicious pleasure? St. John was a fool, of course. But curiosity burned within her, crying to be satisfied. And her heart was lonely. She lifted her chin. "Just one. And then I must go."

"You divine angel." He bent his head to hers and took her mouth.

She didn't know whether she was glad or disappointed. She felt nothing. Nothing! No thrill, no quickening of her heart, no pounding in her temples. Only the awareness that his lips were dry and vaguely unpleasant on hers. She made a move to push him away.

"I'll thank you to leave my wife alone, sir."

Prudence gasped at the chilling voice and whirled to find Ross glaring at them, his jaw set. She was relieved that the night was too dark for him to see the blush of shame on her face.

St. John began to stutter. "N-n-not what you imagine, Manning. I w-w-was merely bidding your wife a good night." He tugged at his cravat, as though it had suddenly become too tight for his neck.

The voice grew icier still. "I choose to accept your explanation, sir. *This* time. Aboard ship, I am not my own man. But, on shore, I'm quite skilled with a sword, and free to use it. Do you understand?"

St. John nodded and fled the deck.

Prudence smiled weakly at Ross. " 'Twas merely a harmless kiss. It meant nothing to . . ."

He cut her short by grasping her firmly around her wrist. "Damn my liver," he growled, "if you *were* my wife, that little scene would have earned you a few unpleasant moments across my knee!" He tugged viciously at her wrist. "Now come below."

She stumbled down the hatchway after him, wondering what she could say to soften his anger. She wasn't certain that—once they were in the cabin alone—he wouldn't carry out his threat, wife or no. The good Lord knew she had behaved foolishly, like a willful child.

She shook free of his hand in the dim passageway before their cabin door. "Ross. Wait. He took me by surprise. I hadn't expected him to do that." She hoped her soft tone would placate him.

His lip curled in a snarl. "Hadn't expected? *Hadn't expected?* Why the devil not? You've deliberately flirted with him for days, all but inviting him under your petticoats! And what do you suppose Hackett will think, if he learns of it?"

She gulped. "I . . . I don't know."

"That the virtuous Mrs. Manning is ripe for the taking." He glared at her. *"Are you?"*

She hung her head. "No," she whispered. "It was a moment of madness. I'm sorry."

He opened the cabin door. "Then get inside where you belong, and go to bed." He slammed the door behind them, stripped off his coat, and threw it across his sea chest. "There will be no more traffic with the swinish lieutenant. He didn't even have the courage to defend his lechery, but ran like a white-livered dog. And no more lingering in the wardroom after supper, if I'm called away to the sick berth."

She had begun to regret her actions. But now, in the face of his high-handed orders, she was sorry she had even apologized! She tugged at the lacings of her gown, climbed out of it, and tossed it aside. "Anything more, *husband?"* she asked sarcastically.

"Yes. Send back the shoe buckles to the lout, so there's no doubt in his mind of your sentiments." His cold blue eyes raked her body; she felt chilled by his glance. "And raise the line of your shift. You have lately begun to show more bosom than a strumpet!"

She gnashed her teeth and swirled away from him, suddenly wishing that her upbringing had allowed her the luxury of swearing.

They readied for bed in silence after that. She couldn't even bring herself to look at him. She knew he watched her as she knelt in her nightly prayer; her simmering anger blotted out all thoughts of God.

She rose to her feet. "I'll climb in now," she said tightly. "You may extinguish the lanterns."

He turned toward one of the lanterns, then paused, his back to her. "Did you enjoy his kiss?" His voice was muffled and dark.

Sweet Mother of Mercy. Was he jealous, as well as overbearing? "Yes. It was very pleasant." Let him chew on *that*, the tyrant!

He whirled to her with a low growl, dragged her to him, and crushed her lips with his. His tongue savaged her mouth with a fiery fury that left her breathless. She quivered in ecstasy and wrapped her arms around his neck, returning his kiss with all the passion in her pent-up heart. His hands dropped to her buttocks and kneaded them through her shift, sending a hot, trembling thrill shooting through her loins, like a bolt of lightning igniting a tree.

This was madness—and she knew it in that part of her brain that wasn't intoxicated with desire. She moaned and pressed her bosom against his chest, feeling the quickening of her heart at the intimate contact. She slid one hand behind his neck and tangled her fingers in the hair at his nape. It was silky and cool, a sensuous delight. And still his burning mouth held hers, until she was breathless.

Suddenly he groaned and thrust her away with such violence that she stumbled and fell against the sea chest. He turned and pounded his fist on the desk. "Damn you," he said with a tortured gasp. "For the love of God, leave me in peace!"

She stared in astonishment, struggling to catch her balance and her breath at the same time. He was bent as though he were in pain, and his face was twisted into a strange grimace. She could scarcely believe her eyes. Could he care for her, after all? Did he feel the same thrill, the same hunger that filled her body and cast reason aside? "Ross," she said tenderly, holding out her hand to him. "Come to bed."

He straightened and glared at her.

She chewed at her lip. Had she meant it as an invitation, if he chose thus to read her words? Oh, wicked Prudence! "Come to sleep," she corrected lamely. *Get thee behind me, Satan.*

His lip curled in disgust. "Mayhap you'd prefer to go to St. John's bed tonight. But I should warn you. He came to me for a cure when we left the Azores. There seems to have been a charming diversion on the island."

"A . . . a cure?"

"Have you ever seen what a visit by Signor Gonorrhea can do to a woman? A burning and swelling in those intimate parts that she has shared so wantonly. With a foul suppuration that can last for weeks, followed by painful ulceration, unless she is treated. 'Tis most unpleasant. But go to St. John, if that's your fancy."

She flinched at the naked cruelty of his words, clearly designed to frighten her. She turned to the bunk, her lip trembling in horror and dismay. "Blow out the lanterns," she said, fighting to keep the pride in her voice. "I wish to sleep."

He gave a short, triumphant laugh. "I thought you might." He strode to the bunk and snatched off his pillow and one of the blankets. "I shall sleep on the floor," he announced coldly. "So neither of us will be tempted."

Prudence paused, her hand on the wardroom door, and glanced up at the sky. It was as gloomy as her mood. That gentle young seaman was dying in the sick berth, his lungs wasting away. And there was so little she could do to bring him peace and comfort.

She longed to cry on Ross's shoulder and pour out her distress. But they were no longer the friends they had been when the voyage had begun. An uneasy truce prevailed, where they spoke as little as possible, and only about the details of their living arrangements. She had persuaded him to return to the bunk after his night on the floor; there was always the danger that Thompson might come in on them, and report back to Slickenham. But the space between their bodies was as wide as the ocean.

He still held her in his sleep. Her only comfort, though she was painfully aware that she was not the woman he sought for warmth and tenderness. She felt a pang of guilt, wondering when—and why—she had come to hate a dead woman.

"Dear lady, you look troubled."

She turned to see Captain Hackett coming down the gangway from the quarterdeck. " 'Tis only . . . a young lad, in the sick berth. Dying. I thought to find a Bible, perhaps, to read to him."

"You're a kind and generous woman, my dear. I must match your kindness with my own. You shall have my very own Bible."

He led her to the great cabin, ushered her inside, and removed his cocked hat. He carefully smoothed his dark hair, then pointed to a small table, upon which sat a decanter and several glasses. "You look pale. Sit down. Let me offer you a Madeira."

She hesitated, then nodded and took a chair. Perhaps the warming liquor would revive her spirits. She sipped it slowly, enjoying its soothing comfort.

Captain Hackett watched her with a benevolent smile on his handsome face—like a doting parent overseeing a child. When she had finished the last drop, he reached for the decanter. "Another, dear lady?"

"No. I feel quite restored."

He crossed the cabin to a far door, opened it, and beckoned her inside. "Then come along."

Behind him, she could see part of a curtained bunk. She felt a vague stirring of unease. "I shall wait here."

"But I have all my books in here. And so many. You might find a diverting novel or two to distract that poor man for a spell."

"Of course." Why should she feel uneasy when he was being so kind? And even when he closed the door after her, she felt safe. After all, most of his books were set in a railed bookcase behind the door. Impossible to reach, with the door open. She exclaimed in delight, seeing some of the titles. "How I wish I had known you had these at the beginning of the voyage! Jonson. And Swift! Two of my favorites."

"Do you read French?"

"Yes."

"Then, perhaps . . . ?" He put a large volume into her hands.

"Rabelais?" She blushed, remembering the bawdy tales. "Oh, he's too wicked!"

"But you *do* read him?"

She nodded reluctantly. That guilty pleasure had cost her half a day of isolation in the dairy. And a scolding from Mama, though Papa had seemed secretly pleased.

Hackett gathered a handful of books from the shelf and carried them across the cabin to a small table beneath the windows. "The light is better here. Some of these might amuse you, or your patient. I've given you my Bible as well."

She leafed through the books. Defoe's *Robinson Crusoe*. The sailor might enjoy that. There were several more novels, and a book of poetry. On the bottom of the stack was a small, finely bound volume. She flipped it open and gasped. It was like the book that Betsy had for her customers—filled with lewd drawings. She clapped it shut and looked at Hackett in horror.

His smile was innocent, with a touch of remorse. "A mistake, dear lady. I hadn't meant to take it down."

"But such a book . . . !"

He shrugged. "There is nothing more painful than the celibate life aboard ship. A man must amuse himself as best he can."

"But how can you . . . ?"

The smile was slightly less than innocent now. "Come, come, dear lady. You're an experienced woman. Surely you're not ignorant of a man's needs." He laughed with an edge of contempt. "Alas, your husband's needs, I should guess, incline in a different direction."

She remembered Ross's words. A sodomite, they had thought him. A lover of men and boys. Scarcely the man who pined for his dead wife, or kissed her so passionately. "That's absurd!" she said with some heat. "Ross is very loving to me, in the way of a man."

He raised a skeptical eyebrow. " 'Tis well-known you share the same bunk. But nothing more."

She bit her lip. How could Hackett have known that? She felt defensive and uncomfortable, willing to lie to put the captain's suspicions to rest. "Of course there's more!"

His smile was cunning and sly. "Then perhaps you have more . . . unusual ways of satisfying him. I should like to hear of them."

She drew herself up with outraged pride. She would hear no more from this vile man. She had very little idea of what he was referring to, but she knew enough to understand that it was wicked. "I'm a virtuous wife, Captain Hackett. Please allow me to pass."

He blocked her way and laughed—one schemer to another. "Odds my life! You expect me to believe that? When you've already set your cap at St. John? Granted him a kiss?" He shook his head. "A foolish choice. When you might have me." He smoothed his already-perfect curls. "You would look exquisite on my arm. A compliment to my own looks."

He stepped toward her. She flinched in alarm and backed away toward the windows. If only one of them were open, she thought in dismay, she could scream. Perhaps the sound would carry to the deck.

He slowly stripped off his coat—a sinuous, dangerous series of movements. His body was wiry, but clearly strong, capable of overpowering her. "I can be very generous to a charming woman. Far more generous than a lowly surgeon."

What had Betsy said about men? "A trinket for a treasure?" she asked bitterly.

"I can buy you far more than trinkets, dear lady." He reached out and tapped the obscene book. "For a woman who is . . . willing to adventure, there could be diamonds."

She fixed him with an icy glare. "Let me pass."

He sighed. "Must we play the 'Outraged Virtue' scene first?"

She stamped her foot. "I *am* a woman of virtue!"

He shook his head and laughed. "A woman of virtue would never come into a man's sleeping cabin. Unless she knew exactly what she wanted."

"Plague take your vile designs! I wish to leave."

"Of course." He smirked and stepped aside. She swept past him to the door. But as she reached for the latch, he grabbed her from behind, his hands snaking up her bodice to grasp her breasts. He spun her around and pulled her close to him. "Let us have an end to games," he growled. "You're neither innocent nor—I suspect—a wife. Manning may be a fool, without the wit to appreciate or enjoy you. But I vowed to have you from the first."

His dark eyes frightened her with their intensity. "Please let me go," she whispered.

" 'Tis a little late for you to play the role of swooning maiden." One hand went around her neck. He tangled his fingers in her hair and held her head immobile. The other hand was at her buttocks, pulling her against his loins. She could feel the hardness of his desire even through her skirts. She gasped as his hot mouth descended on hers.

She moaned in horror and disgust, pounding futilely at his shoulders. She could hear him chuckle in evil pleasure, which only increased her terror. She managed at last to jerk her head away, freeing her mouth. She spit into his face.

He grunted and recoiled. In that moment when his guard was down, she tore herself from his arms, pushed him away, and slapped his cheek as hard as she could. He wiped at the spittle on his face and rubbed his jaw where the marks of her fingers glowed red. To her astonishment, a slow, goatish smile spread across his features.

"Gad's curse," he said with a laugh. "A tiger? What a happy discovery. Well, I shall soon tame you, dear lady. You will sob with pleasure—and pain—before I'm through." His arms shot out and held her in a punishing grip. He lifted her, writhing, and tossed her onto the bunk. While she lay breathless, too stunned to move, he began to fumble with the buttons of his breeches.

She gathered her scattered wits. Once he pinned her with his body, it would be too late to escape. As he released his rigid manhood from its confinement and reached to toss back her skirts, she drew up her knees. Aiming her shoes at his most vulnerable spot, she kicked him with all her might. He staggered back in pain, winded and grimacing.

She scrambled from the bunk, ran to the door, raced through the great cabin, and found the safety of the open quarterdeck. She leaned against the railing, gasping and fighting her tears. How long would it take the villain to recover himself and come after her?

She cast her eyes desperately toward the men on the decks. No one but faceless seamen, who would be too frightened of their captain's wrath to protect her. *Ross.* He would be in the cockpit at this hour. She started for the hatchway.

No. How could she tell him what had happened? She had no one but herself to blame. Ross had tried to warn her. From the first day. And now, after that foolish escapade with St. John, Ross would only conclude that she had deliberately encouraged the captain. What would he think if she told him that she had willingly gone to Hackett's sleeping cabin? That she was an empty-headed ninny as well as a loose woman?

She rubbed her hand across her mouth, still tasting Hackett's disgusting kiss. And the feel of his body against hers . . . ! She shuddered. She should have listened to Ross. Men without women were ruled by their hungers. What was it Betsy had said, in her bawdy way? 'Tis astonishing how a man's pintle springs to attention, like a soldier on guard, when he's not had a woman for weeks. Hackett had made his desires clear—with his words, with his erect manhood.

And St. John. His honeyed words that had seduced her into a kiss . . . were they merely to disguise his coarse desire for more earthy favors? Perhaps—God forgive her for the thought—even Jamie had been driven by his physical needs as well as by his love.

And Ross? She remembered the telltale bulge in his shirt that morning, when he had stared at her bare legs. She had tried to pretend at the time that she was innocent of its meaning, but she was only deceiving herself. He might not *like* her very much, because of the sin she had committed, because she was a burden to him. But he was as horn-mad as the rest.

She shivered. She felt like a fox on a hunt, surrounded by snarling, slavering dogs. There was less than a fortnight until landfall in Virginia. And not a moment too soon, if she was to preserve what honor she had left.

She scurried down to the cabin, determined to keep her wits about her from now on. She might have found it exciting at first, to discover the world of men after her years of country innocence. But far more frightening and dangerous than she would ever have imagined.

Chapter Twelve

" 'Tis blowin' up somethin' fierce, lady. Best you stay below."

Prudence stopped and smiled at Toby Wedge as he overtook her on the hatchway. "And did one of your omens foretell it?"

He nodded his head vigorously. "Aye, lady, that it did. You be minded how yesterday the sun were bright and cheery? Like a gob of butter on your porridge?"

"Indeed." She had felt lighthearted and filled with hope, basking in the lovely day. By God's grace, they would reach safe harbor in a week, if the wind held.

"Well, there was my mate, Gawky, passin' by Cap'n's cabin. And of a sudden, he hears Cap'n fall to whistlin'. Like as not he were happy for the fair weather, same as we."

"And?"

"Body o' me! 'Tis bad luck to whistle on a ship! Like spittin' in the devil's face, d'ye see me? Every tar knows that! And now, faster than a wink, this blow come on us." He sighed. " 'Tis Cap'n's doin', and he not knowin'. The devil is in that man, beggin' your pardon."

She could certainly agree with *that*. But as for the weather . . . Ross had told her they were in the hurricane latitudes, so close to the Virginia shore. And September was the most dangerous month for unexpected storms. However, there was no point in trying to persuade Wedge; he had long since decided that Hackett was the cause of every ill aboard ship. "If it's going to storm," she said, "I'd best see to the men in the sick berth."

"Aye, lady, an't please you." He tugged at his forelock and went on up to the deck.

Prudence turned around and descended the hatchway to the sick berth, taking the route that was most populated with seamen at their chores. Since that dreadful scene with Captain Hackett, she had guarded against being alone and isolated in dim corners of the ship. She had found reasons to accompany Ross on most of his rounds. And when she tended the men in the sick berth, she had invented a giddy, girlish excuse to persuade Richards to walk her back to her cabin.

Hackett had never acknowledged what had happened in his sleeping cabin; indeed, the only change in his smoothly polite manner to her was that he no longer bothered to disguise the lustful glances he sent her way, the burning eyes that dwelt on her bosom.

She had never told Ross. He was still so cold to her. And besides, she feared he might do something reckless that would endanger him. She could only pray that they would reach land before Ross's hatred of the captain could burst forth in some rash act.

The sharp wind and rain were already blowing into the portholes when she reached the sick berth. The moan of the wind was echoed by the groans of the injured and ailing, a mournful sound that she had never quite learned to hear without feeling a twinge of pity. She nodded to Richards, tied on her apron, and began to move among the rocking hammocks.

She greeted a grizzled old tarpaulin with a bandage around his cracked head. He had been here for a week now, hovering near death. But today his color was much improved, which heartened her. She bathed his face and teased him about the girls he would woo when they reached shore, then moved on to the next man.

The storm was building rapidly; streaks of lightning flashed beyond the portholes and punctuated the cabin with eerie bursts of light. Thunder rumbled like cannonballs rolling on the decks, and the rain beat a tattoo against the hull. The heaving seas lifted the ship and cast it down again, causing the lanterns to sway and the slop basins to slide across the floor.

Prudence found it more and more difficult to stand, clutching at the ropes of the hammocks to keep her balance as she moved from man to man. This was the worst storm to hit them on the entire voyage, and it made it difficult to work. There was no hot broth to feed to anyone: the cooks had doused the fire in the galley as soon as the storm had begun to build. And it was next to impossible to change a bandage or give a dose of medicine with the violent movement of the ship.

She heard a sudden, loud crackle of lightning very near to the ship, followed almost at once by a thunderclap that made the vessel shiver and toss upon the sea. Richards spilled a chamber pot he was carrying, and swore viciously; at the same time, Prudence was thrown against a bulkhead.

Richards watched in disgust as the liquid flowed across the deck, then turned to Prudence. "We'll soon be bouncing around like water on a hot pan. There's nothing for it, Mrs. Manning, but to take to our berths until the storm blows over." He found a spare hammock and hooked it up to the beams. "Shall I take you back to your cabin first?"

She shook her head. There was no point in his moving around the ship more than was necessary. And any man who was still standing in this blow would have far more to think about than a woman. She watched Richards lift one leg and spring into the hammock—the only possible way to execute the difficult maneuver—then made her way carefully to the door.

She clung to handholds and railings as she descended to the deck below. By the time she reached the passageway leading to Ross's cabin, she was exhausted from the effort of trying to stay on her feet. She would welcome the snug security of her bunk.

She jumped in alarm. A man crouched in the doorway, muttering to himself. As she warily neared him in the gloomy passage, she made out the gangling figure of Wedge's messmate, Gawky. He was soaked to the skin, his long hair matted around his face.

"What are you doing here?" she asked.

"Oh, ma'am, I be much afeared. He'll die, God love his soul."

Ross? she thought at once. Had anything happened to him? She found herself suddenly breathless. "Is it Dr. Manning?"

"No, ma'am. 'Tis Toby."

"Has he been hurt?"

"Worse than that, ma'am. And me without no one to listen."

"Sweet merciful heaven! What's happened?"

"We was on the deck, me and t'other gunners, lashing down the guns against the storm. Ol' Toby, he were tugging same as us, when the line gives way, and the gun starts to roll."

She let out a cry. "Was he crushed by the gun?"

Gawky shook his head; water dripped from his thin cheeks. "No, ma'am. I springs to his side and throws another line to anchor it. But here comes Cap'n Hackett, bearing down on poor Toby like a man-o'-war after a Frenchy frigate. And he falls to cursing him for a clumsy tarpaulin, calling him lousy son of a whore, and the like. Then he points up to the mainmast. The lower sails is reefed against the storm, of course. But there were one topgallant that tore, and is hanging there and flapping like a big white gull at sunset."

"Can't it be mended when the storm is over?"

"Aye, ma'am. And there bean't danger to the ship, with such a small sail. But Cap'n, he shakes his fist at Toby. 'Get aloft, you ugly swabber,' he says, 'and pull that down.' "

"But Toby's a *gunner*. He doesn't go into the rigging!"

"Lord ha' mercy. That's what Toby is trying to tell the cap'n, and him as good a seaman as ever stepped upon fo'c'sle! But Cap'n, he won't hear. 'You come athwart me once too often, you dog,' he says. Then he says he'll give 'im a hundred strokes if he don't climb."

"Dear heaven! What did he do?"

Gawky scowled. "Ol' Toby, he be as brave a fellow as ever cracked biscuit. So up he goes."

Prudence was growing more horrified as Gawky's story unfolded. "Did he make it safely up and back again?"

"No, ma'am. Cap'n won't let 'im down."

"Not let him down? In this storm?" Prudence nearly screamed the words.

"He even set one of the marines at the mainmast. With a cutlass. Me and t'other gunners, we was set to haul ol' Toby down. But there's him with his cutlass, threatening to part our mainsails if we come near, and there's us, helpless as a frigate without a wind."

Prudence gasped in horror. "Is he still up there?"

"Aye, that he is. Clinging for dear life. Less'n he be blowed away by now."

"God save him." She turned and hurried toward the hatchway, timing her steps to each violent roll of the ship.

She stepped out onto the deck and shrank back into the overhang of the forecastle to protect herself from the raging storm. The whistle of the wind had become a roar, and the rain fell in cold sheets. The guns rattled in their carriages, and the clank of the pump chains blended with the sounds of creaking timbers.

In a few moments, Prudence was drenched from the rain and sea spray, her hair combs blown away, her long curls whipping against her face.

She peered up into the rigging and shuddered. His storm-buffeted face white with terror, Toby Wedge clung to the mast, halfway up, and howled like a crazed dog. A high-pitched, mournful wail that was chilling. With each swell of the ship, the mast swayed dangerously, whipping like a sapling in the wind, until Prudence wondered how the poor man had the strength to hang on.

Impervious to the weather, Captain Hackett watched from the open door of the wardroom, his body braced against the doorframe, his arms crossed against his chest, his face frozen in a malevolent smile. The few officers and men on the windswept deck averted their eyes, clearly too intimidated to challenge the captain. Even the tempest-blown marine standing guard at the mast looked shamefaced. The only one who seemed pleased was the toadeater, Slickenham.

Prudence cast her glance wildly about. Was there no one willing to save Wedge? Through the open door of the forecastle, she spied Ross in the shadows; she heaved a sigh of relief, stumbled inside, and clutched his arm. "For the love of God, do something!"

His face was a frightening mask—jaw set in a hard line, eyes blazing with an impenetrable fire. He clenched and unclenched his fists. "There's nothing I can do," he said coldly. "I tried to reason with the captain. But he's determined to see this through. I think he won't be content until Wedge is dead. And the world is rid of one more grotesque, as he puts it."

She stared in disbelief. "And so you'll do *nothing?*"

His lip curled in a bitter grimace. "Do you know how small a provocation it would take for him to turn on me? This is a military ship. The man has extraordinary powers as captain. I have no right to interfere." His voice was flat and remote.

Her eyes filled with tears of anger. "Oh! Don't you even care what happens to that poor creature? Why can't you countermand his order? Are you too afraid?" She pounded at his chest, sobbing in outrage. "You're nothing but a selfish coward! Only concerned for your own safety! Have you renounced life so completely that you don't mind if others die?"

He seemed about to explode, his body tense with conflicting emotions. He grabbed her roughly by the shoulders and shook her. "You damned innocent fool!" he shouted. "Are you blind to all the subtleties of life? If I were in irons, how long do you think it would be before that villain was in my cabin? In my bunk? Comforting my 'wife'?" His eyes glowed in fury. "You'd be his prisoner and his plaything for the rest of the voyage."

She stared at him in horror. Despite Hackett's attack, she had somehow assumed that a single conquest was all that he wanted of her. "The . . . the rest of the voyage?" she stammered. "He wouldn't dare . . . the other men . . ."

"Like that white-livered St. John?" he said with a sneer. "Do you think he'd protect you? My God, the captain has already offered to increase the sailors' rations if I'll pimp for him! He wants you that much."

"Merciful heaven." She bent her head, her body trembling.

He had no pity. He shook her again, his voice an angry growl. "Is that what you want, damn it? Tell me, and I'll climb the mast myself and carry Wedge down!"

She groaned and leaned her head against his chest. "It isn't right," she said in a choked voice.

He held her close. " 'Tis neither right nor fair," he muttered. "But that's the way of the world. Men have been punished aboard ship ere now, and survived."

Just then, a bolt of lightning sizzled through the air and struck the deck, leaving a charred, smoking spot. Wedge's shrill scream rang out above the din of the storm. Prudence tore herself from Ross's arms. "I can't bear it! Perhaps if I plead with the captain . . ."

"Don't be a fool! Your pleas will be useless. All he wants is your willing body."

Wedge screamed again. Prudence choked back her anguish. "Then I'll go to him! If that's what it takes."

"I forbid it!" he roared, his eyes burning.

"I *will!*" She turned and stumbled toward the door, fighting her horror and disgust. She felt Ross's hand on her arm, spinning her around. She saw his fist descending toward her chin.

"I'm sorry," he said in a tight voice.

The blow, when it came, brought darkness. And blessed release from her agony.

She awoke in her bunk, her jaw throbbing and sore. The gentle swaying of the lanterns showed her that the storm had abated. And some time ago, to judge from her gown, which was already beginning to dry. She staggered from the bunk, sick at heart. Perhaps poor Wedge was dead by now.

She groaned, pushed her tangled curls from her face, and rubbed at her temples. The pounding in her head was almost as painful as her jaw. It was impossible to think clearly while her head hurt so much. She remembered Ross's headache powders in the cockpit; they would surely relieve her. She tottered into the passageway.

She heard the rumble of voices from the cockpit even before she reached the open door. The cabin was crowded with seamen hanging back in the corners and muttering among themselves; their faces were dark and mournful, their voices grumbling with discontent. Prudence froze in horror, her hand on the doorpost.

On the table in the center of the cabin sat Toby Wedge, wrapped in blankets, looking like an old, twisted gnome. His teeth chattered as though he had the ague, and his lips were blue. His thinning hair hung around his pockmarked face in dank, matted strings that clung to his forehead and drawn cheeks. His hair had turned the color of snow.

Only his tar-blackened hands emerged from the blanket, quivering appendages poking out from a trembling mass. The stubby fingers were wrapped in bandages. He shivered and muttered unintelligibly, then burst into laughter—a high, odd giggle that scarcely sounded human.

Ross, bending to him, growled a command to his surgeon's mate. "Hand me that last splint, Bailey." He placed the lath of wood beside one of Wedge's thumbs and began to wrap it.

Prudence spied Gawky's worried face in the crowd of men. She moved quickly to him. "Mother of Mercy," she said in a low voice. "What happened to his hands, Gawky?"

Despite his weather-beaten face, Gawky looked like a little boy about to cry. "When Cap'n finally let us up to him, he wouldn't let go of the mast. We had to break some of his fingers to get 'im down."

"Oh, alas," she moaned. The seamen made a path for her as she stepped to the table. She reached out a shaking hand and stroked Wedge's coarse cheek. "How goes it, Toby?" she murmured.

Ross looked up from his work, acknowledging her presence for the first time. "Save your breath. Wherever his mind is, it's not here."

She refused to allow his cold-blooded assessment to deter her. She put her hand on Wedge's arm. "Toby?"

He looked at her and frowned, his eyes fixed on her long auburn hair, which tumbled loose about her shoulders. "Black-haired be bad," he muttered. "Yellow, worse. But a redheaded woman brings evil." He laughed and stared off into space. "Aye, Maw, that be gospel truth."

She bit her lip. "I'm your friend, Toby."

He chuckled and began to babble, his eyes fixed on a beam of the cabin. He seemed to be holding a conversation with someone—or something—only he could see. "When the sky falls, we shall have larks . . . but I were only . . . a bad omen, d'ye see me?" The grotesque smile had turned to a fierce scowl, which further deformed his unlovely face. He shook his bandaged fingers at Ross. "At a pale man, draw thy knife. From a black man, keep thy wife." He shuddered in sudden horror and then cried out, casting his eyes wildly about the cabin. "Be Cap'n here? Body o' me, be he *here?*" He tried to throw himself from the table and flee.

Ross leapt forward and restrained him. "Rest easy, man. He's not here." He turned and beckoned to Gawky. "He needs more watching than he can get in the sick berth. Put him in his own hammock, and look after him. I've done all I can for his body. His mind is up to God's care."

"Aye, Mr. Manning. Me and t'others will see to him. We'll stand watch every hour, till we reaches land. Our messmate won't never want for naught." He ground his teeth together and jutted his chin. "Poor ol' Toby, what were friend to all. Damn that villain!"

Ross fixed him with a stony glare. "You are not to seek revenge with the captain. Nor think of mutiny. Do you understand? I'll not defend you if you do. I don't fancy watching you hang." He swept the room with an angry gesture. "*Any* of you!"

Gawky dropped his defiant gaze. "Aye, Mr. Manning, we understands."

"What's done is done. We'll be ashore in a week. Hold your tempers and go on about your duties. You're the king's seamen. You owe him your fealty, whatever you may think of Hackett. Now take Wedge to the forecastle. I'll see to his fingers again tomorrow." He took a flask from the medicine chest and handed it to Bailey. "Go with them and stay with Wedge until the dog watch. Give him this brandy until he stops quaking."

Prudence watched, fighting her tears, as the seamen lifted Wedge and carried him from the cabin, their rough hands grown more gentle than she would have imagined. Then she turned to Ross, her lip trembling.

His blue eyes were troubled, dark with remorse. "I'm sorry I had to strike you," he muttered. He reached out and stroked the side of her jaw, then swore softly when she flinched. "Foolish child."

"Wh-what will happen to Toby now?"

"He'll be well cared for till we reach land. Seamen are loyal to their mates. They'll stand his watch for him and see that he's fed."

"And after that?"

"If his wits are still gone, I'll keep him as my servant until I go off to the wilderness, so he'll not become a derelict. After that, I'll put him on a ship bound for England. He can live a pensioner in Greenwich Hospital, among the other disabled and aged seamen. He'll be well tended." His lip curled in bitterness. "Where he'll sit and spout his superstitious nonsense for the rest of his days."

She had reached the edge of her self-control. Her body began to shake. "Is it nonsense? I remember the old wives' tales about red hair. Have I brought naught but evil to the poor man?"

"You? Don't be absurd. Do you think I would have let you go to Hackett? And do you really suppose he would have honored his pledge, even if you'd given him what he wanted?"

"It was my fault!" she cried out. "You would have risked your safety, your freedom, to save him. You would have defied the captain. Except for me." Her guilt was choking her. Her grief burst forth at last in a flood of tears. She sobbed in misery, her heart twisting with pain.

He enfolded her in his arms and held her close. "Prudence. Sweet, brave girl. There was nothing you could do." He held her until her violent weeping subsided, stroking her back and murmuring words of comfort.

At last she lifted her face to his. He pulled out his handkerchief and dabbed at her nose and wet cheeks. His hands were tender, his eyes soft with understanding. He raked his fingers gently through her long curls, combing out the tangled tresses. He touched her jaw, then ran one finger across her still-trembling lips. His eyes had settled upon her mouth, and they glowed with a strange blue light. She felt drawn into his very soul, her grief dissolving into a frightening thrill under that fixed stare, those sensuous hands.

Then he shivered, closed his haunted eyes, and released her, turning away to clutch the edge of the table with taut-knuckled hands. His shoulders heaved for a moment, and then he gave a heavy sigh. When he spoke at last, his voice was low and muffled. "Now that the storm has passed, the fires will be lit in the galley again. Go and change your wet gown. I shall see how soon supper is to be served in the wardroom."

She felt an aching disappointment, as though a door had opened to a wondrous unknown, and then closed again, leaving her bereft. She put her hand on his sleeve. "Ross," she whispered.

He turned, his face twisted in agony. "If you value your safety," he said in a strangled voice, "go away. *Now!*"

Chapter
Thirteen

Ross scowled across the wardroom at Prudence and poured himself another glass of wine. He drummed his fingers impatiently on the table, wondering how much more of this he could endure before he exploded.

Look at her! he thought in disgust. Scarcely the shy, modest country girl he'd carried to the cockpit that first day. She was beautiful, poised, devastating to a man—and the witch had certainly begun to realize it! The way she dimpled prettily as she thanked Elliot for his fiddle-playing. The laughter she shared with that callow midshipman, whose name he could scarcely remember. The rosy-cheeked smiles she gave to St. John.

No more than the smiles of a friend, he noted grimly, after that shameless kiss on the deck. She wouldn't dare! He still wondered why he hadn't taken her across his knee and taught her a lesson that night. Oh, she'd been careful to obey him and not to flirt wantonly again—a minor victory. But it scarcely mattered. Her own natural charm was enough to make a slave of every officer aboard. Officer? Hell! Was there a man in the sick berth who wouldn't willingly die for her?

She was particularly charming tonight, devil take her! Bright and gay and filled with laughter. She had sung half a dozen songs in that lilting voice of hers, and clapped her hands like a happy child when she'd bested Elliot at backgammon. She had even been civil to Slickenham, whom she had always disliked.

Well, he thought sourly, perhaps she had reason to be happy. She was going to her Lord Jamie tomorrow. The ship's master expected to sight Cape Henry before dawn; if the fair weather held, they should be well up the James River before the morning watch was over.

And how many days before she was in that scoundrel's arms? Gazing at him with those trusting eyes—so green they reminded him of a fresh meadow in spring? Would he break her heart, the rogue? Or kiss her and watch the lamplight turn her hair to amber fire, as now it did? Would he take joy in her laughter, the saucy tilt of her nose, the feel of her milky white skin beneath his hands, the soft compassion that colored her words? Or would he only seek to bury his manhood deep within her body, and be blind to her loveliness, her sweet nature?

Ross groaned and squeezed his eyes shut for a moment. *God protect me,* he thought. *One more day.* They would reach safe harbor sometime tomorrow. And then *he* would be safe.

He had been such an innocent with Martha. All those years of courting her . . . so consumed with his studies that he'd scarcely had time to think of his body's hungers; so disgusted with the loose behavior of his fellow students, who satisfied their lusts with any passing wench, that he had refused to succumb. Somehow, he had known that when at last he took Martha in his arms it would be perfect.

The years-long denial of his basest urges, the purity of his untried manhood, had been the gifts he had brought to their marriage bed. But, slowly, they had learned to pleasure each other. He had found himself listening when the talk at the coffeehouses turned to women and all the ways to satisfy them. He had come home, eager to act on his newfound knowledge. And Martha, shy in her innocence, had yet given her willing body to his sometimes awkward attempts. And their passion had bloomed with their enlightenment like a lush flower, nurtured in hothouse nights of lovemaking. He would wake in the morning with her in his arms, and think that Paradise could be no sweeter than what he had found.

Then she was dead. And desire had faded in him as though it had never been there. As a young man—burning, aching for her—he had wondered how the Roman priests could be celibate, and still be at peace with their bodies. Now he knew. His passion had died with Martha, his fleshly needs as vanished as his one true love. He had pledged himself eternally to her in life; it seemed right and natural that his earthly appetites should be buried with her.

He had rejoiced. It made it easier for him to endure the days and weeks and months of grief. If his heart was in torment, at least that pain was not intensified by the sufferings of the flesh.

Until Prudence. He wasn't sure when it had begun to happen, but he found himself haunted day and night by thoughts of her. He would drift into a daydream, and remember the tantalizing sight of her body, the taste of her mouth, the velvet touch of her hand. Then he would bestir himself, and fall to cursing his weakness. And sometimes, half-waking in the dim cabin, he would find her in his arms, and berate himself for not having the moral strength to let her go.

He groaned again. *Forgive me, Martha,* he thought. *Forgive me.* He was faithless even to allow his thoughts to dwell on another woman. And if he should lapse, allow the unthinkable to happen . . .

"God protect me," he murmured under his breath. Only one more day. And then she would be out of his life forever.

"Will you honor us with another song, Martha?"

Prudence smiled hesitantly at St. John, and glanced across the wardroom to where Ross still sat at the table, his wineglass in his hand. He had scarcely stopped glaring at her all evening. He was in a strange, edgy humor; she wasn't sure she wanted to be alone with him yet. But would he allow her to linger for another song?

He had behaved oddly all this past week. Not angry, to be sure, nor even icy cold. He had been tense, abrupt with her, seeking his isolation. As though he carried a heavy burden, secret thoughts that were beyond her understanding. She would almost have preferred his anger to his quiet, contained remoteness—at least she would be reassured that there was still a human soul residing in him.

They had never spoken of Toby Wedge's ordeal since that day. Prudence was still consumed with guilt, and she sensed that Ross blamed himself as well. As for that unfortunate seaman . . .

She had visited him every day in the forecastle. Sometimes he recognized her, most often he didn't. He would sit for hours, spouting gibberish and superstitious flummery, or crouch behind a sea chest, trembling and swearing that the captain was spying on him through a knothole in the bulkhead. In vain, Gawky and his mates plugged the holes with pitch; "Cap'n" was still there, giving him the evil eye.

"One more song, Mrs. Manning. We beseech you. In sweet farewell to a most enjoyable voyage."

Prudence bit her lip and looked at the earnest young officer who bent above her. She turned to Ross, gauging his mood. "Well, perhaps . . ."

Ross bolted from his chair. "No! You've sung quite enough tonight, wife. 'Twill be a long day tomorrow." He hurried to her side, grasped her elbow, and steered her determinedly from the wardroom.

The full moon was bright and cold in the sky, bathing the deck in an unreal glow and filling Prudence with a strange sadness. She should be happy that her search for Jamie was nearly at an end, that her child would be back in her arms before Christmastide. Then why was her heart so heavy?

She cast her eyes about the ship. She would miss the officers and their gallantry, the seamen she had tended—their wan faces brightening at sight of her—the soothing rhythm of shipboard life, for all its discomforts.

She glanced at the man striding so purposefully beside her. *Most of all, I shall miss you, Ross Manning,* she thought. Miss his reassuring presence that somehow made her feel more competent and independent. Miss his friendship, the warm laughter that sometimes shone in his clear blue eyes. Miss the quiet strength that had often sustained her.

And she would never see him again after tomorrow. She had her life and her hopes. Jamie and England. He had his dream of solitude in the wilderness. An ocean apart. She stumbled on the hatchway, her eyes misting with inexplicable tears.

She shook her head to clear away the sadness. You've made your bed, now lie in it, Papa would have said. And was her dear child not worth every sacrifice?

They heard strange sounds as they neared the cockpit. Muttered words, followed by high-pitched laughter, then the angry rumble of other voices. From time to time, the voices were drowned out by the shrill notes of a pipe.

"Oh, Lord, it's Wedge," said Ross, opening the cockpit door.

Toby Wedge sat on the table in the center of the cabin, dangling his squat legs over the side, grinning and mumbling to himself like a madman. In his bandaged hands he held his pipe. Bailey and Richards, their shirts loosened from their breeches, their shoes off, stood glaring at him. Their hammocks were strung in the corner; their faces were red with exasperation.

"What the devil is going on?" said Ross.

Bailey turned. "He wandered down from the forecastle, Mr. Manning. Woke us up, he did, with his infernal piping. And now he won't leave."

Ross strode to Wedge. "Toby," he said gently, " 'tis time to sleep."

Wedge lifted his pipe to his lips and whistled a sweet tune, deftly using those fingers that weren't broken and bandaged. He beamed when he was finished, and nodded at Ross. "Put a morsel o' bread under your pillow, and you be safe from the devil. My life on't."

"Go to the forecastle. To your hammock. Gawky is waiting for you."

Wedge pouted and began to shake his head violently.

Richards sighed. "This is the lay of the land, sir. He's afraid to climb the stairs. We took him to the hatchway, but he looked up and started to shake. Then he scampered back here."

Ross rubbed his hand across his eyes. "My God, not even a flight of stairs?"

" 'Tis a wonder he'll even climb into his hammock, sir, he's that afraid of heights. Thanks to the captain," Richards added, his lip curling in disgust.

"You might as well swallow your resentment," said Ross. "You'll have to sail back to England with him. Both of you."

"Not if I can get another berth," growled Bailey.

Ross put his arm around Wedge's waist and eased him from the table. "Come, Toby. We'll play a game. Close your eyes and I'll take you to your bed."

Wedge complied, closing his eyes and screwing his face into a smiling grimace, like a happy child who shared a secret game. "May dew cures sore eyes. D'ye see me?" he burbled.

"Then you must have Gawky sprinkle your eyes with water in the morning. Come along now." Ross turned to Prudence. "I'll not be a moment."

He led Wedge from the cockpit, while Prudence went on to their cabin.

She sat at Ross's desk, removed her shoes and peeled off her stockings. She was about to rise and work on the fastenings of her gown when an open drawer of the desk caught her eye. Within, she could see the edge of Ross's drawing folio. Impulsively, she pulled it out and opened it.

"Sweet Mother of Mercy," she whispered, thumbing through the pages with ever-increasing agitation. Every other page was filled with sketches of her—sleeping in the bunk, laughing on deck with a group of seamen, busy at her sewing. And each picture executed with a tenderness, a sympathetic grace that took her breath away. Had he watched her so much, and she unaware? She felt confused and strangely joyous. Had she touched his cold heart?

Oh, Prudence, she thought with a sigh, closing the book and carefully replacing it. She had no right to wonder about Ross. She had her son to think of. And that meant Jamie—and no other.

Ross came into the cabin and closed the door, shaking his head. "That poor devil."

"Is there nothing you can do?"

"I'm a surgeon, not a magician. Perhaps when he's ashore, and away from Hackett, his muddled brain will clear."

"How long will you stay in Williamsburg?"

"A fortnight or so. I must resign my warrant, and then see what land there is to be had beyond the mountains. And you?"

She stripped off her gown—Martha's gown—and folded it with care. She must remember to return it to him in the morning. "If there's a stage leaving Williamsburg, I shall go at once."

"And where do you go?"

"My Lord Jamie's plantation. On the shore of the Potomac."

He began to undress, his back toward her. "And you still think he'll be pleased to see you?"

"Merciful heaven! Of course he will."

He turned, a cynical smile on his face. " 'Tis a pity I shall be gone. I should have liked to wager on the faithfulness of your aristocratic lover."

She frowned. "He misses me dreadfully, I'm sure. He loves me."

He laughed, a sharp bark of derision. "As a bee loves a flower, perhaps. As a rutting stallion craves a mare."

She glared at him and tossed her petticoat into her sea chest. He was deliberately provoking her, when she had hoped that their last night together would be marked by friendship. Why did she always have to endure his attacks on Jamie, and feel helpless? She felt the devil stir within her, urging her to strike back.

She thought of the pictures he had so carefully hidden. Did they represent more to him than merely the offhand studies of an artist? She tilted her head at him and smiled archly. "Will *you* miss me?"

He had been about to climb into the bunk. Now he turned, his body rigid, his long, bare legs planted on the deck, his eyes cold. "Do you need one last conquest before you go?"

Despite his icy demeanor, she thought she saw the quiver of a muscle at the corner of his eye. She pressed her advantage. She stretched her arms languidly above her head and pulled the ribbon from her hair. She had worn it loose all week, the side curls caught up on the top of her head in a ribbon bow. She shook her long tresses till they swirled around her shoulders. She felt wicked and restless, hungry for one word of praise from him. For a sign that he regretted their parting as much as she.

"*Will* you miss me?" she asked softly.

He averted his gaze. "Why should I?"

"Whom will you draw when I'm gone?"

His eyes flicked nervously toward the desk. He cleared his throat and frowned. "Why have you worn your hair loose all week?" he said at last.

"I lost my combs in the storm."

"Damn it, you could have asked one of the seamen to carve you new ones."

She shrugged. "I'm sure there are shops in Williamsburg. Don't you like it that way?"

"What have I to do with it?" he growled. "If you choose to toss your curls at the officers and break their hearts . . ." He swore softly. " 'Tis as well we land tomorrow, or Elliot might forget he has a wife."

She felt her anger growing at his sarcastic tone. "What do you mean by such a thing?"

"Your behavior with the men tonight was shameless. Prancing around like a tart on the London docks. A pretty doxy, selling her wares! You call yourself my wife, yet behave like a coquette, though I clearly forbade it! And now you hope to catch my eye at last? One final souvenir of the voyage?"

"Oh!" She stamped in outrage. The deck was rough under her bare foot. "Plague take you, you . . . you tyrant! You have no right to speak to me so! *Forbade?* You're not my husband. Nor ever will be, thank the good Lord!"

"But you didn't mind hiding behind me, when it suited you," he said with a sneer.

She was beginning to hate him, her body churning with emotions she could scarcely contain. "How glad I shall be to be quit of your side. Always finding fault. Seeking my perfection, when your own fails you so often! Whether my hair is up or down, my gowns low or high, I could never please you!"

His lip curled. "And your beloved Lord Jamie. Was your hair long and loose when he met you? Did you toss your curls to catch *his* eye?"

"It scarcely matters. He would not have cared, nor carped as you do!"

He laughed—an ugly, angry sound. "Of course not. You had more intimate curls to tempt him."

She was sputtering in fury. "A pox on you, you villain! You will speak no more of Jamie!"

"I'll speak as I bloody well please!" he exploded. "And perhaps you'll listen, for a change. You're a damned fool to trust in his love. To chase him halfway around the earth in hopes that he'll marry you! I've known men like that. Filled with empty promises. Do you think you meant more to him than just an easy conquest? A simple country girl who was eager to lift her skirts and . . ."

It was too much for her to bear another cruel word. With a shriek, she leapt at him and struck him savagely across the mouth. He flinched, and then his long arms shot out to grasp her by the shoulders. She could feel the bite of his fingers through her thin shift.

"I warned you once before about doing that," he said, his eyes burning. "This time, you'll pay a forfeit." He grabbed her by the wrist and began to drag her toward the chair.

She gulped in sudden terror. She had never seen him so enraged, so tensed with coiled passions. Surely the punishment he meted out would be as harsh and brutal as his raw emotions. Panic gave her a burst of strength. She tore her hand from his grasp, spun about, and raced for the door. His shoes were there. She tripped on them and fell, sprawling on her belly. She tensed in fear, half-expecting the hot slap of his hand on her backsides, then quickly rolled over on her back to protect her vulnerable flanks.

Before she could struggle to her feet, he was upon her, straddling her where she lay. She attacked him with flailing fists, but he snatched at her wrists and stretched her arms above her head, holding her pinned to the deck. "Damn you!" he said, his chest heaving in tortured gasps. "Do you think I'm made of stone? How much is a man expected to endure?"

"Let me up. You're hurting me!" she cried.

His face was tense, twisted into a frightening grimace of suppressed emotions. "Was it deliberate, you witch? All these long weeks of torment? Of watching you charm every man aboard? Of listening to you prattle about your damned Lord Jamie? Well, curse you, tomorrow you'll be gone. Tomorrow you'll be his. But tonight . . ."

He released her hands, curled his fingers around the top of her shift, and tore it open to her navel. Before she had time to collect her wits and push him away, his burning mouth descended to her breast. He savaged her nipple with strong teeth and hot, swirling tongue.

She gasped at the wondrous sensation of his mouth, the intimacy of his tantalizing kisses; she felt her resistance crumbling beneath the fierce assault on her breasts. "No, please . . ." she said, slapping weakly at his shoulders, his bent head.

"Tonight I'll please myself," he muttered, and silenced her mouth with his.

His lips were hard and demanding, grinding on hers with a possessive intensity that left her weak. He forced his tongue deep into her mouth and explored the moist grotto like a hungry man. She shivered at the violence of his whirlwind attack, her senses reeling with every exquisite, darting stroke of his tongue.

His hands were on her breasts, kneading the tender flesh; his rough caresses further inflamed her senses. He drove his knee between her thighs, forcing her legs apart. She felt his hand clutching her furry softness through her shift, and then his fingers assaulted her, plunging deep within her body. She groaned and writhed, arching her hips to meet his relentless fingers.

He lifted his head from the burning kiss, and clenched his teeth in passionate fury. "Did he do this to you, your damned Lord Jamie?"

She was trembling too much to speak. She could feel her shift growing damp against her body. And still the delicious torment continued. She closed her eyes and abandoned herself to the hot waves of pleasure that swept her.

Then his fingers were gone. She opened her eyes to see him fumbling frantically to lift his shirt. He was hard and erect, frightening in his size and power. Not even Jamie . . .

"No," she whispered, torn between her fears and the hungry desire that throbbed in her loins.

"*Yes,* damn you," he growled. His eyes glowed with a wild, maddened light. "For the promise in every kiss you gave me." He clutched at her torn shift and ripped it to the hem. His hands went around her naked buttocks to lift her hips to his savage entry.

She cried out at his first hard thrust, caught by a wild, thrilling sensation she had never known before. His manhood filled her, and the feel of his burning flesh against hers was like a vibrant flame, consuming her. Then he began to move in her—hard, pulsing thrusts that left her breathless. A pounding rhythm of ecstasy that took her to ever-higher peaks of joy and left her sobbing for release, yet wishing he would never stop. She threw her arm across her mouth to still her cries.

He was now thrusting so violently that she could feel the hard deck rub against her back with every wild lunge. Soft, animal sounds burst from his throat, part pleasure, part pain. Through a haze of sensual delight, she watched him.

His handsome face was contorted into a grimace of agony and tension—head thrown back, eyes tightly closed, teeth clenched. He gave a final, frenzied thrust, his body claiming hers in a last wrenching explosion, and uttered a series of tortured cries. Then he was still.

"Ross," she whispered, her voice quivering with passion.

He leaned back on his haunches and stared down at her, his eyes wide with shock. Then his body began to tremble, a frightening, jerking movement that seemed to start deep within his chest and work its way to his arms, his shoulders, his head. He shook like a fevered man. While she watched in horror, the taut expression on his face crumpled into grief, and he began to sob.

"Forgive me!" he cried. "Forgive me." He buried his head in his crossed arms, shaking and moaning as though his heart would break.

Prudence watched him with sorrowful understanding as he continued to weep. This was the man who had prided himself on never shedding a tear at his wife's death. But perhaps the tears had been in him all this time, waiting for just such a violent release.

She eased out from under him, got to her knees, and took him in her arms. His grief was harrowing to behold—the powerful shoulders trembling beneath his shirt, the dreadful cries of pain—a strong man brought so low. "Of course I forgive you," she murmured, fighting her own tears.

He wept for a very long time—heart-wrenching sobs that broke her heart. She crooned words of comfort and rocked him like a child. At last his weeping ceased. She helped him to his feet, led him, unresisting, to the bunk, and urged him to find solace in sleep. He lay immobile, spent and staring sightlessly up at the beams.

She looked down at herself. Her shift was in tatters. She scarcely wanted to stop and find another; he needed her too much. She pulled off her torn garment and climbed into the bunk beside him. Gazing at his empty face, she suddenly thought of Toby Wedge. Was Ross also in some distant realm, lost to her?

She reached out and stroked his cheek with tender fingers, then began to sing a lullaby. A gentle, soothing tune. He sighed heavily and closed his eyes; in a few moments, he was asleep. She pulled up the blankets to cover them, and nestled against him with her naked body—giving and receiving warmth.

She felt strangely triumphant. Had she but known before, she thought in wonder. There had always been a sensitive, passionate heart beneath that cold exterior. She murmured a soft prayer, thanking God that she had been the one to find it.

Chapter Fourteen

Prudence sighed and settled herself more deeply into the mattress, deliberately lingering in that delicious state between sleeping and waking. Her body felt warm and contented, the glow intensified by the memory of Ross's kisses and caresses, his virile hardness within her. She had never thought that lying with a man could bring such pleasure.

She felt a pang of guilty disloyalty that brought her fully awake. God forgive her, she hadn't enjoyed the act with Jamie, though he had been far gentler in his lovemaking than Ross had been. Was it only because she had been frightened and inexperienced? But Ross's savage passion had frightened her as well—yet her body had responded in a way that still astonished her and brought a blush to her cheeks.

She shook off the unwelcome thoughts that crowded in. It was scarcely fair to measure one man against another. Jamie would prove as thrilling a lover when they were husband and wife. She was sure of it.

As for her *moral* conscience . . . She ignored the small voice within her. She felt little shame or guilt for what had happened with Ross. She had been beyond redemption the moment she'd succumbed to Jamie, and God was still punishing her for that. One more sin could scarcely damn her any more than she was already damned.

She closed her eyes and smiled dreamily, remembering the feel of Ross's body on hers, the taste of his hungry kisses. Surely that couldn't have been too great a sin. Not when he had so desperately needed release for his troubled soul, his pent-up heart.

And then—the dear man—to beg her forgiveness! How like him, to take the blame on his own head, as though she herself hadn't secretly yearned for him all these weeks. Hadn't hoped he would take her in his arms, and tell her how much he cared for her, and . . .

No! She mustn't allow such thoughts! She must remember Jamie, try to recapture the passion she had felt for him in those sweet days on the hillside. She groaned in anguish. But perhaps she'd only been lonely and unhappy, an innocent girl, ripe for his soft words and blandishments. Willing to believe in his love because she needed to be loved.

Wasn't that what Ross had suggested—that she was on a fool's errand? And now she was pinning her hopes for the future on Jamie, and saying good-bye forever to a man she half suspected she had begun to . . . Did she dare to use the word "love," even to herself?

She felt torn into a thousand pieces, and each piece a swirling confusion. Perhaps she should tell Ross of the babe, her urgent need to marry Jamie. Would he understand and forgive her for leaving? Would he confess that he loved her, and help her find a way to reclaim her son? Surely, after last night, he had *some* feeling for her.

Use the sense you were born with, Kitten. That's what Papa would have said. The only way she could have her child was through Jamie. There was no point in telling Ross anything. What could he do? If Grandpapa had scorned a country schoolmaster as beneath his family's standing, why would he listen to a mere ship's surgeon? Her only salvation lay in Jamie and his title.

She sighed in regret, putting aside her fanciful dreams. She looked at the clock on the desk: half after eight. She had packing to do, farewells to make. She clambered out of the bunk and stood up, shivering in her nakedness.

She smiled at the sight before her. Even after last night, Ross couldn't abandon his precise ways. There was her breakfast, as usual, laid squarely on the desk. Her basin of water, with soap and towel and tooth powder waiting. He had even folded her torn shift and placed it neatly on the bench. She pulled out her blue muslin gown and her other shift, then turned to her bathing. She scrubbed her face and hands and arms, then soaped her cloth again and washed her thighs and the delicate tuft of hair between her legs.

She had just dried herself and was reaching for her shift when the door opened.

"Your pardon." Ross closed the door and quickly turned his back on her. She could see the flush of scarlet on the edge of his jaw and his ear-lobe. She felt a surge of tenderness at his unexpected, little-boy shyness. Even after the intimacy of last night?

She slipped her shift over her head and stepped into her petticoat. "You needn't stand like that all day," she said with a small smile. "You must have packing."

He turned with reluctance, his face registering relief to see that she was decently covered again. "Yes. I should like to have our boxes on deck before we reach the dock. I have no wish to linger in Hackett's presence."

"I'll give you Martha's gown so you can pack it. I'll not return the ring until we're ashore."

"Yes, that's sensible." He bent and opened his sea chest. "You may keep Martha's stays, since you have no others."

"I thank you. But are you certain you don't want them?"

"No."

She couldn't believe they were speaking like this. As though last night had never happened. And there was so little time left—to tell him how much she cared for him, how their parting would grieve her. "Ross," she began softly.

He turned. She was looking into the eyes of a stranger, cool and remote. "Last night should never have happened," he said. "I deeply regret it. A moment of weakness . . . a foolish lapse."

Was that all it had signified to him? She bit her lip. Surely he didn't mean that. "Is it weakness to need another human being?"

" 'Tis weakness to give in to that need. To be ruled by one's baser passions as though we were no better than the animals."

She shook her head, feeling strangely rebuffed. "I don't believe that," she said.

He raised a condescending eyebrow. "My dear child, how little you know of the weakness of men."

The weakness of men? A few weeks of celibacy aboard ship scarcely explained his extraordinary behavior of last night. He had attacked her wildly, then sobbed in her arms like a helpless child.

"Weakness?" she asked. "Was that all it was?"

He shrugged. "Did you expect more?"

She turned away, crushed. She had expected a little tenderness, at the very least. Now she felt as soiled as one of Betsy's sister whores. "I quite understand," she said, her voice edged with bitter scorn. "Those few weeks of denial must have been very inconvenient for you, considering your *weakness.*"

He sighed heavily, as though she were a difficult child who needed explanations. "Until last night, I had not known a woman since Martha died," he said evenly. "I didn't wish to betray her memory."

"Oh." Her face fell and she sank into the chair. He had not even left her with one single illusion. His impassioned plea for forgiveness hadn't been directed to *her,* but to the ghost of his dead wife. If he felt the slightest remorse, it was because of Martha, not because of the way he had treated *her.* She struggled against her tears.

He relented at the sight of her woebegone face, and knelt at her feet. "Prudence. Dear girl. I'm sorry. We all have moments of madness. But there's no point in making more of it than what it was. I have my sweet memories of Martha. You have your Lord Jamie waiting for you."

"That 'scoundrel' who will break my heart?" she asked bitterly.

"No. That was cruel of me, to fill you with doubts. I feel sure he loves you as much as you love him. Go to him and be happy. As for last night . . . we were simply two lonely people. Dreaming of others. Let's part as friends."

She nodded and allowed him to pull her to her feet. He enclosed her in his arms and held her, and kissed her on the forehead. There was no passion in his embrace, in his kiss. Only tenderness and concern. She thought of Papa, and longed to feel comforted.

But all she felt was a hollow sadness, the thought that she had lost something precious in her life. And she would never find it again.

"Come, Toby, hold fast to my hand. Just one more step." Prudence tugged gently on Wedge's bandaged hand and pulled him into the sunshine of the deck. She still found herself walking with a rolling gait, though they had been at the dock for nearly two hours. "You can open your eyes now, Toby," she said, "and see what a fine day it is."

He giggled in relief and blinked his eyes. He stared up at the sky, then suddenly frowned. "No sunshine but hath some shadow."

"Not today. You shall stay with Dr. Manning, and be safe with him." She smiled. She had been pleased when Ross had said he would take Wedge into the wilderness with him. They were both lost souls who might profit from the companionship.

The deck was bustling with seamen, eager to be free and quit of the ship for a few weeks. Their faces were scrubbed shiny, their clothing brushed and mended. They laughed and joked among themselves, stamping their feet in impatience. On the forecastle, the marines had begun to assemble, lining up in neat ranks to be marched ashore; their scarlet uniforms were bright in the sun. The usual crowd of harlots waved and called out from the dock, grinning in anticipation of their profits. And perhaps, thought Prudence, remembering the London doxies, there were more than a few pickpockets among them.

The sun was strong. She tied on her straw hat and looked around the crowded deck for Ross. Their sea chests and Ross's medical supplies had been piled neatly on the gangway, but he was nowhere in sight. Perhaps he had already gone ashore to make arrangements for his cabin furniture to be taken from the ship. Or to see to the carriage that would take them to Williamsburg.

Beside her, Wedge suddenly let out a thin wail. "Oh, lookee, lookee! The devil's curse be on me now."

She gaped in alarm. He had begun to shake like an aspen tree in a high wind. "Toby! Merciful heaven, what is it?"

"Good morning, dear lady." The silken voice sounded like the slither of a snake above the happy babble of the crowd.

Prudence whirled to find Captain Hackett making his way through the officers on the quarterdeck and bearing down on them. With an anguished cry, Toby Wedge scurried behind Prudence and peered over her shoulder, cringing in fear.

She glared at Hackett. There was no longer a need to pretend civility. They were safely landed. "Go away, you monster."

He laughed—a mocking laugh that turned his handsome face into an ugly mask. "I see only one monster here. That trembling grotesque hiding behind your skirts. What a pleasure not to see his loathsome face ever again."

"Have you no shame?"

"For what? That he's mad as a March hare? He was scarcely more than an idiot when he came aboard. And time has proven him to be a coward as well. I hear he fears to climb a stair, let alone the rigging."

"Only because of you," she said bitterly.

He laughed again. "Because of me? Odds my life, I should be thanked by every captain in the navy. For having spared them the sight of his vile countenance."

"I wish you nothing but ill," she said, fixing him with a cold stare. "May God punish you as you deserve."

He clicked his tongue. "Such ingratitude, dear lady. Had I chosen to be difficult, you would have been *my* whore on this voyage, instead of Manning's."

"I'm Ross's wife!" she cried.

"Spare me that fiction," he drawled. "I only regret that I was unable to prove my suspicions. You cost me many a sleepless night. One slip by your so-called 'husband,' and you would have found yourself tied to my bunk, my hard prick in every orifice of that lush body of yours. You would have paid, thoroughly and well, for your insults to my person. And when I'd had my fill, I would have let the other men enjoy you. Noblesse oblige," he added with a sneer.

She was shaking in horror, her stomach churning with disgust and revulsion. "You vile man. To speak so to me . . ." She turned to Wedge. "Come, Toby, we'll wait near the forecastle."

She felt Hackett's hand on her sleeve, his fingers digging into her flesh. "Such charming outrage. But the voyage is over. The charade is over. I choose to speak to you now as the slut I have no doubt you are. And if ever our paths cross again, I vow I'll have what I want of you at last."

"You will remove your hand from my wife's arm, sir." Ross loomed before Hackett, his face like thunder.

The captain smiled, slid his hand down Prudence's arm and grasped her hand in his. "I was merely bidding this dear lady farewell." He bent to press his lips to her fingers, but she shuddered and pulled her hand away.

Ross's eyes glittered—icy blue crystals. "Did he say aught to disturb you, Martha?"

She bit her lip. He was wearing his sword and had put his hand on the hilt. But until he resigned his warrant, he was still under Hackett's authority, and in peril of his freedom. She shook her head, forcing her roiling emotions to cool. "No. No, of course not. But I find his presence . . . unwelcome."

He took her by the elbow. "Then come. I have a carriage ashore." He turned to Wedge. "You need have no fear. The man cannot harm you, ever again." He bowed to Hackett, his jaw still set in anger. "Your servant, sir."

He led them off the ship and into the waiting carriage. He sat in stony silence, his head buried on his chest, his thoughts seeming to be far away. Wedge babbled disjointedly all the way to town, swearing that "Cap'n" would pursue him and bring evil upon his head forever.

Prudence stared out at the countryside. The trees were tinged with the first soft reds and golds of September. A mournful harbinger of winter. The death of summer. She sighed. Why should her heart be so heavy, with Jamie less than a week away from her? What had happened to the sunny optimism that had kept her from despair all these months?

The carriage reached Williamsburg in a short time; it made its way up Duke of Gloucester Street and stopped at a tavern. The swinging sign above the door read "Raleigh Tavern," with a likeness of Sir Walter, himself, painted below.

Ross stirred himself at last. "I sent someone on to arrange rooms for me here," he said. "The stage north doesn't leave until this afternoon. Come and refresh yourself. We'll have dinner before you go."

They had a quiet, oddly strained dinner in Ross's parlor. Wedge sat alone, at a table near the window, and laughed and talked to himself. Ross and Prudence spoke about trifles, their eyes scarcely meeting. But when she removed Martha's ring from her finger and silently placed it on the cloth between them, all pretense of conversation ceased.

At length, Ross sighed and rose from his meal. "You should go now." He reached into his coat pocket and pulled out a small leather purse. "Here," he said gruffly. "You'll need this."

"Oh, but I can't take it. I have money."

"Not nearly enough," he growled. "Where will you stay at night? In some filthy country inn? Living on bread and cheese until you reach your Lord Jamie? Take it, damn it, and don't begin to quarrel with me again."

She bowed her head and took the purse from his hand. "Thank you." She hesitated. However often she had imagined this moment, she had not reckoned on the pain in her heart, her sad reluctance. "Ross . . ." How could she tell him how grateful she was for all he had done, how dear he had become to her? "I . . . I wish you peace in your solitude," was all she said.

He looked away. "I wish you happiness with your Lord Jamie."

She twisted her fingers together. "Will you kiss me good-bye?" she whispered.

He took her by the shoulders, bent his head, and planted a gentle kiss on her cheek. "The coach is waiting below. I've had your boxes put aboard."

"Thank you." She turned and picked up her straw hat.

Suddenly she felt his hands on her arms. He swung her around and pulled her roughly into his embrace. His mouth was firm and warm on hers, inhaling her lips as though he would never let her go.

She wrapped her arms around his neck and returned his kiss with all the passion in her yearning heart. *Beg me to stay,* she thought, *and I'll forswear my child.*

Instead, he pushed her away from him abruptly and clapped his hands to his sides, curling them into white-knuckled fists. His eyes were dark and stormy. "For God's sake, *go!* Go to the man you love."

Blinded by her tears, she stumbled down the stairs that would take her to the waiting carriage. And Jamie.

* * *

Ross threw down his book and stared out of the tavern window. The night sky was filled with clouds, scudding low. As if to warn of winter, a chill September wind had blown all day and rattled the panes. A dismal tattoo that had frightened Wedge and sent him scurrying to his bed in the little chamber that adjoined Ross's parlor. The first falling leaves of autumn had swirled in the cobbled courtyard below, and the branches of a nearby tree had tapped relentlessly against the glass, like ghostly creatures demanding entrance to his solitude.

He sighed heavily. How would he endure the loneliness of the wilderness, when this past week had seemed like an eternity without her?

One week. And there was nothing left to keep him here. His plans were made, his rough itinerary set. His obligation to the navy was over. He had even penned a note to Martha's cousins in Petersburg, assuring them that he would visit if his travels took him in their direction.

Martha. He threw himself into a chair and took her ring from his waistcoat pocket. He stared at it and tried to remember the softness of her gray eyes, her beauty by firelight, with the flames glinting off her long yellow hair. But the vision kept blurring, the gray eyes turning to bright, laughing green, the hair darkening to the color of the burnished leaves beyond the window.

He groaned and covered his face with his hand. One night of lust, of self-indulgence, and he was lost. A traitor to Martha's memory, giving in to an unforgivable weakness. A hunger he thought he'd suppressed.

But I'm only a man, he thought suddenly, filled with anguish. *No better than any other.* Scarcely the paragon of perfection he had tried to be. And perhaps God had put Prudence in his path to show him the folly of his overweening pride.

Well, he had the rest of his life to atone. The sooner he put Prudence out of his mind, the happier he would be. Buried in the silent stillness of the mountains and woods, he would rededicate himself to Martha's memory, remember again that she was his soul's mate in death as in life. And if his flesh was weak upon occasion, and he found the need to satisfy his body with the warm softness of a female, it would serve as a necessary corrective to his self-conceit. A reminder that he was only human. Surely Martha, watching from above, would understand and forgive.

As for Prudence, he was probably well rid of her, for his pride's sake. He still cringed when he remembered his helpless weeping that night. Thank the good Lord she had not spoken of it—one more weakness that made him burn with shame. He had humiliated himself and his manhood. And her continuing presence would only have reminded him of it. Still, he had to admit that the release of his grief had been helpful; he was sleeping better than he had in a year.

He stood up, threw another log on the fire, and poured himself a small glass of Madeira. He was filled with sudden fresh resolve, his thoughts clear and certain. The temptation of a woman like Prudence was the flame that had tempered his soul and made him stronger, God willing.

He would visit Shields Tavern tomorrow. There was a grizzled woodsman there who had spoken all week of an abandoned cabin on a high peak of the Shenandoah chain. If he could locate it, it would save him the trouble of building from the ground up. He and Wedge could repair it long before the snows came.

He stared into the crackling fire. Even the color of the flames reminded him of Prudence's hair. On the ship, she had washed it with collected rainwater, and the same soap he himself used. But it had always smelled of sunshine, even in the musty cabin. More than once, he had bent to inhale its sweetness while she slept.

No! he thought, *this is the way to madness.* The path to the secret hell that Wedge inhabited. It was time to forget her, once and for all. She was probably sleeping in her lover's arms by now, yielding her soft body to his caresses, sharing the warmth of ardent kisses. Telling him she loved him.

He picked up his book again, determined to finish the chapter before he slept.

A noise at the opposite side of the parlor startled him. Prudence stood in the dimness of the open doorway. She was trembling, and her windblown hair hung wild and loose about her face. Her eyes were large and dark; even from here, he could see the sparkle of tears that reflected the firelight. She closed the door and leaned up against it, her body quivering, her face crumpling into a mask of sorrow.

"I didn't know where else to go," she whispered.

He jumped from his chair and strode to her. "Great God Almighty. What the devil has happened?"

"He . . ." She sniffled and wiped at her eyes. "He's gone. Back to England." She bent her head and began to weep, her body shaking with deep sobs.

"Oh, my poor lass," he murmured, and folded her into the shelter of his arms.

Chapter Fifteen

Ross stroked her tangled hair with gentle fingers. "Tell me everything."

She shook her head. She was still too torn by grief to respond. Jamie was gone. And she would never see her sweet child again. She pressed her face against his chest, sobbing out her misery. "I don't . . . I don't know what I would have done if you . . ." she managed at last.

"Foolish child. We parted as friends. Where else would you go, if not to a friend?" He held her securely until her weeping had subsided. It was the first comfort she had known for days. That long, terrible coach ride back from the Potomac . . . her heart breaking, her tears suppressed for fear that once she started to weep she would never stop.

She lifted her head from his breast and sighed mournfully. "I've drenched your waistcoat."

He smiled in toleration and understanding. "A worthwhile sacrifice. Tell me what happened."

The recollection brought fresh tears. "I . . . I was less than a day from his plantation . . . We stopped at an inn. I asked the proprietor for directions. He told me that Jamie . . . God save me! He had sold the plantation. And returned home." She choked back a sob, overwhelmed by the bitter irony of her life. "He left for England before the end of May! If he came looking for me in my village when he arrived home, I had already gone to London. And no one to tell him where I was." She began to weep again. "My life is over," she moaned.

"Over? Where is the sunshine child who had such bright hopes for the future? And chided me for my darkness? Your life is scarcely over. Your happiness is merely delayed for a little longer."

"I have no strength left to hope."

"Then take my strength for a while, if you need it. Come. You're chilled to the bone. Sit by the fire."

He peeled off his coat and wrapped it around her shoulders, then led her to a chair before the hearth. He knelt at her feet, lifted her skirts to her knees, and removed her shoes and stockings. "Your toes are like ice," he said, rubbing them briskly between his palms. She leaned back in the chair and closed her eyes. Her body was beginning to warm after the coldness of the carriage, but her heart was still frozen, chilled by the enormity of her disaster.

"Where are your boxes?" he asked.

"I left them below." The coachman had refused to carry them up for her. She had counted out her last coins to pay for the carriage ride back to Williamsburg—and nothing left for a tip; he wasn't about to serve her further without compensation.

"I'll fetch them later. Have you had supper?"

"I'm not hungry."

He rose to his feet. "I have a bit of bread and cheese. And you'll take a glass of Madeira to warm you." Despite her protests, he pressed the food and drink on her, assuring her—as a physician—that she would feel better. Then he took the warming pan beside the fire, filled it with glowing coals, and turned to the door of his bedchamber. "You need a good night's rest to restore your spirits. Eat your supper. I shall warm the bed." He disappeared into the next room.

He was right, of course. She felt her hunger for the first time, even as she slaked it. Felt the panic that had gripped her for days slowly fade away. The future no longer appeared so black. Somehow, she would find Jamie again. He had spoken of a house in London. She didn't know where, but she knew of his country seat in Berkshire; hadn't she sent many a desperate letter to that address?

Ross returned to the parlor. "Come. While the sheets are still warm." He pulled her to her feet and began to work on the fastenings of her gown, his surgeon's hands deft and sure. She gave herself over to his tender care, feeling comforted and protected. Like a child finding solace in the benevolence of a parent.

He stripped off her gown and petticoat, then bent to the laces of her stays. She looked down at her bosom as he worked; the confident fingers had begun to slow and tremble. He removed the stays, one hand lingering for a moment to caress her breast through her shift.

She shivered at his touch. And when the hand moved upward to stroke the bare flesh above the line of her shift, she let it stay. He ran his fingers across her neck, explored the hollow of her throat, followed the ridge of her collarbone to her shoulder.

He caught her glance. His eyes were blue pools of desire, his chest rising and falling with labored breaths. He hesitated, then planted a feathery kiss on her shoulder.

She moaned softly and let her head fall back; her body suddenly ached with a hungry need that surprised her. How sweet to be petted and fondled. To pretend that he cared for her, even if he was merely reacting to the momentary desires of the flesh. She fumbled for his hand and placed it on her heaving bosom.

Encouraged by her seeming surrender, he took her mouth in a tentative kiss, his lips closed and stroking lightly across hers. When she responded by opening her mouth, he wrapped his arms around her and plunged his tongue between her lips. His hands slid down her back to cup her buttocks and press her hips against his straining loins. She sighed and slipped her arms around his neck. She would never grow tired of his kisses.

He kissed her thoroughly and deeply, his teasing tongue rousing her senses, his warm, roving hands stirring her body to a hot intensity of longing. At last he untwined her hands from his neck, stepped back, and tugged at the strings of her shift.

He slipped the garment from her shoulders, stopping to kiss the soft flesh exposed, then pushed it down her body to the floor. He explored her naked skin with his hands—soft and sensuous caresses, touching every part of her, that made her tremble. Then he dropped to his knees and put his hands on her hips. His burning mouth tasted the quivering flesh of her belly, then shifted lower to catch the sensitive curls below. He nipped softly at the delicate hairs, his teeth like sharp points of fire, until she cried out in pleasure.

He rose abruptly to his feet and lifted her in his arms. He carried her to the next room and laid her across the bed. The room was in shadow, lit by a single candle. His strong, handsome face, made soft by the dim light, warmed her with its tenderness.

He kicked off his shoes and lay down beside her. His hand explored her breasts, scratching tantalizingly at her nipples until she writhed and strained against his fingers. He traced a path with his hand down her body, stroked her thighs, and gently parted her legs. He put his finger within her and found a sensitive spot, rubbing it with ever-increasing intensity until she was maddened by desire and aching need.

She reached out to his body, hesitated shyly, then placed her hand against his breeches. His hardness filled her with a wondrous joy, knowing his desire was as strong as hers.

He started at her bold caress and jumped to his feet, urgent hands tearing at his clothing. She watched him through half-closed eyes as she drifted in a mist of sated pleasure—and pleasure anticipated. His body was wonderfully formed, the broad shoulders thrilling her with their contained power. And the sight of his erect manhood made her catch her breath, hungering to feel its length within her.

She stretched out yearning arms to him, and sighed when he planted his body atop hers. His hard chest pressed against her breasts, the warmth of the intimate contact—flesh to flesh—a thrill that only increased the mad pounding of her heart.

"Open for me, sweet Prudence," he said in a hoarse voice.

She complied, spreading her legs wide to receive him. His entry was silky and gentle, a soft, sensual glide, a sweet possession that soothed and excited her at the same time. And when he began to move in her, it was with a restrained rhythm that only slowly floated her into a realm of deep satisfaction, every moment a growing delight.

It was just at the end, when his passions overwhelmed him, that his thrusts became hard and driving. She gasped in ecstasy, her body quivering, and felt the heat rise from her loins to her face. She was swept by a spasm of feeling that seemed to explode in her like a great wave crashing against the shore. At the same moment, he cried out and shuddered, his body shaking convulsively in the paroxysm of his final release.

He collapsed against her and buried his head in the softness of her neck. "I had forgot how sweet a woman's body could be," he said. His strong voice shook with emotion.

She sighed. *She* had not known a man's body could bring such delight. For the first time, she wondered if this was the pleasure Betsy took in her livelihood.

He stirred at last, seeming reluctant to withdraw from her. "Sleep now," he said. "There are plans to be made on the morrow." He settled them both within the blankets, took her in his arms, and closed his eyes. His body was warm; the hair on his chest tickled pleasantly against her cheek.

"Ross?" she whispered.

He opened his eyes. "Be at peace, Prudence. We'll find your Lord Jamie."

She reached out and curled her hand around his nape, pulling his head to hers, and kissed him softly on the mouth. "Thank you," she murmured.

But as she drifted off to sleep, she wondered if her thanks were for his friendship, his kind understanding. Or for the sinful pleasure he had given to her.

She awoke alone in the bed to find the sun streaming through the window. And Martha's ring on her finger.

She frowned and touched the gold band, turning it round and round. Why should Ross have done such a thing? Did it make it easier for him to make love to her, if he could pretend that she was Martha? That thought disquieted her more than she cared to admit.

She sighed and sat up, then giggled. As though there had been no pause in their routine, Ross had left her breakfast on a small table beside the bed. Sweet cakes and a pot of tea, resting on a warmer. She was suddenly ravenous; after shipboard food, even such simple fare still seemed like a banquet.

She wrapped the coverlet around herself, took a chair near the table, and poured herself a cup of tea. She was just savoring the last morsel of cake, thickly spread with butter, when she heard the toot of Toby Wedge's pipe in the adjoining parlor. There was a soft tap on the door, then Ross came into the room, swirling off his cloak and tossing his hat on a table.

"It feels like autumn in Gloucestershire this morning. We shall have to buy you a mantle." He smiled. "And combs, I think. Though Wedge has decided to carve you a pair as soon as his fingers heal. But I'm not supposed to tell."

She stared into his face, seeking some sign, some acknowledgment of last night. She saw nothing there but pleasant goodwill and a certain distance. She bit her lip. Lovers by night, but diffident friends by day? She held up her hand and tapped the ring on her finger. "Why did you give this to me again?"

"Because, my dear child, Mr. and Mrs. Ross Manning leave for London in a fortnight, sailing on a merchant ship. In the meantime, it would scarcely do for us to share these rooms as aught but husband and wife."

She found herself trembling. "For . . . for London?"

"Can you think of another way to rejoin your beloved Lord Jamie?"

"But . . . the expense! Are you so very rich?"

"Not at all. But I have enough. Come. Get dressed. We have shops to visit."

Her jaw sagged. "Shops?" she echoed.

"Mrs. Manning can scarcely be seen in the capital of Virginia with shabby gowns. Or appear at social functions. Do you dance?"

She was almost speechless. "A little," she said in a soft croak.

"Good. I had made the acquaintance the other day of a member of the House of Burgesses. He was kind enough to invite me to a ball in honor of the opening of the October session. I declined, at the time. But now that you're here . . ."

She gulped back her sudden rush of emotion. "Why are you so good to me?"

He looked surprised. "I? 'Tis you who are good and kind. And generous," he added.

Generous? she thought in dismay. For the gift of her body, no doubt. That's what he had meant. Her heart sank in disappointment. For the first time, she felt ashamed of her wanton behavior. She drew the coverlet more tightly around her nakedness. "You had a right to last night," she said stiffly. "After all you've done for me."

His brow darkened. "And was there no joy for *you?*"

"Yes, of course!" The words burst from her before she had a chance to think. She bent her head, feeling a hot flush steal over her cheeks.

He laughed—a cynical chuckle. "You're still too innocent, my dear Prudence. You haven't yet learned to dissemble, as most women do."

She covered her eyes with her hand, stanching her sudden tears. She felt no better than a whore.

"Damn my liver," he growled. "There will be no more weeping for your Jamie. I'm prepared to give you over to his tender keeping, but I'll not endure your tears. 'Tis foolish to weep for the past." His face twisted in sudden pain and he turned away abruptly, shoulders sagging. "It cannot be undone." There was torment in his voice.

She stared at his melancholy form. He was not thinking of *her* tears. He was regretting his own. And remembering Martha.

All this time, she thought with remorse, and she had not recalled that he yearned to be alone to mourn in peace. "But what of your plans?" she asked, her heart contracting with guilt. "Your cabin in the mountains?"

"They will still be waiting when I return." He turned, his impassive mask safely in place. "Now get dressed, before Wedge's piping drives me mad this morning."

"Oh, I cannot decide!" Prudence fingered the pale apricot satin gown, then frowned and held up the skirts of the lavender silk.

Ross tipped back in his chair and smiled. "Both of them, of course. You shall wear the apricot to the ball." He turned to the hovering mantua-maker, a long-nosed woman with a haughty air. "As soon as the stay-maker sends over the stays he is fashioning for Mrs. Manning, you may fit the gowns to them. And since the apricot is to be worn to a ball, I want a second stomacher, embroidered in silver. And a flounced hoop."

Prudence stared at him in surprise. It seemed odd for a humble surgeon to concern himself with the niceties of women's fashions. "Are you an expert on female attire?"

He shrugged. "I have the eye of a would-be artist, I suppose." He rose from his chair and replaced his cocked hat, giving the mantua-maker a proud and lordly nod.

She dropped her haughty pose and curtsied humbly. "It will be done to your order, sir. Your custom will always be welcome in my shop. And that of your lady wife."

"Two days' time," he commanded. "I shall expect you or your minions at the Raleigh Tavern, with the gowns. In perfect order." He turned and gave Prudence his arm. "Come, madam."

She felt like a princess as he escorted her out the door. They had spent the day along the length of Duke of Gloucester Street, working their way among the crowds and the bawling peddlers, stopping at a shop every time something caught Ross's eye. He had bought her shoes, a lace neckerchief, a cloak. A pair of tortoiseshell combs for her hair. An armful of fine linen—shifts and stockings and neckerchiefs. Even a carved and painted fan to carry at the ball. She was accustomed to his self-assurance by now, but he had astonished her nonetheless. He had swept into every shop like a man who expected only the finest service. And, consequently, had received it. But the expense . . . !

"I didn't need both gowns," she said. "I already had more than enough, with the flowered calico that we bought this morning."

"My artist's eye again. I couldn't decide which color flattered you more."

"That scarcely seems a reason to . . ."

He cut her off with a wave of his hand. "Enough. Wedge looks restless." He gestured to Toby Wedge, who sat perched on the edge of a horse trough, frowning and muttering to himself. "Well, Toby, are you ready for supper?"

"You've been very patient," added Prudence. Wedge had insisted on spending the day with them, trailing down the street behind them like a loyal puppy. He had smiled, and played his pipe with his injured hands, and babbled on about good omens and bad. All punctuated by happy, childish laughter. But now the smile was gone. "What ails you, Toby?" she said with concern.

He hunched his shoulders and darted his eyes up and down the long street. "He be here. Watchin' me."

"Who is watching you?"

"Why, *Cap'n,* lady."

Ross shook his head. "He's not here."

"Aye, and he is! Just waitin' to get poor Toby."

Ross rolled his eyes. "Great God Almighty, I tell you the man is not here! You're safe from him."

"How can you be sure?" asked Prudence.

"I met Lieutenant Elliot at an ordinary the other day. He told me Hackett has gone to Norfolk to visit friends while the *Chichester* is in port."

Wedge had already found his escape from his nemesis; he was now staring off into space. Lost in a world of his own. "Bare words buy no barley," he muttered.

Ross patted the top of his snowy head. "Yes, yes, of course. But come along, and I'll soon buy you supper."

They strolled down Duke of Gloucester Street, watching the sun set behind the red brick building of the College of William and Mary. Ross seemed in no hurry, stopping to point out the magnificent Governor's Palace, a pretty lane, an orderly garden before a neat, shingled cottage.

" 'Tis a fair city," he said. "Nearly two hundred families, I'm told. I wonder more poor souls, trapped in the squalor of London, don't seek their fortunes in this land."

"Were you here before?"

"No. But I had little save time on my hands when I first arrived. Toby and I wandered the streets like homeless wraiths."

The mention of his name seemed to brighten Wedge, who had moped along, just behind them, kicking at the cobbles of the street. "He that hath most time, hath none to lose," he said cheerily.

Ross sighed. "Aye, Wedge. Sometimes there is more truth than you know in that addled brain of yours."

As darkness descended, they found a quiet inn on Prince George Street, and a snug table in a dim, candlelit corner. Wedge ate his supper before the hearth, still prattling to himself, until the innkeeper's cat came and hopped into his lap. He grinned happily and tucked the animal into the crook of his arm, feeding it morsels of food from his plate.

Prudence looked down at her own plate. Roast goose with oyster sauce. The most costly dish on the menu. And Ross had ordered it for them without a moment's hesitation. *He must have been a very successful surgeon,* she thought. Only accustomed to the best, before he had chosen to renounce his life's work. Jamie, for all his noble title, had been content with an ordinary chop or two, the one time he had treated Prudence to dinner at an out-of-the-way country inn.

Ross glanced across the room at Toby Wedge. "A good man, that. With a strong back. He'll be a fine helpmeet in the wilderness."

"But you had wanted to be alone."

" 'Twill be one and the same. That poor devil. His moments of clarity are few."

"And you'll be content?"

His expression was cool and distant. "Why shouldn't I be? There's little to please me in this life."

"There's your skill as a surgeon! How can you give it up?"

He hesitated, seeming to reflect on her words. " 'Twill be difficult, I warrant. But the peace I find will be worth the price."

She could scarcely comprehend such a dark view of life. "You might as well be dead!" she exclaimed.

He gave a cynical laugh. "That thought has crossed my mind more than once in the past year. Though I doubt you would understand, with your cheerful faith in mankind."

"Why must you stand in judgment of the world? Are you so perfect? Forgive your father and go back to your surgery, where you belong."

He slapped his hand on the table and glared at her. "If ever you speak of my father again, I swear I'll strike you down on the spot!"

She gulped and averted her eyes. There was no reaching him. He would burn with hatred for the rest of his days. She bent to her food, hoping that her passive silence would serve to cool his anger. She scarcely wished to end such a wonderful day on a note of acrimony. She ate in silence; the meal had lost its savor.

At last, she ventured to speak. "You were very kind to me today. I thank you for all my lovely clothes."

He grunted, but said nothing.

She tried again. "Will I meet the governor at the ball?"

He relented, and managed a small smile. "No. I'm told that Governor Sir William Gooch returned to England last fall, because of his health."

Her face fell. "Then I won't get to dance in that beautiful palace?"

"Alas, no. 'Tis closed upon his return. But the ball is being held in the Apollo Room of the Raleigh, where they hold the finest assemblies. And you'll meet His Excellency, Mr. Thomas Lee, the president of the Council of Virginia, who is presiding in the absence of Sir William. And the company will be splendid."

She found it difficult to contain her rising excitement. Prudence Allbright, schoolmaster's daughter, at a great ball! This morning, when Ross had spoken of it, it had seemed unreal. But now, remembering the splendor of all her new finery, she was beginning to accept the wondrous reality. "I can scarcely wait! When is it?"

He shook his head in mock disapproval, but his mouth twitched. "Madcap child. You'll have to curb your impatience. 'Tis not until the twelfth. The night before we sail for England."

She sighed. "Nearly a fortnight? I shall never be able to wait that long."

"Fortunately, they say the theaters here are as fine as any in London. I shall keep you amused." He raised a sardonic eyebrow. "And of course there are the shops. I never knew a woman who didn't think there was always one more frippery she couldn't live without."

She blushed. She had seen an exquisite pair of gloves, but had been too shy to ask him. Not after all his generosity. And he had spent so much money on her already. Still, he seemed to be offering more. "Well, there was a pair . . ." she began.

Across the room, Toby Wedge let out a cry. "A bad omen. A bad omen!" He stared in horror at the cat, who had leapt from his arms and was now standing on the table, licking the remains of his supper.

Ross beckoned impatiently to him. "What is it, Toby?"

Wedge shuffled across the room, shaking his head. "It be a bad omen, when a cat jumps on table. My life on't." He was quivering in alarm.

Ross sighed and turned to Prudence. "I see we shall have to leave before they bring the sweet." He looked down at her nearly empty plate. "Have you almost done?"

She put down her fork and knife and pushed her plate away. "Yes, of course. The sooner we escape Toby's cat, the better for the poor man."

"We'll go back to the Raleigh Tavern and have them send up a sweet to our rooms. And an arrack punch, I think. They say the concoction mixed by our estimable innkeeper, Mr. Wetherburn, cannot be bettered in all the Colonies."

He paid the supper tariff, helped Prudence on with her new cloak, and escorted her onto the street, urging Wedge to compose himself and follow.

The sky was bright with stars, the air crisp and cold, pungent with the scent of dead leaves. They crunched under their feet as they made their way back to Duke of Gloucester Street. The long, straight stretch of road was lit along its entire length with twinkling lanterns, and many a cottage and tavern window sparkled with candlelight.

Prudence breathed deeply of the night air, filled with serene contentment. If Jamie and her baby still awaited, she could have found no better companion than Ross to sweeten the intervening days.

Ross hailed a passing hackney coach, and they returned to the Raleigh Tavern. It took longer than usual to guide Wedge up the stairs, his eyes closed in panic. But eventually they were snugly settled in Ross's parlor, a bowl of flaming punch before them. They sipped the heady brew and nibbled on the candied walnuts that Mr. Wetherburn had provided, all the while recalling with much laughter their adventures in the shops.

Toby Wedge kept to himself. He squatted on his thick haunches before the fire and stared into the crackling flames. No cajolery would budge him, no lighthearted teasing stir him out of his dark mood. The cat on the table had been a bad omen.

Ross sighed in defeat and took up his sketching folio. He looked at Prudence, sitting comfortably in her high-backed grandfather's chair, and opened the book to a fresh page. "Stay as you are," he said. "I want to draw you."

"Let me fetch a bit of mending first."

"Mending?" He scowled. "There are servants in the inn who can do it for you. Damn it, I'll not have you working like a sempstress!"

"I thought you were a tyrant aboard ship. But on land . . . bless me! You should be wearing a coronet, you're so high-handed." She laughed gently to soften the sting of her words.

He glared at her for a moment, then his face relaxed into a sour smile. "I only meant that there's no call for you to work. I can afford to pay for your needs."

"My *need* is for fine needlework, to keep my fingers occupied. Nothing more. 'Tis a gentlewoman's pursuit. Absent that, I thought I might mend."

He made a rumbling noise in his throat, clearly embarrassed by his hasty and peevish words. "I'll give you pocket money in the morning," he muttered. "You can buy what you need."

She folded her hands together, placed them in her lap, and smiled mischievously. "Then you may draw me. Sans needlework, since it offends your delicate sensibilities."

"Saucy wench," he grumbled, and picked up his pencil.

The punch had made her giddy. And wicked. "I see you have a new folio," she said.

"Yes. I've been sketching the houses on the street. And the Governor's Palace."

She kept her voice as innocent as she could. "What happened to your old folio?"

The pencil stopped moving. He glanced up at her, looked away quickly, and cleared his throat again. " 'Twas not my best work," he said at last. "I threw it away."

Liar! she thought. Whatever his feelings for her, there had been too much tenderness, too much care in his drawings of her for him to discard them. "I don't believe . . ." she began.

He cut her off, clearly uncomfortable with the path of her conversation. "Be still," he commanded. "I can't draw you if you chatter."

They spent the next hour in companionable silence. The only sounds in the room were the scratch of his pencil and the occasional mutterings from Wedge beside the fire, mumbling that the cat—a bad omen—was surely Hackett's incarnation.

Changing her pose each time Ross directed, Prudence found his drawing of her a strangely sensuous experience—to know that he studied her so carefully, his intense blue eyes roaming her face and form.

At last he sighed, put down his pencil and rubbed his eyes. "Enough. To bed." He looked over at Wedge. "Come, Toby. Time to seek your rest."

Wedge turned, his unlovely face twisted in dismay. "I *can't,* d'ye see me? Cap'n be in my room. The cat foretold it."

"Nonsense. Come. We'll go in together. I shall look under the bed and behind the cabinet. I'll not leave you alone until you're sure you're safe."

While Ross accompanied a fearful Wedge into his little bedchamber, Prudence waited anxiously in the parlor. "Well?" she asked, when Ross finally emerged from the room.

"I've got him safely tucked in. But he wants the little skylark to sing him a song before he sleeps."

Prudence tiptoed into Toby's small room. He lay in bed—his blankets drawn up to his neck, his large body quivering, his frightened eyes darting about the room. She knelt beside him and stroked his forehead, then began to sing. A gentle lullaby her mother had sung to her many a time.

After a little while, his trembling ceased, his eyes closed. Like an innocent babe, he drifted off to sleep. Prudence kissed him tenderly on the cheek, blew out his candle, and left him to his troubled dreams.

The parlor was empty. The candles were extinguished, the hearthfire banked for the night. She crossed the room and opened the door to the bedchamber.

By the dim light of the fireplace, she could just see Ross. He was sitting up in the bed, the blankets pulled up to his waist. His powerful chest was bare, the naked skin golden in the firelight; his shirt was laid neatly across the back of a chair. The sheets of the bed on Prudence's side had been folded back—welcoming and inviting.

Ross patted the bed beside him and looked at her. His face was blank, telling her nothing. She stood motionless in the doorway, her heart beginning to thump.

He patted the bed again, a little less patiently. "Come to bed, woman," he growled.

Chapter
Sixteen

Prudence hesitated, her surprise warring with her rising desire. His seductive body, those arresting eyes, even the rich, deep tone of his voice—so sure in its command—beguiled her. Last night had been a sensual delight. Had it only been her overwrought emotions that had stirred her? She yearned to know if he could raise her to the same heights of delicious pleasure again.

Still, she wondered, how had it come to this? His easy assumption that her presence in his rooms meant her presence in his bed as well. The small, rebel voice within her balked at acceding to his wishes so easily. He had gone from a man who disdained a woman's caress to a man who demanded a woman's surrender. She pursed her lips and frowned. "Do I have a choice in these . . . sleeping arrangements?"

She steeled herself for his stern arguments, for the authoritative lecture that would crush her resistance. She had retreated more than once in the face of his overbearing manner, yielding to his wishes as she had to Grandpapa.

Instead of anger, his handsome face registered surprise. "A choice? Of course you do. You're not a child."

"Thank you," she said with an edge to her voice. At least he granted her *that*.

His expression was filled with gentle concern. "Does it displease you, to lie with me?"

She hesitated. "No."

"And do you find satisfaction in my embrace?"

She was beginning to waver. "Y-yes."

He held out his hand to her. "Come here."

She moved reluctantly across the room to stand beside the bed. He took her hand in his. His long fingers stroked hers, tracing a path across each knuckle. His touch was as light as the kiss of an April breeze. She shivered, imagining that sensuous touch on her body. Then he turned her hand upward and planted a soft kiss on her palm. "Your hand is as sweet as your lips. Sweet as your nature. You must have been a delightful child."

She chewed on her lip. "No. I was a trial."

He laughed softly. "I scarce believe that," he said. "I find great joy in you. In your nature . . . and in your body. More than I would have imagined."

She was crumbling before the onslaught of his fingers, his tender words. "Ross, I . . ."

He smiled, and she was undone. His dimples made him look like a playful youth. "Come to bed," he whispered.

She nodded dumbly, and moved toward the dimmest corner of the room to shed her clothes.

"Stand before the fire, and let me watch you," he said. "The light makes a wonder of your hair."

As she undressed, she felt as she had when he was drawing her—excited, a little frightened, proud to be the object of his scrutiny. *Oh, Papa,* she thought, *if this be vanity, how can it feel so wonderful? So right and natural?* Even after she stood naked, she lingered by the fire, glorying in his eyes upon her body.

But when he beckoned to her, she returned to the bed and climbed in beside him. She reached down to pull up the blankets.

"No," he said, leaning over to stop her hands. He pressed her back against the pillow and ran unhurried fingers through her hair, arranging the long curls like a halo about her face. He traced the line of her brows, drew his forefinger across the bridge of her nose, stroked her trembling lips as though the artist in him would capture her likeness by the mere touch. His hands moved down to cup her breasts and caress their round fullness. "I should like to draw you like this," he murmured. "You're perfection itself."

His hands were worshipful as they roamed her body, doing honor to every soft curve. She quivered and sighed and closed her eyes, her flesh on fire from his touch. He slid his hands down her breasts, wrapped his fingers around her waist as though he were taking her measure, fondled the triangle of curls, smoothed her thighs and trembling limbs. He stroked her shoulders and limp arms, then drew fluttery, tantalizing circles on her palms that sent shocks of delight pulsing through her body. She moaned softly, praying that his magical hands would never cease their journey.

But he clearly yearned for new territory to explore. He rolled her gently onto her stomach and laid his palm against the small of her back. His hands moved upward to caress her shoulders; then one finger traced an enchanting zigzag down the line of her spine. He scratched provocatively at a spot just below her shoulder blade. "Queer little scar. And climbing a tree? Against your parents' wishes, no doubt."

She nodded in silence, too enraptured to speak. She closed her arms around the pillow and hugged it to her breasts.

"Naughty hoyden," he scolded. She felt a gentle slap to her backside, and then his hands curled around the soft mounds, teasing with sensual caresses. She wriggled in impatient delight, wondering how much more of this delicious torment she could endure.

His fingers burrowed deep between her legs, finding her moist, quivering core. She gasped in ecstasy as his fingers plunged within her. Her body was on fire with desire. She wrenched away from his hand and turned over, spreading her legs wide to receive him. "Oh, please," she breathed.

He gave a small chuckle and leaned back on his haunches. "I only wished for you to be certain that you've made the right choice."

"You villain," she said, wondering how she could feel worshiped and humbled all at the same time.

She looked at his tense body, looming in the dim light from the fire. His member was hard and erect. She thought that he would seek his release at last, and free her own body from its longing. Instead, he hesitated, kneeling above her, then moved away, his expression grown bleak and strange.

"Ross?" She frowned in concern and scrambled to her knees, facing him.

He stared deeply into her eyes, and then he sighed—a sound of yearning and sadness, like a starving man begging for a crumb. He lifted her hand in trembling fingers and brought it to his chest. "Touch me," he said in an uncertain whisper.

She felt her heart constrict in her breast, filled with a sudden understanding and pity. *How isolated and alone we are in this world,* she thought. She had felt a vague loneliness since Papa had died. An unknown and unknowable discontent. Longing for something she didn't even understand.

But Ross . . . For two years he had filled his soul with the daily warmth of an embrace, softly caressing hands, the touch of a woman who had loved him. And since her death, he had renounced it all; his body had not known the sweetness of a woman's hands for a year.

How many nights, she wondered in sympathy, had he lain awake in his empty bed, feeling cold and disjoined from humankind? With Jamie, the act of love had seemed to be the culmination of all his desires; for Ross, it was perhaps merely the adjunct to a far greater need: the warm security, the tender connection to another human body.

And, absent that, he had chosen isolation.

Understanding of his loss guided her inexperienced hands. She prodded him gently onto his back and perched above him, eager to return some measure of the comfort he had given to her. She caressed his face—long, soothing strokes—and watched the haunted look fade from his eyes. She ran her hands along his arms, his shoulders and chest, taking joy from the masculine strength that rippled beneath her fingertips. She circled the soft buds of his breasts and marveled when they hardened under her touch. And when he moaned in pleasure, she bent her head and kissed the rigid points. His body quivered beneath her mouth.

In growing delight, she caressed his body in places that she had thought herself too shy to touch. The segmented ridges of his belly, the soft warmth of his navel, his muscled thighs and hips. And each brush of her fingers was followed by a sigh from him that brought her as much pleasure as when he had touched her.

But there was still one part of him that made her uncertain. Was it too wicked of her to touch him *there?* Would he think her no better than a whore, should she be so bold? She hesitated, torn with fear, then ran her finger along the length of his manhood. The skin was dry and hot, exciting her senses. He groaned and gritted his teeth, his face contorted with sweet agony. Emboldened, she wrapped her fingers around him and gave a hard squeeze.

"Christ Jesus," he muttered. He reached out, put his hands around her waist, and lifted her to straddle his supine body. With a savage grunt, he forced her body down on his erect member, filling her with his fierce hardness. She cried out at the sudden rush of exquisite feeling that radiated from her loins, and pressed down with all her might to enclose him more deeply.

She rode him with all the frenzied passion in her, with nothing but instinct to guide her. His hands kneaded her breasts, hard and demanding, while his hips rose to hers in ever more violent spasms. Her long hair tumbled around her face and brushed against his straining arms, caught in her open mouth, curtained his impassioned face from her gaze. She closed her eyes, the better to focus on the exquisite pleasure of her body.

Of a sudden, the world exploded behind her closed eyes in a luminous glow of color, and a sob of joy burst from her throat. *Let me die like this,* she thought, as she felt his warmth flood her, and her throbbing body slowly stilled to a joyous and heart-swelling contentment.

She awoke to the pungent, welcome smell of coffee. An unfamiliar treat. She stretched luxuriously and glanced over at her waiting breakfast tray. She wondered if Martha had known what a fortunate wife she was: an eminently satisfying lover, and breakfast in the morning. That was a disquieting thought; it filled her with unreasoning envy of a dead woman.

She wrapped herself in the coverlet and sat down in front of the table. The lavish breakfast plate made her mouth water. Eggs and bacon and thick pieces of toast. She poured her coffee and took a tentative sip. Sweetened with a great deal of sugar. He had even guessed that she would like it that way.

She sighed in satisfaction and let her eyes stray around the handsome room. Surely it was the finest in the inn, with polished mahogany tables and inlaid chests, well-upholstered chairs, and fine embroidered hangings at the window and tester bed. Was there another woman in all of Williamsburg who lived as well as she did?

Oh, Kitten! She could almost hear her father's chiding voice. Envy of Martha, and now overweening pride? And surely gluttony, for the joy she was taking in her breakfast. Was there another mortal sin she could commit today?

She glanced over at the rumpled bed and felt her face flaming with remembrance. He had been insatiable last night, scarcely waiting for her passions to cool before taking her body again in unhurried delight. She turned her head away from the bed. Best not to dwell on *that* sin.

Her eye was caught by a pile of packages and boxes near the door. All her purchases from yesterday, save for the two gowns that would arrive tomorrow. Her heart flooded with gratitude for all of Ross's kindnesses. Since Papa's death, she had not known such warm generosity.

But wait. She frowned in sudden, disturbing thought. What was it Betsy had said? A gift for a treasure. A trinket for the chance to . . . the coarse word made her cringe. To poke a woman. Ross had surely paid well for his nighttime pleasures. And if he should demand more of her, how could she refuse? It was her part of the bargain, a business contract, and one she had willingly entered into the moment she had accepted his gifts.

She sighed, more than a little uneasy with her body's warm contentment. If this was whoredom, it was scarcely the cold covenant that Betsy claimed.

Besides, she thought, trying to justify her wanton behavior, to answer the whisper of her conscience, Ross needed her. At least her willing body. When they had finally kissed good night in the early morning hours, she had seen such humble gratitude in his eyes that it had nearly broken her heart. Even without his generous gifts, she wasn't sure she would have refused him last night. Or would refuse him if he asked again. She had restored to him a little of what he had lost with his wife's death. If he went off into the wilderness with more tranquility, thanks to her, she would consider it a bounty. No one could replace his wife in his heart, but she prayed that she had brought him a little peace of mind.

Charity, Papa, she thought. *'Tis naught but charity.* A holy virtue to off-set her woeful failings.

And Ross was helping her to return home. For that kindness alone, didn't she owe him anything he asked of her? Jamie and her baby. She thought of the sweet infant, nestling in her arms, and felt herself over-whelmed with sudden grief. She tried to persuade herself that all would end happily. That it was foolish to be sad.

In vain. The vision of that dear, pink face, eyes upturned to her voice, filled her with a longing that could not be assuaged. Her arms felt empty. Her breasts, that had nursed him, ached with the milk that had long since run dry.

The glorious breakfast no longer tempted her. She pushed aside the tray, buried her arms and head on the table, and sobbed bitterly.

Ross scowled as he mounted the stairs. That damned shoemaker had been insolent beyond belief! Telling him that Prudence's shoes might not be ready in time for the ball. The bloody idiot had almost three days to do the job. And then to suggest that it was *his* fault, for not having thought of the lady's footwear before this . . . Well, damn the man! He'd find another, not so ready to carp!

He scuffed his shoe on the carpet of the stair and swore softly. His foul mood this morning—if he admitted it to himself—had very little to do with the cobbler. It was Prudence who was driving him mad.

They had gone to the theater four times in the week and a half since she'd arrived. And supped at cozy taverns. And walked through the au-tumn twilight, shopped and rode in carriages up and down the cobbled streets. And always she was laughing and happy.

And then, afterward . . . He gritted his teeth. Night after night, she had come to bed at his command. Willingly, joyously. Like a practiced whore. She had allowed him to do things in bed that Martha, even after years of intimacy, had been too shy and fearful to allow. Had touched and caressed him shamelessly, rousing his body to a state of fleshly ex-citement he had not thought possible.

He swore again. Had that damned lover of hers taught her to be so wan-ton? Had she found as much pleasure with her Lord Jamie? Or *more?* That was a disturbing thought. He suddenly felt like an inexperienced fool, cursing his high-minded years of virginity while his comrades had learned how to please a woman.

Not that the little baggage didn't enjoy his lovemaking! Wherever her heart might lie, her body luxuriated in their nightly romps. She sighed and cried out in ecstasy, never tiring in his arms, no matter how often he wanted her.

"Damn my liver," he muttered. Why was he tormenting himself? He was taking her back to the man she *loved*. For all he knew, she was imagining Jamie above her each time he kissed her, or took her trembling body. Hadn't he heard her weeping for her faraway lover? Heartbroken sobs that had driven him away from her door, his soul gnawed by guilt.

It was better to view this interlude as she clearly did: a joining of bodies that brought them both satisfaction. And if she reminded his moribund body of what it felt like to be alive, to be joyous and exuberant, it was one more weakness that he prayed Martha could forgive.

He sighed, feeling trapped and helpless before his earthly needs. Ah, well. A couple of months more with Prudence to sate his lustful hungers. The fire that consumed him would surely burn out, and he would be free. Gratefully he would seek his ascetic solitude in the wilds. And atone to Martha for the sins he had committed against her memory.

He heard the pipe of Wedge's whistle coming from his rooms. And then the sweet lilt of Prudence's voice. It gladdened his heart, set his pulse to racing. He hoped she had put on her lavender gown today. She looked charming in it.

"Oh, God," he groaned aloud. *Forgive me, Martha.* There would be a great many sins to atone for.

Chapter
Seventeen

Prudence glanced up as Ross entered the room, her song trailing away on
a soft note. He looked so troubled and morose it tore at her conscience.
Surely he was dreaming of his cabin in the wilderness, wishing he were
there, instead of postponing his plans in order to take her home. He had
grown cooler, more distant, as the days had gone by, reminding her of
the rigid surgeon he had been when first they met.

It was only at night that he became a different man—hungry, passionate, eager for her to come to his bed. To his arms. His only comfort,
no doubt, while his dream waited on their parting.

She smiled brightly, trying to chivy him into her own lighthearted
mood. Wedge had been almost lucid this afternoon; their merry duets
had added to her cheer. "How can you frown on such a sunny day?" she
teased.

Ross removed his cocked hat and cloak. He smiled halfheartedly, as
though he were unwilling to cast off his gloom. " 'Twill soon be winter,"
he muttered.

She giggled. " 'Twill soon be next year. And the next. But in the meantime, the sun is shining. Shall I finish my song for you? Will that bring a
smile to your chapfallen face?"

He grunted, but said nothing.

She shook her head in vexation. "I'll not have a seeksorrow on such a
pretty day."

Wedge put down his pipe. "Sorrow, no need to be hastened on, for he will come without calling, anon." He intoned the words in a flat, high pitch. His coarse face was screwed up into such a comical yet earnest scowl that Prudence could scarcely keep from laughing.

Ross's face relaxed into an open smile. "Aye, Toby. I'm well rebuked." He settled himself into the grandfather's chair before the fire. "Will you play again, so the lady can finish her song?"

Wedge put the pipe to his lips and maneuvered the stops skillfully. Ross had said that his fingers would be healed in another few weeks. But, in the meantime, he managed quite well.

Prudence finished her song, conscious of Ross's searching eyes on her. It was a simple country ditty, of rustic courtship and seduction, ending happily in a lively wedding, where all the guests got tippled and ended up dancing with the wrong partners. She rattled off the names in the song with such speed and good humor, rolling her eyes at the confusions, that Ross was chuckling by the time she was through.

"You saucy devil," he said, grinning in delight. "Your house must have rung with merriment from morning till night."

She shook her head. "Oh, no! I never sang or danced at home after Papa died. Grandpapa forbade it."

He wrinkled his brow and scratched at his chin. "Not danced? Then perhaps we should see if Mrs. Manning will disgrace herself at the ball." He rose from his chair and held out his hand to her.

She crossed her arms against the bosom of her lavender gown. "Disgrace? Not a bit of it!" She turned to Wedge. "Toby, play us a jig."

As soon as Toby had struck up a tune, Ross stepped forward to make his reverence. He bowed grandly to Prudence, making a small circle in the air with his hand and extending his left leg, foot turned out at the perfect gentlemanly angle. Prudence responded with a deep curtsy. Then they put their hands to their hips and began the lively dance.

Ross was skilled and vigorous, but Prudence matched him with every sprightly step, pleased that she still remembered so well. By the time the dance was through, she was breathless and giddy. She sighed happily and collapsed into Ross's waiting arms. "Well, have I proved myself?" she demanded, between gasps.

"Hmph. All well and good. 'Tis a country dance. But do you know the minuet? Can you play this, Toby?" He hummed a slow melody, beating out the rhythm in the palm of his hand.

"Aye, Mr. Manning, sir." Wedge nodded and began to play.

As lively as he had been in the jig, Ross now measured out the stately paces of the minuet with a grace and elegance that surprised and delighted Prudence. He seemed to grow in stature and regality as the dance progressed, as though he were recapturing a part of his life long forgotten.

It thrilled her to watch him, to match his skillful balances and pacing with her own dainty steps. And when he held her hand to turn her, the other hand at her waist, her body caught fire from his delicate, sensual touch. His blue eyes burned into her, glowing with a sudden hungry desire that made her tremble.

"Enough," he growled, dropping her hand abruptly. He fished in the pocket of his waistcoat and pulled out a handful of coins. "Here, Toby. Go over to Shields Tavern and get yourself an early dinner."

Wedge beamed like a child with a new diversion, stowed his pipe, and scurried from the room.

Prudence frowned at Ross. She had been enjoying the dance. "Why did you . . . ?" she began.

Her mouth was silenced by his eager lips on hers. He kissed her until her head spun, then took hold of her hand and pulled her toward the bedchamber. "Because the more I taste of you, the more I want. And tonight is a long time away."

"But . . . the middle of the afternoon . . ."

"My desires wait not on the clock."

She glanced down at the front of his breeches, seeing the telltale bulge, and nearly made a saucy rejoinder. Then she lifted her eyes to his face. His blue eyes were glowing, his jaw tense. He was hungry and impatient for her. Scarcely in the mood for her levity. She reached for the pins that fastened her stomacher to the bodice of her gown.

But he was too impatient even for that. He plunged his hand down the front of her bodice and lifted her breasts above the line of her shift. He closed his mouth over one nipple, suckling like a starving child. She gasped and let her head fall back, her senses shocked and reeling from the delicious sensation.

Too soon, he released her breast and steered her back to the bed, pushing her down onto the soft coverlet. He groped for her skirts, tossed them back, seized her delicate core with possessive haste and intrusive fingers. His mouth took hers in one hot kiss after another. She was drowning in a whirlpool of pleasure, overcome by his fierce assault.

He fumbled with the buttons of his breeches and swore softly. Then he was plunging into her, hard and demanding, savage in his passionate need. She pounded her fists against the bed in rhythm to his violent thrusts. She could hear the whistle of his breath through his clenched teeth, feel the excited beating of her own pulse in her temples. She cried out and wrapped her legs around his body to draw him in further, and raised her hips to receive every bit of pleasure from his surging, insistent loins. She was floating on a tide of rapture.

The storm was over almost before it had begun. He groaned and gave a last, jolting thrust, then sighed and relaxed against her, his face buried in her tousled curls.

"I never tire of the joy of your body," he said. He rose to his feet and began to straighten his rumpled clothing.

She felt almost too contented to move. But some of the pins of her gown had come loose, and her hair combs were lost in the tumble of the bedclothes. She got up reluctantly, ran her fingers through her long hair, and bent to the fastenings of her gown.

She was suddenly aware that his movements had oddly stilled, that the rasp of his breath filled the silence of the room like the distant echo of a whispered cry. She raised her head to look at him.

He colored—a faint red glow beneath his tan—and looked away. "Why the devil are you so seductive?" he growled. "Even when you pin your gown or smoothen your hair."

She giggled, absurdly pleased that he watched her so minutely. That he wanted her again, and was reluctant to admit it. "Shall I unpin it instead?" she asked with a coy smile.

He grunted and nodded, then tore off his jacket and began to work on the buttons of his waistcoat.

She needed no other encouragement. She undressed at once, noting—

and very close to giggling again—with what careless haste he stripped off his own garments.

When they both stood naked, he pulled her roughly into his arms and held her close, his mouth slashing down on hers in a burning kiss. She felt the quivering, the hardening of his manhood against her body. This time she couldn't suppress the giggle. It began even while his lips were still on hers.

He pushed her away and scowled. "Damn my liver! What is it?"

She felt as wicked and mischievous as the time she and Betsy had sneaked off to the woods to eat unripe pears. She was a naughty little child again, confounding her elders. She pointed to his erection. "Why does that happen?"

"What?" He reeled back, stunned.

She kept her expression innocent. "I mean, as a physician, don't you know the reason?"

He looked as though he didn't know whether to cover his exposed parts or brazen it out. He cleared his throat. "The . . . hmm . . . the circulation of the blood, I believe." His voice was a rumble of feigned assurance.

She gave him a wide-eyed stare. "But why only at certain times?"

He puffed loudly and attempted to appear dignified, a difficult undertaking, considering the fact that he was as naked as a shorn sheep. "This is scarcely a fit topic for a discourse."

"Why not? Can you make it happen? Or does it happen of its own accord?"

His cheeks were starting to redden again. He reached out and tried to pull her into his arms.

She had never seen him so flustered. A fitting revenge, she thought wickedly, for all the times he had treated her with overbearing superiority. "Can't you answer? You, who know everything there is to know about medicine?"

The flush deepened. "The effect a woman has on a man's parts is not fully understood by modern science," he said priggishly, as though he were delivering a lecture to a half-wit.

She was beginning to take pity on him. But she couldn't resist one last deviltry. "Mercy!" she exclaimed, putting her hands to her face in mock surprise. "Does it happen to you every time you take a woman to bed? No matter who?"

His face had become bright scarlet. He clenched his jaws and turned away. His body trembled with emotion.

She bit her lip and frowned. Somehow, the joke had gone too far. She put a gentle hand on his arm. "Ross, what is it?"

His voice was low and strained, as though the unwilling confession were being dragged from him. "Martha was the only woman I ever knew."

"Oh." She sat down heavily on the bed, aware for the first time how she must have wounded his male pride. And Jamie—she had lain with him. Could that thought be torturing Ross as well? Making him doubt his own manhood? Perhaps an honest confession would ease his distress. "Ross. Dear Ross," she said tenderly. "I only gave myself to Jamie twice. And he never pleasured my body the way you do."

He turned, his face brightening with astonishment. "Only *twice?*"

She smiled sheepishly. "I was very near to a virgin when I came to your bed. 'Twas you who taught me the joy to be found in . . ." She was suddenly shy, embarrassed by her own frankness. "In . . . what we do," she finished in a timid voice.

He grinned, relief flooding his face. "And you have proved an apt pupil," he said. "To an uncertain teacher."

She laughed gently, remembering their first impassioned night of love aboard ship. "Scarcely uncertain. I can't imagine that any other man or woman has found greater delight."

He threw himself down beside her on the bed and took her in his arms. He looked suddenly young and happy, his eyes shining for joy. "Well, my little pupil, shall we increase our education together?"

She chuckled, still feeling mischievous. "Only if you promise another lesson tonight. I've grown quite used to our nightly forays."

He kissed her on the breast—a loud, satisfying smack, filled with exuberance. His answer delighted her. "*That,* my little imp," he said, "I can promise you."

"You dance like an angel, Mrs. Manning." His Excellency, Thomas Lee, the president of the Council of Virginia, bowed and kissed Prudence's hand. "In my next correspondence to England, I shall tell Sir William that his unfortunate absence has denied him the chance to meet the most charming lady who has graced these shores in years."

Prudence blushed, flattered and overwhelmed by his words, and opened her fan. "How kind you are, sir." She fanned herself in the coquettish manner that Ross had taught her—though not without warning her against flirting at the same time.

"Have you seen our splendid Capitol, ma'am?"

"Yes. My husband took me on a tour, Wednesday last. A beautiful edifice. And quite new, he tells me."

"Alas, yes. A disastrous fire in 'forty-seven destroyed the first one. And have you seen the Governor's Palace?"

"Only from the outside, of course, Your Excellency."

He bowed again. "I should be delighted to introduce you to the splendor of its many rooms."

"I fear that cannot be, sir. My husband and I sail for England tomorrow, on the afternoon tide."

"A pity. I should have liked you to make the acquaintance of my daughter and her husband. I think you would have enjoyed their company." He beamed like a proud father, then glanced across the room. "Ah, but I see your husband is coming to reclaim you."

Prudence followed his glance. Ross was making his way across the crowded room toward them. He looked perfectly at home amid the elegant surroundings. The restrained perfection of his new white wig, the well-cut, pale blue satin coat that just matched his eyes, the embroidered waistcoat, the long, finely shaped legs encased in black velvet knee breeches and white silk stockings. She had been proud to enter the Apollo Room tonight on his arm.

They had peeked into the room upon more than one occasion, of course. Their own rooms in the Raleigh Tavern were upstairs, in another wing. Ross had even translated for her the motto over the mantel—"Jollity is the child of wisdom and good living"—his Latin being better than hers, owing to his medical training.

But tonight the room glowed with a hundred candles, picking up the gilded frames of the paintings on the pale green brocaded walls. Small tables and chairs were set around the perimeter of the room for the ladies and gentlemen to refresh themselves, and liveried servants moved among the guests in their sparkling jewels and brightly colored satins and velvets, dispensing wine and claret punch. In one corner, an orchestra played for the dancing; it had not stopped since they had come in.

Prudence allowed her eyes to stray to her own apricot gown, with its silver-threaded stomacher. She felt like a grand lady. And her reception by the gentlemen had only added to her glow of pleasure. She had danced with councilmen of the Upper House, had been importuned by burgesses of the Lower House, and had exchanged witticisms with a bewigged, red-faced judge who had declared her a treasure. Even His Excellency, Mr. Lee, the *pro tempore* head of the colony until the return of Governor Gooch, had come back for a second dance.

"I restore your wife to you with reluctance, sir," he said, as Ross approached them. The two men exchanged polite bows; then Lee kissed her hand once again and moved off into the festive crowd.

Ross grinned. "You've made a social triumph tonight, madam," he said. "Every man here envies me. And not a few stopped me to tell me so." His azure eyes ranged her body from the top of her upswept curls to the toes of her brocaded slippers—an intimate, hungry look that made her shiver with anticipation. "Have I told you how beautiful you are tonight?"

She giggled. "Several times. And you're quite handsome yourself, sir."

He cleared his throat. "Humbug."

How she enjoyed making him uncomfortable! Cracking that dispassionate mask to reach the sensitive man beneath. "You're especially handsome when you smile," she said.

He harrumphed again, looking embarrassed.

"You should smile more often and forget your melancholy," she added softly.

She had come too close. He frowned and stared up at the chandelier. "Is your headache gone?" he growled at last.

She felt like a child who'd been rebuked for her sauciness. "Yes," she said in a humble voice. "Your powder worked wonders."

He was on more comfortable territory now. He turned his physician's eyes to her and examined her with care. "Your eyes seem unnaturally bright."

"The excitement of my first ball, no doubt." She laughed suddenly, remembering. "Or do you think it's Toby's bad omen at work?" Wedge had been filled with dark humors all day, predicting all manner of disasters because a black cat had crossed his path that morning.

Ross shook his head. "Sometimes there's truth in that empty brain of his."

"But most often, not."

"Nevertheless, I like not your color. 'Tis too extravagant."

She smiled uneasily. She scarcely had the courage to tell him that she had bought a pot of cerise with her pin money. She clutched at the first excuse she could think of. "We . . . we leave for England tomorrow. 'Tis quite natural that I should be flushed and eager . . ."

He drew himself up, his emotions seeming to congeal into ice. "Of course. I had forgot. Your Lord Jamie."

She felt the pain of his disappointment, though he masked it. *He* had taken her to the ball, had bought her these lovely clothes. Until she found Jamie again, she owed Ross a measure of loyalty and gratitude. She put her hand on his sleeve. "But I'm here, with *you*," she said earnestly. "And I would be honored if you would dance the next reel with me."

He hesitated, searching her face, then relaxed into a smile. "How can I refuse the loveliest woman here?"

He led her to the center of the floor, where the lines for a new dance were forming. It was a sprightly reel, and she danced it with a bright smile on her face, to reassure Ross.

The dance seemed to go on forever—hot and frenetic. She pulled her handkerchief from her bodice several times to dab at her moist brow. She was growing quite weary. As the dance ended and Ross led her from the floor, she leaned into him and stopped, blinking her eyes against a sudden wave of vertigo.

"Damn my liver!" he exclaimed. "You're not well. You've gone pale as a ghost."

The dizziness had passed. She took a deep, steadying breath. "I fear I've danced too much tonight."

"We'll go to our rooms."

"No. I'll find the ladies' tiring-room and rest for a few minutes. That should restore me."

"Damme, but you're stubborn. A good night's rest will restore you. Come along." He took hold of her elbow.

"Fiddle-faddle! I won't miss the rest of the ball because you've suddenly decided to play physician! Mr. Lee said there will be a fine supper anon. I scarcely intend to leave now."

He glared at her. Then his glance wavered. "Well, your first ball . . . and you've drunk far too much claret punch . . ."

She smiled—not *too* triumphantly, that would never do—and blew him a kiss. "Thank you."

He gave a disgusted grunt. "I must be a fool, to give in. I await your return."

She pointed with her fan toward a fat matron sitting forlornly in a corner, and gave Ross a little push. "In the meanwhile, it would be a charity if you danced with that poor lady." She suppressed a merry laugh and headed for the door before he could frame a suitably acid reply.

She maneuvered her hoops through the doorway; they were wider and far more grand than any she had ever worn before. She found the tiring-room at the end of a long corridor, and lay down on a settee while she listened to the chatter of the women around her.

"The most handsome man I've ever seen," said one, stroking rouge onto her cheeks.

Her companion, a fluttery young thing, reached into her bodice and adjusted her breasts so they lay higher against her stays and created a provocative swell to her bosom. "A perfect charmer," she gushed. "He promised to dance with me after supper."

"And did you see his eyes?" asked a third. She lifted her brocaded skirts and tugged at a drooping stocking. "They made me shiver. I'd go back to the gaming room this instant, if he wouldn't think it too forward of me."

"And what would your beau think, if you deserted him?" asked the flighty one. "I have a better plan. When he dances with me, I shall pretend to go faint, and pass him on to you."

"Oh, you sweet pet." The woman in brocade hugged her friend, and the three women went off laughing and plotting a way for the third of their number to entice the unknown gentleman into a dance.

Prudence smiled to herself. They might be gentlewomen, and possibly titled, but they were as silly as any lovesick country girl on the village green.

Still, they had spoken so glowingly of the unknown man that she was tempted to see him for herself. She rose from the settee and smoothed her gown. She was feeling much better now. And surely Ross waited for her with impatience.

She made her way back down the corridor lined with closed doors. A sign above one of the doors caught her eye. The gaming room. She stopped and chewed at the inside of her cheek. What harm? A minute more, that was all. And she had to admit that her curiosity was gnawing at her. She reached out to the door and lifted the latch.

The room was nearly deserted, with a quartet of men just rising from a small card table. She scanned them quickly, looking for this paragon of beauty.

Not the round-faced burgher, surely, thumbing through the cards on the table with a frown of disappointment. Nor yet the grinning popinjay who scraped a stack of coins into the pocket of his gold-braided coat. And certainly not the aging, lank gentleman, as thin and gangly as a stack of twigs ready to blow away in the wind.

The fourth man had his back to her. He was well formed, with a regal carriage and a fine, costly looking powdered wig of full curls. His pink brocaded coat rested on broad shoulders, and the laces at his wrists spilled onto graceful hands.

He turned at the sound of her footfall. "Gad's curse," he said with a sly smile. " 'Tis Manning's harlot!"

She gasped and fell back a step, her hand to her tremulous breast.

The man was Captain Sir Joseph Hackett.

Chapter Eighteen

❦

Hackett bowed gracefully and addressed the other men in the room. "Gentlemen, if you would excuse us." He followed them to the door and closed it behind them. He turned to Prudence. "You're positively glowing, dear lady."

His lascivious eyes scanned her quickly, then came to rest on her bosom. "And dressed like a duchess. You must please Manning very much, for him to go to such expense. Or have you found a richer patron?"

She hesitated, her heart pounding. If he should seek out Ross, heaven knew what might happen! Not unless she could persuade Hackett to be reasonable. Despite the captain's insult, she managed a civil smile. "What happened aboard the *Chichester* is long forgotten," she said. "Ross and I bear you no ill will, but wish only to go our own way in peace."

He smiled, an ugly smirk that contorted his handsome features. "A pretty speech." He sighed and gave a vainglorious pat to his curls, then smoothed the ruffles of his cravat. "So you're still with the lowly surgeon," he said at length. "When you might have had me."

She answered in a frosty tone, disgusted with his vanity. "I am content," she said.

"But, dear lady. Not even a jewel to adorn that lovely neck. I would display you at the finest assemblies in London, not be content with a Colonial backwater. My gratitude for your sweet favors would be as boundless as my purse."

Her lip curled in scorn. "Spare me your vile petitions. I would give myself to the king of Hades before I would submit to you."

He chuckled. "Still that proud defiance. I wonder if you know how much I dream of subduing your spirit. Bringing you to heel like a contented bitch. I've imagined it many times since we parted. You, kneeling humbly on a bed with your skirts raised, and thanking me for every stinging whip stroke that I delivered to your backside." He shook his head. "Gad's curse, the thought of it has become an obsession. Pain and pleasure. And then, afterward, turning you over and drying your tears and plunging myself into you with my . . ."

"In the name of decency, stop!" She was quivering in outrage and horror. She fled to the door.

She felt his hand on her arm, spinning her around. His eyes shone like a hunter at the chase. "Not yet, dear lady. You may not agree to be my whore. A pity. But there's still the matter of unfinished business."

She struggled against his painful grip. "Let me go! You have no business with me. Nor ever shall, you villain!"

"I beg to differ. For example . . ." His voice was indolent, bored, amused. She was totally unprepared for the hard slap that followed—a stinging blow to her cheek that snapped back her head.

"That," he said, "is for the scene in my cabin. You spit in my face, as I recall. And struck me. Like *this.*" He swung his arm in a savage arc and hit her again. And then once more. She tasted blood as her lip split against her teeth.

Her ears were ringing from the blows. In a surfeit of panic, she managed to wrench free of his grasp and make for the door again.

He was too quick. He grabbed her and pulled her against his powerful body, twisting her arms behind her back. She cried out in anguish and he laughed. "And lest you forget the final indignity in my cabin . . ." he said. He raised his knee and rammed it between her legs, a hard, cruel thrust that savaged her even through her skirts.

The pain was so intense she thought she'd faint. "Sweet . . . heaven," she gasped.

He released her, smiling in satisfaction as she moaned and rubbed the bruised bone at her groin. "Odds my life," he said pleasantly, "but I thought for a time you had rendered me as useless as that fool, Lieutenant Elliot."

She staggered backward and leaned against the table. Her body was still so sore, her head so befogged, that she no longer thought of escape. Only of easing her physical torments. She licked at the cut on her lip and winced. "You monster," she whispered.

He shrugged. "But a monster who knows what he wants." Before she could recover herself, he strode toward her, put his hands about her waist; he lifted her onto the table and slammed her shoulders down against the hard wood.

She blinked her eyes and shook her head. Despite the sickening surprise of his actions, her head was beginning to clear at last. She could think again, if imperfectly.

She needed a plan. *Think!* She would never escape him without help, she decided; he was too strong for her. She opened her mouth to scream, praying that someone would hear.

He stifled her cry with the tight clamp of his hand to her mouth. She tried in vain to shake her head free, and clawed at his hand with desperate fingers. *God save me,* she thought.

He pressed close above her, his body planted firmly between her legs. He was too near for her to kick. She cursed her confused mind, that had not warned her to squeeze her knees together before he came so close. She felt his other hand beneath her skirts, snaking up her leg to rest hotly on the bare skin of her thigh. His fingers dug into her flesh—brutal pinches that made her writhe and grunt against the hand that still covered her mouth.

He bent nearer to her. "Does that hurt, dear lady?" he purred. "Save your cries for what's to follow. I vow I'll enjoy your torment as much as your body."

His triumphant face was still too far to reach; she punched at his extended arm with tight-clenched fists that scarcely seemed to deter him. He retaliated by tugging savagely on the curls at her groin. She whimpered softly—in fear as much as in pain; helpless tears sprang to her eyes.

She heard the roar of Ross's voice and sagged in relief. He grabbed Hackett by the back of his coat and spun him around. He tangled one fist in the captain's cravat; the other fist landed squarely on the man's jaw with an emphatic thud.

Hackett stumbled backward, blood oozing from a cut on his chin. His expression was one of amazement—that anyone should dare to strike his person. "I'll have you on report, Manning. By God, I'll have the skin off your back!"

Ross bared his teeth in a feral scowl. "You filthy bastard. You no longer hold sway over me. I'm free to square accounts with you at last. For all you've done." He leapt forward and swung his fist at Hackett's face, opening a deep gash above one perfect eyebrow. Then he struck again.

Prudence struggled to sit up on the table, watching in horror as Ross struck blow after savage blow. His boundless rage was terrifying, all his suppressed hatred of Hackett, the weeks of powerlessness aboard ship, bursting forth in this ferocious attack.

Panting heavily, Hackett stepped back beyond Ross's reach and fumbled for his sword. "I'll slice open your guts, Manning," he said. He pulled out his blade, but Ross grabbed a chair and knocked it from his hand, sending it spinning across the floor.

Hackett grunted and shook his battered hand, then turned and swung wildly at Ross. He struck a glancing blow off Ross's chin—an awkward movement that brought him within reach of Ross's flailing fists once again.

There was no mercy in Ross's cold eyes. He pummeled Hackett again and again, until the captain groaned and sank to his knees. Blood spattered his splendid pink coat, his lip was torn and sagging, his cheek split open. His wig was skewed on his head and smeared with red stains.

Shaking violently, Prudence wrapped her arms around her body; she was horrified by the sight. "In God's name, Ross, *stop!*" she cried.

"Stop?" he growled. "I haven't even begun to avenge poor Toby." He lifted Hackett by the cravat and drove his fist into the man's nose. There was the sickening crunch of bone and Hackett let out a scream of pain.

"What is the meaning of this outrage, sir?"

His Excellency, Thomas Lee, stood in the doorway, bristling with anger. Behind him, several other men craned their necks to see into the room.

Ross released Hackett's cravat and turned, his face carved in stone. "The man is a villain and a scoundrel, sir. He brutalized his men aboard ship and allowed them to starve so his purser could line his pockets. I had men dying in the sick berth, for lack of decent food and water. And this pig refused to intervene."

"Did you file a full report on this matter, Doctor Manning?"

"I intend to."

Lee turned to Hackett with a frown. "Is this so, sir?"

Still dazed from his beating, Hackett had slowly and painfully hauled himself to his feet. Now he dabbed at his ruined face with a handkerchief, wincing when he touched his smashed nose. He straightened his wig, drew himself up—the proud aristocrat—and glared at Ross. "A captain has a right to run his ship as he sees fit."

"True enough." Lee nodded, his face set in stiff disapproval as he turned to Ross. "And scarcely a reason, Doctor Manning, for this uncivil behavior. Captain Sir Joseph Hackett is a guest of this Colony while his ship is in port. If you had a quarrel with him, you might have dealt with the Admiralty direct. Or come to me in my position as president of the colony. I deplore this savagery, Doctor Manning. *Deplore* it, sir! And you a man of healing!" He beckoned to several men behind him. "See that Sir Joseph is brought to a surgeon at once."

Hackett brushed off the supporting arms of the men who had rushed to help. He kept his head erect as he retrieved his sword and headed for the door, though his steps were unsteady.

Lee bowed coldly to Ross. *"Gentlemen* settle their differences with swords, sir. You might anticipate a court action against you. For assault and battery. I myself could be persuaded to speak on Sir Joseph's behalf, sir."

Ross clenched his teeth, returning Lee's bow with exaggerated politeness. "But then, you see, sir, I found this dog in the act of trying to rape my wife."

For the first time, Lee seemed to notice Prudence, sitting on the table with her swollen lip and disordered gown and hair. "Attempted rape, Captain Hackett?" he asked, his voice quivering with outrage. "On the person of this delicate young woman? Damme, sir, that's an entirely different matter. And one that I would be tempted to satisfy myself with a horse-whip!" He made a loud, grumbling sound in his throat. "A man's *wife*, sir. For shame!"

Hackett turned in the doorway, his torn mouth twisting in a smile of contempt. "Wife? Martha Symonds Manning?" He snorted his disgust. "The jade is nothing but a common whore, kept by Manning for his own amusement."

Ross balled his hands into fists. His eyes glowed with fury. "Now, by God, you filthy liar . . . !" He started across the room toward Hackett.

Only the loud clap of Lee's hands stopped him. "We will have no more rough work tonight! As for you, Sir Joseph, you're not merely content to attack this woman, but you must malign her as well?"

"I do not malign *gentlewomen,*" said Hackett with a sneer. "But Mr. Slickenham, my purser, chanced to be in Petersburg last week. He made the acquaintance of the Symonds family, who informed him that Martha Symonds Manning died over a year ago. In England. I scarce know who this trollop is. But she's not his wife!"

Prudence gasped, her face flaming in mortification. The group of men behind Lee stirred at Hackett's unexpected charge, whispering and winking suggestively to one another. She wanted to die for shame.

Ross let out a roar and went for Hackett's throat. Only the intervention of several men kept him from throttling the captain on the spot.

Lee waved his arm angrily. "Get Sir Joseph out of here. Now you, Doctor Manning. You will explain this shameful deception to my satisfaction, sir!"

Ross cast hate-filled eyes toward Hackett as he was led away, then crossed the room to take Prudence by the hand. He looked at her stricken face and stroked her fingers in reassurance.

"This lady is Prudence Allbright, Your Excellency," he said. "A woman of honor who has been traveling under my protection. It is my purpose to escort her back to England. Because of the dangers from lecherous villains, like that rogue you've just seen, I felt it necessary to pass her off as my wife. For her protection."

One of the men in the crowd snickered.

Ross threw him a murderous glance, then bowed to Lee. "I do not wish the lady to be exposed to further scorn and shame, sir. Since we sail tomorrow as Mr. and Mrs. Manning, I should like to prevail upon your good offices—as chief magistrate of the colony—to arrange for our marriage tonight."

Lee looked dumbfounded. "Tonight?"

"Upon the instant, sir."

Lee turned to the man beside him and scratched his chin. "It can be done, I think."

"Yes, Your Excellency. I can fetch a rector at once. As for the license . . ."

"We scarcely need to rouse a justice from his bed tonight. I can grant it myself, can I not?"

"Yes, sir. You have the power."

"Then let it be done. In the meanwhile"—he shooed the assembled men toward the door with an impatient gesture of his hands—"let us give the couple a few moments of tranquility. Your bride looks pale, Doctor Manning. I shall have a servant bring in some Madeira."

"Thank you, Your Excellency."

Prudence had followed the conversation with growing bewilderment. It was unreal. Everything had happened so fast. Hackett's brutal attack, the savage fight . . . and now this. "R-Ross," she stammered in confusion, when Lee and the others had left the room, "I don't think we ought . . ."

"Hush," he said. "Let me find some water for your lip."

"But . . . marriage?"

He gave a gentle laugh and rubbed at his bruised knuckles. "If I must risk life and limb to defend your honor, I might as well have a legitimate reason."

"But our plans . . . *your* plans . . . I won't have you do this." Her brain was spinning with muddled thoughts, and her head had begun to pound again.

"I thank you for your noble intentions. But I'll not have your honor compromised, nor expose you to malicious gossip. Hackett has forced our hand and left us with little choice. Now, be still." He had found a decanter of water. He moistened his handkerchief and dabbed at her lip, his touch gentle and solicitous.

" 'Tis not too grievous a cut," he said. "It will heal in a day or so." He shook his head. "That damned Hackett! Thank God I came looking for you when you didn't return to my side." He smoothed her tousled hair. "My poor Prudence. We'll go to our rooms as soon as the ceremony is over."

For the next quarter of an hour, she felt as though she were in a dream. The large glass of Madeira that Ross had forced her to drink further added to her dazed state. She stood swaying by his side as the rector intoned the marriage ceremony, distant and remote as a spectator at a bizarre scene. Half the guests from the ball had crowded into the gaming room to watch. She heard the flutter of fans, the relentless whispering; it nearly drowned out the sound of the rector's droning voice.

She responded mechanically to her portion of the rite, overwhelmed with the desire to escape this company and seek the blessed solitude of their rooms. Ross gently removed Martha's ring from her finger, then replaced it to seal their nuptials.

It was not until they were in their bedchamber, and beginning to undress, that the mist cleared from her brain. *Sweet Mother of Mercy!* she thought. What had she done?

Jamie! She dropped her stays to the carpet and covered her eyes with her hand. Ross was now her husband. Her husband! How could she marry Jamie and reclaim her child, if she was already married? She was filled with horror and dismay. The enormity of her loss nearly overwhelmed her.

She looked at Ross, standing by the fire in his shirt, his face wearing a self-satisfied smile.

She had never hated anyone so much as she hated him at this moment.

Chapter
Nineteen

He came toward her, holding out his hands. "Come to bed. *Wife.*"

How could he be smiling, when her life was destroyed? "No," she said, her chin thrust out in stiff anger. "I don't want to."

He frowned in bewilderment. "Don't want to?"

The intensity of his searching gaze cowed her. She retreated from her defiance. "My . . . my head hurts again." Avoiding his eyes, she put aside her petticoat and reached up to braid her hair.

"Of course." She could hear the disappointment in his voice. "I'll mix you another powder. And then you can sleep. Perhaps in the morning, if there is time enough, you might wish to . . ."

"Reward you for saving me from Hackett?" She glared at him, her lip curling in scorn.

He fell back a step. "What the devil . . . ?"

"You were disgusting! A brutal animal! Look at your hands—scraped and bruised. Are they the hands of a surgeon? An artist? Or a common brawler?"

"Damn it, I thought I saved you from a rape, not a seduction," he growled. "Are you sorry I interfered? Did you welcome the chance to take the measure of yet another man?"

She hated him for twisting what had happened. As though *she* were to blame. "Don't be absurd. The man is a vile libertine. He makes my flesh creep."

He folded his arms across his chest and eyed her with studied patience.

"Then why this sudden attack on me? Like a petulant child. What have I done?"

"Look at you," she said in disgust. "Do you enjoy playing the scolding patriarch? So superior. So perfect! Well, to me, you're nothing but a high-handed tyrant! You make every decision for me. You order me about. You interfere in my life—with such unthinking self-assurance!—that I want to scream."

The patience vanished. "Christ Jesus! *What* have I done?"

"You never asked what *I* wanted. You never asked if I wanted to be married to you! All you could think about was your stupid pride. Caught in a lie by His Excellency. Shamed before a roomful of . . . of petty bigwigs!" She fairly sputtered the words.

"*My* pride? Damn my liver, it was *your* reputation that concerned me. Your pride and honor. Did you expect me to let them think you were nothing but my whore?"

"Well, wasn't I?"

He looked stunned. He swore softly and covered his eyes with his hand. "And the last weeks?" he said in a hesitant voice. "They meant nothing to you? Was your pleasure feigned . . . because you thought yourself my whore, and nothing more?" He looked up at her, his face dark with uncertainty, resentment. "You came to my arms, to my bed, every night. I thought it was your joy as well as mine."

She felt her face flaming. Whatever her quarrel with him now, she could scarcely deny that her body had welcomed his.

"Was it your joy?" he asked hoarsely.

She nodded, then cursed herself for giving him even a crumb of comfort. Not after what he'd done! "But it was your joy, as well," she said with a sour frown. Once he'd rediscovered the pleasures of a woman's body, he had certainly availed himself of her services, the lustful dog! "And fair recompense for all you've done for me."

"Recompense? My God, what are you saying?"

She parroted Betsy. "A gift for a treasure. A perfectly agreeable business contract, as far as I was concerned. Until you spoiled it," she added bitterly.

He was roaring now. *"Business* contract?"

She wavered in the face of his fury. Her own words sounded so cold, so calculating. "W-well, you were kind to me," she stammered. "And bought me gifts, and . . . and I was grateful."

He grunted in disgust. "And so you deigned to give me your body. A 'business contract,' after all. Well, I was grateful to *you*. And not only for the pleasure of sharing your bed. You gave me a purpose in life, when I thought I was dead. What a fool I was—not to understand you had the instincts of a trollop, if not the experience. Scarcely worth the necessity of a marriage."

Marriage. Her lip curled in bitterness. "I hate you," she burst out. "I wish to heaven you had thought of another way to save your pride and my honor tonight. And now you've ruined my life."

"And mine? What of mine, damn it? I turned my life upside down for you. I've exchanged my blessed solitude for a life with a woman who tells me she hates me."

"Why shouldn't I? I told you I had to go back and marry him. Why couldn't you understand?" Her eyes filled with tears of frustration.

He whirled away from her and began to pace the room, his bare feet slapping angrily on the floor. "If it's the child you're carrying," he muttered at last, "I'll claim it as my own."

She gasped in shock. "Child? Oh, you fool! I'm not carrying his child!"

He stopped in mid-stride, turned, and grabbed her savagely by the arms. "And still you want to marry him?"

Her rage and pain were beginning to choke her. "Yes!" she cried.

He shook her roughly. "It's time to forget your damned Lord Jamie! *I'm* your husband, now. Live with the reality of that, instead of your foolish dream. Both our dreams are beyond recapture. Best we try to make a life together. Forget your Jamie!"

"As you've forgotten Martha?" she asked in scorn.

He was suddenly, frighteningly, still—his teeth clenched, his cold blue eyes glowing with an angry fire. "Upon reflection, I think that we will seal our vows properly tonight. In the conjugal bed." His voice was deceptively soft, hiding emotions she could only guess at. Passion? Fury? Or the desire to avenge his pride by humiliating hers?

"You'll not touch me," she said, her voice beginning to tremble.

"You're bought and paid for. A business contract, isn't that what you said? And I scarce have been repaid in full for what you cost me. You'll begin tonight."

"No, I'll not!" she shrieked.

"Yes, by God! Whether your 'business' is marriage or whoredom, I have a right to you now!"

He released her arms to tangle his fingers in her loose hair and pull her toward him. He slammed her against his hard body and ground his lips down on hers. His moouth was hot and possessive, demanding her surrender, sapping her strength. She struggled against him and knew she fought her own desires. She felt his hands on her shift, pulling it upward to expose her naked flanks to his searching touch, and writhed against the caresses that would defeat her. The tantalizing penetration of his fingers that would make her long for his body.

She was quivering in helpless submission by the time he released her, her whole being on fire from his draining kisses, his expert hands. In a haze of anticipation, she allowed him to strip her garment from her, and passively watched, admiring his lithe strength, while he pulled off his shirt.

Then he smiled. A smile of triumph? she thought with a sudden jolt of anger. He had ruined her life, and she allowed him to vanquish her with a few kisses and caresses? As he moved near to hold her again, she raised both her hands to his bare chest and gave him a violent push. "You have a right to me only when *I* wish it!" she cried.

A low growl came from his throat. "And you do," he said with a fierce scowl. "And you will!" His arms shot out to grab her.

She felt herself being lifted, tossed over his shoulder like a sack of grain. She pounded on his back in helpless fury, her swaying hair nearly touching the floor as he carried her across the room. Then she was on the bed, scrambling on hands and knees to escape him.

His hands were around her waist. She braced herself to keep him from turning her onto her back and finding her vulnerable core. If it was the last thing she did, she would deny him satisfaction tonight. Their wedding night, she thought bitterly. Let the villain know the pain of denial tonight, though it scarcely matched her own pain and loss.

"My stubborn wife," he muttered, as she kept her body rigid and fought his attempts to turn her. "Do you think to prevent me? Were you so shy, little shepherdess, that you turned away when your charges coupled in the fields?" His voice behind her sounded almost amused. He tightened his hands around her waist.

Her head jerked up in stunned surprise at his unanticipated, conquering entrance, the hard manhood that found its customary sheath within her. He filled her deeply, and stirred her stubborn body to new and unexpected heights. And when he began to rock against her hips, plunging again and again with ever-quickening strokes, she was undone.

She wanted him tonight. Would want him every night for the rest of her life, if he would but inflame her body as now he did. She moaned with every deep, possessive thrust, the sweet tension building within her until she clenched her teeth to keep from screaming her joy. Never stop, she wanted to cry aloud. Sweet heaven, let him never stop!

Just when she felt herself ready to explode in a starburst of passion, he withdrew, leaving her shaking. "Ross?" she whispered. And then, "Ross," with a desperate note to her voice. Surely he wouldn't leave her like this— waiting and unsatisfied. She rolled over and spread her knees in invitation.

He knelt between her legs, his chest rising and falling with labored breaths, but made no move to take her again. He stared at her, searching her face for a sign. His skin glistened with the sweat of his exertions.

"Yes, I do," she said with a sob of frustration.

If this was surrender, it was a surrender her body craved. Ross took her mouth in a conquering kiss, then plunged his shaft into her, awakening her senses anew. She closed her eyes and abandoned herself to her pleasure. There was nothing but the feel of him within her. No past. No future. Only the pounding rhythm that spiraled her to a realm of delight that blotted out her dark thoughts.

The bone at her groin was still sore from Hackett's cruel blow. But the jolt of pain that accompanied each of Ross's impassioned thrusts only served to intensify the sensations in her burning loins. Molten fire radiated to every part of her body, ignited by her throbbing core. She dug her nails into Ross's back, spurring him to ever more frenzied thrusts. She needed to be possessed, consumed, overwhelmed. Savaged by passion.

Only that sweet torment would obliterate the ache in her heart. They climaxed together in a joined cry of ecstasy.

With release came remembrance. Her baby. Would there ever be enough nights of lovemaking to compensate for that loss? She felt the hot tears fill her eyes even before Ross had withdrawn from her. And when he rolled off her and flopped against the pillows, sighing in contentment, she gave way to her grief. She curled herself into a ball of misery and sobbed bitterly.

He sat up in alarm. "Prudence. What is it?"

She could only shake her head and weep. What could she say? She had no one but herself to blame. She could have spoken up, *should* have, to stop that absurd marriage ceremony. Ross had meant well; it was only her fear of scorn and shame that had kept her silent. Marry in haste, repent in leisure. And she would have the rest of her life to repent.

"Prudence, don't cry," he said, gathering her into his arms. "I'm . . . I'm sorry I forced you. It seemed the only way to make you forget Jamie. And you will. He'll be a sweet memory in no time. Nothing more."

The mention of Jamie's name only made her wail the louder, heartbroken cries that seemed to disconcert Ross. He held her more tightly in his arms and rocked her, murmuring tender words of comfort.

At last she stilled, exhausted by her grief. He lifted her to her pillow and covered her and kissed her forehead. "We'll make a good life together," he said, lying down to take her in his arms again. "You'll see."

There was nothing she could do except leave Ross as soon as she reached London.

Prudence sat up reluctantly in bed, wishing she could sleep and hide from her troubles forever. Last night, locked in his sweet embrace, her body filled with warm contentment, she had found it easy to pretend to herself that she could be happy with him. That the choice for her future had been made for her, and she could accept it.

But she had awakened in the cold, early hours of dawn, her thoughts churning anew. What did that choice mean? To accept carnal joys in exchange for the bliss of being with her son, watching him grow to manhood. To fill her nights with passion so the days would not be so bleak and empty. She could hear Papa's voice in her ear. Short pleasures, Kitten, long lament.

And her tears would never stop until she held her baby in her arms again. No embraces—however impassioned—would fill the emptiness, the need to cuddle the dear creature she had carried in her womb.

Ross had left her breakfast, as usual. She made a face, staring at the brimming plate. She had no appetite this morning. And her head had begun to throb again. The result of all those tears, no doubt. She climbed out of bed, relieved to see that Ross hadn't yet locked his medicine chest for travel, though his sea chest and the rest of his boxes were already packed. She mixed herself a headache powder, drank it down, turned to her morning ablutions.

She frowned into the mirror, examining her face with care. There was nothing like grief to impair a woman's looks, she thought ruefully. Dark circles ringed her eyes and her cheeks were sallow. Her lip was still swollen from Hackett's blow, and she had even discovered the beginnings of a small pimple on her forehead. She left a few curls loose at her brow to cover the spot, then finished dressing.

She was just folding the last of her linens into her sea chest when Ross entered. He seemed distant and distracted, scarcely meeting her eye—as though the passions of last night had left him as drained as she.

"The carriage is below, whenever you're ready," he said, his voice flat and devoid of emotion.

She straightened and turned. "I've finished my packing."

"I spent an hour with His Excellency, Mr. Lee, this morning. I gave him a full report of Hackett's conduct aboard the *Chichester*. He intends to send it on to the Admiralty in London."

"I'm glad. If he can be punished, poor Toby will not have suffered in vain."

"Lee tells me that Hackett has been relieved of his command whilst he is recovering from . . ." He cleared his throat and turned away.

She felt a pang of guilt. "Ross, I'm . . . I'm sorry for what I said last night. Were I a man, I would have beaten the villain as savagely."

"No. You were right to chide me. I shouldn't have allowed myself to lose my head that way."

She laughed gently and glanced at his discolored knuckles. "Well, your hands will remind you of your folly for some time to come, I'll warrant." She smiled into his eyes, her thoughts drifting back to the passions of the night, and then blushed. His eyes were so blue and intense they made her tremble.

He seemed equally uncomfortable with the sudden intimacy of their locked gaze. He turned away and busied himself with his boxes, as though his already-fastidious packing had left him with anything to do. "I don't much like London," he said at last. "As I recall, neither do you."

"No," she replied, mystified by his sudden shift in the discourse. " 'Tis too crowded and foul. At least in summer."

"And dismal in winter. There are some pleasant villages in the Cotswold Hills, near the city of Cirencester. 'Tis sheep country, so you wouldn't feel a stranger."

"Why do you speak of it?" He was talking in riddles.

"I shall set up my practice there. There's a need for surgeons in that region."

"I thought you wished to give up medicine. Too imperfect, you said."

He sighed morosely. "A wife needs to be maintained. And I have spent much of my inheritance these past weeks."

She felt a twinge of guilt. He too had had second thoughts about the wisdom of their marriage. His obvious unhappiness only strengthened her resolve to leave him. They would both be the better for it. She would find Jamie. And Ross could use the rest of his money as he had intended. For his solitary ease. He could return to the quiet and peace he so clearly desired. To the memories of Martha.

It was a strained carriage ride that took them from Williamsburg to the harbor and their ship. Only Toby Wedge seemed oblivious to the mournful regrets and guilt-ridden memories that hung in the air like a dark cloud.

Wedge had been frightened, at first, when he'd learned they were going on a ship. But Ross had dealt patiently with him, explaining that they were leaving the land that harbored the feared "Cap'n Hackett." Now he babbled happily to himself as they traveled to the ship, occasionally stopping his mutterings to ask a question about the autumn countryside, the harvested fields—moments of lucidity that heartened Prudence.

He suffered a brief bout of terror when he saw the *Chichester* lying at anchor, but Ross reassured him, pointing out the merchantman *True Heart*, on which they were to sail.

After some delay to get their baggage transferred, they came aboard the *True Heart* at last, as the bright afternoon sun shone down. It seemed an excellent ship—not nearly so large as the man-of-war *Chichester*, to be sure, but far more splendid. Their quarters were the finest on the ship: a spacious, airy cabin on the quarterdeck.

"How glad I shall be to have sunshine," said Prudence, smiling as she looked around the cabin, with its wide bank of windows.

" 'Tis far different from a surgeon's hole," agreed Ross. He turned toward Wedge, who was muttering into space, a distracted frown on his face. "Now that we're under weigh, let me settle Toby in his cabin next door. Poor devil. I fear the disruptions of the day have quite put him out of his mind."

When the two men had gone, Prudence took off her straw hat, laid her cloak across a chair, and examined her surroundings. The paneled cabin was filled with Ross's furnishings from the *Chichester*—his desk and padded chair, his food locker and bench. To these had been added a large, round table in the center of the room, surrounded by four chairs. She knew that Ross had seen to the purchase of a cow and several cages of chickens, and arranged for one of the crew to be their cook; they could entertain the captain and mate in elegant style on the voyage.

But there was one new piece of furniture that gave her pause. A large, curtained bunk that dominated the cabin. *Sweet heaven!* she thought, as she realized the implications of that looming bed. Six weeks, at the very least. Of passion-filled nights, and a restless husband who might also wish to idle away a languid afternoon on those sheets.

And what would she do if he made her pregnant? For all she knew, she was already carrying his child. She didn't expect her flux for another week, and she could feel the dread building within her, imagining the nervous anticipation that week would hold.

"It cannot be," she whispered aloud. It would be trial enough, when she returned to England, to leave Ross and seek for Jamie. But to complicate her life further with another child . . . She shivered at the frightening thought. Jamie would renounce her for certain.

She sighed with regret. As difficult as it would be, she would somehow have to persuade Ross to defer his pleasures until they reached home. She sighed again. And deny herself the thrilling pleasure of his body. A wrenching denial; the mere sight of him had begun to stir her senses every time he appeared.

She dropped to her knees and clasped her hands in prayer. "Dear Lord," she murmured, "if Thou wilt but return my child to me, I pledge on my honor to forswear henceforth any sweet congress with this man. Thou knowest that a marriage entered into falsely, for the pleasures of the flesh alone, is less than sanctified in Thy sight. Cleanse Thou me from my secret faults, and hear my prayers."

She rose to her feet, feeling renewed and strengthened. Surely God would look kindly upon her sacrifice. But . . . she swallowed the small lump of fear in her throat . . . how in the name of heaven was she to tell Ross of her decision?

"Are you pleased with the cabin?"

She turned and saw him in the doorway. His expression was guarded, uneasy. Could he be feeling guilt over forcing her into the marriage? She decided to gamble on the chance—to play on his conscience, God forgive her. She pursed her lips in a frown of disapproval. "In point of fact, I'm not. I'm still quite vexed with you, because of last night. You seduced me into an intimacy that was . . . unwanted. You took advantage of my weakness in a most ungentlemanly way."

She waited for him to respond. When he kept silent, his face frozen, she lifted her chin at a proud angle and continued, praying that she could brazen this out. "A wife has rights a whore has not," she said haughtily.

"And so?" he growled, closing the door firmly behind him.

Sooner broken, sooner mended, she thought. She blurted the words quickly, to have them done with. "I wish for you to arrange for a hammock or a trundle bed on the voyage. I prefer not to share the bunk with you."

"By the beard of Aesculapius, not share the bunk?" His eyes glowed with anger. "What new childish mischief is this?"

Heaven preserve me, she thought, beginning to quake. Perhaps she should try another tack, to smooth his ruffled feelings. " 'Tis . . . 'tis only that I find sleeping aboard ship less than comfortable. When we're settled in our cottage, on dry land, in the Cotswold Hills . . . which plan I find very agreeable, by the way . . ." She was babbling worse than Wedge. "I shall welcome our lovemaking in our own home," she finished lamely. A patent lie. There would never be "home" for them; only for her and Jamie. She gave Ross a smile full of promise and hope, praying that she had placated him.

He didn't intend to be placated. His brows drew together in a fierce scowl. "May I know the reason for this . . . this sudden female reticence? After all we have shared, you are now to play the part of a coy maiden? And I'm expected to agree?"

She felt like a naive fool, lost in male territory she could scarcely understand. She yearned for Betsy's counsel. Betsy's wisdom. "Y-yes," she stammered.

"I think not, madam. You have much to learn about marriage, God knows. But surely, even in that country village of yours, the women know of a wife's duty to her husband."

Curse him, he *would* take that superior tone! As though she were an idiot child! She stamped her foot in annoyance. "I know that a wife is not her husband's slave. Nor he her tyrant! I wish to sleep alone, for my comfort, until we reach England. Are you so unfeeling as to deny me that?"

She could hear the crunch of his jaw. "We will share the same bunk," he said ominously.

"And I say no. If you choose to be difficult, *I* shall sleep in a hammock. This marriage was your idea, not mine." That seemed to have an effect on him. His stony glance wavered. She was certain that she had won the argument, that he would trouble her no more on the voyage. But perhaps one final nail to seal the box? "I'm sure you would not have shown Martha such disrespect." She put a deliberate note of accusation into her voice.

He blanched, but said nothing.

The victory was hers. She tried not to flaunt her triumph as she pointed to a spot under the wide windows. "I think a trundle bed would fit very nicely there."

She had miscalculated. He took her roughly by the shoulders and glared at her. "There will be no trundle bed. Nor hammock! And you will speak no more of Martha. She was an agreeable wife. In every way."

She hated Martha with a passion that blinded her to reason or prudence. She broke free of his grasp and strode angrily to the window to stare out at the receding shoreline. "I have no doubt she was as perfect as you yourself," she said waspishly. "Jumping at your every command, to exalt your manhood. Telling you how wonderful you were. In and out of bed. I regret I'm such a disappointment, next to your *agreeable* Martha."

She heard the sharp intake of his breath through his clenched teeth, and then he spoke—cold and menacing. "More to the point, Martha never gave me cause to think that a man should treat his wife with aught but gentleness. But then, I had never met a petulant child-woman until you. 'Tis time for you to behave like a proper wife. Forget your fanciful dreams and be prepared to do honor to your husband."

She whirled to challenge him. "And if I don't agree to your high-handed demands?"

"It goes against all my instincts as a gentleman. But I begin to think it would give me great satisfaction to . . ."

She curled her lip in scorn. "To rape me whenever you want me?"

"To spank you like a child," he said grimly.

She trembled at the cold threat in his eyes and turned away.

She heard the sound of the door being opened behind her. "Be prepared for one or the other tonight," he said. "I'm for the forecastle, now. I'll see you here at six bells. The captain has invited us to dine with him." Then he was gone.

She sank to a chair, quivering. *Oh, Prudence,* she thought. How had she managed to get herself into such a pickle? She had insulted his fragile masculine pride, maligned his dead wife, stubbornly refused to lie with him. If she'd had a grain of common sense, she would have told him the truth about Jamie and the baby long since. Perhaps there were some cunning women who could twist men to their purposes with lies and willful demands. Hadn't she seen her stepgrandmother get her way with Grandpapa many a time, with her artful wiles? But clearly, innocent Prudence Allbright was not a member of *that* sisterhood!

She spent the rest of the afternoon in a ferment of dread. She wasn't at all sure he didn't mean what he'd said. And if he'd meant only to frighten her, he had succeeded.

What were her alternatives? The pain and humiliation of a child's punishment, as against the danger of a pregnancy. She feared the harsh cruelty of his angry hand. But if he touched her with loving hands, she feared her surrender even more. If she abandoned her resolve, allowed him to get her with child, God would never forgive her.

It didn't help that her head was throbbing again, that the rocking of the ship had brought on a spell of nausea. She paced the quarterdeck to clear her head, but the air was chill, and she retreated to her cabin, shivering.

They dressed for supper in cold silence. She was filled with a depressing weariness that made every movement a trial. She picked at her meal, tried to be pleasant to the captain and his mate, and the several other passengers who had been invited to his table. But her thoughts were already turned toward Ross and a frightening, unpleasant reckoning she could scarcely avoid.

She followed him meekly into the cabin. Watched as he closed the door, lit another lantern. He turned to her and folded his arms across his chest.

"Well," he said, "have you decided?"

She felt her pulses racing madly. Her head was befogged, spinning with confused thoughts. What to do? From somewhere in that mist she could hear Papa's scolding voice. Honesty is the best policy, Kitten. She sighed and took a step toward Ross. It was time to tell him the truth.

The deck whirled beneath her feet. Her knees ached so much she could scarcely stand. She blinked her eyes and stared at Ross. His face seemed so far away, beyond a deep chasm she was forced to cross.

With a soft moan, she crumpled to the deck.

She awoke to find him undressing her with gentle hands. He carried her to the bunk and placed her between the sheets.

She struggled to sit upright. Had her silence persuaded him that this was what she wanted? "Ross, no. I can't . . ." she began in a quavering voice.

He pushed her back against the pillows. "Hush," he said. "You're quite ill."

She took a shallow, gasping breath. "Is it serious?"

His face was creased in a worried frown. "I fear it could be the small-pox."

Chapter
Twenty

Her delirious cries were breaking his heart.

Ross crossed the cabin and bent over Prudence, grateful she had stilled at last. Her beautiful face was scarcely recognizable. Large red blotches and oozing pustules had swollen the delicate features into a grotesque mask that was more hideous to look upon than Wedge's face. He cursed his impotence as a physician. He cursed her unknown family, that hadn't had the sense to have her engrafted with the smallpox lymph when she was still a child. Did they know so little of modern medicine in the countryside?

He himself had saved scores of children and adults from the scourge. 'Twas such a simple operation—learned from the Turks. A small scratch, treated with the foul pus from a sufferer, bound and left to form a scab. And then . . . a few aches and pains, racing pulses and nausea, perhaps a day or two of fever. But the patients *lived;* moreover, they were no longer susceptible to the smallpox contagions that might sweep their villages and kill hundreds of others.

He swore softly. She must have caught it from that filthy, ragged peddler in Williamsburg. The woman had sold laces in the street. Prudence had held the pieces up to her sweet, pure skin, and had only changed her mind when the cost seemed too high. He swore again, cursing his own stupidity. He should have realized at once: the peddler-woman's cheeks had been covered with pale white indentations. The signs of recent pox. Surely she had just come from her sickbed.

He wrung out a cloth in a basin of water and pressed it against Prudence's forehead. At least her fever seemed to have abated. He had lived in dread those first few days—while she thrashed and moaned and shivered—seeking in vain for the eruptions, the dusky red spots that would signal release from the first crisis. Better to have pox on the hands and face than in the heart, and kill the whole body.

He had sent for a red cloth from the purser to wrap her shivering body, and a large brazier to set by the bunk to keep her warm and start the sweat to flowing. He had plied her with drink—water and the largely ineffectual nostrums he had mixed—and comforted her fears in those few times when her mind had been clear enough to understand what was happening.

It was odd. She feared only to be scarred. But when she spoke of death, her fever-wracked eyes were clear and calm, putting her faith in God. He remembered her devout prayers, night after night, and was glad she had the comfort of her faith to sustain her. He himself had spent more than one hour on his knees in the week since she'd fallen ill.

He had been grateful when the pustules had finally appeared, covering her face and arms and breasts. And even when they had swollen and deformed her sweet flesh, he had felt hope. But these past two days . . . the frightful delirium . . .

Oh, God, he thought for the hundredth time, *don't let her die.*

"Here be your dinner, sir."

He looked up as Wedge entered the cabin, bearing a steamy stew. "Thank you, Toby. Have you eaten?"

"Aye, sir."

He seated himself at the table and began his dinner while Toby scurried to his food locker to fetch him a large mug of ale. He didn't know what he would have done without Wedge.

The captain had wanted to turn back to Virginia as soon as he had learned of Prudence's illness. But Ross had assured him he would stay in quarantine, confined to the cabin with her until she should recover. Wedge, with his pockmarked face that attested to his immunity, had become his invaluable go-between. He had refused to climb the hatchway from the galley, of course. But he waited patiently on the main deck for each meal to be delivered into his hands, and had even conquered his fear enough to climb the few steps of the gangway to the quarterdeck. "I be brave for the little skylark," he had said.

Wedge waited in silence for him to finish his dinner, then picked up the empty bowl. He shook his massive head. "Will the lady die?"

Ross frowned and looked up at the childlike expression on the man's face—so trusting, so hopeful. "Of course not," he said. There was no point in disturbing Wedge with his own dark fears.

"There were a rat on the lines this mornin'. A bad omen, d'ye see me?"

He sighed tiredly. "Her life is in God's hands, not your omens, Toby."

Wedge's expression turned fearful, his eyes widening like great saucers. "But if Cap'n should be lurkin' in the ship, and bringin' his wicked curses down upon her head . . . !"

"Christ Jesus," he muttered. "Will that damned villain haunt you all your life?"

"Body o' me, a man never know . . ."

He stood up, his face set in a stern frown. "Go to your cabin," he ordered. "Now that your bones are almost mended, you promised to make hair combs for the lady."

Wedge hung his head like a repentant child. "Aye, sir." He shuffled to the door, then turned, his eyes filling with tears. "Death devours lambs as well as sheep," he mumbled, and left the cabin.

Ross groaned and covered his eyes with his hand. Even that simple mind could comprehend the danger, for all his optimistic words. And if she should die . . . He groaned again. Her last memory would be of his cruel threat to chastise her. He burned with guilt, wishing he could take back the shameful words.

He had never meant them. The thought of raising his hand to her was inconceivable. But he had felt helpless and frustrated, hoping to frighten her into obedience. A clumsy attempt to deal with her changeable ways, when reason seemed to fail.

She was so foreign to his few experiences with women. Docile and willing one moment, then filled with saucy rebellion. An angelic innocent with an imp lurking beneath. How the devil was a man to get a woman like that into his bed without playing the tyrant, as she called him?

Not that his conduct—absent tyranny—made him proud of himself. He cringed in shame, remembering how he had taken her that night in anger, like a lustful, savage pig. He was no better than Hackett. What had happened to his vaunted self-control?

Well, when she was quite recovered—he murmured a prayer that it be so—he would make a fresh start. He wanted her in his bed. He needed the pleasures of her sensuous body, her passionate embraces. But more than that, he realized with a start. He wanted to hear her soft laughter when she was pleased with their lovemaking, see the glow of contentment in her remarkable green eyes. He wanted their future together to be as sweet as she was. But how was he to win her trust again, after all that had happened between them?

He eyed his hammock, strung in the corner of the cabin. Lord, he was tired. Perhaps he'd take a nap for a short while. She seemed to be resting comfortably.

She cried out suddenly and began to twist about on the bunk. He hurried to her side. She had begun to moan and thrash in pain. He ached for her, aware of the agony in her swollen joints—a pain that reached her even in her delirious state. He lifted her puffy wrist and felt her pulse; her heart was racing.

"Hush, sweet lass," he murmured. "Hush."

He bathed her face with cool water, opened her shift to press the moist cloth against her heaving breasts. He lifted her head and brought a glass of water to her trembling lips, grateful that they hadn't been asea for so long that it had turned foul and undrinkable.

And still she tossed and cried out, tears pouring from her swollen eyes and staining her blotched face. "Oh, Jamie. Jamie!" she sobbed. "I need you."

He soothed her, settled her back into peaceful sleep. Then he turned with an oath and flung the wet towel across the cabin. Was he a fool, to dream of a placid life with her, when that damned rakehell still ruled her heart? He regretted the first moment he'd seen her, regretted the hasty marriage that she so clearly abhorred. Regretted most that his body, having tasted the pleasure of hers, was now loath to give it up.

And that sweet future he had envisaged. He laughed bitterly. Would he spend his nights like a craven husband, on his knees, begging for her favors? Or brutalizing her until she submitted? Or—what was worst to contemplate—taking advantage of her body's willingness to be pleasured, while her heart dwelt elsewhere?

No! He had his pride. He had lived the life of a monk before she had come along; he could do it again. A celibate marriage was better than being cuckolded by a memory. Better than taking her into his arms and seeing Jamie reflected in her eyes.

And he still had his memories of Martha. They would have to be enough. He groaned in anguish. But why was her image fading from his sight, from his dreams?

Prudence grimaced and wriggled in her bed. Her face was a burning torment, the flesh crawling as though it were covered with vermin. She tried to raise her hands to scratch it, then frowned. Why were her hands tied to the sides of the bunk?

She turned her head and looked about the cabin. It was night. A single lantern hung from a ceiling beam; beneath it sat Ross, reading a book and puffing on his pipe. She inhaled the warm scent of tobacco. It was somehow comforting and natural, reminding her of the cozy evenings she had spent with Papa, while they read together. She sighed and closed her eyes. She could drift on a tide of ease, remembering those gladsome days.

Ease . . . But only if she could scratch her face! She opened her eyes again. "Please, Ross," she whispered. Her voice was hoarse and dry, a soft croak that bewildered her. "Will you release me?"

He looked up from his book, smiled, and put down his pipe. "Is that Prudence, come to life again?" He crossed to the bunk and groped for her wrist. "Your pulse is normal. How do you feel?"

"Dreadful!" she said. "I itch all over."

"The pustules have begun to dry up and form crusts."

"Is that why I'm tied?"

"If you scratch in your sleep, you can spread the infection. It seemed wise to prevent that."

She strained against her bonds. They cut into the crusty skin of her wrists. "Please. 'Tis most uncomfortable."

He nodded reluctantly. "But only until you sleep again. And *don't* scratch."

"I promise."

He carefully untied the bandages, and watched—the concerned physician—as she put tentative hands to her face. "Remember, don't scratch."

"May I have a mirror?"

"No. 'Twill only distress you needlessly."

She touched her face, feeling the rough scabs that covered her from forehead to chin. "Oh, alas! So many?"

"The swelling has gone down. Be grateful." He laughed gently, with no malice in his voice. "You looked like a puffball when the pustules first appeared. But you've passed the worst of it."

"By God's grace," she murmured. She explored her body beneath her shift with trembling fingers, shocked at the number of scabs she found. Her trunk, her arms and legs. Even a few crusty spots on her belly. Her armpits and groin were sore; she discovered large, hard lumps within the moist cavities. "It hurts here," she said.

"That too will pass. Do you want a drink?"

She nodded. Her mouth felt dry, her lips cracked and painful to the touch. She ran her tongue around the inside of her mouth. Thankfully, there were no pustules there. She had heard of more than one villager dying when the air passages were swollen and blocked.

Ross poured her a glass of water, and supported her shoulders while she drank. She made a face. "It tastes terrible."

"We should reach the Azores in two or three days. And take on fresh water. You should sleep now. Is there anything more you want?"

Her eyes darted to the covered chamber pot in the corner of the cabin; then she blushed and looked away.

His penetrating eyes followed her glance. He crossed the cabin and returned with the pot. He pulled back her blanket and started to raise her shift.

Burning with embarrassment, she pushed at his hand. "No, please."

He smiled in tolerant understanding. "Don't be shy and foolish, Prudence. You have lain abed for three weeks now. I've washed your body, and cleaned your face when you vomited. Your . . . bodily functions are scarcely unknown to me by now."

There was comfort in his voice, sympathy in his face. She *was* being foolish. He was her husband, after all, as well as a doctor. And she had served the seamen in like manner when she had tended them in the sick berth. And felt no shame. She nodded and allowed him to set the pot beneath her bared hips.

When she was finished, he stowed the chamber pot and covered her again. "You must try to sleep now."

She frowned, remembering what he had said. "Three weeks?" It was inconceivable.

He shrugged. "And a day."

"Will I recover?"

"I think so." He smiled, his eyes crinkling in satisfaction.

"And will . . . will I be scarred forever?"

The smile faded. "We shall only know that when the scabs begin to fall off."

She closed her eyes, fighting her tears. To be scarred and ugly. Jamie would never want her then. "Oh, sweet heaven," she sobbed, giving way to her unhappy fears. She wept softly, wishing he would put his arms around her and give her comfort.

Instead, he took her by the shoulders and shook her. "Damn my liver, why do you weep? You have your *life*. And you have your sight! I've known men to go blind, when the pox infected their eyes. And you have your voice, to sing your songs." He softened his tone, stroked his hand along the side of her cheek. "And your heart is still as pure and sweet," he said gruffly. "I care not a farthing what happens to your face. You're still the same Prudence to me. Beautiful and good."

She trembled at the look in his eyes. She had never felt more lovely, more cherished. "Ross," she whispered.

He made an odd, grumbling sound in his throat and turned away. "You need a change of linen and bedding. It's been several days. If you're not too tired . . ." His voice had become the voice of a doctor, cool and remote.

She felt the distance between them. "No," she said, dismayed at his sudden, bewildering withdrawal.

The effort of moving from the bunk—though he carried her to a chair—made her weary. By the time he had changed her bedding, sponged her itching face and limbs, and helped her into a fresh shift, she was exhausted. She settled herself against her pillows and reluctantly allowed him to tie down her hands, then followed his precise, graceful movements as he folded the soiled linens into a neat pile. "What do you do with them?"

"Wedge takes them on deck and boils them, to rid them of the pestilence. Sleep now."

She was tired, but not ready to sleep. She owed God a prayer of thanks for her life. For Ross's tender care, that had seen her through the crisis. She felt strangely reborn and ridiculously content, her senses alive to the joy and infinite wonder of life. The scent of the pipe that he had relit; the warm glow of the lantern that cast a golden pool on the deck; the soothing rocking of the ship. *May I walk before God in the light of the living,* she prayed.

She cast her eyes around the cozy cabin and sighed in gratitude. She felt as snug as she had in her little dormer room in Winsley. She couldn't take in enough of her warm, friendly surroundings.

Her roaming eyes stopped at a dim corner, then opened in amused surprise. She began to giggle.

He looked up from his book. "What is it?"

She laughed again. "A *hammock?* Here?" The joke was too delicious. It had taken an illness for him to accede to her wishes. "I thought you said there would never be a hammock in this cabin," she teased.

She had thought he would share the joke, admit that they had both behaved unpleasantly that day. Instead, he stared at her, his eyes grown cold and distant. "I order you to sleep," he growled.

"Damn my liver, Pru, keep still!" Ross's voice was more amused than irked.

Prudence wrinkled her nose and wiped a soap bubble from her cheek. "How can I, when you're determined to get soap in my eyes?"

She ignored his mocking snort and shifted her knees on the deck of the cabin. She leaned her head lower over the large tub so the foaming lather from her hair wouldn't drip on the floor. "How good that feels," she said with a grunt of pleasure.

Kneeling above her, he rubbed briskly at her scalp until it tingled, then swirled her long tresses into a soapy mass on top of her head. "I promised you I'd save you a barrel of water from the Azores. Hold still while I rinse." The water that poured over her head was warm and soothing; Ross had arranged for their cook to heat it in the galley.

He wrung out her rinsed hair and twisted it into a towel, then leaned back on his heels and grinned. "You look like a maharajah."

She returned his smile. "I feel like a princess. To put on a gown again, and stays! After all this time."

"Five weeks to the day since you fell ill."

She looked over to the chair upon which rested her beautiful apricot satin gown. Ross had forbidden her to wear aught but her shifts until every scab had fallen off, lest the pox contaminate her garments. "Oh, how I should like to dance today!"

He frowned. "You will sit quietly, and walk on the deck for a quarter of an hour. And nothing more. Or you'll find yourself back in bed in a trice."

She made a face at him. "Tyrant."

"Physician," he corrected primly. He stood up and helped her to her feet. "Let me look at you." He examined her face with care, fingering a small indentation beside one eye. "You were very fortunate. One little scar. And you can wear a black patch on it, as the ladies of fashion do. It will look charming."

His fingers were soft on her face. She found herself remembering his kisses, the feel of those fingers on her trembling flesh. She turned her head away from his hand. Wicked Prudence! Hadn't she made an oath to God?

"Sit on the bench. I'll comb out your hair."

Her hair was woefully tangled from the long weeks she had lain in bed, but his touch was gentle as he worked at the snarls and wet, twisted strands. She felt as luxuriously comfortable, as pampered as a great lady with her maid.

He took a very long time at the combing—gliding, sensuous strokes that awakened her senses—but at last he laid down the comb. "It can dry in the sunshine at the window," he said. His voice sounded oddly strained.

He helped her to dress, bending to tighten the laces of her stays and teasing her because her illness had made her so thin. "We shall have to fatten you up," he said, laughing and measuring her slim waist with his long-fingered hands. His arms below their rolled-up sleeves were sinewy and powerful, covered with a light fuzz of hairs. She ached to run her fingers along their length. She had forgotten how the mere sight of him, his gentlest touch, could stir her.

When he reached out to help her pin her gown to her stomacher, she could bear no more of this sweet torture. She turned away from him. "The pox has not made me helpless," she said, fighting to keep the tremor from her voice. "I can do it myself."

There was no way to avoid his help with her shoes and stockings, however. Bending over with the unaccustomed tightness of her stays made her dizzy and weak. The intimacy of his fingers as he pulled her stockings above her knees and tied her garters brought a blush to her cheeks. As though she were still a virginal innocent, enjoying the forbidden caresses of a lover.

When she was dressed at last, he examined her critically and nodded in satisfaction. "You're a right fair sight, lass." He led her to a cushioned bench beneath the windows and seated her so the gentle breeze and bright warming sunshine would dry her hair.

There was a tap on the door, and Wedge shuffled into the cabin. "Be you finished with the tub, sir?"

Ross smiled. "Aye, Toby. Take it away, and then come back with your pipe. Perhaps the lady would like to sing."

Wedge frowned. "Sing before breakfast, cry before night."

Prudence gave him a reassuring smile. " 'Tis the middle of the afternoon, Toby."

He looked bewildered, as though he were digesting her words, and then he grinned in comprehension. "Aye. So it be. And the little skylark shall have her song, an't please you."

She sang a lilting, merry song that matched her mood: the sun filled the cabin with golden brightness, she had recovered her health, and she was dressed in her beautiful gown. And Ross sat and watched and listened as though everything about her delighted him.

But when she had finished, she sagged back on her seat, winded. "I fear I'm not as strong as I thought."

Ross hurried to her and felt her pulse. " 'Twill be another week or so before you're fit. Perhaps you should go back to bed now."

She pouted at him. "You promised I could walk on the deck."

He wrinkled his brow. "Very well. But only when your hair is dry. I'll not have you taking a chill. In the meantime, I order you to sit here quietly. Toby, amuse the lady with your tunes."

While Wedge tootled his lively airs, Ross pulled out his folio and a crayon, and began to sketch the seaman as he played. Prudence sighed in contentment and stared out the window at the ship's wake far below. The waves foamed and sparkled in the sunshine, and the briny scent that carried to her nostrils was crisp and refreshing. The air was surprisingly mild for November—Saint Martin's Summer, Papa had always called it, from the French custom.

She ran her fingers through her damp hair, fluffing the long tresses to catch the breeze. She was content just to enjoy the day and Ross's companionship, suppressing the nagging voice that whispered that England and Jamie—and her parting from Ross—were less than a week away.

At last he put down his crayon and looked sheepishly at Wedge. "Poor Toby. Your fingers must be aching by now. The bones are still fragile. I should have told you to stop long since."

"And my hair is dry," said Prudence, as Wedge put away his pipe. "May I take my walk on deck now?"

"Of course." While he rolled down his sleeves and reached for his coat, Prudence smoothed her hair with a comb. She was loath to pin it up; after her weeks of confinement, she wanted to feel free to the very top of her head. But Ross's warning glance, and the memory of the sailors' hungry eyes as she came aboard, made her choose propriety. She twisted it up and fastened it with the combs that Wedge had carved for her, and was rewarded by a beaming smile from his simple face.

Ross bowed grandly and held out his arm. "Madam, will you walk?"

They made their way along the passageway and onto the quarterdeck,
Ross supporting her with his arm. The weather was even more glorious
from this vantage. The strong breeze snapped at the sails, and the sky was
a crystalline blue, clear and cloudless. The sun was so bright it almost
made her eyes water, with a warmth that soaked into her cabin-weary
bones.

At Ross's direction, Wedge scampered back to their cabin to fetch a
chair for Prudence. She protested that she didn't need it, but Ross
frowned. "Unless you sit, you'll go back to bed. I'll not endure your stubbornness."

She gave him a mock scowl. "You've had too many weeks of playing
the tyrant, unopposed. Prudence the invalid was forced to endure it. But
you see I've quite recovered my strength. And my self-determination."

He stirred uncomfortably and looked abashed. "I dislike to be called
tyrant. Am I truly so harsh with you?"

She saw her advantage. "If I sit now, do you promise not to give me
any more orders today?"

He nodded unwillingly. "Agreed," he grumbled.

She wondered if it was too wicked to profit from his moment of weakness. "And for the rest of the voyage?" she asked with a sly smile.

He shook his head and growled in annoyance. "Imp! I give you a pearl,
and you want the whole string."

For a moment, she feared she had pushed him too far, and tensed herself for his anger. Then he grinned, his eyes lighting up, and her heart
leapt in her breast. How she basked in his smiles, gloried in the ability to
make him laugh. She wondered if he had laughed with Martha.

He took out his pipe and lit it, then leaned against the railing of the
quarterdeck, nodding greetings to the sailors on the deck below. Several
of the passengers passed by and expressed their delight at seeing Mrs. Manning up and about again. Their concern only added to Prudence's sense
of well-being.

She stole a glance at Ross. He stood gazing up at the foremast, his strong
profile outlined against the blue sky. She never tired of looking at him:
the stubborn jaw, the proud flare of his nostrils, the heart-stopping blue
of his eyes, the mocking arch to his eyebrows. His tied-back hair ruffled

in the breeze; the golden summer streaks had faded from the sandy brown locks.

And his skin was no longer a warm tan, she realized with a start. How many weary nights had he watched her while she lay near death? How many days of sunshine had he been denied, while he nursed her? And with such tender care. She remembered waking many times—fevered, terrified. And he was there. Calm, soothing, comforting.

And he had *always* been there. From the very first. To support and protect her. To give her strength and bring her joy. To make her feel beautiful and wise and clever, and quiet the uncertainties that gnawed at her heart.

Oh, Papa, she thought suddenly, wishing she had his counsel. *Is this love?* To laugh when he was happy, and grieve for his pain? To listen for his footstep, and know that life would not begin until he came through the door?

Jamie had been a skyrocket; the brightness had faded almost at once. But Ross had begun as a friend, loyal and true. And the wonder and joy in her heart had grown with each passing day, with such gentleness that she'd scarcely noticed it. Like a fire slow to start, yet growing to a bonfire that sometimes consumed her with its passionate flame, then settled to a cozy warmth that enveloped her with comfort, the sense that she belonged near its protective heat.

Yes, she thought, *this must be love.*

And what of him? Did he love her? *Could* he love her? He had been so warm, so playful and kind these past few days. Surely he must feel something for her besides the desires of the flesh. The obligation he felt toward their marriage, if nothing else. He had said he wanted to make a future together. Wasn't that a beginning that could lead to love?

She felt a surge of optimism, of bright hope. Perhaps there was a chance to stay with him and realize her dreams at the same time. She would tell him everything. He would stand by her against Grandpapa. He had neither wealth nor title to impress her grandfather, but surely he could do *something.* He had never failed to be her protector, to save her from the darkness. With his help, she would have her child again.

And he had a generous nature. It might be difficult, painful for him, but she felt sure that he could eventually accept another man's child as his own.

And then, perhaps, if she saw the warmth in his eyes, she would find the courage to tell him that she loved him.

He turned his head and smiled down at her. "You're blooming like a flower in this sunshine," he said. "It gladdens me to see it."

He *did* love her. He had to love her, when he looked at her like that. She found herself blushing, filled with unbearable happiness. "Ross . . ." She hesitated, searching for the words that would reveal her heart.

He seemed not to have heard the tender note in her voice. He frowned and looked up at a drifting cloud. "The wind is freshening. Come inside."

"No. Let me stay a little while longer."

"You should have a cloak, then. I'll send Toby."

"Let me fetch it. I feel quite fit." And it would give her the time to find a way to speak to him, to breach that wall she still sensed was there.

"You'll stay," he said sharply.

She pursed her lips. "There are no steps to climb. I'll walk slowly. And you promised not to give me any more orders today."

He grunted. "A rash promise. But"—he waved his hand in the direction of their quarters—"go, if you insist."

She made her way slowly down the passageway to their cabin, holding to the wall to support her shaky steps. She found her cloak in her sea chest and threw it over her shoulders, then clicked her tongue in annoyance. The button was hanging by a thread. One strong tug of wind on the deck and she would lose it.

She remembered Ross's sea kit. It would only take her a minute to find needle and thread and fasten the button securely. She knelt before his sea chest and opened the lid.

She gasped in shock, her hand going to her mouth. There on the top of the chest was Martha's gown, lovingly folded and tied with a pink ribbon. But it was the pair of stays tied in with it that curdled her heart. The very shade of green as the silk gown, and trimmed with the same rosebuds.

He had seemed so indifferent when she had kept and worn Martha's stays in Virginia. As though they were a faded memento that no longer held significance for him. But at some time during those weeks in Williamsburg—while he bought gowns and trinkets for Prudence and made her think she was valued by him—he had taken the care to have Martha's ensemble restored.

She closed the chest and rose unsteadily to her feet, trembling in every limb. What a fool she was to think she could ever win his heart. Hadn't he told her, all that long time ago, that Martha was the only woman he would ever love? She touched the wedding ring on her finger. He hadn't even given her a ring of her own. She was simply Martha's inferior replacement.

She squared her shoulders, struggling to hold on to her pride. She had been right all along. Jamie was her salvation. Her *only* hope to reclaim her child. She would go to him. Be his mistress, if need be . . .

No! Her son deserved a name. Why should her sin be on his innocent head? Better that God punish *her* on the Day of Judgment. She would marry Jamie, and pretend that the marriage to Ross had never taken place. And if she shrank at the thought of bigamy, she would remind herself every day of her wicked life that she had done it for her child.

But . . . Oh, Ross! How would she endure the long years without him? Survive the loss of her dearest friend in this world? *Dear God,* she thought, anguished, *why dost Thou bring these trials to Thy poor servant?*

She buried her face in her hands and wept.

"Are you determined to prove Toby right?"

She turned to find Ross in the doorway, his face dark with concern. "Wh-what?" she said, blotting at her eyes.

"Sing before breakfast, cry before night." He frowned. "I should never have let you tax yourself so much today. And now you're weeping and shaking like a leaf. Come. To bed." He reached for her gown and began to work on the pins.

She allowed him to undress her like a child and carry her to the bunk. She felt empty and helpless, her heart ripped by pain.

Why must he be so kind, when he could never love her?

Chapter
Twenty-One

The fog was so thick that the lamps from the forecastle appeared as pale yellow halos of light in the murky gray that filled the nighttime sky. The ship rocked gently at anchor; the soft creak of its timbers and the plash of the river current against its hull seemed like eerie, disembodied voices whispering of sad finality.

Prudence shivered at the sounds. Her dream of happiness with Ross was ended. She touched Toby Wedge on the arm and pointed aft. "The quay is that way?"

"Body o'me, no, lady. We only be in Limehouse Reach. London and the Custom House be around that bend in the Thames. When the fog lifts in the mornin', and we gets under weigh again, you'll see it."

"But there's land there."

"Aye. Limehouse and the East India docks."

She shivered again. It was so cold and damp that she could see the puffs of their breath mingling with the fog. But beyond the whiteness lay the shoreline of the suburbs.

She was grateful for the fog. She had spent all of last night in a ferment of worry, knowing the ship had reached the mouth of the river. How could she escape Ross once they docked at the Tower stairs? But this morning's thick mist had halted their progress up the Thames, and given her time to form a plan.

She had enlisted the aid of the captain's mate, and discovered a capacity for guile in herself that had appalled her. She had smiled archly at him, told a fanciful tale of wishing to get to London ahead of her husband and surprise him with a waiting carriage. A secret, she had said. He had nodded and grinned to be part of the conspiracy, and put a weathered finger to his lips for silence. At the start of the second watch—midnight—he would be waiting to take her over the side and row her ashore in the ship's boat.

She still had enough pin money to pay him for his pains and hire a hackney coach to take her to London and Shoe Lane. She prayed that Betsy wouldn't be entertaining one of her customers tonight. The sooner she collected her hidden cache of money—and Jamie's ring, of course—the sooner she could be out of the city and on her way. She wondered if her uneasy excitement was for the joy of reclaiming her child. Or the fear that Ross might find her if she lingered.

"You have my bundle, Toby?" she asked.

"Aye, lady. Safe stowed in my cabin, an't please you." He giggled like a child. "Mr. Manning'll be mightily pleased at his gift."

"Yes." She felt a pang of guilt for having deceived such a simple creature. She had packed surreptitiously this afternoon, wrapping her clothing in a bundle. She regretted leaving her sea chest behind—the precious gift from Wedge and Gawky and their mates—but it couldn't be helped. Ross would notice the missing chest. She had told Wedge only that the bundle held a gift for Ross. One she wished to present to him at the stroke of midnight, as a memento of their voyage.

She sighed, feeling the long night weighing heavily on her soul. "What time is it?"

He frowned and scratched his white head in perplexity, as though her question were beyond his ken. "I heard two bells when I came out," he said at last.

Nine o'clock. Three hours to go. She would go mad. "I shall knock at your cabin door just before the second watch," she said. She turned her eyes toward the unseen shore, hearing the ghostly chimes of a distant church bell. "Do you have family ashore, Toby?"

That seemed to confuse him. He looked down at the deck, scuffed his shoe against the boards, frowned and grimaced. "My Maw be dead, I think. And my Paw . . . he flitted the first time he cast his glims on this face o' mine." He stared off into space, suddenly distracted by his memories. "Aye, Maw," he said with a gentle chuckle, "I be your faithful Toby. A silk petticoat I'll fetch you from the Indies."

She patted his arm to bring him back to reality. "Doctor Manning will take good care of you."

It was too late. He was lost in his own world again. He looked at her with blank eyes and tipped his head to one side like a bewildered puppy. "Take time when time cometh, for time will away," he said mournfully. He sighed and wandered off in the direction of his cabin.

She watched him go. There was more wisdom in his ramblings than he dreamed. Soon she would be gone. She had chosen a mother's love over her heart's desire. She had made the dreadful decision to abandon Ross, to break the laws of God and man. She had begged God's mercy for her wickedness.

But . . . Take time when time cometh. She still yearned for Ross, till her heart felt as though it could hold no more pain. She had been well for a week now, and still he strung his hammock in the corner of the cabin. He had not spoken a word about his conjugal rights, but had slept apart from her as though he found it fitting and natural.

She had been afraid to ask him the reason why, to trespass on his cool reserve. She tried to tell herself that he still feared for her health, but she lay in bed night after night, filled with loneliness, and ached for his embrace.

God forgive my weakness, she thought. One more sin. The breaking of her solemn vow. She would go to Ross's arms tonight, if he would have her. Give herself one last memory of their passion, to carry her through the long, cold years.

Her eyes were wet with tears by the time she stumbled into their cabin.

Ross looked up from his reading, then rose quickly to his feet. "What is it? You've been weeping."

She gulped back her misery. "No. 'Tis only the fog on my face."

He pushed back the hood of her cloak, cupped her chin in his hand, and stroked at her tears. "Yes, of course." He hesitated, his eyes searching her face, then kissed her wet cheeks. "The fog tastes of salt," he said with an understanding smile.

She gazed at him in an agony of longing, praying he would see the desire in her eyes.

"Poor Prudence," he whispered. He bent his head and took her mouth in a soft, tender kiss.

She sighed at the sweetness of his lips and wrapped her arms around his neck, returning his kiss with all the passion in her and pressing her breast against his.

As though he feared the intimacy of her straining body, he stiffened and pushed her away. "I should never have let you go out in this fog," he growled. "You're trembling from the cold. Go to bed. 'Twill be a long day tomorrow and I fear you've not recovered your strength."

Her heart sank. She hadn't the courage to speak her mind. What if he should refuse her? She watched him seat himself again, retreat behind the cool distance of his book. Then she slowly began to undress. But when at last she stood shivering in her shift, she found her desires too strong to ignore. Braving his wrath—and the pain of his possible rejection—she crossed the cabin in her bare feet and pulled his book from his hands.

"What the devil . . ." he began.

"I don't want to sleep," she said boldly.

"Cards? A game of draughts, perhaps."

"No."

He pursed his mouth in annoyance. His firm, inviting lips made her heart jump. "Damn my liver, Pru, are you determined to be vexatious tonight? Shall I read to you, then?"

She twisted her fingers together and stared at a spot on the deck, fearful to see the look in his eyes. "Come to bed," she said softly.

He frowned up at her. "I'm not ready to string my hammock yet."

"Why must you string it at all?"

He cleared his throat, his cheeks reddening. "You still need your rest, and . . ."

"The bunk is lonely without you."

He raised a skeptical eyebrow. "But uncomfortable to share. Isn't that what you said? The hammock, as I recall, was *your* idea. We'll share a bed in our own home, you said."

She cursed her intemperate words. Was that the reason he had avoided her—because he feared *her* rejection? "I . . . I've changed my mind. I don't want to wait."

"I do," he said, his eyes cold and hard. "A proper house on dry land, a large bed . . ."

Large enough to keep from touching her? she thought in dismay. Was that what he meant? Could it be that he didn't *want* her anymore? Ever? She bit her lip. "Must I beg you?" She wondered if she sounded as desperate as she felt.

He leaned back in his chair and stared at her with as much dispassion as he would give to a diseased patient. He laughed mockingly. "It would seem that—now that you're well—you've rediscovered your appetites. And, willy-nilly, I'm expected to accommodate you."

She felt the heat rising in her face. He made it seem as though she were a voluptuary, insatiable in her desires. She nearly turned away, nursing her humiliation, her wounded pride.

A pox on her pride! she thought, as he stretched out his hand to retrieve his book. Let him think what he would. She wanted him. She wanted their last night together. And if it meant she must behave like a shameless hussy, so be it!

She pushed aside his reaching fingers and sat on his lap, twining her arms around his neck and stroking the soft curls at his nape. He stirred uneasily, but she took his face between her hands and pressed her mouth against his.

He grunted and jerked his head free. "I order you to bed," he said hoarsely.

"Not without you." She brushed her lips against his cheek, his stubborn chin, and found the softness of his earlobe. She nibbled delicately at the tender flesh, and was rewarded by an involuntary gasp from his lips.

"In God's name, leave me be," he growled.

"You're my husband," she said, and kissed his lips again before he had time to turn away. He held his mouth rigid, but she ran her tongue along his lower lip until he groaned and opened his mouth to her. She slipped her tongue between his teeth and explored the moist, warm cavity with sensuous strokes, remembering how much pleasure he had brought to her in the same manner. She thrilled to the feel of his quivering body beneath her embrace. She closed her eyes and lost herself in the wonder of his mouth.

When she lifted her head at last and opened her eyes, she saw that his chest was heaving, his breath coming in labored gasps. With trembling fingers, she untied his cravat and worked on the buttons of his shirt, gliding her hand beneath the fabric to caress the hairy softness of his chest.

He struggled to push away her searching hand, but he was clearly weakening. "God Almighty," he said in a strangled voice, "I don't want this."

She shifted her position on his lap so she could reach and open the buttons of his breeches. He was hard and throbbing even through the folds of his shirt; she fumbled with the cloth until she touched his bare flesh, then closed her hand around his pulsing manhood. He gritted his teeth and let his head fall back, his eyes squeezing shut in the agony of his pleasure. "Must I show you the way?" she whispered.

"You witch," he said, and clasped her to his strong chest, returning her kisses with wanton fervor. He lifted her in his arms and carried her across the cabin, tossing her onto the bunk with hungry impatience. He tore off his clothes and threw himself beside her, pushing at her shift to bare her to the neck. His burning mouth found her bosom, his roaming hand her quivering core. He ravaged her with his mouth, his teasing fingers—until she thought she could endure no more sweet torture. She pulled off her shift, then grasped his member again and guided it toward her eager cleft.

His growing need matched her own. He pulled her beneath him and plunged himself within her, wringing a cry of delight from her lips. He rode her with a wild passion that roused her to peaks of fulfillment again and again, yet left her greedy for more. She moaned and writhed, raising her hips to meet each frantic thrust.

But when his pulsing entries quickened in an ever-increasing tempo to find his own release, she pushed gently against his chest. "Not yet," she gasped. "Please. I want it to last forever."

He stopped his frenzied movements and stared down at her, his hands tight on her waist. "If God gives me the will," he panted. He rolled her onto her side and curled up behind her, adjusting her body to his until he had found her soft grotto again. She clutched at the pillow, kneading it in rhythm to his pounding thrusts. She had not thought a body could feel such joy.

He seemed determined to pleasure her to the point of madness. Each time he seemed on the brink of his own climax, he would withdraw, shift their bodies with sure hands, and enter her again, contriving to reach new places within her that made her quiver in ecstasy.

By the time he allowed himself his own satisfaction, her head was spinning, her thoughts drained of all but the exquisite feel of his hard manhood, his fiery kisses and caresses. He shook with a final, wild spasm, then groaned and collapsed against her bosom. "Will that suffice you until tomorrow, you minx?" he asked, his voice shaking.

For the rest of my life, she thought, and clasped him to her breast, never wanting to let him go.

He fell asleep in her arms, his face nestled against her neck. She felt the softness of his breath on her cheek, the warmth of his flesh against hers, the strength of the arms that still curled around her, even in sleep. *I must remember every bit of this,* she thought. Her last moment in Paradise.

She lay quietly, drifting in and out of sleep. Each time she wakened, she tightened her arms around him, needing every last second of sweet possession. It was only when she heard the ship's bells tolling the lateness of the hour that she sighed and reluctantly eased herself out of his arms.

She watched him as she dressed. His hair ribbon had come untied in the frenzy of their passion; she bent and brushed a stray lock from his face. How soft and young he looked in sleep. How dear and vulnerable. He exhaled softly and turned onto his back. He seemed to smile.

"Dream of your Martha," she whispered, "and never know how much I loved you."

No! She choked back a sob. *Think of me sometimes, Ross,* she thought, anguished. *By God's grace, let at least a part of me remain in your heart.*

She put on her cloak and turned to the door. Then she stopped, her hand on the latch, remembering. She took Martha's ring from her finger, held it to the light of the lantern. POR TOUS JOURS. For always.

With a heavy sigh, she placed it on the table and hurried out the door to Toby Wedge's cabin.

The movement of the ship woke him. Ross stretched in contentment and opened his eyes. They were under weigh again, and the angle of the sun streaming through the windows showed him that the morning was well advanced.

He sat up and looked around the cabin. Prudence was gone. Waiting on the deck, no doubt, eager for the sight of London Town.

He frowned. Eager? Or filled with dismay? He remembered her tears of last night. Had she been weeping for her Jamie, knowing him so near, yet so unattainable? He wondered if she would ever forget the rogue.

Still . . . the remembrance of her passion last night gave him hope. Never had she been more fervent, never more eager to please and be pleased. Not even making love to Martha had ever brought him such satisfaction, God forgive him. Perhaps he and Prudence could have a marriage, after all.

He felt a sudden twinge of uneasiness. Of hatred for the unknown Jamie. *Or at least the physical satisfactions of marriage,* he thought ruefully. *If nothing more.* Whatever was in her heart, her body responded to his with a fervor that took his breath away. A man could do worse.

Clearly—despite her cold rejection of him the first day they'd come aboard the *True Heart*—she wanted him. Perhaps her petulance that day had been because she was angry at their marriage, wanting to lash out at him in the only way she knew how. And then, she was already infected with the smallpox; perhaps her mind hadn't been quite clear or rational.

He rose from the bunk, his spirits surprisingly high, his body refreshed. The future no longer seemed so grim. The passion of a fiery woman in his bed might compensate him after all for his lost solitude, his abandoned plans. His heart might be desolate, but his body would be satisfied.

Wedge had brought him a pitcher of warm water; he washed and shaved, wishing all the while that Prudence would come through the door. For a change, his optimism would match hers.

He went out on deck, glorying in the bright day, the sun that glittered in the crisp November air. He could see the Custom House and the Tower stairs in the distance; they'd be making anchor very soon. But where the devil was Prudence?

He found Wedge and put the question to him. All he got for his pains was a silly giggle and a strange allusion to some sort of gift. Clearly, the man's mind was wandering today, heightened by his fears of going ashore. He stopped several of the seamen, growing more concerned by the minute. No one seemed to have seen Prudence this morning.

The mate hurried past him, intent on the final preparations for their landing. He halted the grizzled seaman in his progress, his hand a tense clamp on the man's arm. "Have you seen Mrs. Manning this morning?"

The mate looked strangely disconcerted, his eyes evading Ross's sharp glance. "There be much to do, Mr. Manning, sir. I can't be noticing every passenger."

The mate's obvious discomfort made him uneasy. "Where is my wife?" he insisted.

The man tugged at his neckerchief. "It were a secret, sir."

"Damn it, tell me!"

"The lady . . . wished to surprise you, sir."

"And so?" he growled.

" 'Od's blood and bones, I gave me oath to keep the secret. But I'll tell," he added quickly, as Ross clutched him by the sleeve again and glowered. "I rowed Mrs. Manning ashore last night. That I did, sir."

His blood was beginning to boil. "Ashore? And not a word to me? Curse you for a miserable grub!"

The mate looked aggrieved at the insult. "It were at her request, sir," he said sulkily. "The lady wished to surprise you with a waiting carriage when we lands."

He forced his anger to cool. The man had only done as he was asked. It was Prudence who deserved the brunt of his rage. And, by God, she would have it! What had possessed the imp to think that he would be pleasantly surprised by her disappearance? By her taking upon herself a chore that should be his?

He stomped back to their cabin to finish his own packing. Damn the contrary wench! To leave that way, to rise from their bed, still warm with passion, and sneak off into the night!

He threw his clothing helter-skelter into his sea chest, too vexed to take his usual care. His eyes were caught by her sea chest, sitting in the corner of the cabin. Had she packed, or was that chore to be his as well? He strode across the deck and threw open the chest. It was empty.

He felt a shiver of dread as he looked around the cabin. Not a ribbon, not a carelessly abandoned vial of scent. Nothing to show that she had ever shared this space with him.

And then he saw Martha's ring. Sitting alone and almost unnoticeable on the wide expanse of the table. He groaned and sank into a chair. Only a fool would misunderstand what Prudence had meant by that act of finality.

She was gone—for good and all, the confounded jilt. He felt as desolate and angry as he had when Martha had died, with no one upon whom to vent his pain and rage.

She had *used* him, all this time. He had been her means to return to England. To her damned lover. And the passion she had brought to his bed? A business contract, she had called it. And he had been too besotted by her allure to take her at her word. Too innocent of the ways of a cunning female to understand what was happening.

He heard an unhappy sigh from the doorway. Toby Wedge stood there, quaking and wringing his hands together.

"What is it, Toby?" he snapped.

"I be afeared to go ashore, sir. Cap'n be waitin'."

"No he's not!" He felt assailed from all sides.

"But there were a jackdaw what flew out from land and circled the mast, then lit on the ship's bell." Wedge shook his head, his eyes wide with fright. "A bad omen, that. My life on't."

Ross slapped his hand on the table in frustration. The sound was like the crack of a pistol. "Damn it, Toby, the captain is in America! There's no danger, no curses! No bad omens!"

He bent and leaned his head on the table. Except for the curse of the first moment he had seen her face. Who would have thought those pure green eyes masked the dark soul of a devil?

Chapter
Twenty-Two

The large wagon rumbled along Thames Street, its heavy wheels rattling on the cobblestones. Ross sat beside the driver, his head sunk to his chest, his brain teeming with dark thoughts. He made a grumbling sound that echoed the noise of the wheels, and glanced over his shoulder in irritation.

"God Almighty, Toby," he muttered, "put away that damned pipe. Your tweedling is driving me mad."

The back of the wagon was piled with Ross's baggage and furnishings from the ship; Wedge sat proudly perched on an armchair in the middle of the jumble of possessions and surveyed the streets of London as though he were a child inspecting a new toy. At Ross's harsh tone, his face fell. "Aye, sir," he mumbled, and stuffed his pipe into his pocket.

Ross felt a pang of remorse at the man's crestfallen face. Poor Toby— to bear the brunt of his foul mood. He sighed and pulled out his pocket watch. Half after four. Another hour to stow his belongings in the warehouse near Paul's Wharf. And then what?

He felt lost, cast adrift in a sea of confusion and roiling emotions, his life turned upside down. What the devil was he to do now? He didn't even know where to begin to look for her. If she'd told him the name of her village in Wiltshire, he didn't remember. And her beloved "Lord Jamie," the viscount from Berkshire? Even knowing she was going to him didn't help. Half the aristocracy in the county probably named their sons after past kings, in hopes of winning more favor at Court.

He could return to America, he supposed. Continue on the path from which he had been so rudely diverted. But somehow, solitude no longer seemed so attractive. With Martha's death had come dejection, the hunger for peace and quiet. But Prudence's disappearance filled him with unreasoning rage, a restlessness that needed outlet in action, or he would explode. He had spoken to Prudence of going to the Cotswold Hills, of resuming his practice. Would he be content as Ross Manning, surgeon, again? Thrown back into the tumult of human suffering?

He sighed once more. As soon as his goods were safely stored, he would take Wedge and look for an inn for the night. Perhaps in the morning he would be rested and ready to make fresh plans.

He looked around the bustling street, feeling oddly disconnected from its teeming, noisy humanity. A mail coach careened past the wagon, filling the air with the clamor of its postilion's horn, and scattered a flock of pigeons on the street. The clatter of hammers was joined by the dull thud of mallets as carpenters and stonemasons swarmed over a half-built church.

He glanced down a side street to where peddlers had set up their stalls. The alley rang with the hawking cries of the vendors, the strident voices of customers, the laughter of the children who played amid the crowds. There were shrill-voiced harlots, as well, eager for a coin or two from the free-spending buyers. And whining cripples on little carts, or hobbling about on crutches, their outstretched hands begging for a penny.

The sight of their twisted bodies touched his conscience. So much misery. It seemed a pity to abandon his skills. There might be peace for him in usefulness, after all, though happiness elude him.

The clerk in the warehouse was efficient and competent. Ross was pleased that the captain of the *True Heart* had directed him to this place. He had his baggage set aside and waiting; as soon as he found lodgings for the night, he would send for his clothing and necessaries. He took Wedge by the elbow and steered him out into the street.

"Come, Toby. Let's see if we can find ourselves a hackney-coach. I remember a clean inn on Fleet Street."

They moved down the crowded street. It was a slow progress: there were no coaches in sight, and Wedge dragged his heels, distracted by every shop window and pie-seller. He stopped, his eyes lighting with hopeful, child-ish enthusiasm as they reached the alley with its array of stalls and goods.

About to tug impatiently at Wedge's sleeve, Ross hesitated. He still felt an edge of guilt for his surly treatment of the man all day. Perhaps he'd buy him something, some little child's gimcrack, to keep him amused.

He stared in shocked surprise, his pulses racing. Could it be? Among the throng, he had caught sight of a flash of apricot satin. The woman was at some distance from him, and her head and shoulders were covered by a hooded cape, but there was no mistaking the gown. Prudence!

He turned to Wedge with an urgent frown. "Toby! Go back to the warehouse and wait for me there. Do you understand? Can you find your way?"

Wedge looked confused for a moment, then smiled and nodded. "Aye, sir."

He hurriedly fished in his waistcoat pocket and pressed a coin into the man's hand. "Buy yourself a pie while you're waiting. But wait for me! No matter how long."

The smile became a grin. "Aye, sir!"

He watched to be sure that Wedge turned back, then raced into the alley, elbowing his way through the crowd. The woman had vanished by the time he neared the end of the narrow street. He felt a moment of panic, then sighed in relief as he spotted her again, just rounding the corner. He reached her at a gallop, took hold of her arm, and swung her around.

"Are you looking for a tousle, my fine cove?" The woman who smiled archly up at him was blond and pert, her face painted and powdered with all the artfulness of a skilled whore.

He felt a jolt of disappointment, then dismay.

"You're a right strapping lad," she said. "I could give you an hour or two of pleasure."

He scowled down at her dress. There was no mistaking it—even to the silver-threaded stomacher. "I don't want your services," he said in disgust.

She frowned at the hand that still gripped her arm. "Then let me go. A lady has a right to be on the streets unmolested. I'm as good as you, for all your hoity-toity ways." She struggled against his steely grip. "Cursed rogue! Must I call for a bailiff?"

He wanted to choke the little baggage. "Where did you get that gown?"

She thrust out her chin in defiance. "I didn't steal it!"

He felt a moment's relief. He had pictured Prudence lying in some dark alley, wounded or dead. *"Where* did you get it?" he said again, and gave her arm a savage shake.

"From a friend!" she said hotly. "And 'tis not for sale, if that's in your thoughts."

By the beard of Aesculapius, he would go mad! "What friend?"

"What's it to you?" she sneered.

"Prudence?"

She gaped at him. " 'Od's fish! How did you know?"

He cast his eyes down the street and saw the hanging tankards of a tavern. "Come!" he said, pulling on the girl's arm. "We'll talk."

She dug her heels into the dirt between the cobbles and thrust out her hand. "I don't talk—nor do anything!—without a shilling."

He muttered an oath and slapped the silver coin into her raised hand, then dragged her—grumbling in protest—to the tavern. He found a quiet corner, threw down his hat and cloak, and glared at the wench across the table.

"Now," he said, "Prudence Allbright gave you the gown?"

"Yes," she said sourly. "Only this morning."

"Why?"

She rolled her eyes as though he were a half-wit. "I *told* you. We're friends."

He curled his lip in an expression of disbelief, his eyes raking her painted face. Why would an innocent like Prudence traffic with a strumpet?

She drew herself up in proud disdain. "I may be beneath the likes of you—a haughty cove, if ever I saw one. But Pru and I are friends for all time, whatever our circumstances. We grew up together."

"In Wiltshire?"

"Yes."

"What's your name?"

"Why should I tell you?"

"Because I'll break your arm if you don't," he said through clenched teeth.

"No need to be uncivil, my high-handed popinjay," she said, glaring at him. "I don't owe you a farthing."

"Damn it, your name!"

"Elizabeth Berridge," she said quickly. "But they call me Betsy."

"And where do you live?"

"Shoe Lane."

"Do you know . . . ?"

She interrupted him with a contemptuous toss of her yellow curls. "I'll not answer another question till you tell me who *you* are."

"Only her husband," he said bitterly.

"Pshaw! What a crackbrain. She doesn't have a husband. I left her not ten hours ago. On her way to find her sweetheart and marry him."

He stared in stunned surprise and alarm. *"Marry* him?" He fairly shouted the word.

" 'Tis what she said. And as soon as possible."

"That can't be! She married me in Virginia!"

It was Betsy's turn to look surprised. "She told me some of what happened since we were parted. The accident aboard ship, the voyage to Virginia. I knew by her garments that she had been well cared for. But"—Betsy stirred uncomfortably—"a woman of the game don't pry. And she didn't tell me about you."

He felt like a cast-off dog. "Clearly I was of no great importance to her," he muttered. "Just the means to get her home again."

She shrugged. "A man has to be good for something. A gift for a treasure."

He swore softly. This was the little trollop who had filled Prudence's head with nonsense. "You saw her this morning?"

"And glad I was to see her. She vanished last summer like a snowflake in the Indies. I thought never to see her again in this world. Then bold as life, there she was on my doorstep. She came to get the money I was keeping for her. And Jamie's ring. His pledge of marriage."

That cut him to the quick. "He even gave her a ring," he said, his heart curdling with bitterness. "And now she's off to commit bigamy, no doubt.

As though our vows had never been spoken." He sighed heavily. "She must love him very much."

Betsy seemed almost pleased at his dismay. " 'Od's fish, of course she does! He was all she spoke of when she came to me in London last June."

He signaled to the barmaid. He needed a drink. "I should have understood. I found her weeping many a time. For her Lord Jamie, I suppose."

"Or for her child."

"The one who died?"

Betsy's gray eyes widened in shock. "Who told you that?"

He was bewildered by her tone. "She said that she lost the child."

Betsy snorted. "Aye, that she did. To that psalm-singing, sanctimonious old goat of a grandfather of hers."

He couldn't believe his ears. "What do you mean? The child is *alive?*"

"God willing, he still is. For her sake."

He felt as though he'd been hit in the pit of his stomach. "Tell me about it," he said hoarsely. "All of it."

Betsy helped herself to the wine the barmaid had brought, pushed back the hood of her cape, and settled herself more comfortably into her chair. She was clearly animated by the importance of her tale. Her power over Ross. She ignored the impatient drumming of his fingers on the table and began her account, eyes shining like a malevolent gossip sharing the latest news.

"We were a rum pair, she and I. She was innocent and pure and God-fearing, whilst I . . ." Betsy shrugged. "A trial to my widowed mother from the day I was born. Pru was the only one in the village who didn't treat me with a high hand, no matter how many scrapes I got into. She was my loyal comrade, always looking for the happy side of life, and . . ."

"Yes, yes, I know," he snapped. "Have I not lived with her these past four months? Get on with it!"

The saucy wench refused to be hurried. She gave him a withering glance and took a dainty sip of her wine. "She was close to her papa. When he died—oh, it's near to two years, now—she was beside herself. I never saw her so low."

"And then?" he prompted.

"All in good time, my fine gentleman. You might not fancy a romp between the sheets with such as me, but you'll hear me out. For as long as it takes me. And treat me like a lady, not a whore. Or you'll see my heels out that door faster than you can spit!"

He gnashed his teeth. "Continue with your story. *Madam,*" he added sarcastically.

She snorted. "I'll wager *you* never took a fancy to a tart. Too low for you to stoop?"

He groaned and rubbed his eyes with his hand. He was behaving like a prig, when all he wanted was news of Prudence. "I beg you, in all humility, to go on."

She softened her tone, clearly stirred by his anguish. "After Pru's father died, she had only her grandfather, Squire Hammond. And his bitch of a wife. A miserable old widow who drove her first husband to the grave. What a pair! They embraced John Wesley, and consequently kept Prudence on a short tether. Always dragging her to church and chiding her for a sinner. Lord love me, I would have gone mad. They even scolded her for laughter. But she endured, though her spirit was nearly broken. The old squire was a fearsome man, ruling Burghope Manor like a miserly king. She trembled and obeyed the tyrant. What could she do?"

He frowned up at the beams of the tavern. "She called me tyrant, sometimes."

"Were you?"

" 'Tis my way," he muttered, filled with remorse. "I reckon that Jamie was kinder to her."

"I never met him myself. To my way of thinking, the cullion only wanted one thing of her." Betsy sighed. "But I never saw her so happy. She would sneak away from the manor sometimes, and we would meet. Oh, the laughter and sweet whisperings, as she told me all about him. He had promised her marriage, you see, and she had faith in him."

He nodded. "Yes. That would be Prudence's way. How long . . . ?"

"Jamie? Only a fortnight. And then he was gone."

"To America?"

"Yes. He had a small inheritance, he said. But she never doubted that he'd return."

"She looked for him in Virginia. He had sold his plantation."

"She told me this morning. All in tears."

"And the child?"

"It was dreadful when she realized she was carrying it. Not that she was afraid, mind you. But—God-fearing as she was—she felt shame. 'Will God punish me, Betsy?' she would ask. I tried to entreat her to put an end to it. I knew an old crone in Limpley Stoke."

He clenched his fists. As a surgeon, he'd treated more than one unfortunate maid who had endured the butchery of some old crone. "Thanks be to God she didn't listen to you," he murmured.

"How could she—with her faith in Jamie? He had given her his ring. His promise to return and marry her. She wrote him desperate letters, but he never answered. We plotted together to leave the village, run away to London before her condition showed. But her grandfather's steward—a mean little worm! He had seen her and Jamie in the fields. He tried to blackmail her in exchange for her favors. But when she refused, he went running to his master."

"And the squire?"

"They were horrid to her. He and the sanctimonious old bitch. They scorned her for a willful, immoral child. They called down all the curses of heaven upon her. They dragged her to church for hours on end and forced her to listen to sermons from the self-righteous old clergyman. 'Od's fish, I think they would have beat her, but for her condition! And for the rest, they kept her under lock and key."

He swore softly, filled with Prudence's agony.

"I used to climb a tree to whisper with her at her window. They would make her stand for hours in a corner until she fainted. And all to force her into telling the name of her lover. But she stood fast. Never a word passed her lips."

Betsy sighed again. "After a while, the squire got it into his head that a marriage of convenience, as he called it, was the only thing that would redeem her in his sight. He's a cheeseparing old bastard, but he was prepared to pay a local lout to marry her and save her honor." She snorted in disgust. "*Her* honor. I'll wager the proud fool was only thinking of his own reputation."

"And she refused, of course. Because of Jamie."

" 'I can't, Betsy,' she told me. ' 'Tis against God.' She was so sure of her Lord Jamie's pure love that she thought it a sin to betray him by marrying another."

Betsy bent her head and wiped at a tear. "I blame myself for what happened. I should have been there to succor her. But"—she twisted her fingers together—"there was a soldier, you see. I ran off with him. He was a liar and a son of a bitch. I should have known. He set me up here in London. Begged me to 'entertain' his friends. When I found out he was taking money from them, I threw the wretch out."

"Did you return to your village?"

"How could I? When everyone knew what I'd done?" She laughed bitterly. "I think my Maw was well rid of me."

"And Prudence?"

"I had written to her and told her where I was. A kindly servant managed to slip my letters to her. She answered but once, her letter filled with despair." Betsy was beginning to tremble. "Then, after months of silence, she turned up at my lodgings this summer. Like a whipped dog."

"God save her," he muttered. "What happened?"

Betsy began to weep, her tears staining her painted face. "She had given birth to her son. And those . . . those bloody cruel villains. They let her nurse it. Learn to love it. And then, one day, she went to find him in his cradle. And he was gone."

"Gone?"

"They had sent him off to foster care. They told her she would never see her babe again. 'Tis the Methodist belief, you see, that a child of sin is yet unblemished."

He lowered his head, fighting his own tears. "Oh, God. Prudence."

She touched his arm in sympathy. "Forgive me if I was saucy to you before. I thought you were"—she shrugged in weary worldliness—"a man like any other."

"More like a blind fool." How had he failed to see beyond Prudence's sunny face to the grief within?

She smiled in understanding. "I don't even know your name."

"Ross. Ross Manning. But the child . . . ?"

"The proudful old squire never reconciled himself to having only a daughter and a granddaughter. He intends to raise the boy as his own. In his own image, to carry on his line. Prudence humbled herself, begged him on her knees. She would marry anyone he chose if she could keep her baby. The cold-hearted bastards refused, of course. They called her Mary Magdalene and dragged her to the edge of the village. All the pious folk were watching. Not a soul lifted a hand to help her."

Betsy began to cry again. "She told me they . . . they threw clods of dirt and cursed her as she passed. Her grandfather said she was never to return. Or he would have her stripped naked and horsewhipped in the village square."

"Christ Jesus." He groaned and buried his head in his arms.

"That's why she needs Jamie and his wedding ring."

He lifted his head. "What do you mean?"

"He's a great lord. A viscount, she said. Only he can demand his son back from the squire."

"But I'm her husband. *I* can demand the return of the child."

"You don't know the squire. He's a man of importance in the village. He scorns his inferiors. Prudence's father was the schoolmaster, and a fine, churchgoing man. But the squire treated him like a dog. He always cursed his daughter for marrying so low. I'm sorry, sir. But as rare a gent as you may be, you'd be powerless against Squire Hammond. He has money and influence. And the law would find for him, you may be sure. It will take a noble title—Jamie's title—to force him to give up the boy."

He was devastated by Betsy's story, imagining how desperate Prudence must have been. Small wonder she had raged at their marriage, seeing her child lost to her for good.

He scowled, suddenly filled with unreasoning anger. "We lived together for months. She shared my bed. Why the devil didn't she tell me the whole story? Damn it, she allowed me to think the child was dead! Why didn't she trust me?"

Betsy laughed gently. "She's too innocent, too sweet. She sees only the face that people turn to the world. And I suspect that you can be quite overbearing, and filled with stern judgments."

"Absurd," he muttered uncomfortably.

"You looked at me and saw a whore, without any thought to who I was." There was no accusation in her soft voice, but he cringed at the truth. "My eyes are not as clouded as hers," she went on. "Life has given me clear vision, if not wisdom. And so I see what she didn't."

He raised a quizzical eyebrow. "Which is?"

"You love her," she said simply.

"Rot and nonsense!" How could he fall in love again after Martha? And so soon? It would be a betrayal of all they had shared.

"Why did you marry Pru, then?"

"Circumstances forced us. Nothing more. But damn it, she owed me the truth because I'm her husband! She had a duty to tell me."

Her eyes were soft with worldly understanding. "If you'll have it that way. But what will you do now?"

"Find my wayward wife," he growled. "And bring her home where she belongs. She left this morning, you say?"

"The bells of Saint Paul's were sounding eight."

"And she'll go to Jamie, of course. Her true love."

"Without a doubt."

"His name and title?"

Betsy made a face. "I know not. She never told me, you see. He lives in Berkshire. That's all I know."

He pounded on the table in frustration. "How the devil am I to find him?"

"It were best you let her go. Whatever her mad scheme. It would break her heart to lose her child for good and all."

"I'm her *husband.* That ought to carry some weight with the squire."

Betsy looked doubtful, chewing on the edge of her lip. She frowned in thought and curled a lock of her blond hair around one finger. "There is a way," she said at last, "though I'm fearful for Pru. If your interference should cost her her child, she'd never forgive you."

"What way?" he said impatiently.

"If she finds Jamie, they'll go to our village to challenge Squire Hammond. You can wait for her there. Winsley. Near Bradford-on-Avon."

"Yes, of course. I never thought of that. Burghope Manor, you say."

He slumped back in his chair, drained. So much to consider, so many compromises in life. He looked across the table at Betsy. She was right, of course. He was far too judgmental. It had blinded him to Prudence's suffering. Blinded him to the good heart behind Betsy's painted face. She was young and pretty, and circumstances had cast her out on the streets, to live a life of degradation and the diseases that ultimately destroyed her kind.

He fished in his coat pocket, pulled out a large sack of coins and tossed it on the table. "In God's name," he said gruffly, "give up your trade. There's naught but death in it."

She smiled, her clear gray eyes shining in gratitude. She put the purse into her bodice, stood up and covered her head with her hood. "You're a good man, Ross Manning. Did she know that?"

He laughed bitterly. "I doubt it. She was always dreaming of Jamie. Speaking of him. She never even saw me."

Betsy turned to go. "I wish you good fortune. And love, if you're wise enough to seek it." She hurried to the door of the tavern and went out into the evening air.

He sat brooding for a long time, thinking of what the woman had told him. He had only one choice, though it wrenched his soul. He couldn't let Prudence go against the law by marrying again. And—if he let himself dwell on it—the thought of her in Jamie's arms filled him with rage. For better or for worse, she belonged to him.

He paid for the wine, threw on his hat and cloak, and returned to the street. He allowed himself a moment of uneasiness, praying that Wedge would have the sense to wait for him, then went down to the river. A cold mist hung over the water. He found a uniformed waterman to row him to the new Westminster Bridge, and sat in the boat like a dead man, his thoughts in turmoil. God help him, this was the only way.

It was dark by the time he climbed the stairs leading up from the river. He hailed a link-boy with a flaring torch of pitch and tow to light his way, then strode purposefully past the Parade and the House of Commons to Downing Street. He looked up, his stomach tightening when he saw the sign on the door of the brick town house.

"JASON MANNING," it read. "PHYSICIAN." He hesitated, torn with anguish.

Just then, a carriage pulled up, and a graying man stepped from the building. Ross clenched his fists and intercepted him as he was about to step into the coach.

"Jason," he said coldly, "I've come back. I need your help."

Chapter
Twenty-Three

⌇⌇⌇⌇⌇

"What do you want, woman?" The porter scowled at Prudence through the iron bars of his gate.

She glanced down at herself. She must look like a ragamuffin, with her bundle of clothes and her dusty gown and cloak. She was almost sorry now that she'd given her apricot satin to Betsy—her prettiest gown. Then she chided herself for an ungrateful friend. Anyone but Betsy might have disappeared with her money long since. Still, what would Jamie think of her bedraggled state? Her lavender gown that was far less fine than the apricot?

The trip had taken longer than she thought; the mail coach had been slow, stopping at every village along the way. And the cost for everything had been dearer than she planned. She had used the last of her money to pay the landlord of the coaching inn last night, with scarcely a tester left over for breakfast, let alone a carriage ride. She had walked all the way this morning from Newbury, contriving only to beg a ride for the last few miles of her trip. A kindly farmer, on his way to Lambourn Downs, had allowed her to sit in the back of his rickety cart.

But she was here at last. And she wasn't about to let a haughty porter keep her from Jamie! Not after all she had endured. She brushed off a bit of straw from her skirts and faced the man proudly. "I'm here to see James Arnott, Viscount Lord Swindon."

He gave a coarse snort. "And you'd disturb His Lordship on a Sunday?"

Courage, Prudence, she thought. She raised her voice. "See here, my good man. 'Tis a matter of grave importance. His Lordship would be quite vexed if he knew you barred my way."

He looked skeptical, wavered, then shrugged and opened the gate to her. She sailed through, her head held high, and marched down the long, straight drive leading to the great house, conscious of the man's eyes on her all the while.

After all of Jamie's boasting, Swindon Hall was a disappointment. Though grand, it had fallen into a state of disrepair, with loose tiles on the roofs and crumbling bits of masonry. The unraked lawns were covered with autumn leaves, the late-blooming flowers needed tending, and half the trees of the drive were dead.

Still, there was scaffolding against one wing of the house, and a fresh coat of paint on the door; clearly Jamie had come into some money and had embarked on a course of restoration. Perhaps the decrepit old house was the reason he had sold his plantation.

Her heart was pounding by the time she lifted the heavy door knocker. The supercilious footman who opened the door eyed her up and down as though she were a speck of dirt. He shuddered, and the curls of his elaborate periwig quivered on his shoulders. "Yes?" he inquired with a curl to his lip.

She shifted her bundle uncomfortably from one hand to the other. She reminded herself that if this proud creature had to *work* in a great house, he was no better than she, for all his high airs. Her clothing had been fine enough for the gentry in Virginia; for all the wretch knew, she could be a duchess traveling incognito. She lifted her chin, used the same regal tone that had cowed the porter. " 'Tis Mistress Prudence Allbright, to see Lord Swindon. I regret I have no appointment, but I've come up from London unexpectedly."

He bowed, sufficiently impressed. "Come this way, madam." He ushered her to a small parlor and bowed again. "Please wait."

She drew upon unfamiliar reserves of dignity. " 'Tis a most urgent matter," she said. "I trust His Lordship will receive me at once." She nearly laughed aloud at his awed expression as he left the room. Surely the self-confident, dignified woman who could command such respect was a far cry from the Prudence of a few short months ago—the timid country girl who had deferred to all signs of authority. She wondered how much she owed to Ross's faith in her strength and self-possession.

No! She mustn't think of Ross. That part of her life was over and done with. It would only grieve her to dwell on the past.

She glanced around the small parlor. It was fine enough, she supposed, with its handsome furniture and patterned carpets. Still, the windows were bare of draperies, and there was a dearth of paintings on the walls; clearly, it was not the grandest reception room in the house. Well, when she was married to Jamie, she would see to it that visitors were received in finer surroundings, no matter how humble their station.

"Madam." The footman stood in the doorway, the haughty smile back on his face. "His Lordship informs me that he will not see you today. He is about to dine. Come back tomorrow."

Not see her, after she had come so far? And to be repulsed for the sake of a *dinner?* She pulled Jamie's ring from her finger and thrust it angrily at the servant. "Give him this. I have not come all this way to wait until tomorrow!"

She dismissed him with an imperious wave of her hand, but when he had gone, she crumbled. How could Jamie not wish to see her?

Perhaps he had watched from a window, seen her on the drive—a weary foot-traveler, not worthy of his attention. She inspected herself in a large mirror over the mantel. Oh, alas! Her cloak was covered with dust, and unruly tendrils of hair peeped out from the hood. She put down her bundle, took off the cloak, and swiftly redressed her hair, smoothing the curls and arranging several long ringlets in an artful fashion over one shoulder. She straightened her bodice, brushed the last lingering wisps of straw from her skirt.

She tried to ignore the trembling of her hands; she was more nervous about this interview than she cared to admit to herself. It had been more than a year. She had changed. Had he?

" 'Tis the girl from Winsley, I believe."

The voice from the doorway made her jump. It was soft and faintly petulant. She turned to face Jamie.

James Arnott, Lord Swindon, closed the door behind him and stared at her, a sour expression on his face. He wore a violet-colored frock suit, and his dark hair was elegantly dressed and powdered. He was as handsome as she remembered him—the sparkling dark eyes, the aquiline nose, the soft, full mouth.

But the faint whiff of alcohol that reached her nostrils explained the sparkle, and the mouth drooped in a sullen manner. She remembered a god; the creature who stood before her, eying her with distaste, was a sulky child. She wondered if he would ever grow into the man that Ross was.

"Well," he said, "why have you come, after all this time?"

She reminded herself that she needed him. That his love was all that could comfort her into the bleak future. She smiled warmly, hoping to brighten his mood and bring back the lover she had known. How to begin? "The . . . Swindon Hall is as beautiful as you told me about, that . . . that day in the meadow," she stammered, too shy to get to the point at once. "And I see you're restoring it. Did you realize a good profit from your plantation?"

His eyes narrowed. "Have you come for money?"

"Of course not!" How could he think such a thing?

"Then why are you here?"

"Did you never receive my letters?" she cried.

He pulled a silver snuff box from his waistcoat, tapped a bit of the brown powder onto his fist, and inhaled sharply. He grimaced, nose twitching, and caught the sneeze in a lace-edged silk handkerchief. "Not until I returned from America."

"But why did you not answer then? Your letters would have found me." *Her* letters had been desperate, but circumspect, for fear that they would fall into her grandfather's hands. She had only begged Jamie to return to her on a matter of urgent importance.

He shrugged. "You said, in your letters, that you were going to London. I assumed you were long gone by the time I read them. How was I to reach you?"

That sounded reasonable. It quieted the fears that had haunted her. The dreadful thought that he had received the letters before he went away—and ignored them. Foolish Prudence. Was he not still her Jamie?

The man who had pledged his love forever? "I followed you halfway across the world," she whispered.

"How touching," he drawled. "And now, here you are. What is this urgent matter that brings you to me today?"

"You must help me."

He stifled a yawn. "My dear girl, I have no obligation to you."

"You *must!* We have a child."

His eyes opened in startled surprise. Then they lowered and he looked at her warily. "Are you certain it's mine?"

Her lip began to tremble. What had happened to her sweet Jamie? "Of course I am. Do you think I could forget your loving promises? Do you think I could endure torment and shame, but for the joy of presenting you with a son?"

"A son?" His handsome face broke into a wide smile, reminding her of the Jamie of old. "My God, a *son!*" He took her by the hands and brought them to his lips. "Prudence. Bless you. A thousand times!"

She felt proud and remorseful all at the same time. How could she have doubted him, even for a moment? He had only been taken by surprise at her appearance after all this time. Perhaps her months of silence had even persuaded him that she no longer cared for him. "He's a beautiful child. Strong and robust," she said.

He cast an eager glance around the room. "Where is he? Did you bring him?"

She pulled her hands away and turned her back on him, frightened and ashamed to tell him the truth. "No," she said in a low voice. "I . . . I haven't seen him for months now."

He put his hand on her arm and spun her around to face him. "What the devil do you mean? Haven't seen him? Is he well?"

She couldn't meet his intense gaze, the dark eyes filled with accusation. "My . . . my grandfather refused to let me keep him. He disowned me for my sin. And now he intends to raise the boy as his own."

He muttered a string of foul oaths. "The damned villain!"

"I know he would give up the child if you were there. He couldn't refuse. I never told him your name. But when we stand before him, and

I claim you as the child's father, he wouldn't have the courage to refuse. Not in the face of your title and influence."

The smile returned to his face. "Of course. I'll twist the rogue's tail for him! We'll leave for Burghope Manor at once." He laughed for joy, throwing back his head in delight. "A son! Heaven smiled upon me this day!" He pulled her into his arms and gave her an exuberant kiss.

God forgive her. She tried to remember how his kisses had thrilled her. But she felt nothing.

He released her and tugged impatiently on the bell cord. When the footman appeared, he barked orders in a sharp voice. His carriage was to be brought round at once. Well furnished with dinner for himself and the lady. He turned to Prudence. "I must make my excuses to my dinner companions. I'll not be a moment." He grinned again and hastened from the room.

He returned almost before she had had time to put on her cloak and pick up her bundle. He dashed into the room, swirling his greatcoat around his shoulders, and hurried her to the waiting coach.

They flew along the highroad, the coachman having been spurred on by Jamie's promise of a purse of gold should they reach Winsley under three hours. Jamie lowered the blinds against the slanting afternoon sun and attacked their hamper of food with gusto. Prudence was almost too elated to eat, but she sampled the roasted chicken and nibbled at the almond biscuits, and accepted a small glass of wine.

Jamie was content to finish the bottle. He poured the last of the wine into his glass, ignoring the ruby liquid that sloshed over the edges in rhythm to the rocking coach. He smiled expansively and held out a small box to Prudence. "Have another macaroon."

She shook her head. Her stomach was churning with excitement. At last! To hold her sweet child again. She could scarcely believe it was happening.

Jamie finished his dinner and leaned back on the velvet cushions, watching her through heavy-lidded eyes. " 'Pon my soul, but I'd forgot what a fine-looking wench you are."

She blushed and looked down at her hands.

He laughed at her modesty. "Still as shy as ever? I recall the first time

I saw you, up on that hill, with the wind in your hair. Do you still sing your songs?"

"There was precious little to sing about, after you'd gone," she said with a sigh.

"But you were my pretty sweetheart, and now you've given me a son." He patted the seat beside him. "Come and sit with me."

She moved across the carriage and seated herself primly at some distance from him. But he put out his arm and pulled her close.

"Give me your sweet mouth," he said in a hoarse voice. "My pretty Prudence."

She hesitated, then lifted her head reluctantly to his. If she was to be his wife, she would have to learn to accept his kisses. And much more.

His mouth was hard and possessive, grinding down on hers with a hungry impatience that repelled her. Had she ever been so young, so foolish as to imagine that she loved him?

He seemed not to notice her strained reserve. He kissed her thoroughly, his tongue invading her mouth, then leaned back against the cushions and sighed in pleasure. He put his hand on her skirt and rubbed it suggestively along her thigh. "Is the rest of you as sweet as I remember?"

She tried to push his hand away. "No, Jamie. Please don't . . ."

He gathered her into his arms. "Prudence. Sweetheart. How I've ached for you, all this long year. You gave me only a taste of your charms. I hunger for more. Will you not succor a starving man?" His eyes were warm and loving, filled with the same tender yearning that had conquered her before.

She bit her lip, torn with indecision. Sooner or later, she would have to allow him to make love to her. By tomorrow at this time, they'd be married, in all likelihood. And then her body would belong to him forever. She sighed in surrender, and kissed him resolutely on the mouth.

He held her close, grunting in the enjoyment of her kiss, then lifted her and laid her across the seat of the carriage. He threw his body on top of hers and kissed her face and neck and bosom, moving his hips against hers in jerking spasms that bespoke his impatience.

She tried desperately to respond, to tell herself that she owed him this. Her willing body in exchange for the joy of having her child again. But when he lifted himself from her and began to raise her skirts, she shuddered. It was too soon, with the thought of Ross's sweet lovemaking still fresh in her mind. She pushed at him and struggled to sit up. "No, Jamie. Not now. Not here."

He pouted and tried to force her down again, his hands clutching her breasts. "You said you loved me once. Was it a lie?"

"No, of course not." Heaven knew it had been true a year ago. " 'Tis only that . . ." Sweet Mother of Mercy, what could she say?

The speeding carriage rocked over a bump in the road and gave a jounce that sent him tumbling to the floor. She saw her opportunity. She gave a shy laugh. "How can we make love, with the carriage bouncing so?"

He scrambled to his knees and imprisoned her in his arms once more. "I shall hold you very tightly," he growled.

"No, please. 'Tis most uncomfortable, and . . . and . . ." She crumbled and began to weep, her heart aching for Ross.

He released her, sat back on his haunches, and glowered at her. " 'Pon my soul, I remember you as an agreeable girl. Not given to silly tears, nor coyness."

She wiped at her wet cheeks. "I'm a mother today," she said simply, "and all I can think of is my dear child. Forgive me. Perhaps tonight, after I've seen him again, held him in my arms . . ." She hoped he could read the promise in her eyes.

He grumbled and settled himself into the seat opposite her. "I trust you will be more yielding later," he said sulkily. "And in better humor. When we stop at an inn for the night, I'll expect your compliance."

"You shall have the Prudence you remember," she said with a heavy sigh.

He grumbled again, crossed his arms against his chest, and closed his eyes. In a few moments he was snoring softly.

She raised the blind beside her and stared out at the countryside. The bleakness of the landscape, with its nearly denuded trees, mirrored the emptiness in her heart, and the sunshine mocked her dark thoughts.

She had counted on Jamie's love, had dwelt on her sweet memories of him as a bolster for her courage. And surely he had wooed her as charmingly today as he had all that long time ago. But was it her love he wanted? Or only her body? Was his tenderness merely a calculated scheme to win her favors?

Betsy had called her innocent. Ross had called her blind to Jamie's cunning entreaties. And surely Jamie's sullen disappointment today was more the behavior of a thwarted child than an understanding lover.

No! For her own future peace of mind, she mustn't allow such thoughts! She had to believe that Jamie loved her. Perhaps she had spent too much time with Ross. She was beginning to see the world through his cynical eyes.

She brightened as the carriage neared Winsley. The villagers had been cruel and contemptuous when she left, but it was still her childhood home, the repository of many a dear recollection. There were the stubbly fields where she and Betsy had romped amid the summer grain, stealing a stalk of wheat to munch as they ran and laughed under the sun. There were the sheep-dotted meadows, rising to the rolling hills where Jamie had knelt to pledge his love. There the village green, its spreading trees still clinging to a few pale yellow and umber leaves. They cast lengthening shadows across the smooth lawn.

And Papa's schoolhouse. She gulped back her tears at sight of the old stones. How many happy memories it held, the secrets of her youth locked within its walls.

Jamie roused himself when the coach stopped abruptly. He yawned and stretched and frowned at her. "What is it?"

The door opened and the coachman stuck in his head. "We're at Winsley now. Where does Your Lordship wish to go?"

Prudence directed him to the shadowy, tree-arched lane that led to Burghope Manor. The ivy on the mellow, buff-colored stone walls of the house was now a deep red, and the dormers, rising to peaked slate roofs, reflected the thin November sun in their mullioned windows. There was smoke coming from only a few of the chimneys: Grandpapa was too miserly to light many fires until the snows fell.

Her heart thumped as they pulled up to the arched portico with its welcoming benches on either side of the door—a courtesy to weary travelers that had been installed by a more generous previous occupant. Trembling,

Prudence tucked her arm through Jamie's and allowed him to knock.

To her relief, the door was opened by Old Meg, the only one of Grandpapa's servants who had ever been her friend. It was Meg who had managed to slip her Betsy's letters, in those long, dreadful months of imprisonment.

The ancient face twisted into a happy, toothless grin. "Mistress Prudence! What joy to see you, luv. And welcome you are to the manor! Come in."

Prudence hesitated. "Does he . . . does he still curse my name?"

The kindly face fell. "We bean't allowed to speak of you, miss. But come along. How can he refuse to see you, and you bloomin' like a rose?"

Jamie growled and pushed his way into the entrance hall. "He'll bloody well see *me*, or I'll know the reason why!"

The old servant had been too delighted at Prudence's appearance to pay Jamie any mind; now she stepped back and in deference she bobbed politely. "Of course, sir. Come this way."

Meg led them to the oldest part of the house, and ushered them into a snug parlor. It glowed with a myriad of colors from the setting sun that still shone through its stained glass windows. The old woman bustled to the fireplace—a huge Gothic arch with Latin words painted on the stucco above it—and lit a fire in the grate. "I'll tell the squire you're here."

Prudence paced nervously when she had gone. She didn't fear for her safety—not with Jamie here. But Grandpapa had always managed to intimidate her, to reduce her to a helpless, cringing child. She prayed not to shame herself before Jamie.

She heard the ominous clump of Grandpapa's cane coming down the passageway, and then he lumbered into the room. His gouty foot was bandaged, and he winced with every step.

Prudence's heart sank. When his foot was troubling him, he was even more terrifying.

He was supported by his wife. Her thin, aging face was wrinkled in disapproval, with lines cut deep into her cheeks from her nostrils to her chin. Her mouth was white around her tight-pressed lips, and her pale eyes glittered malevolently. She guided her husband to a chair and urged him to sit.

The old man shook her off, too angry even for that. He glared at Prudence, twitching with rage; his full, old-fashioned wig shook with the movements of his ponderous body. He lifted his cane and jabbed it toward Prudence.

"You dare to come into this house, jezebel? And on the Lord's day? Have you no shame? You sinful baggage! I'll have you pilloried!"

Prudence flinched, his words like sharp blows to her conscience.

Jamie growled and leapt forward. "I'll not have you speak to Prudence that way!"

"*Silence,* sirrah!" the old man roared. "You've come to lend her support, I'll wager. But do you know what this . . . this creature is? A whore! A *whore,* sir! She has broken God's commandments, brought dishonor to this house with the sin of uncleanliness. Evil fornication!"

He gestured toward the fireplace. "Do you see that inscription? Archbishop Cranmer himself had it inscribed, two hundred years ago." He translated the Latin in a pompous, stentorian voice. " 'Lord, I have loved the habitation of Thy house, and the place where Thine honor dwelleth'. There is no longer honor in *this* house, sirrah, thanks to that shameless strumpet!"

His voice was like thunder, as frightening as Prudence remembered it. His face had turned purple, the veins swelling on his forehead. Even Jamie seemed cowed. But, strangely, Prudence felt her strength growing. For all his cruel words, he was simply a noisy old man, without the power to hurt her further.

"Grandpapa . . ." she began, willing her trembling to cease.

He jerked his head sharply toward her, his eyes narrowing with a withering look of disgust and rage that had frozen her in terror many a time. "I had put aside a fine dot for you, to bring to a husband. But you're your father's child, worthless and ungrateful. And now you dare to return, when I forbade it?"

She refused to be intimidated, to allow him to make her feel godless and unworthy. She put her hand on Jamie's sleeve. "This man does you honor by coming to your house, Grandpapa," she said boldly. "This is Lord Swindon."

The old man sneered. "A wanton actor you've hired for this farce, no doubt."

Grandpapa's wife gave a sniff of disdain. "Now may the good Lord bring down His wrath upon the pair of them," she said, and cast her eyes heavenward.

Jamie found his courage at last. He fished angrily in his pocket and pulled out his card, which he thrust toward the old man. "You will receive us with honor, Squire Hammond. I'm not in the habit of being insulted by my inferiors!"

The sight of the engraved card wrought a stunning transformation on Grandpapa. The redness of his face subsided to a fleshy pink, the scowl melting into an obsequious smile. "Your Lordship. I had not dreamed . . . The girl has been a liar and a rebel since the day she was born. A stranger to the values of thrift and hard work and honesty. You must forgive me if I naturally assumed . . ." He frowned at his wife. "Abigail. Quickly! A chair for our honored guest."

Abigail gave a cringing curtsy to Jamie, her face a mask of servility, then ushered him to the best chair in the room. She helped her husband to sit, and propped a little footstool beneath his bandaged foot. She even managed to nod coldly to Prudence and point to a stool in the corner.

Prudence ignored her and took the armchair next to Jamie. She felt oddly released from the past, despite Grandpapa's calumnies. She had nothing to fear from him. He would part with the child without a quarrel.

The old man leaned back in his chair and smiled, his fingers entwined across his round belly. "Now, Lord Swindon, will you take a dish of chocolate with us? I regret I cannot offer you Madeira or canary on the Lord's day, but I trust our humble fare will suffice."

Jamie pulled out his silver box and helped himself to his snuff. Abigail opened her mouth to protest, but Grandpapa silenced her with a hard stare.

Jamie sneezed delicately and dabbed at his nose. "Canary," he said in a firm voice.

The smile was frozen on Grandpapa's face. "Canary it shall be. Abby, take out the decanter."

Abigail looked horrified, as though Jamie had just smeared paint on the gates of Heaven. "But husband, the Lord's day . . . !"

The old man clenched his teeth. " 'Tis a great day when a viscount honors us with his presence. You will serve our guest!"

Prudence felt the old rebellion stir in her breast. "I shall have a glass as well," she said, as Abigail made her way across the room to a sideboard. God forgive her for the sin of pride, but it gladdened her to see them both humbled at last.

"Now, Your Lordship," said Grandpapa, as Abigail reluctantly filled two glasses with wine and set them on a tray. "How may I serve you? Set me a task, that I may show my devotion."

Jamie flicked a speck of dust from his satin waistcoat, clearly enjoying his position of superiority. "I've come for my son," he said.

There was a loud crash. Abigail stood like a statue, dumbly staring at the tray on the floor. The liquor made a large puddle at her feet, sparkling ruby among the shards of broken glass.

Grandpapa began to stammer, his face turning red again. "Your son . . . it can't be . . . I . . ."

Prudence felt the cold hand of dread on her heart. "Is he here? Is he alive?" she cried.

Grandpapa groaned and cast frantic eyes at his wife. "He's gone!" he cried at last. "His father, Lord Longwood, came and took him away."

"*Gone?* Oh, sweet heaven," whispered Prudence, horrified.

Jamie swiveled his head to her; there was accusation in his dark eyes. "How many gentlemen have you gulled with your lies, hoping to find one who might rescue your child?"

She shook her head in desperation. "I don't know any Lord Longwood!"

His lip curled in disgust. "You lying bawd. How many other men did you spread your legs for?"

She clutched her hand to her mouth and choked back a sob. "He's *yours*, Jamie. I swear it! He has your black hair. I never lay with another. I'll swear it on the Bible!"

Her anguish seemed to convince Jamie of her sincerity. He rose from his chair and glowered down at her grandfather. "Are you such a fool that you'd give away my child to any man who comes through your door?"

Grandpapa put his hands on the arms of his chair and attempted to rise. "See here, I'll not be insulted! Lord Longwood gave me irrefutable proofs of his paternity." His mouth twisted with injured pride. "The blackguard threatened me with the charge of kidnapping if I refused to turn over the boy. He even forbade me to see the child ever again. My own flesh and blood!" He slapped on the arms of his chair in rising outrage. *"Me!* The squire of this village, honored by my neighbors, friend to the great lords of Bath!"

Jamie's eyes were bulging in anger. "Important though you may be, I'll see you ruined for this blunder. By God, I will, sir! You'll be a beggar on the streets before I'm through with you."

Grandpapa had managed to struggle to his feet at last with the aid of his cane. He drew himself up and pounded the stick on the floor. "Leave my house at once!" he bellowed. "You disturb my rest on the Lord's day! You threaten me, insult me to my face, and use this shameless whore as your confederate. You think to trick me into giving up that which isn't yours? I'll wager you're merely the hussy's lover, viscount or no, allied with her for your own dark purposes. For my part, there is no doubt that I've given the child to his true father!" He pointed his cane toward the door, his hand shaking with outrage. *"Go, sir!"*

Jamie clenched his fists and uttered a string of foul blasphemies. Abigail recoiled in pious horror and covered her ears. "There's nothing further to be gained here," growled Jamie, and stormed to the door.

Prudence stumbled along behind him, trembling violently. It was too much to bear—to have her hopes and dreams shattered in such a dreadful way. She felt her head spinning. When they reached the outside portico, she stopped and put a hand to her dazed eyes, unable to go on. The evening sky seemed to crowd in on her. "Jamie," she murmured incoherently, and crumpled to the ground.

She came to on the bench of the portico to find Old Meg bending over her, a small vial in her hand.

"Here, luv," said the old woman. "Take another whiff of this smelling bottle. You'll feel better in the twinkling of a bedstaff."

Prudence wrinkled her nose at the pungent odor from the bottle and looked toward the drive. Jamie was already climbing into his carriage. She rose to her feet and hurried to him as quickly as her unsteady legs would allow. "Jamie, what's to be done now?" she asked in dismay.

He turned in the doorway of the coach. His eyes were strangely cold and distant. "I met Longwood years ago. A decent enough chap. I'm sure I can persuade him to be reasonable and admit he made a mistake. Some sort of joke, perhaps. A drunken wager with another spark."

She managed a thin smile, a whisper of hope returning. Of course. Surely that was the explanation for this Longwood's bizarre behavior. More than once, Betsy had told her stories of wild pranks and abductions, when some young lord was in his cups. Longwood could have heard the tale of the child in the village, nodding over his ale, and lit upon his capricious scheme.

Jamie glanced up at the sky and furrowed his brow in thought, speaking softly as though he were talking to himself. " 'Twill soon be night, and I'm hungry. A stop at an inn . . . I'm not sure of the way to Longwood House. My coachman can inquire. And if the villain is abed when I arrive?" He muttered an oath. "So much the worse for him."

She held out her hand to him. "Help me up, please."

He laughed sharply, pushing at her outstretched fingers. " 'Pon my word, I don't need *you.*"

She began to stammer. "I . . . I don't understand."

"Your grandfather was another matter. I needed you to swear I was the father. But Longwood?" He shrugged. "I can take him to court if I must. Since you say he's never met you, he can scarcely describe the mother of 'his' child. But I think this can be settled without the law. One gentleman to another." He reached behind him in the coach and tossed her bundle carelessly to the ground.

She gasped in horror. "You can't do this!"

"Why not?" he sneered. "All I want is my son."

She shook her head, bewildered by the frightening change in him. "But . . . but marriage! You promised to marry me!" she shrieked.

"Must I deal with your hysterics? My dear girl, I *have* a wife. A rich heiress from Virginia. A gentlewoman of my own class. Why in God's name would I want a common country wench?"

"Jamie, for the love of heaven!" She clawed at the carriage door, desperate to pull herself aboard.

He gave her a violent shove that landed her on the gravel of the drive.

He sat down in the carriage, slammed the door, and shouted to his coachman. "Drive on!"

She struggled to her knees and watched the retreating carriage disappear into the lane. Then she bent her head and began to weep, sobbing at the utter ruination of her plans. *Oh, Ross,* she thought in desperation, *what am I to do now?* She should have trusted him. She should have told him everything. Instead, she'd pinned her hopes on a love she had only imagined in her childish innocence.

After a few minutes, she sniffled and wiped angrily at her tears. This would never do—to weep like a ninny. Think. *Think!* Jamie planned to stop for supper. If she could get to Longwood before he did, explain herself to the man, tell him the joke had gone too far, all might still be well. But how to do it, without a penny in her pocket?

Grandpapa! He had a coach. And the fresh memory of his humiliation at Jamie's hands. She would humble herself, beg his forgiveness for her sins, promise any atonement. Surely he couldn't refuse. He would exult to see Jamie defeated.

She turned and hurried toward the door of the manor, feeling a measure of calm at last. A loud voice from the lane startled her.

"Aye, Mr. Franklin! That be Mrs. Manning. My life on't."

She whirled to see Toby Wedge trotting toward her, followed by a bewigged man in a dark frock coat.

The man halted in front of her, puffing from his exertions. "Mrs. Manning?" At her stunned nod, he broke into a wide smile. "Gads, ma'am. I feared we would never find you. But this fine tarpaulin here, simple though he may be, assured me he could pick you out. And here you are!"

She frowned. Why was he wasting her time, when she had urgent business with Longwood? "What do you want?" she demanded impatiently.

He bowed low. "Permit me to introduce myself. William Franklin, lawyer."

Her thoughts were whirling in her brain. Why was Wedge here in Winsley? "What business do you have with me, Mr. Franklin?"

"Why, as to that, ma'am, I've been sent by Doctor Ross Manning. Your husband, I do believe. 'Tis my responsibility to return you to him at once."

Sweet heaven. She must have told Ross where she had lived—and not remembered. The stubborn fool. Why couldn't he leave her in peace? Was his masculine pride so hurt at her leaving that he would go to any lengths to get her back?

"I cannot go with you at this time, Mr. Franklin," she said with dignity. "My husband will have to wait on my return."

"But, ma'am, he specifically said that I was to brook no delay. No delay whatsoever."

"A pox on his high-handed ways! Always interfering! As though I belonged to him." She took a deep breath and collected her thoughts. "Mr. Franklin, I swear that I'll accompany you in a day or so. I give you my oath on that. You may wait here in Winsley for my return. But now I have an urgent matter that cannot be postponed."

The smile still lingered on his face, but his eyes had turned cold. "May I remind you, Mrs. Manning, that you *do* belong to him? And you're a runaway wife. Liable to prosecution under the law. 'Twould pain me to do so, ma'am, but I'm prepared to have this simpleton hold you until I can fetch a constable. With manacles, if you make it necessary," he added in an ominous tone.

"Toby wouldn't do such a thing," she said defiantly. "Not to me."

Franklin turned. "Mr. Wedge. I order you to keep this woman a prisoner until I return."

"Aye, sir." Wedge shuffled toward Prudence.

"Toby, I beg you," she pleaded. "Let me go."

He hung his large head. "I can't, lady. D'ye see me? Mr. Manning, he told me to hark to every word Mr. Franklin says. And not to let you weigh anchor from my sight, less'n Mr. Franklin gives me the nod. Or 'twould be a bad omen."

Franklin took her gently by the arm. "I think you had better come with us, Mrs. Manning. My coach is just down the lane."

She groaned in despair. "If he wanted to destroy me," she said bitterly, "why not simply send an assassin with a dagger?"

Chapter
Twenty-Four

The waning moon had set an hour ago. Prudence gazed morosely out of the window of the speeding carriage, watching the villages and hamlets pass by. Her soul was as black as the night. Her heart was empty. Not even the thought of seeing Ross again could cheer her.

Franklin put away the remains of the supper. "Are you certain you'll not eat anything, Mrs. Manning?"

"I'm not hungry."

He grunted in disapproval. "Come. Be of good cheer. We should reach our destination well before midnight. Doctor Manning will greet you with joy, I have no doubt."

She stared at him across the carriage. The swinging lantern hanging above them accentuated the planes of his good-natured face. She hated him. "Will you enjoy our happy reunion?" she asked, her lip curling in sarcasm.

" 'Gads, ma'am, I trust it *will* be happy. Doctor Manning seemed most eager and elated to have you restored to him."

"Eager?" she asked bitterly. "Or vengeful?"

He frowned in bewilderment. "Ma'am?"

"Mr. Franklin, can I not touch your heart? I fear my husband's greeting will be far less benevolent than you suppose." She gulped, imagining Ross's wrath. He must be furious, if he could arrange such a cold-blooded abduction. To send a lawyer, with the threat of arrest, instead of coming for her himself. She sighed. "I am prepared to accept . . . whatever awaits me. But—just for one day—let me go, to do what I must. He need never know. And I promise to return."

The lawyer bristled. "I have my instructions, Mrs. Manning. And my honor."

"Then come with me, if you fear I'll not return. Never let me out of your sight." Franklin's presence would give her courage with Longwood, and his knowledge of the law might help to persuade the lord of the rightness of her cause.

He shook his head firmly. "It cannot be done, ma'am."

"Oh! Then curse you for a flint-hearted, stubborn old mule!" she cried, and burst into unhappy tears.

Wedge had been sitting quietly huddled in a corner of the coach ever since he had finished his meal. Now he stirred, animated by her violent sobbing. He shifted uncomfortably in his seat, screwed up his face in shared misery, and wiped at his own tears. "Don't be sad, Maw," he said. "Ol' Toby'll come back to you."

Prudence stopped her crying abruptly. The poor man. His addled brain must be spinning in confusion after all the disruptions of the past few days. And now her tears, while doing nothing to ease her pain or soften Franklin, had driven him to his distant realm.

She leaned forward and patted him on the arm. "There, there, Toby. All will be well. We shall soon join Mr. Manning. 'Twill be like it was, on the ship. The three of us, together again."

He stared blankly at her. "There were a screech owl tonight. A bad omen. Some calamity, d'ye see me?"

She shivered, infected by his superstitious fears, and lapsed into silence. He pulled out his pipe and began to play, a mournful tune that sounded like a dirge to her grieving heart. She sighed, closed her eyes, and drifted into a fitful sleep.

She awoke feeling more hopeful. She had dreamed of Ross. God had set more troubles in her path to test her, but perhaps Ross could think of a way to help. She suddenly felt the need for his comforting arms.

At last the coach stopped at an imposing gatehouse. Prudence saw a gilded crest atop the intricately wrought iron gates. A liveried porter saluted the carriage and opened the gates, and they passed through into a long, tree-lined drive. Prudence could see, through the gloomy night, the dark, looming shape of a large house in the distance.

She frowned. "Where are we, Mr. Franklin?"

"This is Castle Bridgewater, the country seat of the marquis of Bridgewater. Doctor Manning is here."

A *marquis!* Ross must be in the man's employ, as his private physician. And if—by God's grace—Ross was in favor with his master, Lord Longwood and Jamie would be powerless against a marquis's influence. She felt her hopes growing with every turn of the carriage wheels.

Still, she thought, chewing petulantly on her lip, she wouldn't be in this pickle in the first place, except for Ross. But for her capture, she'd be at Longwood House by now. Holding her dear son in her arms. Even with the help of Ross and the marquis, it could be *months* before she recovered her child.

She was seething by the time they reached the massive front door. The impossible meddler! She would tell him a thing or two, that she would! How dare he upset her plans?

She swallowed an unexpected lump of fear. Now that the moment had come, she was beginning to reflect on Ross's humors. She found herself praying that he wasn't too angry at her for leaving.

Her fears were scarcely quieted when Franklin allowed her to step down from the coach and didn't follow. He smiled blandly at her questioning look. "I leave you to your husband, Mrs. Manning." That sounded ominous.

Her dread grew as a stone-faced footman took her cloak and led her silently through a great hall to a small door. She felt like a condemned prisoner going to her execution. She knew firsthand the power of Ross's anger; she had never experienced the force of his hand, though he had threatened more than once.

The footman knocked on the door, opened it for her, then withdrew. Squaring her chin, she sailed through the doorway.

Ross stood in the center of a small library, his hands folded across his chest. He was well dressed in a fine velvet suit, and his hair was tied back and powdered.

No doubt his new master pays him well, she thought sourly, then hesitated, waiting for him to speak. It wouldn't do to rush into a tirade until she could gauge his mood.

"How nice of you to come, wife," he said. His voice was cold and sarcastic, his eyes wary.

She breathed a sigh of relief, quieting her fears. She could deal with his coldness. "In your usual high-handed manner, you left me no choice," she snapped.

His eyes narrowed. "And is your beloved Jamie following close behind, panting to get you back?"

The mention of Jamie reminded her of her child. And her simmering resentment. "You tyrant! I didn't need your cruel interference!"

"Interference, madam? Is it interference to keep my wife from folly? From dishonoring herself with another man?"

For the first time, she noticed how haggard he looked, his face drawn, his eyes sunken as though he hadn't slept since they'd parted three days ago. And was that *jealousy* in his voice, for all his icy demeanor? "Sweet Mother of Mercy," she breathed. "Are you jealous of Jamie?"

"Haven't I a right to be? I had to listen for months to your stories of him. Your sickly sweet recollections. Your shameless yearnings. Even after you pledged yourself to me, I saw him in your eyes. And then I find you gone, your marriage ring abandoned. To go to him, of course," he added bitterly.

She had never considered it—how much she must have hurt his self-esteem. "I had no choice," she said gently.

"And then, not content with making a cuckold of me, you intended to marry him. As though I had never existed."

She was desperate to see the haunted look vanish from his eyes. "No, Ross, I . . ."

His clenched fists were the only outward sign that his anger was rising. His voice remained icy and distant. *"Did* you intend to commit bigamy?"

She hung her head. "Yes," she whispered.

He swore softly. "Did you love him so much? Hate me so much?"

"Oh, why can't you understand?" she said in frustration. " 'Twas not meant to hurt *you.* We had a child together. The only way to reclaim him was with Jamie's influence." She prayed her words would soften his pain and anger.

"Why did you never tell me the child was alive?" There was neither understanding nor forgiveness in his tone.

She sighed tiredly. "What could you have done? And now, because of your meddling, the good Lord knows if I'll ever see him again."

"Is it that you thought I could do nothing? Or that you couldn't stay away from *him?*"

"Jamie was just the means to an end, I tell you."

He turned away. "Do you love him?" he said raggedly.

She felt helpless to reassure him, to mend his wounded pride. "I was young, trusting—oh, Lord! how innocent. Yet I think a part of me knew, from the very first, that he wasn't what my overwrought heart imagined him to be." Her voice caught on a sob. "But . . . but I wanted my child so desperately that I was ready to live with a broken heart for the rest of my days."

He turned back to face her, his eyes filled with doubt. "What do you mean?" he growled. *"Do you love him?"*

How could he be so dense? "Oh, you muttonhead!" she cried. "Of course not. I love *you!"*

His eyes widened in stunned surprise and wonder. "You love . . . me?"

She brushed at her tears. "It pained me so to leave you that morning on the ship. I didn't want Jamie. I wanted you. To be your wife. To lie with you at night, warmed and held. But I had to choose between the two pieces of my heart. What could I do?"

"Pru," he whispered, his face flooding with relief and joy. He pulled her into his arms and kissed her, his mouth sweet on hers. She twined her arms around his neck and returned his kiss, feeling secure at last. This was where she belonged.

But when he released her mouth and began to rain soft kisses on her bosom and neck, her trembling chin, she remembered her troubles. She pushed at his shoulders, struggling in his arms. "Ross. No, wait. You must help. My child . . . Some madcap lord took him away—only for a joke! And now Jamie is hurrying to claim him tonight. But not for me." Her voice shook with the burden of her grief. "He's *married,* Ross. Married. All those months I counted on him . . ."

"Yes. To be sure." He kissed her cheek and nibbled on her earlobe.

How could he be so indifferent to her misery? "In heaven's name, Ross . . . !"

She heard loud shouts and scuffling noises coming from the closed door. There was the sound of a fist striking flesh, and then the door burst open. Jamie stood on the threshold, his eyes wild, his carefully coiffed hair unkempt.

Ross released Prudence and stepped back, his jaw set. "What is the meaning of this intrusion?"

Prudence clapped her hand to her mouth in horror, trembling in every limb.

The footman staggered in behind Jamie, rubbing a red mark on his jaw. "Your pardon, sir. I couldn't stop him."

"Yes, of course." Ross waved the servant away and turned his cold eye on Jamie. "Who are you, sir?"

Jamie stuck out his lower lip like a sulky child, smoothed his hair and tugged at the edges of his coat. "We have met before, sir. I regret you've forgot the occasion." He gave a stiff bow. "I am James Arnott, Viscount Swindon."

Ross's mouth twitched in amusement. "The infamous Jamie, I take it?" He returned the bow. "Your servant, sir. What do you here?"

Jamie glared back at him. "See here, Longwood, I'll not beat around the bush with you! What the devil have you done with my child?"

Ross raised a mocking eyebrow. *"Your* child?"

Jamie pointed a finger at Prudence, his hand shaking with rage. "I don't know what this creature has been telling you, but I can attest to the fact that I sired her son!"

Ross made a growling noise in his throat. "This 'creature,' sirrah, is my wife, Lady Longwood. You will address her with all due respect. Or I'll have you thrown out."

Prudence stared at Ross, her head spinning. She could scarcely believe her ears. "R-Ross?" she whispered.

He looked down at her with a sheepish smile. "Sorry, my dear. We both had our secrets."

"*You?* Lord Longwood?"

He shrugged. "I always have been."

Jamie stamped his foot. "Damn it, I want my child!"

Ross looked at the other man as though he were a bug under his feet. "What makes you think he's yours? I am willing to swear in a court of law that I dallied with Prudence last year, leading to the happy issue of our son. I suspect my lady wife would concur with that." He grinned unexpectedly at Prudence. "On the hills above your grandfather's farm, was it not, my sweet?"

She nodded, still too stunned to fully comprehend what was happening.

" 'Pon my soul, that's a foul lie!" sputtered Jamie.

"You claim to be the child's father," said Ross evenly. "Prudence has a scar on her person. Could you tell the court where it is? And the child, a birthmark. I'll wager you can't describe it. But *I* can. I left that hypocritical grandfather of hers dumbfounded." He took Prudence by the hand and kissed her fingers. "My poor lass. To be forced to live with that vile old man."

Jamie made a move toward Ross, his hand upraised in a fist. "Now see here . . ."

Ross skewered him with an icy stare. "You don't really intend to challenge me, do you, Swindon? I would guess that your forte lies in seducing unsuspecting women, rather than standing up like a man, with a sword in your hand. However, I'll be happy to oblige you."

Jamie crumbled at the challenge in Ross's eye and looked away.

Ross pointed to the door. "I'm sure you can find an inn at Cinderford tonight. Then go home to your own wife and lick your wounds."

Jamie began to blubber, his face distorted like a spoiled child's, twisted and ugly. "You don't understand, Longwood. I . . . I contracted the mumps in America. I can never sire a child again. I need an heir. My son! I appeal to you, sir." He sniffled and wiped his nose with the back of his hand. "God willing, you and Prudence will have children, whilst I . . ."

Ross's lip curled in disgust. "You miserable cur. Do you expect my sympathy? You found an innocent, trusting girl and seduced her for a moment's pleasure. Then left her to suffer for your lechery. You've caused her enough grief. Go home to your barren house. May your villainy haunt you till the day you die."

Jamie fell to his knees, sobbing. It sickened Prudence to think that she'd loved him for even a moment.

Ross laughed coldly. "Damn my liver, Pru, what did you ever see in this bloody weakling?" He strode to Jamie and jerked him roughly to his feet. "I trust you'll leave now, sir. If not, it will be my pleasure to have you tossed out."

Jamie slunk from the room like a whipped dog, weeping all the while.

Ross turned to Prudence with a grin. He looked smugly pleased with himself. "Now, Lady Longwood, I was kissing you, I believe."

She sank into a chair. "Lady Longwood," she said in wonder.

"You're a countess, you know."

"I can't believe any of it! I don't understand. All that time we were together . . ."

"I renounced a great many things when I renounced my father. Including my title."

She looked around the handsome library for the first time, noticing the superb furnishings. "And the marquis of Bridgewater?"

His expression hardened. "My father."

"But . . . but you said he's a surgeon, as you are. But you're an *earl,* and he's . . . I never heard of such a thing. Noblemen taking a profession. It isn't done."

He shrugged. " 'Tis a peculiar family history. I'll tell you someday."

He had returned to his father's house. It gladdened her. "You made peace with him, then. And forgave him."

The face was harder still. "I took back my title and my income," he growled. "But forgive him? He killed Martha. I shall never forget that. Nor forgive."

"Then why did you return to him?"

" 'Twas the only way to help you, and wrest the child from your grandfather."

Her heart flared with hope. "You made such a great sacrifice for me? Why?" *Tell me that you love me,* she thought.

He turned and fiddled with a vase on the table behind him. "Because you're my wife, and I had a duty to you." His voice darkened to anger. "And I wasn't about to see you commit bigamy with that dog!"

She couldn't accept that. Her heart wouldn't allow it. If it cost her her pride, she would ask him outright. She stood up resolutely. "Now see here, Doctor Ross Manning . . ."

She stopped, her hand going to her mouth. What had he said? Wrest the child from Grandpapa. "My baby," she said, her voice quivering. "He's here!"

He turned with a tender smile, his eyes bright. "I wondered when that would occur to you." He strode to the bell cord and tugged at it, then gave rapid orders to the footman. "Rouse the nurse and have her bring down her charge. Apologize to her for the lateness of the hour, but . . . his mother wishes to see him."

Mother. How sweet the word! She paced the room, trembling in happiness, then turned and ran into Ross's arms. "Bless you," she whispered.

He kissed the top of her head. "I took his nurse away from your grandfather, as well. A young widow. Mary Hunt. She says she knows you."

She nodded. "From . . . from the village."

"How old is he now?"

"Six months. And nine days." She had never stopped counting the time.

"When did you see him last?"

She couldn't stop the tears. "He was only six weeks when . . ."

"I've brought the boy, Your Lordship." Mary Hunt stood in the doorway, clutching a squirming bundle.

Prudence gasped, her heart stopping, then held out her hungry arms.

Mary laughed and knelt, placing the baby on the carpet. "He's only just learned to crawl. I can't keep him off the floor, he's that lively."

Prudence dropped to her knees and watched her child scramble to her across the floor. The last distance of that yawning chasm of time that had kept them apart. He gurgled happily, his dark curls tumbling over his forehead, his little face wreathed in the sweetest smile she had ever seen. She scooped him up and pressed him to her breast, while the joyous tears poured from her eyes. She kissed him and hugged him, examined every feature of his dear face, her heart overflowing with tender love.

She looked up at Ross with streaming eyes. "I don't even know his name," she sobbed.

He knelt beside her and wiped at her tears. "They baptized him Peter."

"Oh, Ross," she said, filled with grief for the lost months. "I missed so many milestones in his life."

His voice was hoarse with emotion. "There will be many more. You'll not be parted from your son ever again."

She felt a momentary flicker of unease. *Your* son, he had said. Would he ever love and accept Jamie's son as his own? She shook off her fears. She had her child again—and the man she loved. She thanked God for her happiness.

Peter began to whimper in her arms. Mary hurried forward. "Beggin' your pardon, Pru"—she stopped and blushed—"Your Ladyship. But 'tis the middle of the night. The babe needs his rest."

Reluctantly, Prudence rose to her feet and handed her child to Mary.

The woman smiled. "Don't you fret, ma'am. I nursed him since you left Winsley. I'll tell you stories of him to warm your heart. Never fear." She cuddled the baby close to her and left the room.

Filled with inexpressible joy, Prudence threw her arms around Ross's neck. "How can I ever thank you?"

He kissed her gently. And then not so gently. "I can think of any number of ways," he said with a good-humored leer.

There was a soft tap on the door. Prudence turned to see a middle-aged man standing there. He was clad in a dressing gown, and his graying hair was covered with a cambric nightcap.

He was tall and dignified, with a proud carriage and an unexpectedly sweet smile. Prudence had thought that no man's eyes could be more blue than Ross's, but the older man gazed at her with eyes that were a dazzling azure. But where Ross's were cold, his were filled with warmth. And a shadow of sadness.

"May I come in?" he said. "I heard a commotion that roused me from my bed."

Ross stiffened. Prudence could hear the crunch of his jaws. "Prudence, permit me to introduce Jason Manning, the marquis of Bridgewater."

Prudence started to curtsy at the grand title, but the marquis laughed. "From my daughter-in-law, I deserve a kiss. Prudence, is it not?"

She nodded shyly, crossed the room to him, and kissed him softly on the cheek.

"Upon my conscience, Ross," he said. "Your wife is a beauty." He smiled to Prudence. "You are welcome at Bridgewater Castle, my dear. Both of you. Damme if you're not."

Ross scowled. "I shall speak to my banker tomorrow about advancing me funds. The sooner I can refurbish Longwood House, the happier Prudence will be."

She looked around the handsome room. "Oh, but I'm quite content here until . . ."

Ross cut her off with a frigid stare. "I am not," he said coldly.

The marquis's smile faded and his face fell. "As you wish," he murmured.

The air was heavy with Ross's animosity. Prudence was conscious of the fact that he hadn't even introduced the marquis as his father. She tried desperately to think of something to say, to bring back the smile to the elder man's face. "If this fine room is any example, I should be pleased to have you give me a tour of the castle, Lord Bridgewater."

He held up a graceful hand. "Please. You can scarcely call me that. Not if you're now a member of the family."

"How shall I address you, then?"

He gave a heavy sigh. "You might call me Jason, as Ross does."

Ross snorted mockingly. "Did you know, Pru, that 'Jason' means *healer?*"

The marquis's face turned white, and his hands began to tremble.

Prudence glared at Ross. How could he be so cruel? She touched the marquis softly on the arm. "I shall call you Father, if I may." She pursed her lips in anger when Ross uttered a low growl.

The marquis looked from one tight face to the other and gave a little bow. "I've grown quite weary. I leave you to your happy reunion." He shuffled to the door; he seemed to have aged a dozen years.

Prudence whirled to Ross when the marquis had gone. "How could you?"

"The traffic between my father and myself is not your concern," he said in a hard voice.

"But how can you . . . ?"

He groaned and covered his eyes with his hand. "I beg you, Pru, don't vex me with this."

She felt a twinge of remorse. He had done that which he had sworn never to do—reconciled with his father. And all for her happiness. She had no right to be ungrateful, to chide him for deep emotions she couldn't begin to understand. "Forgive me," she whispered.

He cradled her face in his hands and stared deeply into her eyes. All the pain of his past griefs glowed in the depths of his own blue eyes. He reminded Prudence of a wounded animal who needed tender comfort, loving, and care.

"Take me to bed," she said.

He bent and kissed her. Softly, at first, and then with hungry intensity as his passion grew. The painful moment was forgotten. Smiling with joy and gladness, he lifted her into his arms. "Would Your Ladyship care to see your apartment?"

She giggled and held tightly to his neck. "Is this how the aristocracy behaves? Like ruffians?"

" 'Tis fitting treatment for a saucy wench. Even if she is a countess."

Her stomach gurgled; she screwed up her face. "This countess is hungry. I never ate a crumb of supper. Your horrid Mr. Franklin . . ."

He scowled. "By the beard of Aesculapius, was he uncivil to you? And starved you, as well?"

"He was naught but punctilious. Filled with moral rectitude. And there was supper, though I couldn't eat a bite."

"Thinking about that 'madcap lord'?" He grinned and carried her from the room. The footman covered his smile at the undignified sight of the master holding his lady; he listened obediently while Ross ordered a supper for Her Ladyship to be brought to his rooms.

Prudence had never known such grandeur and luxury existed. Two sleepy footmen sprang to attention at the door, then scampered away when Ross dismissed them for the night. Ross's drawing room was a vast, cavernous space, ablaze with candles. The furniture was elegantly gilded, and the brocaded walls displayed huge paintings. The thick, floral carpet made a silken sound beneath his buckled shoes as he carried her across the room. She could see the starry night beyond the velvet draperies at the windows. She felt like an enchanted creature being carried through a magical land.

He kicked open the door to his bedchamber. At once, his *valet de chambre* sprang forward. The man was dressed in a frenchified manner, with a laced velvet coat, a flowing cravat, and a fashionably styled bag-wig. His face was unnaturally pale: he was clearly obliged to artifice for the purity of his complexion.

"Your Lordship," he said in a faintly accented voice.

"Seek your rest, Marais. I'll not need you tonight."

"But, Your Lordship . . . !"

Ross gave a dry laugh. "Marais, *mon vieux.* Though I know there are gentlemen who would lie helpless abed—like beached turtles—without a valet to dress them, I assure you I am not one of their kind. I can prepare for bed myself."

"But milord, I only wished . . ."

Ross's voice was less patient now. "If you wish to continue to serve me whilst I'm in this house, you will obey me. Go to bed!"

The valet looked aggrieved, but he bowed and backed out of the room.

Ross set Prudence on her feet and grunted. "One would think a Frenchman could appreciate the dictates of *amour.* Remind me, when we hire our servants for Longwood House, to get a sturdy Cornishman for a valet. No matter the fashion for French fops. As for you, Lady Longwood, I'll arrange for a waiting-woman in the morning. For tonight"—he gave her an enthusiastic kiss and a leer—"you'll have to content yourself with my ministrations."

She felt playful and lighthearted. "I never yet found fault with your services. Though you took far too many opportunities to undress me aboard ship!"

He struggled against his smile. "Merely in my position as surgeon, you understand," he said priggishly.

She returned the mock-formality of his tone. "Of course, Doctor Manning. And tonight you wish merely to see if I've recovered from my illness."

"Imp!" The grin burst forth unrestrained. He tugged at the pins of her gown, his fingers growing more hasty by the minute. "You look charming in that gown, as usual. But damme if I have any patience with it tonight."

She chewed at her lip. He had always preferred her in the apricot. "I don't have the satin gown anymore," she said, abashed. "I gave it to my friend, Betsy, in London."

"I know. How did you think I found you, and learned about your child?"

She stared in surprise. "By my faith, I never thought of that until now!"

"A loyal friend, your Betsy. We shall have to have her at Longwood."

He finished undressing her—with many kisses and caresses along the way—then carried her to the curtained bed and placed her tenderly between the sheets.

It took him less time to shed his own clothing. She allowed herself the shameless pleasure of admiring his lithe body. He was eager and ready for her. She felt a shiver of delicious anticipation.

He swore in vexation at the sound of a knock at his drawing room door. He rummaged in an armoire, hastily threw on a dressing gown, and stamped—barefoot—into the other room. When he returned, he was carrying a tray and chuckling. "Marais seems to have recovered his French sensibilities. He positively simpered when he handed this to me."

She had never felt more pampered and petted. He sat on the edge of the bed, feeding her like a child. She played little teasing games, clamping shut her lips and refusing each tasty morsel. He would kiss her and tickle her until she gasped and laughed and opened her mouth. By the time she declared herself genuinely satisfied and he put aside the tray, they were both laughing and merry.

His lovemaking was as lighthearted as his mood. She had never seen him so playful, so young and exuberant. They romped and fondled each other, settling into burning kisses that erupted into gales of laughter from one or another. Ross tossed her about on the bed, molding her pliant body to his and teasing her with gentle thrusts of his manhood that had her begging for more and declaring that he was the greatest rogue she had ever known.

She was weak with laughter and ecstasy by the time they found release in a wild, final burst of frenzied passion. They rolled away from each other, panting and spent.

At last Ross sighed and dragged himself from the bed. While he searched for nightclothes for them both—so Marais would not be too impertinent in the morning when he found them—Prudence knelt beside the bed.

Oh, Lord, she prayed, *I thank Thee for Thy blessings. Thou has given me the happiest day of my life. Thou hast opened up a bright garden, an Eden, for Thy humble servant. May I be worthy of Thy goodness.*

Ross extinguished most of the candles in the room, then carried the last one to the bed, shielding it with his hand, and set it on a small table. He was about to climb in beside her, when he stopped and frowned in thought.

"What is it, Ross?"

He knelt beside his pile of discarded clothing and fished in the pocket of his waistcoat. "Now, madam," he said sternly, lifting her hand to slip Martha's ring onto her finger, "you will *not* return this to me ever again."

He lay down and embraced her, snuffed the candle, and was soon sleeping soundly.

In the dark, she could hear the screech of an owl from Bridgewater Park, mournful and foreboding. Toby's bad omen. She felt the ring on her finger and turned it round and round in unhappy distraction. He would never be able to love her fully. Even after she had declared her love, he had kept silent. She stifled a cry of pain, feeling the burning tears seep from her tight-closed eyes.

God had shown her an Eden. But there was a serpent in its midst. And the serpent was the ghost of Martha.

Chapter
Twenty-Five

The cold January rain beat relentlessly against the windowpanes, but within the snug morning room of Castle Bridgewater all was warmth. Prudence sat cross-legged on the floor, her back to the fire, and rolled a large ball to Peter. He laughed happily, revealing his recent front teeth, and pushed it back to her with chubby hands.

He was so adorable, she couldn't resist the urge to hold him close. She held out her arms, and he scooted across the carpet into her embrace. While she smoothed back the dark curls from his forehead, he burbled his child's gibberish and poked at the black patch that covered the pockmark beside her eye. She played peekaboo with her hand before her face and was rewarded with peals of happy laughter.

His nurse, Mary, clicked her tongue. "Take your breakfast, milady. 'Twill grow cold." She gestured toward the table set in the center of the room and the footman who hovered near a food-laden sideboard.

"In a little while," said Prudence. "It warms my heart so to see him laugh." She shuddered. "When I think of what might have been . . ."

"Aye. The old squire were always harking to Mr. Wesley's words. 'He who plays when he is a child, will play when he is a man.' "

"What nonsense. As if God would begrudge the joys of childhood." She laughed again as Peter squirmed out of her arms and crawled off to explore the shiny pull of a cabinet drawer.

Mary shook her head. "He'll soon be walking. I never saw such a strong, healthy bantling."

Peter was now sitting up and tugging at the pull with both hands. To his shocked surprise, the drawer gave way, tumbling him onto his back and spilling the contents to the floor. He howled in alarm. At once, Mary ran to him and scooped him into her arms, soothing him with her gentle voice. The footman scrambled to pick up the scattered objects.

"Damn my liver, Pru, will you give that child of yours the run of the house?"

Prudence rose to her feet and turned. Ross stood in the doorway, a cryptic smile on his face. She wondered what he was thinking. He had never played with Peter, had seldom seemed to notice him in the nearly two months since they'd been at Castle Bridgewater. He had examined him with some regularity, but it had merely been with his careful physician's eye, to ensure that the child would not fall ill.

Was he uncomfortable with the bother of children in a house? Or was his cool reserve only because this was *Jamie's* son, with the dark curls that would always and forever be a galling reminder? That child of yours, he had said, as though he never intended to be a father to the boy.

Prudence waited until Mary had discreetly retired with Peter. The woman was scarcely blind to the undercurrents in the room, the tensions that had simmered for weeks, like a stew on the edge of the boil.

She turned to her husband. "Good morning, Ross," she said softly. She blushed and looked down at her shoes, remembering the passion in his bed last night. He was always ardent and hungry for her when they retired after supper. And as passionate and satisfying a lover as she could want, night after night.

But since they had been at Bridgewater, he had grown increasingly cool during the day. Tense and distracted. So far away from her that she wanted to scream in frustration. She prayed that it was only the strain of living with his father that had created such distance between them. But she couldn't forget that his fervent dream had been for isolation, for the complete and permanent rejection of his father. Did he resent her and Peter because they had forced him to compromise his principles, disrupt his life? Perhaps his impassioned lovemaking was only a compensation for him, to quiet his disappointment.

He seemed not to notice her blush. He nodded a greeting and ambled to the breakfast table. "Have you eaten?" When she shook her head, he motioned for the footman to hold out her chair. "Come and join me."

She watched him heap his plate with food, her stomach churning. While he dived into a well-broiled chop, she picked at a piece of toasted bread and forced it down with a little tea. She hoped Ross wouldn't interrogate her in his maddeningly professional manner, the dispassionate tone he used when he was concerned about her health.

She knew she must be carrying his child, of course. She had missed her menses in December, and too many mornings had been spent clutching her queasy belly and hoping she wouldn't vomit. But how could she tell him? His behavior with Peter made her wonder if he wanted children at all. And, if he did, would the prospect of his own offspring turn him even more against *her* child?

He looked up from his plate and frowned. "Why do you not eat?"

" 'Tis the . . . the weather," she lied. "A whole week of rain. Most dispiriting. I have no appetite."

That seemed to satisfy him. He nodded. "The rain has vexed us all. I hope the sun shines before Toby begins to drive me mad. I've scarce seen him so distraught, so sunk into gloom and abstraction. And when his faculties are clear, 'tis this 'bad omen' or that 'bad omen.' My God, he's even begun to speak of Captain Hackett again, swearing the man is lurking around every corner, waiting to harm him."

"Poor Toby." She had hoped that the steady familiarity of his days at Bridgewater would restore him to his former self. But he dogged Ross's heels like a forlorn puppy; and when he was dismissed, he sat in the garden or in his little room, staring vacantly into space or tootling on his pipe. "But you'll take him to Longwood House today, as usual," she said.

He sighed. "Can I go anywhere without my shadow? Perhaps when we're settled in, I'll see if the clerk of the stables can use his help. Something to keep him busy."

"Will you ride today?"

"I wish I could. I need the exercise. But with this weather . . . and Toby

. . . I'll take the phaeton. At least controlling a spirited horse should rid me of some of this lethargy."

"How soon do you think we can move to Longwood House?"

"A fortnight, I should guess. They put up the damask in the eating parlor yesterday. A very handsome silk from France."

"Oh, I should like to see that," she exclaimed in delight. "I haven't been there in days. Perhaps I'll drive over this afternoon in my pony cart."

He scowled. "Not unless it stops raining."

"Oh, pooh!" She tossed her head. "I shall use an umbrella."

"Damn it, Pru, why must you always be so stubborn? 'Tis a long ride, and not good for your health in this weather. You might take a chill. You're looking far too pallid of late. I like it not."

She hated it when his voice took on that superior, domineering tone. The doctor who had all the answers. Did he guess at her condition? "Perhaps my complexion would improve if I had a cheerful husband!" she snapped. "When you're not disappearing to Longwood for hours at a time, you're glouting around here like a bear with a thorn in its paw."

"By my faith," he growled, slapping his hands on the table and rising to his feet.

She welcomed his anger. Perhaps if they had a good quarrel, it would help to clear the air. Anything was better than his distance. "You're as disagreeable as first you were aboard the *Chichester!*" she taunted him.

"Now, by God . . . !" His face was beginning to turn red.

"Upon my conscience, Ross, have I come for breakfast at an inopportune moment?"

The crimson glow faded. Ross turned to his father with ice in his eyes. " 'Tis your table, Jason. We can scarce keep you from it."

The marquis sighed. "I suppose it would do no good, in your present mood, to tell you that you are most welcome."

Ross settled back into his seat and picked up his knife and fork, glowering as he attacked his chop. "Tell it to my wife. I trust she will be more agreeable to you this morning than she has been to me."

The marquis took the seat the footman tendered and sipped at a cup of chocolate, watching his son. "You're late for breakfast this morning,

Ross. I don't usually have the pleasure of your company, but find you long gone to your house."

Ross grunted, his head bent to his food. "I shall be more timely tomorrow."

Prudence flinched at the look of pain that crossed the marquis's face. But he calmly started in on the filled plate the footman had set before him, seeming as though his breakfast were the only thing on his mind. "In point of fact," he said at last, putting down his fork, "I'm glad you're here. 'Tis my habit, as you know, to go down to London in February and March. To open up my office. I would know your plans. Do you intend to practice there as well?"

"If I do, you may be sure it will be as far away from you as possible."

The marquis paled and motioned to the footman. "Take this away," he said in a ragged voice.

Prudence pursed her lips in anger. Ross's behavior toward his father had made their stay at Bridgewater well-nigh unbearable. Christmas had been a nightmare of cold silences and tense, prickly conversations, even when the marquis's holiday guests were present. Ross had even returned his father's Yuletide gift.

Prudence turned away from her husband and smiled at the marquis, making her smile as warm as possible. "I wasn't hungry either, Father. But our appetites will be sharp when we dine together this afternoon."

He answered her warmth with a smile of gratitude. "And you'll sing for me, I trust. I never tire of your charming voice."

Ross glared at his father. "How fortunate you are. She saves her shrewish tirades for me." He rose from his chair before Prudence could respond, and stalked to the door. "I bid you both good morning." With a final angry glance at Prudence, he stormed from the room.

The marquis covered his eyes with his hand. "It only gets worse," he muttered.

She reached across the table and put her hand on his. "Perhaps, when we move to Longwood, he'll see things more clearly from that distance. And rid his heart of its bitterness."

"I had hoped, when I spoke of London, that he would wish to join me in my practice, as he did in happier times." He looked at her with a sad smile. "Ah, well."

"How odd that you should be physicians, with your titles and honors."

"A family tradition."

"So Ross told me, though he never gave me the reason."

" 'Twas a long time ago. In the days of Good Queen Bess. At the time, Owen Manning was just a humble country doctor in Cinderford. The queen, on a royal progress through Gloucestershire, had the misfortune to fall ill. She sent for a physician. As luck would have it, my esteemed ancestor. He served her so well that she persuaded him to move to London, where he performed many services for Her Majesty through the years. Over the course of time, she honored him with the title of earl of Longwood, and then marquis of Bridgewater. Owen built the first Castle Bridgewater, and died there in the fullness of his age, a year before his beloved queen breathed her last."

"That explains the *first* Doctor Manning. But what of you?"

"There was an obligation that came with the queen's favor. There must always be a Doctor Manning, down through the generations. So it was stipulated, and so it was done."

"A heavy imposition."

"Not at all, my dear. While others of our class waste their lives in dissipation and debauchery, we have always been useful. SERVE MANKIND is the motto beneath the Bridgewater crest, you may have noticed."

"And Ross?"

"He was a credit to the Manning family. He embraced his studies at the Royal College of Physicians with joy and zeal. I would that I had been such an apt pupil."

"I've seen his skill." She laughed ruefully. "And his temperament, as well."

He shrugged. " 'Tis very difficult, I suppose, when one reaches perfection with so little effort, to understand the weaknesses of others. I could have wished, sometimes, that his heart was as well tutored as his mind. And then, to be sure, he's a proud man. Not given to suffering fools gladly."

The marquis gazed at the rainy day with a faraway look in his eyes, then went on at last. "He worked in my dispensary when he was still a boy, learning to mix nostrums—as I had, with my father. Then, later, he served his surgeon's apprenticeship with me. They were happy years, forging a bond between us." He sighed. "And then he met Martha."

Prudence felt a morbid chill, as though a specter had just passed through the room. She went to stand by the fireplace, holding out her hands to warm them at the blaze. Her ring glinted gold in the light. "I know he loved her very much," she said softly.

The marquis looked at her with knowing eyes, then turned away. "She was the only love for his life, he used to say. Longwood House was a crumbling ruin at the time, but he restored it for her."

She picked at her pain, helpless to stop herself. Like a child worrying a scab until it bled again. "Was it . . . such a very great love?"

" 'Tis not for us to see into the human heart. But I saw compassion in him as a doctor that had not been there before. Martha brought that to him, I think."

She flinched, fearful to hear more, yet hungry to know. "Will you . . . tell me about her? How she died?"

He stood up and began to pace the room, his agitated footfalls making a swishing noise against the carpet. "I murdered her," he growled at last. "Hasn't Ross told you? Did you think that his demeanor to me was caused by a mere foolish quarrel?" The sardonic twist to his mouth reminded her of Ross.

"Oh, but that can't be so!" Somehow she had hoped that Ross's story was wrong. That the kindly man before her was guilty of an accident, and nothing more.

"Thank you, my dear, for the goodness in your heart. Your faith. But I was as cocksure and proud as he, in my time. Martha had a cancer in her womb. I wanted to operate. Ross thought we should wait. We quarreled for weeks over it."

She smiled in understanding. "I suspect you were also as stubborn as he."

His shoulders sagged. "I was many things, in those days. Until God taught me humility."

"And so you operated."

His eyes filled with tears. "Ross was away, tending a patient. Martha was in terrible pain. The poor creature. I had given her every narcotic at my disposal, and still she suffered. She begged me to release her from her agony, to rid her body of the foulness that was killing her. I agreed." He groaned and wiped at his tears. "So confident of my skills, dear Lord . . ."

"I pray you, don't go on," she said, weeping with him. "It brings you too much grief."

"Do you know how quickly a person can bleed to death when an artery is severed?" he asked bitterly.

She put her arms around him and held him to her bosom, desperate to bring him comfort. He was shaking like the rain-tossed branches outside the window. "Perhaps it was only because you cared so much, for Ross's sake. Your hands were unsteady—fearing to fail."

He pushed her away with a low growl. "I was reckless and clumsy! It should never have happened. But I took an oath not to practice surgery ever again. I dispense medicines. I minister to gouty old men. But I have never picked up a scalpel again. Nor ever will." His chest heaved with a deep sigh. "I deserve my son's contempt."

She felt helpless before his suffering. "No! God can forgive all. Why shouldn't we?"

"Sometimes I think that Ross blames himself. Perhaps if we had operated sooner . . ."

"Would it have made a difference?"

"No. Her poor body was spread through with the disease. But *I* was the instrument of her death. Not God's hand. And for that, Ross rightly holds me to account."

She wondered which man suffered more, the son or the father. "When did she die?"

"A year last July."

"And then he went to sea."

"He spent a month in London, I heard. Wandering the streets like a wraith. Stumbling with drink and accosting passersby with accounts of my villainy."

"You're not a villain!" she cried. She snatched at his hand and pressed her lips to his trembling fingers. "You're a good, kind man—who makes me proud to call him Father."

He searched her face, his eyes bright with fresh tears. "I wonder if my son knows what a treasure he has." He sighed again and gave a deep bow. "Permit me to withdraw. This morning has quite taxed my strength."

She watched him go with a heavy heart, then made her way up the great staircase to her rooms, which adjoined Ross's. Across the passageway was the door to Bridgewater's apartment. *So close,* she thought sadly, *yet so far apart.* For all the proximity of their three suites, they might be dwelling on separate, windswept isles of some exotic sea.

She was so distracted by her mournful thoughts that she didn't see Ross's valet Marais until he was almost upon her. He stopped and gave her an ostentatious bow, his slim hand making florid circles in the air. "Lady Longwood."

She acknowledged him with a smile. Even with all his airs, she had found him to be a likable young fellow, a penniless Frenchman who had discovered—much to his surprise—that the English nobility would pay a premium for his services, his affected ways.

He cleared his throat delicately. "I have done as you requested, milady."

"And . . . ?" She felt a pang of guilt for their conspiracy, the desperation that had driven her to go behind Ross's back.

"After a careful search of His Lordship's effects, I have discovered that which you are seeking."

Her lip trembled. "The . . . the gown?"

"*Hélas,* yes, madam. Wrapped in silver tissue and placed in a carved chest."

Oh, Ross, she thought, fighting her tears. He could not have broken her heart more had he built a shrine to Martha's memory. She struggled to preserve her dignity. "Thank you, Marais. I shall see that you're paid for your troubles."

He looked horrified. "Madam, no! In affairs of the heart, I do not expect compensation, you understand."

For all his youth, there was a worldliness about him that invited her confidences. "Do you understand the human heart, Marais?" she said with a sigh.

"I like to think so, milady."

"Then tell me, how does one contend with a ghost?"

His eyes widened in surprise. "Ah! That is not what I had supposed. It is not the ordinary . . . domestic problem. But is your ghost different from a living rival? A woman has arts that can charm a man, if she but use them. And turn him even from his memories."

"And the contemplation of a faded old gown?" she asked bitterly. "Why must he keep it?"

"Milady, in my country we have a maxim. *The heart has its reasons which reason does not know.* If I may be forgiven my presumption, you would do well to put such thoughts from your mind. They are beyond our comprehension. Strive instead to be the living embodiment of his joy."

She dismissed him with her thanks and stepped into her drawing room. It was sumptuously furnished—a room fit for a princess. And the armoires in her bedchamber beyond were filled with a dozen new gowns. But her exalted position in this household was a hollow triumph. Without Ross's love, she had nothing.

She picked up her needlework and sat before the window, filled with a weary lassitude. After a few minutes, the sewing dropped from her fingers, and she slept.

When she awoke, she saw that the rain had stopped. She felt refreshed from her nap, and the recollection of Marais's words gave her renewed hope. She was Ross's *living* wife. She had confessed her love, and he had accepted it. And though they had never spoken of love since that night, he must know her heart was constant. Surely, someday, he could learn to love her in return.

She summoned her waiting-woman and ordered her pony cart to be brought round to the door. She snatched up her gloves, threw a fur-lined cloak over her shoulders and pulled up the hood, then hurried from the house.

The fresh air revived her spirits further, and the cold mist that had descended on the earth made her feel as though she were being borne through a clean, white tunnel to a land of hope. She would begin her campaign to win Ross's heart today. A humble apology for her sharp tongue at breakfast. And perhaps a request that they move into Longwood House at once, even before it was finished. Alone together, they might rediscover the happiness they had shared in Virginia.

She looked up. Ahead in the fog loomed the ruins of the first Castle Bridgewater. It had been destroyed in the civil wars, Ross had told her, and was nothing but a shell. Still, the high, massive towers and crumbling walls always filled her with awe. The very silence of the stones echoed with the remembered clash of weapons, the shouts and cries of armies.

Just beyond the castle lay the Manning chapel, its low surrounding wall enclosing the gravestones and tombs of generations. Prudence nearly lost her resolve when she saw Martha's grave. It was banked with fresh flowers from the greenhouse at Bridgewater. The bright colors glowed against the winter-seared earth, even through the mist. She wondered how often Ross knelt there and prayed.

Courage, Prudence, she thought, and urged her pony around the curved drive that led up to Longwood House. She heard an odd, whirring noise from somewhere in the dense whiteness before her. And then the house came into view.

Tobias Wedge stood at the open door, his eyes wide with fear. His body trembled violently.

"Toby! Sweet heaven, what is it?"

He wiped the sweat from his brow with a shaking hand. "Body o' me, lady. You come out of the fog like a ghost ship from the bottom of the ocean."

She took him gently by the arm and led him inside. The ground floor was deserted; the noises of workmen came from the floors above. "I've come to see the house," she said. "No fright in that."

He shook his head. "But there were three ravens on the drive, black as a night at sea. They flew away. And then *you* came, d'ye see me? A bad omen, that."

That had been the sound she'd heard. "Nonsense, Toby. There are hundreds of birds in this park."

"But there were *three.* That were always a sign of death, my Maw told me. And Cap'n . . ."

"No more, Toby," she said with an exasperated sigh. "You're safe. Now let me see what changes have been wrought since last I was here."

She looked around the splendid entrance hall, with its marble pillars framing arched doorways on either side. Above each doorway was set a sculpted representation of an earl's coronet: eight silver-leaf balls set on gilded rays alternating with strawberry leaves. The floor had been inlaid with black and white marble tiles since her last visit, and the massive fireplaces had received handsomely carved mantels.

She disregarded the formal drawing room on the left, with its dark paneling and ruby velvet walls; it had been finished a week ago. She turned instead to the eating parlor on the right, eager to see the wall coverings of which Ross seemed so pleased.

She was scarcely disappointed in the room; the pale blue patterned damask glowed even on this gloomy day, and the corners of the ceiling were festooned with stucco carved into motifs of the four seasons. Elaborate plaster swags of fruits and flowers, designed to frame paintings, were set at regular intervals along the walls.

"Oh, how lovely," she exclaimed. "I shall delight to play hostess in this room." She suddenly wanted to see Ross, to tell him how pleased she was with what he had done. "Where is His Lord . . . Mr. Manning?" she corrected herself. Wedge was still unable to understand the reality of Ross's title. In his confused mind, Ross would always be the ship's doctor, and nothing more.

He pointed toward the ceiling. "Mr. Manning be aloft."

There were almost a dozen rooms on the floor above, she knew. And the same number in the attic story. "But *where?*" she asked.

He screwed up his face and twisted a hank of white hair between his fingers. Then his eyes lit up and he smiled. "The green room! That were a pretty pickle this mornin'! The mantelpiece be listin' to starboard."

"The green room?" She had seen no green room on her last visit. She swept out of the eating parlor and headed for the broad, divided staircase that led to the rooms above. "Come, Toby. You'll have to show me."

She was halfway up the stairs before she realized he hadn't followed. She glanced behind her to find him at the foot of the stairs, gaping up the steep flight with an expression of terror on his face. Cursing her own forgetfulness, she retraced her steps, pocketed her gloves, and took him by the hand.

"Close your eyes," she said. "I'll lead you."

He looked at her, his face breaking into a child's grin of relief and gratitude, and closed his eyes. She took him firmly by the hand and guided him upstairs, assuring him that he had nothing to fear.

When they reached the top, Wedge opened his eyes and led her to an intimate closet that adjoined Ross's bedchamber. From its appearance, Prudence guessed that he would use it as an office and informal reception room. The walls were covered in shagreen leather and a paneled wainscot of rich, dark mahogany. The carved mantelpiece, of the same wood, was topped by a slab of gray-green marble.

Several artisans were attempting to reset the stone. Ross stood back, squinting, his arms folded across his chest, and gave directions in a firm, somewhat testy voice. "No, no," he said, "over to the *left* side." He allowed his gaze to stray unwillingly to Prudence, as though her presence were an added burden on an already-difficult day. "Well?" he said with a scowl.

His eyes were wary and guarded; he had clearly not forgotten their quarrel. She found herself loving him for his stubborn, foolish pride. "The rain stopped," she said gently. "I wanted to see the house. And you." She crossed the room, unfolded his rigid arms, and took him by the fingers. She tugged at his hand, trying to draw him from the room.

"Name of God, Prudence," he said. "What are you doing?"

"Come with me."

He gestured angrily toward the mantel. "This must be done right. That bloody carpenter . . . He had to add nearly an inch to the right side."

She reached up and stroked the side of his stiff face. "Have a little pity for human imperfections. Besides, they can restore it without you."

"But . . ."

"Come!" She pulled him, muttering his protests, to the empty dressing room next to the closet, and closed the door behind them.

He shook his hand free of hers. "May I ask the purpose of this, madam?" he growled.

"Only this." She put her arms around his neck, pulled his head down to hers, and kissed him firmly on the mouth. He resisted for a moment, but when she tickled his lips with her tongue, he groaned and surrendered.

He wrapped his arms around her pliant body and held her close, returning her kiss with a fervor that left her trembling.

"Witch," he grumbled, releasing her at last, though she still clung to
his neck. "Have you come to ask a favor?"

"No. I came to beg your pardon for my sharp tongue."

His face relaxed into a smile of pleasure. "I much prefer your soft
tongue. In every way."

"Then you shall have it," she whispered, and kissed him again, her eager
mouth joining with his in a breathless exploration.

His hands roamed her back, curled tantalizingly around her bottom
to hold her close to his swelling loins. He trailed kisses down her neck,
buried his face in the linen at her bosom. "I could wish it were night," he
murmured, his voice a hoarse growl of longing and desire.

She felt strong, aware for the first time of her power over him. Perhaps
Marais had been right, and she had been too naive to use the arts granted
to her sex. She twined her fingers in the curls of his nape, stroked the soft
flesh of his neck. "Why must we wait? Come home with me now."

His body tensed. "Don't be absurd."

She gave him a coy smile. "You've reminded me more than once that
I must learn to be a countess. And demand what I want. Is it forbidden
a countess to be made love to in the daytime? If she wants it?"

"And be forced to dine with my father? I spend my days here to avoid
that ordeal. 'Tis only through the strongest effort of will that I can endure facing him across the supper table."

"Ross, dearest. You have a good heart. Why can you not forgive him?
He lives in a world of grief and remorse. He's as proud as you are, but I
think he would humble his pride for one kind word from you."

He pushed her roughly away from him. "Is that why you came? Did
he send you to beg his cause?"

"I came because my heart breaks for both of you. Do you give honor
to Martha's memory with such obduracy? You've told me she was a good
and loving woman. Who even forgave a lout for a broken toe. Remember? Would *she* not have forgiven your father?"

His jaw hardened. "Madam, you go too far."

She lowered her head, her eyes filling with tears. Why did she try to reconcile him with his father, when her own situation was so unbearable? When she was reduced to begging for his warmth and tenderness? Competing with a ghost.

"Then come home with me now because I . . . I want you," she said, choking on a sob. She couldn't say the word "love" and humiliate herself further. "We can dine in your rooms, if that will please you. But come home now, I pray you."

He wavered, clearly moved by her tears. "Poor Prudence. I've been more than neglectful these past few weeks. And you've been sweet and patient with your glouting bear of a husband, as you called me."

The warmth in his eyes heartened her. She gave him a seductive smile and rubbed her finger across his lips. "We shall make the clouds vanish this afternoon."

He grinned. "I shall exhaust you, madam." He gestured toward the closet. "Only allow me to finish . . ."

"No," she said, pouting as prettily as she could. What untapped powers lay at her command, if only she had the skill to use them? And he was weakening. She could see it in the heavy rise and fall of his chest, the hungry gleam in his eye. "If you don't come now, I shall lock myself in my dressing room until supper."

His face was a study in indecision. "Name of God, Prudence . . ."

"Now," she announced firmly.

"You siren," he said with a sigh, reaching for her. "Will you quite conquer me?"

Just then, there was a loud crash from the closet, followed by the excited babble of voices. "Damn my liver!" Ross cried, pounding one fist in the palm of his other hand. "The bloody fools have broken it."

"Then let them order another."

"But I want to see . . . Wait for me below."

She stamped her foot. "You ungrateful dog! You might find my dressing room locked tonight as well!" She swirled on her heel and stormed into the closet.

The marble mantel was smashed into a thousand pieces. Clearly, there was nothing to be done but to replace it. The workmen stood in a nervous knot, muttering soft accusations at one another. Wedge looked as though he were about to cry.

Ross barreled out of the dressing room and swore at the sight of the ruined stone. "Pru, wait a little longer." His voice was thick with exasperation.

She tossed her shoulder at him. "I gave you a choice. You took it. Enjoy the afternoon in your *perfect* house!" She ran from the room and down the stairs, furiously pulling on her gloves as she went. Her anger held until she had regained her pony cart and left the drive behind. Then she sagged in her seat. She had been vanquished by a ghost. And now she was even to be defeated by his sense of perfection.

Still, she thought, calling on her reserves of optimism, he had weakened, if only for a moment. She had almost conquered him. Perhaps she'd spend the afternoon in quiet contemplation, recalling Betsy and her coquettish ways. By God's grace—and a studied artfulness!—she might win Ross's heart yet.

The fog was almost as thick as before, heavy white clouds that oppressed the land. She drove slowly, straining to see the road ahead. There were clear patches now and again, which made the going easier. Still, there was an ominous heaviness in the air, compounded by her troubled soul, that gave her a shudder of unease. The cold seeped through her cloak, ran down her spine like icy fingers. The thick fog no longer seemed as benign as it had earlier.

She heard rustling noises somewhere on the road ahead of her, and gave a start. Wedge's three ravens? Presaging disaster? Her flesh prickled with unreasoning fear. She wished now that she had waited for Ross.

Then she laughed softly. It was only a misty January day. How foolish, to let Toby's omens frighten her. The woods were alive with winter birds and small creatures. No more than that.

She gave a shriek of alarm and horror: a dark figure in a long, hooded cloak loomed out of the whiteness and blocked the way. He looked like a raven, stark against snow. He leapt forward and grabbed the bridle. The pony shivered to a stop, his ears flattening against his head in terror.

"Let me pass," said Prudence, her trembling voice echoing hollowly in the eerie mist. Sweet heaven, why did she have to sound so frightened?

The figure laughed—a chilling sound from beneath his enveloping hood. He seemed like the specter of Death, only lacking a scythe. "Gad's curse," he said. "They told me that you came this way nearly every day. But who would have guessed you would fall into my hands so easily, dear lady?"

She gasped at the familiar voice. She raised her whip to strike at him, but he curled his gloved hand around it and pulled it savagely from her grasp. The hood fell back to reveal his face. It was a grotesque, scarred travesty of his former beauty.

"Sweet Mother of Mercy," she whispered.

"There will be no mercy this time, dear lady," said Captain Sir Joseph Hackett.

Chapter
Twenty-Six

Still holding the pony's head, Hackett stepped nearer to Prudence and glared up at her, his dark eyes glittering with an evil light.

She recoiled in horror at his face. A long scar jagged across one cheek and a corner of his mouth drooped with an odd puffiness. The black arch of his right eyebrow was interrupted by a ridge of bare skin, and his once-proud, perfect nose was warped, the nostrils flattened against his face. The bridge bent at a sharp, hawklike angle, which added a note of ferocity to his grotesque features.

"What . . . what are you doing here?" she stammered.

His mouth twisted in the mimicry of a smile. "I see you are admiring my looks. I owe them to your husband."

She felt a pang of guilt, despite the man's villainy. She had been the cause of his beating, after all. The reason Ross had been pushed over the edge. And for a man of Hackett's vanity to suffer so, for the rest of his life . . . ! "But couldn't the surgeons . . . ?"

He laughed bitterly. "The surgery practiced in the Colonies is primitive, to say the least. But I am beholden to your husband for the loss of my commission, as well. And my career."

"What do you mean?"

"The son of a bitch made a full report to Mr. Thomas Lee, the president of the Council of Virginia." His lip curled in scorn. "A dog among men, in his own right. That esteemed gentleman—who seems to have taken a fancy to you—saw that a full account of my so-called 'disgrace' reached the ears of the Admiralty in London. I had no choice but to re-sign from the navy. For the sake of my family's honor."

That seemed a dreadful punishment, even for Hackett's acts of cru-elty. "Surely Ross can do something . . ."

"Ah, yes. The great Lord Longwood. Who would have guessed? A scurvy surgeon! I knew of his title in Virginia, of course. The Symonds family was quite eager to share the gossip of his renunciation of his fa-ther, though no one seemed to know the reason why. I came back to Eng-land and searched for him. And bided my time. Quite by accident, last week, I learned he had reclaimed his title and family estates. And so I came to see you, my dear countess."

She felt a chill of fear. He was so filled with hatred. "Perhaps Ross can compensate you for what you've lost . . ." she ventured.

"I don't need his golden reparations," he said with a sneer. "I have wealth aplenty of my own."

"Then what do you want of us? What's done is done."

"Not quite." Before she had time to collect her wits, he had leapt up into the seat beside her, twisted her hands behind her back, and tied them securely together.

"Sweet heaven," she gasped, struggling against her bonds and cringing away from his leering face, "what do you intend?"

He pushed her down on the seat and straddled her, his muscled legs strong against her thighs. Her wrist bones pressed into the wooden plank, painful even through the soft leather of her gloves. The savagery in his burning eyes made her tremble.

"For months I've dreamed of you," he said thickly. "And of my revenge. And you shall be the instrument, my sweet." He removed his gloves as though he were a gentleman about to partake of some delicacy, then tugged at the strings of her cloak and spread it wide. At the sight of her tremulous bosom, his eyes lit up, filled with a hungry lechery that was frightening. He caressed her neck; then he curled his fingers around her throat and pressed softly on her Adam's apple.

For all the frantic pounding of her heart, she felt an icy calm. "You vile coward," she said in contempt. "Will you kill me because you haven't the courage to challenge Ross to a duel?"

"Courage?" He gave a scornful bark. "Odds my life, I have no doubt I should kill him in an instant. I doubt he sharpened his skills whilst he was a surgeon. But his death would scarce satisfy me."

"And mine will?"

"You, dear lady, are an entirely different matter. 'Twas not only *revenge* that filled my thoughts these past months. My dreams were haunted by you—and my thwarted passion. I have but two desires—you, and his suffering." His hands left her throat to plunge into her bodice. He squeezed her breasts, his fingers rough and coarse on the tender flesh.

She writhed beneath him, helpless tears springing to her eyes. "You'll be hunted down like a dog for this."

"Somehow, I doubt that. I planned this with care, you see. I traveled incognito. When I vanish, no one will ever be able to prove that I was here."

"I beg you, let me go," she whispered. Perhaps there was still some small spark of compassion within him.

He sighed. "Gad's curse. I had forgot how beautiful you are. Even in tears." He caressed her breasts more gently, his eyes softening into a mockery of a lover's gaze. His hands made her flesh crawl, and his sickly smile was more loathsome than his frowns.

"If you intend to rape me," she said in cold disgust, "do it and be done. And then go away and leave us in peace." The prospect of it horrified her. The intimacy of his vile flesh against hers. But if there was no stopping him, at least she would maintain her dignity. She closed her eyes and composed her face, steeling herself for his assault.

He gave a shout of laughter that made her eyes fly open. "A proud answer, dear lady. But has it not yet occurred to you that *I* pull the stroke oar? Not you?" He rummaged in his coat pocket and drew out a length of rope. "When I take you, it will be with pain and humiliation. Not for me a woman who submits with noble fortitude. A wench is more tantalizing when she is broken and sobbing. *That* is when I find my satisfaction in her."

"Then you shall never find satisfaction in me," she said boldly.

"We shall see." He carefully tied the rope into a sailor's knot, lifted her head, and slipped the noose around her neck. He climbed off her and stood up in the cart. "Now," he said, giving a tug on the rope that nearly choked her, "we'll take a little stroll. Climb down."

Trembling and gasping against the constricting rope, she obeyed. "Where are you taking me?" she asked, when they stood on the mist-shrouded road.

He smiled slyly, turned his back, and started down the road, pulling on the rope so she was forced to follow. The fog was beginning to clear in this direction; she prayed some traveler or shepherd would see her distress and come to her aid.

After a few minutes, he stopped and turned, a malevolent grin on his face. Curse the devil, he was enjoying every minute of this. "Are you not the slightest bit curious as to how your husband will suffer?"

She held her chin at a proud angle. "He is a man of honor. He will never forgive—nor forget—this stain to his name. That will be suffering enough."

" 'Tis his heart I mean to wound, not his pride." He laughed—an ugly sound. "Gad's curse, how he'll suffer. When he finds his beloved wife dead. I should like to be there to see it."

She stumbled in horror and fell to her knees. At once, the rope tightened around her throat. "You mean to kill me?" she choked.

"My dear countess, did you think I intended you to live to tell the tale?" He pulled savagely at the rope and she struggled to her feet. "Come along," he ordered, "before I'm tempted to give you a taste of what your husband did to me."

They made their way along the road, Prudence skipping to keep up with his long strides lest she falter and the rope go taut. Her mind was teeming with wild schemes. How to escape him? She wrenched at the rope that bound her wrists. If only she could free them, she might have a chance to loosen the bond on her neck, race for the woods, and disappear into a lingering patch of fog.

She looked up. The ruins of Castle Bridgewater loomed before them. Hackett dragged her to the rotting door of one tower and started up the stairs. They were wet from the rain, their stones worn and uneven from countless feet.

The climb was difficult and exhausting, with her hands bound so tightly. Prudence slipped on the second landing and fell heavily on her side. She could feel the cold damp of the granite through the thin silk of her gown. Hackett swore viciously and jerked her to her feet.

"Where are we going?" she panted.

He pointed up the flight of stairs to the open roof, one arm raised in a languid gesture. "To love's aerie, dear lady. After that . . . ?" He let his arm drop with a frightening suddenness and smiled at her. "Do you understand?"

She gasped, filled with fresh panic, and began to scream. Her throat grew raw, but still she cried out, praying that someone would hear.

He laughed and clapped his hands, his mouth curved into an evil smile. "Bravo, my dear. You know just how to please a man. I can feel my prickle growing harder with every cry. Pray continue, as long as you wish. 'Twill only increase my virility."

She clamped her lips shut. She had no desire to prolong the vileness of his rape. *Dear God,* she prayed, anguished, *if I must die, let my agony be brief, and ended soon.*

They reached the top of the tower at last. It was a small space, perhaps three yards square, bounded by a low, crumbling wall. The wind whistled through the chinks of the stones, and wisps of lingering fog drifted past. Prudence could see the ground far below, the empty road beyond. She shuddered in despair.

Hackett's eyes glittered with hatred—and lust triumphant. "Kneel," he said, "like the bitch you are."

She was desperate to delay the moment. Perhaps someone would come. "No," she said defiantly.

He gave an angry pull to the noose. She gasped and choked, seeing spots before her eyes, and sank to her knees. She felt his boot on her shoulders, savagely pushing her down until her forehead touched the floor. She could smell damp, molding stone and rotting wood.

She felt him lift her skirts and cover her bound hands with the fabric; then she felt the cold air on her bare legs and buttocks. She felt his hands spreading the soft mounds. "No!" she shrieked. "You cannot!"

He was already panting in breathless anticipation. "In a moment, my sweet bitch, you shall have cause to scream."

She tried to move, to roll over on her side. But his hand was tight on her hips, and the other still held the choking rope taut.

She heard a shout from the distance. Hackett muttered a foul oath and released her body. In a moment, she found herself jerked to her feet. He pulled her to the edge of the wall and pointed to the road. "It seems you're to have a champion."

She nearly wept for joy: Ross raced along the road in his open carriage, Wedge by his side. The sound of her shouted name drifted up to the windy tower. "You depraved villain," she spit at Hackett. "You may throw me to my death, but your evil will be punished!"

He glanced hurriedly around the walls, and smiled when he saw an iron ring set into the stone. He tied Prudence's neck rope to the ring, and stepped just out of her reach.

She could see over the edge to the ground far below. Still crying her name, Ross had brought his phaeton to a halt and was now racing toward the tower, with Wedge lumbering behind. She sagged with relief, then started in fear as she heard an ominous click. Hackett had pulled a pistol from his coat, cocked it, and was now aiming it at Ross.

"Take care, Ross!" she screamed. "He has a pistol!"

Her warning came too late. The weapon barked in Hackett's hand and Ross jerked back and crumpled to the earth, an awful red stain spreading over his coat front. Wedge ran to him, knelt, then looked up in horror, his face twisted with despair. He began to howl like a mournful dog over its fallen master.

Prudence sagged against the wall, sobbing. He couldn't be dead. He *couldn't*.

"Upon my soul," crowed Hackett. " 'Tis a bounty! The son of a dog as well as his bitch!"

She felt helpless with grief and rage. "You'll not escape man's justice."

"And who will tell, when you're dead?" he sneered. "That madman? They told me, aboard ship, that the simpleton saw me around every corner. Does he still?"

She bit her lip. He was right. Who would believe Wedge's story? Just one more wild fancy, they would say. The ravings of an idiot, obsessed with his nemesis, mistaking a common brigand for his feared "Cap'n."

Hackett gave an evil chuckle. "Your face gives you away, dear lady." He put down his pistol and advanced toward her. " 'Tis time for my reward—for killing your husband." He wrapped his arms around her waist and pulled her savagely against his body, bending his mouth to hers.

She turned her head from his foul kiss and screamed down to Wedge. "Toby! For the love of heaven, save me!"

Hackett waved one arm mockingly toward Wedge. "You foul swabber!" he called. "Are you still afraid of heights? Come, fool. You babbling bedlamite. You miserable cur! Come and save your mistress, if you dare!" He laughed in cruel delight.

Wedge shrank in terror at the ugly taunts. He turned away, moaning, and wrapped his arms around his body, rocking in a frenzied rhythm to give himself comfort. He seemed to be babbling at some unseen presence.

Hackett laughed again. "Now, dear lady, with that helpless idiot out of the way, I am free to enjoy you at my leisure."

He grabbed her hair in one strong fist and pulled it back to bring her mouth close to his slobbering lips. She shivered at the cold look in his eye, then cursed herself for a fool. She wasn't completely helpless. Not when he held her so close. She raised her knee and drove it into his groin.

He released her and groaned in pain, which gave her a measure of bitter satisfaction. A small victory. As soon as he had recovered himself, he raised his fist and swung it against her chin. She felt the crunch of her jaw, saw the smirk on his ugly face. Before the darkness closed in on her.

When she came to, she was lying on her back, her skirts pulled up to her waist. Hackett stood between her parted legs, working at the buttons of his breeches. She moaned and shook her head, still dazed from his blow. Her arms ached from being twisted behind her for so long.

Hackett smiled and preened, smoothing back his raven hair. "We shall begin in this position," he said. "Accustom you to the feel of my hard pintle within you. You might even enjoy it. The ladies have complimented me upon my prowess."

"I shall curse you with every breath," she said in revulsion, fighting against her choking fear.

"Save your breath for the pain and torment that will follow. You'll find I'm not a gentle lover." He tugged at the tails of his shirt and reached into his breeches to free his organ. "Gad's curse, but I've dreamed of this moment!" he crowed.

Prudence heard a crying noise from the stairs, like the squawk of a wounded gull, and turned her head. Wedge stood in the doorway, weeping like a child. His ruddy face had become as white as his hair, and sweat poured from his brow. He quaked from head to foot and swayed unsteadily, his breath coming in painful gasps.

Hackett muttered an oath; his eyes darted to the pistol on the other side of the tower. In that moment, Wedge let out a roar.

"You lubberly son of a whore!" he screamed, and threw himself at Hackett, propelling them both to the wall and over the edge. Prudence heard the dull thud of their bodies far below.

She lay quivering in horror, sobbing hysterically, nearly out of her mind from all that had happened. It was only when she thought of Ross that she recovered her senses. Oh, dear heaven, she thought in renewed panic. What if he were still alive, and needing her help?

She struggled to her feet and tore desperately at her bonds. It seemed useless. Hackett had tied them tightly around her gloves. Her *gloves!* Perhaps there was a way. With great difficulty, she pulled the gloves from her hands and discovered that she had a little play between her flesh and the rope. The cord was rough and scratchy; by the time she had managed to pull her hands free, her skin was rubbed raw.

She allowed herself a moment to look over the edge and see the two smashed bodies below. Then, with a shudder, she raced for the steps, tearing the noose from her neck as she ran.

Ross lay in the same position as he had fallen, his eyes tightly closed, his face ashen. His bright red blood oozed from a gaping hole in his chest.

She cried out in anguish and knelt beside him, cradling his dear head in her lap. "Ross," she sobbed. "You can't die. I love you."

His eyelids fluttered, the merest flicker, and her heart leapt for joy. She kissed him and rocked him, smoothing back his hair and calling his name until he groaned and opened his eyes. "What . . . what happened?" he said in a weak, breathless croak.

"Hackett shot you. We must get you to help. Lie still. I'll fetch the carriage." She lowered his head to the ground and ran toward his carriage. She took the horse by the bridle and led the snorting animal back to where Ross lay. "Can you get up? I'll help you."

By the time she had got him into the carriage, half-dragging, half-supporting him, he had recovered his mental facilities. He looked down at the hole in his chest and muttered an oath. " 'Tis close to the heart, I think," he gasped. "Pull my handkerchief from my pocket."

She did as he asked, and watched in dismay and fascination as he wrapped it around his hand and drove his fist into the wound. She cringed at his involuntary cry of pain.

"Can you handle the horse?" he mumbled.

"By God's grace." She picked up the reins and urged the horse into a gallop. The phaeton careened down the road. She fought to keep control of the spirited animal, scarcely allowing her glance to take in the swooning Ross, lest they veer from the road.

"Open up!" She was screaming to the porter even before they reached the gates of Castle Bridgewater. He threw open the gate and stared at Ross in horror as the carriage flew past. Then he cut across the field to the house, shouting as he ran.

By the time she pulled up to the door, there was already a commotion, with grooms and footmen running about. The marquis raced from the house and scrambled into the carriage. His face paled when Ross pulled his fist from the wound to reveal the bloody cavity. "You, there, Sam!" the marquis yelled to one of the grooms. "Take the reins and get us to Cinderford and a surgeon posthaste!"

Ross put his bloody hand on his father's sleeve. "No time. You do it," he panted.

The marquis began to tremble. "Sweet Jesus, I *can't*. I haven't operated since . . . since Martha. And my eyes . . . I can't even read without the aid of spectacles."

Ross gritted his teeth in pain and glared at his father. "Damn my liver!

'Tis simple enough. Take out the bullet, then cauterize, to seal the vessels. You taught me how, years ago."

The marquis hesitated, shaking his head and looking helplessly first at Ross, then at Prudence. His face twisted in agony. "I haven't the skills I once had. I daren't risk your life. My hand might slip . . . so close to your heart . . . Dear God, don't ask me!"

Ross's blue eyes glowed with an unfathomable light. "You can do it," he said tightly. "I *want* you to do it. I'll not survive the ride to Cinderford. And if you wait for a surgeon to be fetched, I'll be dead. You know that as well as I."

Bridgewater nodded reluctantly, then squared his shoulders in determination. He leapt from the carriage and began to bark orders. In a few minutes, Ross lay on the table in the morning room, his eyes closed with exhaustion. Prudence cut his coat and waistcoat and shirt, and carefully turned back the edges of the fabric to expose his wound. She cringed at the damage to his poor body.

Bridgewater washed his hands and tied on his surgeon's apron, all the while supervising the placement of his instruments. He nodded crisply as a large charcoal brazier was set nearby, into which he placed an iron rod. He gave orders for Ross to be bound to the table with wide leather straps, and set a footman close by with a sponge to stanch the flow of blood. He directed Prudence to feed Ross a large glass of brandy and stand by his head for comfort. His voice was calm and assured, but Prudence could see the panic lurking in his eyes.

When all was prepared to his satisfaction, he took a deep breath and picked up his scalpel.

Ross frowned. "Mind the axillary artery."

Prudence pressed her fingers gently to his lips. "For once, my love, don't be the doctor."

Despite his earlier uneasiness, Bridgewater's hands were sure and deft as they probed for the bullet. "Several of the ribs are shattered," he muttered. "I'll have to remove the shards, and hope that the remaining bones knit together." He sounded as detached as Ross when he was treating a patient. He picked at the bits of bone, dropping them into a bowl as he pulled them out. They made a metallic click when they landed. Prudence flinched.

Ross writhed in pain and struggled against his restraints as the operation went on, gnashing his teeth to keep from crying out. "Christ Jesus," he mumbled at length, "let me die."

Prudence mopped his perspiring face and kissed his lips. "No, my love. You mustn't wish that. You have to live. For our child."

His eyes widened in wonder. "Pru?" The smile on his face turned into a grimace of agony as Bridgewater dug deep and produced the bullet at last.

The marquis turned to the brazier and pulled the glowing rod from the fire. Prudence trembled at the thought of that diabolical instrument touching Ross's dear flesh, but she found herself pressing down on his shoulders to hold him steady beneath its fiery assault.

Ross jerked violently against the leather straps and let out a roar as the iron sizzled into the wound; then he sagged against the table, gasping, and closed his eyes. The reek of burning flesh filled the air.

Prudence kissed his sweat-stained brow. " 'Tis finished, my love."

He raised his head and looked at the wound, examining it with a critical eye. "As good a job as I could have done myself," he said hoarsely. "Perhaps better."

The marquis had begun to tremble again, as though the strain of the past half hour had finally unnerved him. "Do you think so?"

"I do." Ross lifted an unsteady hand and clutched at Bridgewater's sleeve. His eyes were beginning to glaze over, but Prudence read forgiveness and understanding in their depths.

"Thank you," he said in a choked voice. "Father."

Chapter
Twenty-Seven

Betsy stood at the window of the morning room of Castle Bridgewater and cast her gaze toward the broad expanse of lawn and trees. The early crocuses dotted the grass—great profusions of purple and yellow—and some of the bare trees were already shimmering with a reddish haze. She turned from the window and grinned. " 'Od's fish, Pru. I can scarce believe this will all be yours someday."

Prudence handed a gurgling Peter back to Mary Hunt and returned Betsy's smile. "I can scarce believe you're *here*. When I wrote to you at Shoe Lane and received no reply . . ."

Betsy snorted. "Trust that French devil, Marais, to ferret me out in my new home."

"Was it a fine house?"

"The grandest bawdy house on Drury Lane! And I was the grandest madam, thanks to your husband's generosity. With as pert a gaggle of girls as you've ever seen." She sighed. "How glad I was to be rid of men and their lewd demands."

"I always thought you enjoyed your calling."

Betsy shrugged—a worldly-wise gesture, filled with a knowledge beyond her years. "We find the good in what we have. When I was a whore, I accepted it. But when I was a madam, I gloried in my freedom from the lustful needs of the foul sex." She wrinkled her nose. "You shall find me a happy spinster a dozen years from now, cousin."

Prudence giggled. Ross had insisted that Betsy be passed off as her cousin, to ensure the proper respect from their friends and neighbors. Besides, he had told her, if Betsy was to live with them from now on, a blood connection would make explanations simpler.

She still couldn't believe it. Betsy had been with her for a week now, and they still sat up for hours, cross-legged on her bed, and laughed and shared gossip, just as they had as children. She blessed Ross from the bottom of her heart.

He had even had the wisdom to send his valet on the search for her friend. Since Marais didn't view Betsy's trade in the same scornful light as an Englishman, he was prepared to keep a discreet silence, to be understanding and sophisticated about Betsy's former life.

Betsy stirred restlessly, her sparkling eyes dimmed like a gray sky under rain. "Still, I miss the city sometimes. Perhaps it's the weather." She frowned out of the window. "Will spring never come?"

" 'Tis only a few weeks away."

"Will you stroll in the park with me?"

Prudence pursed her lips. "There's a chill in the air yet. And my father-in-law thinks it wouldn't be good for me, in my condition."

"Are you happy to be pregnant again, Pru?"

She smiled and rubbed her still-flat belly. "Delighted."

"And Ross?"

"I've never seen such joy in his eyes as when we speak of the child." She ignored the finger of unease that scratched at her vitals. What would happen to Peter's standing in the household, once Ross had his own child?

Betsy eyed her shrewdly. "And you're happy with Ross?"

"Oh, Betsy, why shouldn't I be? His health grows stronger every day. And he's made peace with his father. Why shouldn't my life be perfect and happy?"

Betsy gave a snort of derision. "You're talking to *me*. And I'm not a blind fool."

Her voice trembled and she played nervously with the ring on her finger. "Why shouldn't I be happy? He's good to me. And kind."

"Hmph! And still thinks he's in love with his dead wife." She put her arm around Prudence's shoulder. "Never mind, little Pru. He loves you—even if the chucklehead is too thick to know it."

"I wish I could be sure," she said sadly.

"Of course you . . ."

Betsy was interrupted by a light tap on the open door. William Franklin stood there, his face set in a formal smile. He bowed politely to Prudence. "Begging your pardon, Your Ladyship, but I thought I'd pay my respects before I go."

"How kind of you. Allow me to introduce my cousin, Elizabeth Berridge." Prudence made the introductions, and was surprised to see Betsy's eyes light up when Franklin bent and kissed her hand.

"Oh, Mr. Franklin," she said with a coy smile. " 'Tis such a chill day. Allow me to send for a sack-posset before you go out into the cold."

He blushed to the edge of his neat wig and gave a dismissive flutter of his hand. " 'Tis scarcely necessary, ma'am. I thank you for your kindness. But I have a pressing engagement in Cinderford."

Betsy smiled winsomely and put her hand on his sleeve. "Another time, perhaps."

"Yes, yes, of course," he stammered. "Another time. I look forward to it. Indeed I do." His face was now flaming. He gave a jerky bow—"Your servant, Mistress Berridge. Your Ladyship."—and retreated, nearly tripping over his feet as he escaped through the door.

Betsy stared at Prudence, wide-mouthed, the sparkle returning to her gray eyes. "Who was that handsome dog?"

"A lawyer. He's done some service for Ross in the past few weeks. He's come to Bridgewater several times. I think Ross means to hire him as his secretary once he's on his feet again. If the man will have it."

Betsy grinned. "A delightful prospect."

Prudence clicked her tongue. "You shameless hussy! I thought you said you weren't interested in men."

"I said I'd be a spinster," said Betsy indignantly. "But where's the harm in a flirtation or two?"

Prudence laughed. "Then perhaps I should tell you. Marais came to me, only this morning, in the strictest confidence, and told me that he thinks you're a *belle dame.*"

"Pshaw! That one! He's a vexation, that he is!"

Prudence frowned. "Does he treat you disrespectfully? Because he knows your history?"

"Lord love you, no. He keeps trying to get me into his bed! He says he can teach *me* a few tricks. And he pinches me, the rascally devil! He sneaks up behind my back and . . ."

"Merciful heaven! Why don't you complain to Ross or the marquis?"

Betsy grinned wickedly. "You're still as innocent as ever, love. Why should I?"

Prudence shook her head. There was still so much she had to learn about the ways of men and women. She looked forward to long talks with Betsy in the weeks ahead.

A footman tapped at the door and came in, bearing a letter. "The post, Your Ladyship."

"A letter for me?" Who could be writing to her? She ripped open the letter, perused it quickly, and chewed on her lip in thought. "I must talk with Ross," she said at last.

Betsy waved her out of the room. "Go to him. If it's not too windy out, I'll take that stroll." She grinned. "Perhaps I'll ask Marais to accompany me."

Prudence hurried up the stairs to Ross's rooms. She could hear the rumble of voices as she made her way through his drawing room to his bedchamber.

"Damn my heart, Ross, you'll not be up and about until I give you leave!"

"I'm scarcely a child, Father."

"I speak to you as your physician, not your father. If I must, I shall put sleeping draughts into your food, to keep you in your bed until the wound is properly healed."

Prudence suppressed a laugh. How alike they were. And didn't even know it! She marched into the bedchamber, her hands on her hips. "This bickering is good for neither of you," she scolded.

The marquis turned to her, his eyes imploring. "Make him stay in bed until his ribs are healed," he said. "If we're to go down to London in the fall, I want a healthy partner beside me in the surgery."

Prudence crossed the room to the bed, leaned over Ross, and gave him a firm, resounding kiss. "Do as your doctor says, or I'll not come with you. And then what will you do for a nurse?"

Ross grumbled, then smiled in sheepish surrender and looked at his father. "And what does milady's doctor say about her condition?"

"If she has a healthy delivery in August, she should be fit to travel by the end of September. For the present, your lady is blooming."

Ross looked skeptical. "I shall have to see for myself, when I'm fit enough. A few tests, perhaps . . ."

Prudence rolled her eyes. "If I'm to be doctored to death by the two of you, I shall go off into the woods to have my baby!"

Ross leered. "That wasn't quite the test I had in mind."

While Prudence blushed furiously, the marquis cleared his throat and tried to hide his smile. "Ahem. I think 'tis time for me to leave." He permitted himself a small, contented chuckle as he left the room, closing the door behind him.

"Now, you imp," said Ross, holding out his arms, "come and give me a proper kiss."

She sat on the edge of the bed and lifted her mouth to his. He held her as tightly as his injured body would allow, his hands soft at the nape of her neck. His kiss was thorough and impassioned; by the time he released her, she was trembling and longing for the day when they could share a bed again.

"Now," he said, "to what do I owe this visit? I thought you and Betsy would come up for tea later."

She fished in her pocket and pulled out her letter. "I just received this from Abigail. Grandfather is dying."

His eyes filled with dark remembrance. "Will you mourn him, the sanctimonious scoundrel?"

" 'Tis not that. They shall be forced to sell Burghope Manor within the fortnight. Jamie made good on his threat, and managed to reach all of Grandpapa's creditors. How can I see them turned out of their home?"

" 'Tis no more than they deserve," he growled.

"Please, Ross, have a little pity. Judgment is mine, saith the Lord. I thought we had embraced forgiveness and buried the last of our anger when we buried poor Toby Wedge." It had been a sad funeral, with pipers to play over Toby's coffin.

He sighed, relenting. "You have a more forgiving heart than I. But I'll send Franklin with instructions to buy the manor, and allow them to stay."

"You don't fool me," she said. "Beneath that cold facade lies a warm heart. Damaged though it very nearly was by Hackett's bullet."

He grunted, unwilling to concede the point. "I'll do it only because it will rankle Jamie to have his malice undone."

She stroked his forehead tenderly. "Of course, my stubborn darling. If you'll have it that way. But you look tired and drawn. You shouldn't have Franklin to visit. You can discuss your business when you're quite yourself again."

He took her hand and pressed it to his lips. "It was too important to wait. I've asked him to arrange for me to adopt Peter."

She gasped, her eyes filling with happy tears. *"Adopt?"*

"If he's to be the next doctor in the family, he needs the Manning name, by the terms of the queen's compact."

"Oh, Ross," she said, her heart overflowing with love for him. "But what if the child I bear is a son?"

"No matter. He may inherit the title, but the honor of being a surgeon goes to Peter." His voice took on a hoarse note. "I want him to apprentice with me."

She leaned against his breast, weeping for joy. "Why are you so good to me?"

He stroked her bent head, his hand gentle on her curls. "Because he's your beloved child. And he should be mine as well. Because I love you," he added simply. "Did I neglect to tell you that, along with all my other failings?"

She lifted her head, her eyes streaming. "You love me?"

"I've lain in this bed for weeks, fevered and in pain. Dwelling on death and thinking how foolish I was to cling to the past, when I had a treasure for the future. You brought me joy and hope, Pru, when I had none of my own. My little shepherdess, you guided me to the sunshine. Great God, you brought me back to life! Do you know how close I was to killing myself when first I met you?"

She caressed the side of his face, fresh tears springing to her eyes. "Ross. No."

" 'Tis true. I had done with life. And yet . . . Do you remember all the nights I held you aboard ship, when you thought I was asleep? You were warm with the gift of life, and I began to imagine I could live again. You once spoke of the crone in your village, and her winter wine. 'Twas your warmth that melted the ice from my heart. It would not have happened without you." His voice was thick with fervent emotion. "You saved me, Pru, when I didn't think it was possible."

"Oh, Ross. I think I've loved you forever. Or should have." Despite his dear words, his heartfelt confession, she still felt a whisper of doubt. Did he say "love" and mean "gratitude"?

He smiled, as proud of himself as a little boy who has shared a secret. His eyes were warm on her face. "Am I not to get a kiss, for such tender sentiments?"

"All the kisses you can take," she murmured, and melted into his embrace.

His mouth claimed hers in a hungry kiss, drifting from her lips to her cheeks and nose and closed eyes. At last he grunted and pushed her gently away, holding his hand to his chest. "I suspect all that pounding isn't good for my heart, as yet. And I burn to be well enough to show my love in more . . . vigorous ways. And *soon*, God help my suffering body!"

It wouldn't do to excite him too much yet, though she wished their kisses could go on forever. "You look tired. Sleep," she said firmly, rising from the bed and crossing to the door.

"Wait." He stretched out his hand to the table beside his bed, which contained his sketching folio, a decanter of water, and several small items.

"You don't intend to draw me again," she said in a mock-scolding voice. "You're impossible, Ross Manning."

She smiled in spite of herself, remembering the picture she had come across only last week. Drawn aboard the *True Heart*, the day he had pretended to draw Wedge playing his pipe. Instead, he had sketched her with her hair like a radiant halo about her face, drying in the breeze from the window. If she had seen the picture then, she thought, limned with such tender skill, she would have guessed at his love.

He lifted a box from the table. "Come here."

She returned with reluctance. He had been so close to death—he still needed his rest. "What is it?"

He tapped the bed beside him, and waited until she seated herself again. "Franklin has been very helpful," he said mysteriously. He lifted her hand and pulled Martha's ring from her finger. "We shall bury this with her," he said. " 'Tis fitting." He opened the box.

Within was a small gold band with a sky blue sapphire set in the middle. On either side were the names Ross and Prudence. She gasped in heart-stopping joy, and started to put the ring on her finger.

"There's an inscription inside," he said in a choked voice.

She held up the ring to the light of the late afternoon sun, weeping afresh at the words. She kissed him with all the love in her heart, and allowed him to slip the ring on her finger.

He ran a hand over his eyes. "By the beard of Aesculapius, I *am* tired." He pulled back the coverlet and patted the bed with his palm. "Lie with me until I fall asleep. As we did aboard ship, my sweet Pru."

She nodded, took off her shoes, and crept in beside him, curling her body to his. He held her as tightly as he was able, his arm loosely draped across her. She felt warm and secure.

As she drifted off into a sleep of contentment, she thought again of the words on the ring. The dearest pledge he could have given her.

ALL I REFUSE, AND THEE I CHOOSE.

If you enjoyed THE RING
you will also enjoy Sylvia Halliday's
SUMMER DARKNESS, WINTER LIGHT
published for the first time in paperback
March, 1996
On sale wherever Zebra Books are sold.
The following is a preview chapter.

Chapter One

∽⟨⟨⟨⟩⟩⟩∽

The wrought-iron gate was newly painted. Allegra ran her fingers over the smooth curliques, followed the cool, sinuous curves to the oval medallion that held the Baniard coat of arms. The carved leopard still raised a broken front paw. But after more than eight years of fresh paint—glistening black layers piled one upon another—the jagged metal edges had become rounded, gentle.

"Curse them all," Allegra muttered. "Every foul Wickham who ever lived." She clenched her teeth against the familiar pain. If only sharp memories could be as softened and gentled as the old iron gate. She reached into the pocket of her wide seaman's breeches and pulled forth a worn, lace-edged square of linen, yellow with age and mottled with stains the color of old wine, the color of dead leaves. Papa's blood—staining the proud Baniard crest embroidered in the corner.

Wickham. Allegra's lip curled in silent rage and bitterness. If there was a God of vengeance, a just God, her prayers would be answered today. Her stomach twisted with the pangs of hunger, and her feet—in their broken shoes—ached from the long morning's climb through the Shropshire hills, but it would be worth it. She reached under her shabby coat and waistcoat and fingered the hilt of the dagger tucked into the waistband of her breeches. All her pain would vanish when she confronted John Wickham, Baron Ellsmere, false Lord of Baniard Hall. When she saw his look of surprise, then fear, then abject terror in the breathless, time-stopped seconds before she plunged her dagger into his black heart.

A sour-faced manservant came out of the lodge next to the high stone wall that enclosed Baniard Park. A thickly curled gray peruke covered his round head, and he wore a handsome livery of blue velvet trimmed with crimson—the Ellsmere colors, no doubt. He squinted up at the morning sun, peered through the bars of the gate and shook his fist at Allegra. "Get off with you, boy. You have no business here."

Allegra jammed her three-cornered hat more firmly over her forehead to shield her face from the gatekeeper's gaze. Her masculine guise had protected her clear across the ocean and through the English countryside all the way north from Plymouth. Still, to be discovered now, when vengeance lay so close at hand . . .

"I ain't doin' no harm, your worship," she mumbled, keeping her naturally husky voice pitched low, her accent common. "Just come up from Ludlow, I did. It were a long climb. And I'm fearful hungry. Thought I might beg a farthing or two of His Lordship."

"Pah!" said the gatekeeper with a sneer of contempt as he scanned her stained and ragged clothing. "Do you think milord can be bothered with the likes of you? A dirty-faced whelp?" He scowled at her dark eyes, her raven-black hair braided into a tousled queue, and her face still deeply tanned from the Carolina sun. "Leastwise not someone who looks like a black Welsh Gypsy," he added. "Be off, lest I give you a good rap on the ear."

Years of cruel servitude had taught Allegra how to feign humility, even while her heart seethed with rebellion. "Have a crumb o' pity, your worship," she whined. "I be but a poor orphan lad."

"Be off, I say." He pointed across the narrow, dusty road to a footpath that wound its way through a small grove of trees. "That way lies the village of Newton-in-the-Vale. There's a fine workhouse that will do well enough for you. A good day's work for a good day's bread, and none of your sloth and begging."

Allegra rubbed at her hands, feeling the hardness of the calluses on her palms and fingers. She wondered whether this self-satisfied, overfed man had ever known *real* work. Heigh-ho. There was no sense in quarreling with him. She shrugged and plodded across the road. The trees were thick in the coppice, crowded close together; their dark, summer-green leaves

and shade soon hid her from the gatekeeper's view. She waited a few minutes, then stepped off the footpath and doubled back through the trees,
treading softly so as not to alert the servant. Just within the shelter of the
coppice, she found a spot that concealed her presence while commanding a clear view of the gate.

By King George upon his throne, if she had to wait all day for Wickham she would!

She heard the noise of a coach from somewhere beyond the gate—the
rattle of harness, the squeaking of wheels—as it made its way down the
long, tree-shaded drive that led from Baniard Hall. In another moment,
the coach appeared in view and stopped at the gate; the team of horses
snorted and stamped, eager to proceed. At once, the gatekeeper hurried
to take hold of the iron gate and swing it wide. Allegra heard the word
"Milord" uttered in deference, noted the blue and crimson Ellsmere colors on the coachman's ample body. Wickham's very own coach. Without a doubt, the villain himself was within.

Allegra's heart began to pound in her breast, like the thud of distant
thunder before a storm. After all this time . . . She started to rush forward, then checked herself. No. No! She mustn't let her impatience cloud
her judgment; she must think clearly. The coach was moving quite slowly
through the open gate. Out of the view of the gatekeeper and coachman,
she might be able to hoist herself onto the empty footman's perch in the
rear and cling to the coach until it stopped and her enemy alit. But that
might not be until they reached a village and the coach was surrounded
by crowds. And then the job would be impossible.

She remembered a crumbling section of the wall that surrounded the
park, where the stones had loosened. Perhaps she could make her way onto
the grounds from there, wait for Ellsmere to return. No. The wall might
be repaired after all this time. And, besides, she couldn't wait another
minute. She laughed softly, ruefully. She had endured the long, slow years,
the years of nurturing her hatred in patient silence. And now, to her surprise, she found that the thought of a few hours' delay had become unbearable.

What to do? The frown faded from her brow as a sudden thought struck her. She would accost him now, present herself as a harmless lad, win his sympathy, worm her way into his favor. He wouldn't recognize her after all this time. And then, when his guard was down, her dagger could do its work.

"Milord!" she cried, and dashed in front of the carriage. The coachman shouted and tried to avoid her; she held her ground and leapt away only at the last second. It had been such a narrow escape that her shoulder burned from the friction of rubbing against a horse's flank, and a passing harness buckle had torn the sleeve of her coat.

She began at once to howl. " 'Od's blood, but my arm be broken!"

She heard a string of foul curses from within the coach, then a deep voice boomed, "Stop!"

As the coach drew to a halt, Allegra clutched at her arm and bent over in seeming pain. Though she continued to wail, all her energies were concentrated on observing the man who sprang from the coach. She'd seen him once before—that long-ago, sweet summer at Baniard Hall. The summer she'd turned nine. The summer before the nightmare had begun. A man of stature, proud and haughty and cruel.

He was even taller than her misty memory of him, and the years had clearly treated him with kindness. His dark-brown hair was still untouched by gray. He wore it simply, unpowdered and tied back with a black silk ribbon. His pugnacious jaw had a bluish cast, as though he'd neglected to take a shave, and his dark and somewhat shaggy brows were drawn together in a scowl, shading pale-brown eyes. His well-cut coat and waistcoat of fine woolen cloth covered a solid, muscular torso, and his legs were strong and straight. The fact that he looked so young made her hate him all the more: Papa had aged a dozen years from the time of the trial to the day they had been herded aboard the convict ship.

"Damned fool," growled the man. He sounded more annoyed than angry, as though it was a bother merely to deal with the lower classes. "Why the devil did you run into my coach, boy? I should break your neck, match it to your arm." He stepped closer and thrust out his hand. "Show it here."

The simmering hatred became a red mist before Allegra's eyes: the red, bloody dream that had kept her going through all the hellish years, through the shame and the suffering and the loss of all she'd held dear. She felt strength coursing through her body—the strength of righteous anger that poor Mama had never been able to find.

Now! she thought. For her pledge to Mama. For all the lost Baniards! There would never be a better opportunity. The gatekeeper was busy with his gate and the coachman was too fat to scramble down from his perch in time to save his master.

Allegra snaked her hand inside her coat. A quick thrust with her dagger and then—in the chaos of the unexpected, the confusion of the servants—she'd make her escape into the woods. "Die like the dog you are," she choked, and drove the knife upward toward his breast with all her might. With all the fury in her pent-up heart.

"Christ's blood!" he swore. He wrenched his body to one side and just managed to dodge the murderous blade. At the same moment he caught Allegra's wrist in a punishing grip and twisted it until she was forced to drop the knife. His lip curled in disgust. "Good God. You're not a fool. You're a bloody lunatic! Do you fancy the gibbet, boy?"

She bared her teeth in a snarl. "It would be worth it, to see you dead."

He laughed, an unpleasant sound, lacking in humor or warmth. "What a tartar. How does a boy learn such passion at such a young age?" He drawled the words, as though strong emotions were scarcely worth his own effort.

"I learned from villains like you," she said. She eyed her dagger lying in the dusty road. If she could just reach it . . .

"Oh, no, boy. You'll not have a second chance." Reading her intentions, he quickly stooped and retrieved the knife.

"Curse you!" Allegra felt her stomach give a sickening lurch. She had failed them all. All the ghosts waiting to be avenged. How could she have been so hasty and careless? Would there ever be another chance to redeem herself? Another chance to do what she must, and then learn to live again? In her frustration, she raised her hands to spring at the man's throat; she grunted in surprise as she felt her arms caught and pinioned behind her back. She struggled in vain, then twisted around to glare at the man who held her—a somber-looking young man who had stepped from the coach behind her. He was dressed in a plain dark suit, the garb of a steward or clerk.

"Hold your tongue, bratling," he said, "unless you mean to beg His Lordship's mercy."

"His Lordship can rot in hell, for aught I care!" She turned back and spat in the direction of the tall man. "In *hell*, Wickham! Do you hear?"

"Wickham?" The tall man laughed again and idly scraped Allegra's blade against the stubble on his chin. It made a metallic, rasping sound. "Wickham? Is that who you think I am?"

"You're the Lord of Baniard Hall, aren't you?" she challenged.

"That I am. But Wickham was ruined by debts nearly two years ago. The last I heard, he was in London."

"No!" She shook her head in disbelief, feeling her blood run cold. "Curse you, villain, you're lying to save your skin."

The steward gave a sharp jerk on her arms. "I told you to hold your tongue, boy," he growled in her ear. "This is Sir Greyston Morgan, Viscount Ridley. Baron Ellsmere sold the Hall to His Lordship a year ago."

"I don't believe you." But of course there was no reason to doubt him. She examined the tall man more closely. What a fool she'd been, allowing her passion to blind her to reality. He didn't just appear younger; he *was* younger, and considerably so. Perhaps in his early thirties. Wickham would be almost as old as Papa would have been today, or at least nearing fifty. She'd forgotten that, still seeing the man through the eyes of her childhood.

All the fight drained out of her. She sagged in the steward's grip, filled with an aching disappointment. To have come so far, and then to find another obstacle in her path, another barrier before she could sleep in peace . . . She stared at the viscount, her dark eyes burning with frustration and resentment. He should have been Wickham. "I curse you as well, Ridley," she said bitterly. "A pox on you."

"Now, milord," said the coachman, climbing down from his box, "if this isn't a rascally lad who needs a few hours in the stocks to teach him manners! Shall we deliver him to the beadle in the village?" He looked for agreement toward the gatekeeper, who had finally joined them.

Ridley looked down at Allegra's petite frame and shook his head. "He's just a slip of a boy. The stocks would kill him. A mere ten minutes with a mob hurling garbage and filth . . ."

"But you can't let him go, milord. He tried to kill you!" said the gate-keeper.

Ridley smiled, a sardonic twist of his mouth. "So he did, Humphrey. And I note you took your time coming to my rescue." His icy glance swept his other servants as well. "The lot of you. Slow as treacle on a cold day. Very shortsighted. If you'd let him kill me, you'd have had to seek honest employment for a change." He shrugged, ignoring his servants' sullen frowns. "Well, the lad wasn't the first to wish me dead. However"—he slapped the broad width of Allegra's dagger against his open palm—"the boy does have an insolent tongue, and for that he should be made to pay." He nodded at his steward. "Loose him, Briggs. I'll deal with him myself."

"But . . ." Briggs hesitated. "Do you think you're fit, milord?"

A sharp laugh. "Sober, you mean?"

"I didn't mean that at all," said Briggs in an aggrieved tone.

Ridley's eyes were cold amber. "What a damned bloody liar you are, Briggs. Now, do you want to keep your position? You'll not find another master willing to pay so much for so little. Loose the boy, I said."

"As you wish, milord." There was pained resentment in the steward's voice, but he obeyed.

The moment her arms were freed, Allegra looked wildly about, seeking a path to safety. There was none. The three servants hemmed her in, and Lord Ridley stood before her, a cold smile of determination on his face. He slapped the flat of Allegra's knife more sharply against his hand. Again, and then once more—a decidedly menacing gesture, for all his smiling. "Damn me to hell, will you, boy? Spit on my boots, will you? Someone has neglected your education, it would seem. I intend to remedy that." He slipped the knife into his boot top and advanced on Allegra. His long arm shot out and wrapped around her waist. With the merest effort, he lifted her and tucked her under his arm, like a farmer carrying a squirming pig to market.

Allegra writhed in his strong grip. "Bloody villain. Spawn of hell! Put me down!"

"If I were you, boy, I'd hold my tongue," he said dryly. "I have all day to educate you, and every fresh insolence will only earn you another painful lesson." He turned toward the woodland path.

"Where are you going, milord?" asked the gatekeeper, Humphrey.

"To find a suitable 'schoolroom.' Don't follow me. Grant the lad privacy in his humiliation." Ridley laughed, a sharp, sardonic bark. "Besides, you shall hear his howls anon."

He carried Allegra into the grove of trees and stopped at last when he found a fallen log in a small clearing. He sat down and slung her across his knees with such force that her hat flew from her head and landed in a patch of bright green ferns.

Allegra grunted and wriggled in powerless rage, punching at his legs, his thighs—anything within reach of her flailing fists. It was like beating back a tempest with a lady's fan. His strong arm held her firmly against his lap. She felt his other hand at her rump, turning up the skirts of her coat; then his fingers were curled around the top of her breeches.

She struggled more violently to free herself. She didn't fear the thrashing—not even with the flat of her own knife, which the villain clearly intended. Punishment was nothing new to her. But if he saw the pale flesh of her backside, the womanly curves, he'd guess at once. And then what? What could she expect from this cold-hearted devil of a viscount? God save her, she hadn't guarded her virtue against the greatest adversities only to be raped by a man with nothing better to do on a July morning! With a superhuman effort, she wrenched herself from his lap and tumbled to the ground.

He reached down to pull her back. By chance, his hands closed over her breasts. "Christ's blood," he exclaimed, and dropped down beside her. "A *woman*, begad!" While she struggled in helpless frustration, he rolled her onto her back, straddled her and pinned her wrists over her head. With his free hand he explored her body, threw open her coat and tattered waistcoat and fondled her breasts through her full linen shirt. It was a leisurely, searching examination that clearly amused him. His mouth twisted in a smirk. "A very pleasing shape. May I assume your other parts are equally feminine? Or shall I find out for myself?"

She squirmed in disgust at his touch, her eyes flashing. "Let me up, you plaguey dog!"

He shook his head and laughed. "To think I very nearly beat you like a child. I should have realized . . . all that passion. Not childlike at all. But why waste your fire in anger? Why foul your lips with curses, when they could be put to better use?" He bent down, his face close to hers. His breath smelled of liquor, sour and pungent.

"Cursed rogue," she muttered. "Drunken sot. I would rather the beating than the kiss."

"Perhaps I can oblige you with both," he said, and silenced her mouth with his.

His lips were hard and demanding, rapacious in their greed, the desire for self-gratification. And when she groaned and bucked beneath him, Ridley chuckled deep in his throat, as though her struggles only increased the enjoyment of his mastery over her. Without releasing either her lips or her hands, he shifted his body so his considerable weight pressed upon her breast and his free hand rested on the juncture between her legs.

Allegra had a sudden, terrifying memory of Mama, gasping in pain and grief as Squire Pringle violated her frail body. She could hear again the animal sounds she'd heard, night after night in the dark. Hear her mother's heartbroken sobs as the master, satisfied once more, slunk away to his own bed. *No!* It mustn't happen to her. She was stronger than Mama. Hadn't she survived until now?

Despite her rising panic, she forced herself to think clearly. If Ridley wasn't completely drunk, he'd certainly had a great deal to drink this morning. His senses would be dulled, his reflexes numbed by alcohol. Surely she could outwit him if she put her mind to it.

With a sigh, she relaxed under him in seeming surrender. She even managed a moan of pleasure when he began to stroke her inner thigh, his large hand hot through her breeches. He grunted his contentment, softened his kiss, eased his hard grip upon her wrists. How easily gulled men could be, she thought. And if he was anything like the lecherous pigs in Carolina, no doubt he enjoyed kissing in the French manner. She prayed it was so. She parted her lips beneath his, hoping he'd understand and respond to her invitation. To her satisfaction, he immediately opened his own mouth and thrust his tongue between her lips and teeth. She waited a second—fighting her disgust—then bit down with all her might.

He let out a bellow and flew off her as though he'd been shot, sitting up to clutch at his bloody mouth. "Damned bitch!" he roared.

She gave him no chance to recover. She scrambled to her knees and drove her fist into his diaphragm with all her strength. He recoiled in agony and doubled over, gasping for breath. She was on her feet in a flash. She snatched up her three-cornered hat, pulled her knife from his boot top and turned toward the footpath. Her mouth was bitter with the taste of his blood; bitterer still with the knowledge that time was passing and she was no nearer her goal. Her stomach burned with hunger, and London and Wickham were long miles and days away. Somehow, that made her hate Ridley all the more. Ridley, with his careless, shallow lechery. What did he know of true suffering?

She retraced her steps to where he still sat, rocking in pain. "Filthy whoremonger," she said, and spat his own blood upon his bent head. When he looked up at her, she was pleased to see that the cold, indifferent eyes were—for the first time—dark with rage. "Laugh that away, Ridley," she said. "If you can." She turned on her heel and made for the safety of the trees . . . and the direction that would take her eventually to London and Wickham.

And bloody vengeance.

Sir Greyston Morgan, Lord Ridley, late of His Majesty's Guards and survivor of many an incursion against the Mogul Empire, gingerly rubbed the sore spot beneath his ribs and muttered a soft curse. He pulled out a handkerchief and wiped the spittle from his hair, grunting at the pain that small effort cost him. The absurdity of the whole episode served to temper his anger. "Ambushed, begad," he said, beginning to laugh in spite of his discomfort. He stuck out his tongue and dabbed at it, marveling at the amount of blood on the snowy linen. It was a wonder the virago hadn't bitten his tongue clean off!

"Are you hurt, milord?" Jonathan Briggs stood on the edge of the path, frowning in concern.

Grey struggled to his feet and glared at his steward. It was one thing to be outwitted by a wench. It was quite another matter to be caught at it by a servant. "Damn it, I thought I told you not to follow."

"We heard you cry out, milord." Briggs looked around the small clearing. "Where's the boy?"

Grey took a tentative step forward, relieved to discover that he could breathe almost normally again. "The 'boy,' Briggs, turned out to be a woman." His tongue was still bleeding; he stopped to spit a mouthful of blood against the base of a tree. "And a damned shifty bitch at that."

Briggs watched in dismay. "Was the wench responsible for this? I'll send Humphrey after her."

"No. Let her be. I'll wager she's halfway to London by now."

"What's to be done now, milord?"

Grey moved slowly to the steward and leaned his arm on the man's shoulder. "Help me back to the coach and open that bottle of gin."

Briggs shook his head in disapproval. "But, milord, do you think it wise, so early in the day?"

He swore softly. "You tell me what's worth staying sober for, Briggs, and I'll stay sober. Until then, you'll keep me supplied with all the drink I need. And no insolence. Is that understood?"

Briggs pressed his lips together and nodded.

By the time they'd reached the coach, Grey was feeling a good deal better. At least his tongue and his ribs were feeling better. He wasn't sure of anything else. There was something disturbing about the woman. Something about her eyes, so large and dark and filled with pain . . . "Damn it, Briggs," he growled, "where's that gin?" He snatched the small flask from the steward's hand and took a long, mind-numbing swallow. Why should he let the thought of a savage creature with a dirty face get under his hide?

"Do you still want to go down to Ludlow, milord?"

"Of course. The blacksmith promised to have that Toledo blade repaired by today."

"Are you sure you don't want someone to go after the woman?"

"I told you, no!"

"But she tried to kill you. What if she should return and try again?"

"She wants Ellsmere, not me." He smiled crookedly. "I pity him if the witch should find him." He took another swig of gin and shrugged. "Besides, if she should return to kill me, I'm no great loss."

"Nonsense, milord. You're a great man, admired and respected by your tenants and servants. Everyone in the parish honors Lord Ridley."

Grey threw back his head and laughed aloud. "Such kind flattery, Briggs. You do it well, as befits a man of honor. But how difficult it must be for you. To serve a man you don't even like. You're the second son of a knight, aren't you? You were predestined to inherit nothing from your father except his good wishes. Well, a house steward is a fine calling for a man with few prospects and a good education. And money speaks with a loud voice, as I've learned." He leaned back in his seat and tapped his long fingers against the bottle of gin. "How much am I paying you?"

"Forty pounds, milord," murmured Briggs. He watched in silence, his solemn eyes registering dismay, as Grey downed the last of the gin.

The liquor stung Grey's injured tongue, but he was beginning to feel better and better. He chuckled softly. "What a disappointment I must be to you, Briggs. I think your upbringing was better than mine, though I, too, was the second son of a title. I regret that I don't suit your ideas of proper nobility here in Shropshire. But if you can learn to hide that look of disgust on your face, I give you leave to take another thirty pounds per annum. If not"—he shrugged—"it's simple enough to buy loyalty elsewhere, if one has the money." He laughed at the sullen look Briggs shot at him. "God's truth, I think if my brother hadn't died and left me his fortune and title, you'd be pleased to knock me to my knees at this very moment. But you're too much a gentleman for that. Too respectful of a man's rank, even if he's undeserving. Eh, Briggs?" He laughed again as the steward reddened and turned away.

Grey closed his eyes. The rocking of the coach soothed him. And the gin had done its work. It was good to feel nothing but a comfortable hum in his brain. There was a surfeit of passion in the world, a stupid waste of emotion. He hated it. Hated caring, hated feeling. It was better to be numb than to suffer with rage and pain, one's soul exposed to the agony of the human condition. Raw flesh held to an open flame. Like that ragged, dark-eyed creature, who burned with an intensity he couldn't begin to understand. That he didn't *want* to understand.

"Briggs," he said suddenly. "Do you remember the red-haired serving wench at the King's Oak tavern in Newton? Find out if she's still as agreeable as before. If so, pay her double what you did last time. Then see that she's waiting in my bed tonight."

"Yes, milord." Briggs's voice was sharp with disapproval.

Grey opened his eyes and smiled cynically. "She's a shallow, greedy whore, Briggs. I know. But—like the gin—she gives me what I want. Forgetfulness."

And plague take all sad-eyed creatures who overflowed with more passion than their hearts could safely hold.

ABOUT THE AUTHOR

Sylvia Halliday is the author of more than a dozen award-winning historical romances under the pseudonyms Ena Halliday and Louisa Rawlings. Her Louisa Rawlings books include *Forever Wild*, a finalist for the RWA Golden Medallion, *Promise of Summer*, which received the *Romantic Times* Reviewers' Choice Award, and *Wicked Stranger* which was a finalist for a 1993 RWA Rita Award. Born in Canada, raised in Massachusetts, Sylvia Halliday now makes her home in New York where she is at work on her next historical romance which will be set in Colorado.